Also by Rebecca Rothenberg

The Bulrush Murders

The
Dandelion Murders

Rebecca Rothenberg

THE MYSTERIOUS PRESS

Published by Warner Books

A Time Warner Company

MYSTERIOUS PRESS EDITION

Cover design by Jackie Merri Meyer
Cover illustration by Theresa Fasolino

The Mysterious Press name and logo are registered trademarks of
Warner Books, Inc.

 Mysterious Press Books are published by
Warner Books, Inc.
   1271 Avenue of the Americas
   New York, NY 10020

Ⓦ A Time Warner Company

Printed in the United States of America

Originally published in hardcover by The Mysterious Press.
First Printed in Paperback: December, 1995

10 9 8 7 6 5 4 3 2 1

The
Dandelion Murders

women who were not as beautiful as Large, and set as

Hector Cedillo stumbled, cursed violently in Spanish, and steadied himself against a post. Maybe this shortcut wasn't a good idea, he thought, rubbing a bruised shin. And maybe that last beer at El Aguila hadn't been such a good idea either. If he hadn't had that last beer, he wouldn't have gotten into a fight with that stupid Okie who always came into the bar to pick a fight with a Mexican. (He wondered who had won, rubbed sore right knuckles, and decided he had.) He wouldn't have missed a ride home with Juan. He wouldn't be wandering through this damned vineyard in the dark.

And he wouldn't have had to pay for his bender tomorrow. Usually he didn't drink on a Sunday night; he had to be up at four-thirty for work. But, hell, he was entitled to a few beers once in a while. He worked like a dog all week under a sun that would fry tortillas, and the beer helped him forget the aches in every joint and every muscle in his body, and this flu that he couldn't seem to shake, and memories of his mother and four sisters, to whom he sent all his money, only saving out a little for himself and Lupe, and the future—

He paused in this litany of woes to think about Lupe, who lived in his hometown five hundred miles to the south and was sixteen and pure as the Virgin she was named for. His eyes filled with tears at the thought of her—or maybe it was just the flu. His eyes and nose were running like faucets these days; he could rent himself out for irrigation. A one-man irrigation system. The idea made him laugh so hard, he stumbled again. And then he began to think about some other women who were not as beautiful as Lupe, and not as inno-

1

cent, and a whole lot closer. Hector was nineteen, and even working seventy hours a week in the fields of the San Joaquin Valley didn't quell his ardor. Take those two women at the bar tonight . . . Maybe he should go back to the bar. Only that would require threading his way back through these vines, which he most definitely did not want to do.

If anyone should have felt at home in this particular place, it was Hector. He must have spent thousands of hours in the vineyards over the past few years. Hell, he'd even worked here this spring, he thought. Yeah, he remembered these vines, thirty-year-olds, he reckoned; remembered pruning them to four or five canes in January, tying them to the wires, digging the furrows, piling up the berms . . . He fuzzily admired his handiwork. Grapes were good money, if you were fast and skilled, and a hell of a lot easier on your back than stoop labor. He was becoming a sort of specialist in grapes.

But it was different at night. At night the vineyard became a cemetery: the T-shaped lattices, rows of crosses; the dark vines whispering and winding along their wires, little Christs nailed to those crosses . . . And he, Hector Cedillo, had nailed them there.

Jesus, what an idea. He really shouldn't have had that last beer. He lurched forward and stumbled again; the moon was bright, but the ground, booby-trapped by his own ditches and berms and irrigation pipes, was in shadow. He forced himself to slow to a cautious crawl, but damn! he wanted out of here. Thank God the vineyard ended about twenty yards ahead. Beyond that was the friendly shelter of an orange grove and beyond that the highway. Maybe he could even pick up a ride; it was only midnight—

Something huge rose up before him, white as the moon, man-shaped and faceless.

Hector gave a grunt of disbelief and terror. His heart slammed twice against his ribs, then seemed to stop beating altogether, the way it did sometimes.

The thing didn't move, didn't make a sound. Hector stared at it with blank panic for what must have been thirty seconds; then, because he was young and resilient and cocky and too drunk to sustain any emotion, even terror, for long, he addressed it.

"*¡Hombre,*" he said, "*que susto me dió! ¿Que hace usted?*" (He was careful to use the polite form of the verb.)

No reply. Maybe it was an Okie ghost. "Man, what you do here?" he said in uncertain English.

Still no response. The figure moved toward him slowly, paused with what would have been indecision in something less menacing, and raised its right arm. Hector saw that it carried some kind of wand. Suddenly he was afraid again.

Involuntarily he stepped backward. "Hey, man, *hombre,* easy, *todo está* okay," he gabbled.

His heel caught on a pipe, and he fell heavily. And then the figure was over him, closer and closer, until it filled the sky. The last thing Hector saw was its upraised arm, blotting out the moon.

Chapter 1

"Strike two!" The shrill exclamation came drifting in from the back yard, followed by a deeper male voice.

"Choke up on the bat a little, Shannon," Sam said, and Claire looked out the kitchen window just as he leaned forward and released the softball. It moved in a slow, fat arc toward the towheaded boy, who watched anxiously and slashed at it wildly a half second too soon. It landed with a thud at his feet.

"Strike three!" piped his little brother gleefully. "One away!" Taken with this phrase, he began to chant, "*One-awayoneawayoneaway . . .*" while doing a sort of war dance, bent-legged, dragging his toes in a circle. The boxy white sneakers at the ends of his skinny legs made him look impossibly thin and oddly graceful, like a stork in ski boots. Both boys dressed identically—T-shirts, Day-Glo shorts that reached to the tops of their knees, baseball caps turned backward (a perennial emblem of rebellion, from the Dead End Kids on)—and when they had first arrived they had seemed completely undifferentiated. But now she was beginning to see that eight-year-old Terry was already better coordinated and more athletic than his ten-year-old brother. Shannon, stocky and ungainly, was, she hoped, the intellectual.

The boys were up from Los Angeles to visit their dad in "the country," if you could apply that epithet to the vast expanse of the San Joaquin Valley, which—Claire sometimes thought—managed to combine the bleakness of rural life and the charmlessness of suburbia. Luckily, Sam didn't actually live *in* the Valley but along its eastern edge, in the dry hills that marked the beginning of the Sierras. It was here in Kaweah County that Sam and the boys' mother, Debby, had grown up, married, reproduced, and separated, and it was here that the boys returned every summer like swallows, or locusts: last year in May, before Sam and Claire had gotten together, this year waiting until August, when the heat was intolerable anyway. And next year . . . well, next year, if, God help her, she was still in Kaweah County, Claire would arrange to be on a Mediterranean cruise. Or better still, in Maine, she thought dreamily, remembering a childhood of cool dark woods and rocky beaches. . . .

And rain. There were places in the world where water came down all unbidden from the sky instead of on schedule through a sprinkler nozzle. Here only dust came out of the air, especially now, when the pickers, human and otherwise, moved through field and orchard, stirring the dry earth into gray clouds like powdered bone.

Commotion outside interrupted her reverie. Shannon was now advancing on Terry, brandishing the bat, and she retreated from the window just as Sam rushed to intervene. One week down, three to go, she thought morosely, collapsing on the living room couch. After a moment she retrieved the issue of the *Journal of Agricultural Biology* she had flung down on arriving from work and picked idly at the address sticker: "Dr. Claire Sharples, P.O. Box 323, Riverdale, CA." Futile to bring it home, really—it was impossible to think coherently with the kids screeching around like small antipersonnel devices.

At least she could escape to the lab during the day; Sam had taken the week off to be with them, carting home a pile of paperwork that was, naturally, gathering dust on the corner of the coffee table. But then Sam didn't seem to find them as irritating as she did. He just worried about them incessantly, which was in itself irritating—Were they having a good time? Was he fulfilling his fatherly duties? Could he even maintain a relationship with them? etc. etc.—not to mention his qualms about them growing up in Los Angeles, which constituted a whole other catalog of anxieties.

Well, tomorrow, Wednesday, life would regain some sort of order. The kids would begin staying with a neighbor dur-

ing the day, and Sam would return to work—to the Citrus
Cove Agricultural Experimental Field Station down in the
Valley, where Claire was in transition from effete academic
researcher to can-do hands-on plant pathologist and Sam was
the local UC Extension expert on stone fruit (peaches, nec-
tarines, plums).

The screen door slammed and Sam walked in, wiping his
glasses on his jeans, his damp T-shirt clinging to him in a
very compelling way. She grabbed the tail of his shirt as he
passed, peeled it up, and kissed his stomach. "Mmmm," he
responded, bending down to her, then straightening swiftly
as the boys came spurting into the room.

"Dad, can we go down to the Mini-Mart and play Nin-
tendo?"

"Yeah, please, will you take us?"

"I thought we agreed that you guys would play ball while I
worked this afternoon," Sam said weakly, a note of pleading
creeping into his voice. Claire hated that helpless tone. It was
so uncharacteristic. Whatever his other failings, Sam was
resolute, resourceful, decisive—except with his kids. With
his kids he was a patsy. Especially when they resorted to that
magic phrase "Mom always lets us . . . ," usually followed
by some outrageous clause: "Mom always lets us ride our
bikes on the freeway"; "Mom always lets us watch *Texas
Chainsaw Murderers on Sorority Row.*"

Sam, of course, exercised reasonable restraint, but he ago-
nized over every denial, terrified of estranging them. His
children realized this very well, thought Claire sourly, and
now she waited for them to move in for the kill.

"It's too hot to play catch. I feel sick!" stated Terry.

"Yeah, and we're bored," his big brother added, and
watched his father flinch; what if Mom knew they'd been
sick and bored at Dad's house?

Sam looked at her in dismay. "I really have to read some
of this before Saturday," he said, indicating the pile of docu-
ments. "At least these reports on pesticide residues. I'm supposed to talk about them at the open house."

The open house was the major event of the field station's
liturgical calendar; otherwise she wouldn't have acquiesced.
There was a brief silence, and then she replied ungraciously,

"All right. I'll take them." She ignored his grateful smile and stomped out of the house, feeling like a sullen ten-year-old herself. Shannon and Terry swooped down the stairs before her and piled into the car.

The road down to the tiny settlement of Riverdale wound through steep bleached hills that were shaded by dark-leaved oaks and studded by gray boulders. The kids sat in the back of the Toyota and talked animatedly about various arcane elements of little-boy culture. Some mysterious objects called "transformers" loomed large in their world.

"What are 'transformers'?" Claire asked brightly. As usual she sounded forced and condescending even to herself, and also as usual her conversational gambit fell on unresponsive little ears. "Don't try so hard," Sam kept saying (well, how hard *was* she supposed to try?). "It'll come eventually. Right now they don't have too much use for females, I'm afraid. It's not really personal, it's the age. And Chuck's influence." Chuck, their stepfather, was fourth on Sam's list of kiddie worries, items one through three being too much TV, not enough fresh air and exercise, and the corrupting atmosphere of L.A., respectively.

"Toys," Terry muttered reluctantly.

"Little-kids' toys," Shannon added in a lofty tone designed to provoke his brother, who immediately shot back:

"Then you must be a little kid, 'cause *you* played with mine this morning!"

"I was just looking at it!"

"Liar! You were so playing with it—*ow!*"

Claire sighed and turned on the radio.

"Somebody should leave," Reba McEntire warbled, "but which one should it be? You need the kids. . . ." KCW, the country station out of Bakersfield. Claire furiously twirled the dial; Sam must have been driving the Toyota.

Ah, there it was. "*Y volver, volver, volve-e-rr,*" she crooned along with the theatrical male singer—she was trying to teach herself Spanish from the local Mexican stations—"*a tus brazos otra vez. . . .*"

"Oh, yeah, like you're way cool . . . *not!*" came Shannon's taunt from the back seat.

Scuffle. Muffled thumps. "Stop it . . . stop it . . . *Claire!*" somebody wailed—Terry, who was more willing than his brother to appeal to her alleged parental authority. "He put his toe on my toe!"

She didn't even laugh; that's how anxious the boys made her. "Well, um, Shannon," she began uncertainly, "don't put your toe—"

Too late; there was a crescendo of shrieked accusations, and in the rearview mirror she saw limbs flail as elbows were placed in other people's eyes and toes on other people's toes.

"Terry . . . Shannon . . ."

It was hard to remember that she had liked the idea of Sam having children. It had seemed to give him a kind of stature that she lacked: he had moved on to the adult phase of the species, while she was forever stalled in adolescence, a thirty-four-year-old teenager. In fact, before the boys had come she had even entertained fantasies of herself, warm, nurturing, maternal (qualities she had never aspired to possess), cookin' up dinner for her menfolk . . .

That was in the abstract, of course. In the flesh these particular boys quickly made clear, through retching noises and other amusing reactions, that they despised her healthy, vegetarian, no-sugar-or-cholesterol meals, and after three days she had refused to reenter the kitchen. Now they were subsisting on frozen pizza and fast foods, which suited Shannon and Terry—and, she suspected, Sam—just fine.

Uh-oh, Terry was crying in earnest. "Are you all right?" she called worriedly. "Terry, what videos do you want to rent?" Her voice stretched desperately over the din, unheeded. Of course unheeded; nothing she did worked with them. Maybe if they had been younger—

And a little less male.

Because they were *so* male, these boys; that had surprised her. She had expected them to be softer somehow, but they seemed to be little concentrated pellets of all that was most competitive, most aggressive, most macho in male culture. And she was already drowning in a testosterone sea out here, even more than at MIT. With a few exceptions her colleagues were male, her clients were male, even her friends, such as they were, were men.

Terry had stopped crying, and now both boys were giggling. She shifted down for the hairpin turn that meant they had almost descended the thousand feet or so to Riverdale. As they rounded the curve the hills opened out suddenly, and to the west they looked out across the lead-colored sea of pollution that settled into the Valley every summer. Ah, yes, fresh air, she thought sardonically. And as for exercise and TV, sliding around on the floor of the car were five videos she was returning to the Riverdale Mini-Mart. Sam had held out about twenty-four hours before the anguished wail of his offspring had sent him rushing down to rent a television—his first—and a VCR and $20 worth of movies.

The road dead-ended into State 170, Riverdale's main street, and she turned right and pulled into the Mini-Mart's parking lot. The kids sprinted into the market and headed for the video game, but Claire halted by the front door and looked east.

Just beyond town the highway began to snake up the long western slope of the mountains. From this side the huge batholith of the Sierra swelled gradually to a fourteen-thousand-foot crest, then plunged abruptly in a sheer vertical escarpment, like a tremendous wave of granite forever poised to crash down on Nevada. And if it weren't for the kids, she could be up there, in the high country somewhere, settled under some alpine tree—lodgepole or limber pine (*Pinus contorta, Pinus flexilis,* Sam's voice corrected, in her head)—instead of in a damned convenience store parking lot, waiting for two crazed preadolescents to run out of quarters.

Well. She slipped back into the car and flipped through her journal.

The radio's program of *Música de Jalisco* had ended, and a crisp male voice was reading the news. Since this particular station, Radio Campesino, served the Valley's Spanish-speaking farmworkers and often reported events that no one else bothered to cover, she listened hard, frowning in a doomed effort to snatch some meaning from the torrent of words. But it was beyond her. "*El Presidente de Mexico yah*dala *yah*dala *yah*dala *con los Estados Unidos yah*dala *yah*dala," a pause, "*yah*dala *yah*dala *Hector Cedillo . . .*"

Eck-*TOR* Say-*DEE*-yo. Switching off the radio, she carefully repeated the syllables, savoring the voluptuous *r* and trying to remember who he might be. Minor functionary of the Mexican government? Central American despot/democratic leader? Freedom fighter/terrorist? Shrugging, she immersed herself in an article on *Entyloma seritonum,* an obscure fungus—smut, to be precise—in which she had developed an unnatural interest.

Twenty minutes later she looked up with a guilty start, remembering the kids, and walked to the window. Terry was now sitting on the floor reading a *Masters of the Universe* comic book, but Shannon was still at the throttle of *Super Mario Brothers in Hell,* his face set and fanatical like a kamikaze pilot's.

Or like Sam's, she thought, surprised. Superficially the very blond boys bore little resemblance to their father, who was thin and dark, but Sam had that same expression of rapt attentiveness when he was examining some scrubby little specimen of native flora. Or sometimes when he was looking at her—which made up for a lot, but not for everything.

"Help me pick out some new movies," she said. After some bitter negotiation during which they traded vetoes, Claire on grounds of excessive violence and degradation of women, the kids on grounds of dumbness, they grudgingly compromised on three cassettes, *Ernest Saves Christmas* (Terry), *Home Alone* (Shannon), *Alien III* (both). As they left, the lady behind the counter gave Claire a smile of maternal complicity, which she returned weakly, feeling like a fraud.

Frozen pizza for dinner and then some serious television watching: this was the nightly routine that had been established during the previous week. Claire read, and Sam pretended to read. Like many people who rarely watched TV, he was fascinated by it and attempted to disguise this by making perfunctory scathing comments from time to time. But, being Sam, what he chose to object to was not, say, the inane scripts or the cardboard characters; it was the botanical inaccuracies.

"Look at that!" he said tonight. "They're supposed to be in Korea and there's *Quercus agrifolia* all over the place! Obviously Malibu Canyon or somewhere like that!" And later, "I don't believe it! Washington, D.C., and there's a goddamn *Umbellularia californica* in the front yard!"

"Da-a-ad!" the kids complained, and, "Sa-a-am!" Claire screamed silently. This was Sam at his nerdiest: slumped on his chair, television glittering in his lenses, hands folded across his thin chest (at least he was wearing the T-shirt instead of his workday uniform of pale green polyester shirt and strange trousers). How had it happened that after years of exposure to his type—in high school science classes, college biology, graduate school microbiology—without the slightest attraction, she had found Sam irresistible? Was it heat stroke? His beauty of character? Or his pheromones?

All three, maybe, but mostly the latter, which was another black mark against the boys. Since their arrival she and Sam had barely shaken hands. He was preoccupied and reluctant to express affection in the kids' presence—and since there was no privacy, not even a lock on the bedroom door, it was impossible to escape their presence—and she was sulky. Not exactly a good atmosphere for sex or even a decent argument, the two mainstays of a relationship.

She tolerated two hours of Family Life, then announced abruptly, "I have to go to the library," and bolted.

Back down the hill. The sun was descending toward the Valley, slowly, like a fat man lowering himself into a tub of dirty water. By the time Claire reached downtown Parkerville, eleven miles below Riverdale, a glorious toxic pink sunset was smeared across the sky. The library was in fact the only reason she had found for visiting downtown Parkerville, and evidently everyone else felt the same: serious shopping was done in the suburban malls or in Bakersfield to the south or Fresno to the north, and Parkerville, like grander cities before it, was dying from the inside out. Broad, shady Main Street was now generally deserted; only the bars and the squalid old hotel that housed farmworkers were thriving.

And, of course, the library.

She drove around this cinder-block structure, which the city in its wisdom had just erected in place of the delightful thirties-era mission-style building that had preceded it, and finally parked. Before her was an old Volvo encrusted with ancient bumper stickers: BUY ORGANIC and BOYCOTT COORS peeked out from under MONDALE-FERRARO, which was half-covered by US OUT OF CENTRAL AMERICA, which shared space with EARTHACTION! which overlapped I KNOW WATTS WRONG in a sort of pentimento of hopeless liberal causes.

In Cambridge, or Berkeley, or Eugene, this was a run-of-the-mill vehicle, maybe, but in Kaweah County there was only one person to whom it could belong. And in fact she nearly crashed into him as she rounded a corner at a brisk pace.

Emil Yankovich threw up his hands in an odd protective gesture—not, she thought unhappily, at the impending impact, but at the sight of her—and dropped his library books.

"God, Emil, I'm sorry. Here, let me help."

"N-n-no!" he stammered fiercely, but it was too late; she had already stooped to help retrieve his books and so found herself knee to knee and eye to eye with him as he did the same. He croaked something through a constricted throat, and his brown eyes rolled like a trapped . . . animal's. Cow's, she had been thinking, but that was unkind, even though there *was* something bovine about him when he was like this, paralyzed by self-consciousness, gagged by a stutter.

There was a time when he had been relatively fluent and relaxed with her.

Then she had blown it.

"*Desert Solitaire,*" she read from the cover of the book she had picked up. Once, months ago, she had run into Emil (though not so literally) at the library, and he had also been carrying *Desert Solitaire.* "Again? You must have this memorized!" The sound of her own overly cheerful voice, sprightly as a kindergarten teacher's, made her wince. It was the way she talked to the boys, and she knew it was the way women always talked to Emil. He reddened, mumbled something, and pulled away.

"I haven't quite finished *Monkeywrench,*" she continued. Actually she had been unable to get past page three, but she was hoping to reestablish their rapport. "I'll bring it by your house when I do." She gave him her best smile.

"You c-can k-keep it," he said brusquely, and swept past

her toward the street. She felt a flash of disappointment and anger; it was humiliating to have once patronized someone and then find that you needed them more than they needed you.

Quickly she dumped this week's load of sci-fi, procured another armful—between these and the videos she shouldn't have to speak to anyone in her so-called family for a week—and stepped back out into the sultry night. Emil's Volvo was still there, and she saw his lone figure standing under a streetlight by a newspaper vending box, reading the paper. When she called to him he jerked upright but didn't look in her direction. Instead he slid into his car and drove away.

Angry all over again—he had heard her all right—she found herself automatically picking up the paper he'd flung, in a most un-Emil-like gesture, to the ground. (*Litter! Waste!*) As she headed for the recycling bin she scanned the headlines.

The *Parkerville Sentinel*'s front page was as usual culled from the papers of bigger cities: Fresno, Bakersfield. FRESNO REPORTER AND SENATOR TRADE CHARGES IN LIBEL CASE, she read. MORE KILLER BEES SIGHTED NEAR BAKERSFIELD. BODY FOUND IN CANAL IDENTIFIED.

Ah, a body in an irrigation canal. This was the local method of choice for the disposal of awkward corpses in Sam's rural paradise. "The nude body of the man discovered Monday afternoon in the Friant-Kern Canal has been tentatively identified as Hector Cedillo, 19, a Mexican national."

Claire frowned, then remembered—the radio. That's what the broadcast had been about. Eck-*TOR* Say-*DEE*-yo, poor kid; not a head of state, just a statistic. She read on. "Cedillo apparently drowned last Sunday night, August 14. Police speculate that the victim may have stumbled into the canal while intoxicated. On August 1 another Mexican national, Juan Perez, drowned in an irrigation ditch about four miles north of Parkerville."

The end. One lousy inch. It was a typical *Sentinel* account, and one that made her grit her teeth. There was the usual inexorable logic of the police—the guy was Mexican and therefore drunk—and the whole story was an inch long. The Lions Club elections had gotten three, and a whole column was devoted to the upcoming classic car show, at which, by the way, for a dollar a swing you could beat on a vehicle donated by Ernie's Auto Wrecking, and bashers would considerately be provided with safety glasses.

She knew by now that the death of a "Mexican national" (read "unperson") didn't rate much copy in Parkerville. A couple of "Mexican nationals" get drunk and fall in a ditch? Knife each other on a Saturday night? Disappear from the face of the earth and turn up six years later in a shallow grave? Oh, well, They don't value human life as We do. In a county that was upward of 40 percent Mexican in some seasons, it was astounding how few Anglos even spoke Spanish. It seemed to be regarded as a degraded language; the high school kids took *French*, for God's sake—

Claire realized that she herself didn't speak Spanish. But she was really going to learn.

Maybe that would make a difference in how she felt about this place—that and the farm adviser job Ray Copeland kept dangling in front of her. Because the Mexican farmworkers constituted a culture and a community that attracted her— that, to be frank, she romanticized, as was her wont—but that so far remained politely and implacably closed to her.

Of course, not long ago it had seemed to her that all of Kaweah County had bolted and barred itself against the interloper from the east. Before she had moved out here a year and a half ago she had been warned about the insularity and the racism.

And the heat. Most definitely the heat. But not about the violence, she thought, glancing at the paper before she tossed it into the recycling bin. Maybe they were related. Because a year ago on a blistering summer day her almost friend Tony Rodriguez had died, violently, precipitating upheaval, violent, in her own life.

And now here she was, she thought as she sped up the hill, somehow involved with a man she had thought she disliked, somehow installed in an environment she more or less abhorred, and what was to have been a brief sojourn in the California countryside, a sabbatical from acadamic politics at MIT and Boston winters, had apparently become a life, *her* life, in fact. . . .

She halted in mid-panic attack, reminded herself that she was not indentured to the field station or to Sam, not exactly; that she could leave any time; that anyway, "a life" was literally more than Hector Cedillo had, poor guy.

At home the living room couch had already been unfolded so Shannon and Terry could go to sleep. The adults sat on the front porch in silence for a while; then they too went to sleep.

Chapter 2

State Highway 170 ran due west along the Kaweah River, a mere stream by East Coast standards that nevertheless had sliced a deep canyon down through the granite of the Sierras. West of Riverdale the canyon opened out into a shallow valley, and the river, now dammed and heavily tapped, "creeked" along, sometimes vanishing in dry summer. But a swath of green through brown marked its course: willows, cottonwoods, alders, sycamores. The people of the eastern San Joaquin Valley—the Yokuts, then the Spaniards, then the Mexicans, then the Americans—had all learned to search among the dull green live oaks for the broad bright leaves of these riparian trees. They meant water—several feet underground, maybe, but there all the same.

Twelve miles west of Riverdale the highway and the river ran down into the Great Central Valley itself, but on Thursday morning, as always, Claire turned south before that point, skirting Parkerville, following the westernmost range of Sierra foothills through the orchards. The hills rose around her like West Texas, bare, dun-colored, close-cropped by cattle and horses. Then, just as arbitrarily, the neat rows of trees appeared again. Apricots. Peaches. Pears, pomegranates, pistachios. Olives, almonds, walnuts, and plums; oranges, grapefruit . . .

And finally, just north of the field station, the grapes began.

Claire had photographed these vineyards in January, when the dormant vines had been as lifeless as walkingsticks and

their bare, T-shaped lattices, strung together like bonsai tele-
graph poles, ran off toward the blue mountains.

But that was winter. Months ago those mountains had
faded behind a curtain of smog/dust/don't-ask haze, and
now, in August, the lush vines drooped under their heavy
purple burden. It was the time when growers turned a worried eye to the sky lest a freak summer storm mar the unholy
predictability of Valley weather; it was the time when strings
of old cars, towers of empty wooden flats, and green portable
toilets materialized along frontage roads; in short, as any
five-year-old in Parkerville could tell you, it was harvest
time.

There was not a soul in sight in the vineyard, but there
were the cars and the flats and the toilets; somewhere, somebody was busy in this field. Beyond the last of the vines was
a windbreak of shaggy eucalyptus and then another vineyard.
Now *this* looked truly deserted, and the explanation might lie
in what seemed to be a "For Sale" sign driven into the sloping ground just off the highway. Claire slowed to read, actually wondered for an instant why a realty company would
choose a skull-and-crossbones as its logo, then skidded to a
stop on the shoulder just beyond the sign.

Even then she didn't know what she was seeing. At first
she assumed it was a routine notice: the state had begun to
require growers to post bilingual signs when they sprayed,
notifications of date sprayed and date of safe entry and/or
harvest. But this was different. "DANGER-PELIGRO," it
warned in four-inch letters. "NO ENTRY—SE PROHIBE
ENTRAR." And below, "This field has been found to be
contaminated with an unregistered pesticide and presents a
Health Risk to Humans. Do not enter until further notice."
There was a number for further information; then the text
was repeated in Spanish and signed by the county agricultural commissioner.

Wow! This was big news! And bad news, for whoever's
field had been declared off limits right at harvest time. Of
course, it served the bastard right for spraying poison—cor-
rection, *unregistered* poison, it was all poison—on table
grapes. Whose vineyard was this? Sam would know, or Mac
Healy, the extension expert on grapes, or Ray . . .

Suddenly remembering that she was standing twenty feet from a field that presented a Health Risk to Humans, she dove back into her car, rolled up the windows, and drove to work.

Sam's blue Plymouth Valiant was already parked in the station's lot; he had left early to take the boys to his old friend Linda's, who had two boys of her own. Ordinarily she would have stopped by his office to share a cup of morning coffee and some conjugal affection, but relations were presently so strained—or, to be accurate, she was so resentful; the strain was all on her side—that she was tempted to walk straight downstairs to the lab. On the other hand, she was very curious about the vineyard. Her dilemma was rendered moot when Ray Copeland, the station manager, stuck his head out of Sam's office and waved her in.

"We're just sort of finalizing plans for Friday," he said enthusiastically, handing her a printed flyer. "What do you think?"

Avoiding Sam's welcoming smile, she glanced at the agenda for the Citrus Cove Annual Harvest Open House. Ray Copeland, Station Manager, opening address: "Integrated Pest Management and You." Dr. John Hardy, UC Davis, keynote speaker: "The Future of California Agriculture." Sam Cooper, UC Extension expert, "Pesticides: Use, Abuse, Misuse." Staff, tour of lab (this was Claire), greenhouses, and orchards. Barbecue and picnic.

Ray was watching her anxiously. What did he expect her to say? The open house was exactly the same every year, as far as she could tell. It was part of their mandate: Reach Out to the Community. The growers told the University of California scientists their concerns, and the scientists hawked their latest research projects like so many Kitchen Magicians and Ginzu knives, and Claire suspected that both groups went home unshaken in their belief that the others were overpaid eggheads or hidebound oafs, respectively. Mostly it was an excuse for a barbecue.

"Looks fine," she said, and his round face resumed its usual expression of naive good nature.

"Good, good," he said happily. "Hope you have the lab all dusted and sparkling for the tour."

Claire supplied banter, as required. "No, I figure people should see it under normal working conditions—encrusted with mold and crawling with disgusting life forms."

Ray cackled delightedly and walked out, calling as he left, "Let me know if you have any other last minute suggestions."

Sam propped his legs up on his desk. "How about a pool on how many growers in the audience will be bankrupt by the next open house?" he muttered in a mildly malicious tone; Ray's unflagging sweetness could get to you. Caught off guard, Claire burst into laughter, which Sam incorrectly interpreted as a friendly response. He reached out a long arm, snagged her hand, and kissed the palm.

Claire was not unmoved, but she was nursing a nasty grudge and was fully capable of cutting off her nose to spite her face. In fact, it was her favorite thing to do. She suffered her hand to lie limply in his for a moment, then primly retracted it.

"Did you drop the kids at Linda's?" she asked coolly.

A flash of what might have been anger passed across his face; then the shutters came down. It was a mistake to compete with Sam in the concealment of emotion. The very lenses of his eyeglasses could become opaque.

"Yes," he replied politely, "I'm picking them up at five." He unfolded the newspaper and started reading.

"Oh," said Claire, wondering dimly at her own capacity for making herself unhappy. A pause, a restart, "Do you know anything about that contaminated vineyard I passed on the way to work? Whose grapes are those?"

Sam had opened his mouth to answer when a low rumbling, like a cranky outboard motor, vibrated in the hall. Curious, Claire stepped outside just in time to witness the genesis of a major ruckus.

Emil Yankovich's big brother, Bert, his feet planted wide and left hand clenched into a fist, was waving a piece of paper under poor Ray Copeland's nose. "It's a goddamned lie!" Bert roared in that ruined basso profundo—Bert had inhaled Camels and Valley dust all his life, and his chest sounded like the silt was up to his clavicle and rising. "You tell those morons to clean out their little machines, Ray! They don't know what the hell they're doing!"

He turned on his heel and stalked impressively down the hall toward Claire, heavy boots echoing ominously. His jeans were caked with mud, and his gray workshirt, stretched taut around his massive torso, was already stained with sweat.

"What's the story?" Claire whispered to Sam, who had come up behind her.

"That's what I was about to tell you. County Ag paid Bert's vineyard a little surprise visit on Monday. And as you may have noticed, they slapped him with a citation for using CONKWEST on his grapes—his table grapes, the Red Flames."

"CONKWEST?"

"Phosthion. It's a strong organophosphate, like parathion. And not authorized for food crops."

"Oh."

"He'll try to deny it, of course. Claim County made a mistake."

Unfortunately, Bert's credibility in this area was in the low single figures. He was a known abuser: of pesticides, workers, land, his liver, his lungs, his ex-wife, even his brother.

In fact, it was hard to believe Bert and Emil Yankovich *were* brothers, except for that shared preposterous last name. It was as if one had been raised by wolves—or Bert raised by wolves, and Emil stolen at birth by a roving band of hippies. The schism ran through every part of their lives, but especially their work: Bert had inherited his father's prosperous little vineyard and built it into a thousand acres of diversified crops, while Emil tended his twenty acres of organic grapes with scrupulous, not to say obsessive, correctness.

"Bert!"

She looked up in surprise at the sound of Sam's voice. He had slipped past her and was strolling down the deserted hall. Everyone else had sensibly slunk back into lab or office; it was *High Noon* in the corridor, and Claire suddenly felt a certain amount of alarm. Sam was a tall man, but Bert had it all over him in volume and surface area, and besides, rage became him; he slipped into it like a comfortable coat. If ever Parkerville were called upon to personify the seven deadly sins, Bert

Yankovich, with his hot blue eyes and booming James-Earl-Jones-with-emphysema voice, could certainly be Anger. (No role for Claire there . . . unless overintellectualizing got promoted from irritating habit to sin.)

"Somebody's asking for a major lawsuit here, Sam," Bert was growling.

"Could be," Sam agreed. "Any way that stuff could have been sprayed on an adjacent crop and sort of . . . floated over?"

"You know damn well what the adjacent crops are," Yankovich said. "My grapes on three sides, and the highway on the fourth!"

"Mmm." Sam was silent for a moment. "Been having trouble with leafhoppers?" he asked presently.

"Everybody has trouble with leafhoppers," Bert shot back. "And I use MONITOR, same as everybody. EPA- and state-approved."

"Strong stuff, all the same. Ever think about trying Cryo-Lite? Or leaf cutback? A lot of people have been having luck with—"

"Don't give me that IPM crap," Bert interrupted rudely. "I run a business, not some experiment in organic living like my brother. I use what works!"

"Like CONKWEST?" Sam said with a trace of anger.

"*No*, goddamn it! I don't want to have to tell you again! I didn't spray that stuff, and either County's completely incompetent or I've been set up. And *that* wouldn't surprise me," he added darkly. "There's a lot of people around here would like to see me go under. Now where's that fool Mac Healy?"

He shouldered past Sam and continued down the hall, attending to Claire no more than to a water fountain. She caught a glimpse of his face; it was creased with a thousand tiny seams and gray under the sunburn, and suddenly she felt a stirring of sympathy for Bert Yankovich. Say what you will, Sam had once told her, nobody works harder than Bert. Maybe he's got his farm managers and his foremen, but he's out there every day, all day. And she could well believe it. He was as drawn and weary as . . . as his brother. Right now he looked like his brother. Somehow this carried the weight of a revelation, like the moment she had noticed that Shannon resembled Sam.

Bert had turned the corner in pursuit of the hapless Mr. Healy. "Whoa. Mad Bull Yankovich," she said to Sam.

"That son of a bitch."

Ray had come up beside them. "He does deny it," he said hesitantly.

"Sure he denies it. He's looking at a hefty fine, or even confiscation of his crop!" Sam snarled.

"It is possible there was some lab error—"

"Bullshit! I'm sorry, Ray, but it's just the kind of thing Bert would do, and you know it! He's been having trouble with leafhoppers; he just figured he'd zap 'em with CONKWEST and that it would break down by harvest time. I bet he sent his workers back into the field a half hour after he sprayed, too."

"Even so," Ray said doggedly, "CONKWEST is hard to detect unless you know exactly what you're looking for. Call Bill at County and see if you can find out what the story is, will you?"

So Sam headed for his office and in a few minutes reappeared and shrugged.

"Guys at County stand by their testing. Says they found fourteen micrograms per cubic centimeter of the stuff, well above the safe residue level. They'll repeat it, but they were acting on a tip, so they knew what they were looking for."

"A tip!" echoed Claire. "From whom?"

"Anonymous," Sam answered. "They think Cathy Bakaitis took the call late on Friday, but she's on vacation."

"That's right," murmured Claire, "she's at Tahoe." Cathy was, through a series of flukes, acting county agricultural commissioner and one of the few nodes on Claire's flimsy new girls' network of local female scientists.

"It doesn't quite make sense," Ray was saying slowly. "Bert tells us that field was picked last week. We would have had workers dropping like flies with that concentration of phosthion."

"How do we know we don't?" said Claire. "It takes a while for those reports to come in from clinics and hospital ERs."

"Well, if it is true," Ray began, then concluded in a rush, "I hope they nail him to the wall!"

Nail him to the wall? Ray never expressed so much as tempered disapproval. Claire and Sam gaped at him in astonishment.

"I mean it," he said loudly. His voice broke under the unaccustomed strain, and he continued quietly but ferociously, "Sometimes I get so tired of people like Bert Yankovich! We devote our lives here to developing ecologically sound alternatives to these dangerous pesticides—"

(Here Claire had to suppress a cynical smirk at Ray's revisionism. The current philosophy of the Agricultural Extension System was indeed admirable: integrated pest management, which emphasized management of pests—rather than eradication—through biological control and sparing, carefully timed use of narrow-spectrum pesticides. But it had not always been so.)

". . . and we publicize these methods," Ray was saying "We . . . we explain them carefully to the growers, we're here to help—and then Bert turns around and does something like this. It makes me very angry. Bert seems to positively enjoy flouting the regulations."

"He probably does," said Sam. "Bert thinks the government interferes too much in the life of private citizens. He wants to abolish income tax, stuff like that."

"Oh, yes, I hear that all the time from some people," Ray said bitterly. "But I notice they never complain when it comes to federal price supports, or tariffs, or soil banks, or water subsidies. Damned whiners!" He hiked up his trousers, looked them both in the eye, and stomped away.

Claire goggled at his retreating back for a moment. "I've never seen Ray so . . . ," she began, then remembered they were mad at each other. "Agitated," she finished, clamped her mouth shut, and headed downstairs to her lab.

Her lab. Whenever she became nostalgic for MIT she reminded herself of how many years, and how many grant proposals, it would have taken her to have her own lab if she had stayed. Today Bob Higgenlooper, the new expert nut—whoops, nut expert—had left a present on the counter: four plastic grocery bags full of almonds. Not brunch, but work. Claire and Bob were studying hull rot, a fungal disease that occurred right before harvest, when the hulls of almonds began to split. It was Claire's job to examine these nuts, which had been treated with varying amounts of fertilizer and water over their growing season, for signs of disease. Sometimes the naked eye was enough: the nut meat was blackened and rotted. If not, a quick look under the microscope might show the fur of fungus. But if both these passes were negative, she tossed the nut in a plastic bag with damp filter paper to see if it would grow something with a little encouragement.

So she spent a whole afternoon doing this and wasn't bored. Okay, sort of bored. It was the kind of work an undergrad research assistant could have done and was certainly a far cry from the cutting-edge pure science she had been doing back east. But the novelty of her new job hadn't dissipated—not entirely. She still liked the work, especially the field work. (And since her grant ran out in September, and Ray had offered her a permanent staff position as farm adviser/plant pathologist, she was about to have to decide just exactly how much she liked it.)

At six she left the lab by the back door and took her customary turn around the station's grounds, walking quickly past the familiar projects: soil solarization (some kind of sprayed latex, an adjacent area spread with plastic sheeting, and a control area of bare earth); pistachios, flagged to indicate some kind of treatment, for pests or fungus; Mac Healy's comparison of three different pruning systems for grapes. All very worthwhile, but not why she was here.

She was here for the peaches.

From her lab window she had monitored them since spring, watching the branches become furred with green, then leaf out, and the fruit set and swell until now they were big as softballs, rosy as dawn over the Sierras.

There were no peaches like the station peaches, and they tormented her. Because they were strictly forbidden, they were all Sam's, at least until he finished his trial of organically grown versus non-organically grown yield. She gazed at them longingly, then headed for home.

But the noose of claustrophobia started to tighten again after dinner at Sam's (Chicken McNuggets) and the first hour of TV (reruns of *The A Team*). The library again? A movie?

Just as she was feeling a little panicky the phone rang.

"Claire?" The line echoed with distance.

"Hi, Sara," she said listlessly, and then, with fervor. "Sara!" A vision of salvation, a temporary way out of unpleasantness, had just formed in her head.

Sara Ashe and her husband, Steve, were old friends from Boston who had moved out to Los Angeles about a year ago when Steve had gotten a faculty appointment at UCLA. A devout New Yorker, Sara had regarded her tenure in Boston as exile to the provinces, so her feelings about the move to Los Angeles were unprintable.

"How's life in Lotus Land?" asked Claire, baiting Sara, which somehow she could never resist.

"Appalling," Sara replied languidly, but added, surprisingly, "It has its compensations, however."

"It has?"

"Oh, you know, balmy breezes, Thai food . . . Claire, I got a job!" she crowed, unable to contain herself. "I mean, a real job, a writing job, reviewing movies for the *L.A. Free Press*. It's an 'alternative' paper—you know, a smidgen of leftist politics among the ads for tanning parlors and colonic irrigation—but it has the best entertainment news in the city."

"Sara, that's wonderful!" For a freelance writer a regular paying job, however modest, was downright miraculous.

"I know. I'm ecstatic. If only I thought someone in this city could actually read, my happiness would be complete. But listen, how are you?"

"Fine."

"And Sam?" Only an old friend would have noticed the slight constraint in her voice.

"Fine," Claire said brightly; then, "His kids are visiting."

"Mmm. That must be hard."

"A little," she said guardedly.

Some history lay behind this short exchange. On their trip out to California, Steve and Sara had spent one memorable evening with Sam and Claire. For reasons known only to himself, Sam had chosen dinner to present a long and excruciatingly boring exposition of some minute, possibly nonexistent difference between two types of obscure sedges. Only two people at the table had even seen a sedge, and only one cared. Then, during dessert, Claire had had to explain to Steve, who had been a colleague at MIT, that she was not exactly on the cutting edge of research but in fact spent much of her time testing local crops for brown rot, little leaf, shothole, stunt, smut, wilt, and other similar homely afflictions with pithy Anglo-Saxon names.

Sara and Steve had been exceedingly polite and somewhat bewildered, obviously wondering what the hell she was doing living with an asocial eccentric in a total scientific and cultural backwater. Since these were questions that crossed Claire's mind from time to time, she felt a little defensive with them, but now she ruthlessly quashed any such delicate sensibilities. She needed a favor.

"Listen, Sara—that invitation still open?"

"Of course, any time."

"How about this coming Monday? I know it's short notice, but I have to drive down to UC Riverside to talk to some people about a project, and I could just scoot over to L.A. Maybe stay till Wednesday." She really did have to confer with Allen Okamoto, and after all, why deal with things when you could just . . . split. Make some personal space. Run away.

Sara's enthusiasm seemed unfeigned, and they worked out the details. Claire hung up the phone feeling euphoric. Monday she would be eating Thai food, basking in balmy breezes, engaging in sparkling adult conversation about, oh, new movies, and books, and politics . . . The thought of lemon-grass-and-coconut-milk soup sustained her until bedtime. On Friday she finally sent for her boxed set of *¡Speak Spanish Like a Diplomat!* tapes.

And she and everyone around her prepared for the open house.

Chapter 3

It was Saturday, it was open house, and the belt buckles were here. Turquoise and silver, enameled American flags, brass, with hammered initials three inches high or the names of chemical companies: Monsanto, Pennwalt, DuPont. And the hats: caps, favored by the younger men, with more company logos—International Harvester, Caterpillar, John Deere & Co., or, occasionally, 5th Airborne, USS *Maddox*—and traditional cowboy models with braided bands or silver conchos, perched on top of the seamed faces of the older men. Claire craved her camera as she looked out across the crowd packed into the station auditorium.

The visitors were restless. Sam was speaking, and his tenor voice with its hint of Oklahoma twang was clear and resonant, but the dismal catalog of pesticide dangers he recited was boring, and they had sat through forty minutes of speeches already and were men of deeds, not words. So their boots, and hats, and big buckles proclaimed; she was always amazed at how universally the cowboy aesthetic prevailed on these ceremonial occasions. Some of these people were, indeed, longtime cattlemen, but how about Bert, first-generation Yugoslavian vintner with, rumor had it, an ag degree from UC Davis? Bert too was resplendent in snakeskin boots, cowboy hat, and silver concho belt. Even Ray had donned a string tie for the event.

The few people who weren't in western regalia stood out like cacti in a grotto of orchids: Sam, behind the podium, in sport jacket (polyester) and sport shirt (Dacron). Herself, dressed-for-moderate-success. Emil, in Greenpeace T-shirt and Birkenstock sandals. Like her, he was standing in the back of the room near the exit, and she caught his eye and smiled. He squirmed and looked down at his feet.

Sam was telling cautionary tales. There was the one about the worker who, after accidentally contaminating himself with a pesticide, had stripped, showered, and was laughing with the paramedics when he keeled over dead. There was the one about the worker who had been mixing pesticides and instead of tossing a perfectly good coverall into the bin to be burned, had worn it home and thrown it in with the family laundry. He, his wife, and his three children had all become seriously ill. He reminded them that the LD^{50} of some common pesticides was three or four drops—and then he reminded them what "LD^{50}" meant : Lethal Dose 50, the dose at which 50 percent of experimental animals died. Finally he recalled an incident last summer, in which a whole dormitory of kids at Parkerville Community College—not merely farmworkers, whom some considered expendable, but the sons and daughters of his audience—became ill because a nearby grower had sprayed without warning them.

"Education, compliance, disclosure," he summed up. "That means making sure your workers know what they're using and what precautions they should take—"

"Wait a minute, Sam," Bert Yankovich called loudly. "I'm already posting signs in English *and* Spanish every time I spray something! What the hell do you want from us, bilingual announcements every time we take a shit?"

General laughter from the crowd, and Sam grinned, too, but raised a pacifying hand. "Now, Bert, spray notification is a perfectly reasonable piece of legislation; that's the *minimal* information you—"

"It's a waste of time and a pain in the ass!" Bert interrupted emphatically. "Signs in Spanish? Most of these boys can't even read! 'Specially them Indians, what-do-you-call-'em, Mixtecs." Several people guffawed; Claire saw Wayne Harris, sitting with his wife, Suzie, and their three kids, smirk as if at a dirty joke. "Anyway," Bert continued, "why the hell don't they learn English? My father came over here at sixteen, and *he* sure—"

"You fucking hypocrite, Bert!"

A high voice rang out from the back of the auditorium, and to her astonishment Claire saw that the speaker was Emil. The crowd was shocked into silence by his venomous tone and choice of adjectives, and Claire heard Bert say, "Emil," in a low, warning, oddly intimate tone. But it was too late; Emil was lit and spinning.

"You f-fucking hypocrite," he repeated, trembling with emotion, his stutter giving full weight to the offending word, "you c-could p-pay p-people enough to stay here for a w-while! B-but you'd rather g-get Ruben Moreno to bring you a nice fresh crop of illegals every season"—here there was a strangled noise from the second row—"and b-both of you use them and d-discard them! And then you c-c-complain that they d-don't speak English!"

"You shut your mouth!" roared Bert, stung into fury. His face was scarlet under the snow white Stetson. "I suppose I should have kissed César's ass, like you! You make things worse for every grower in this county! Why don't you go back to the loony bin, you little—" Here he lunged forward and had to be physically restrained from clambering over the rows of folding chairs to get at his brother.

The two men glared at each other for a moment; then Emil wheeled abruptly and left the room. Claire saw the man in the second row, a dapper middle-aged Latino, looking after him murderously. Ruben Moreno, presumably, she thought, whoever and whatever he might be. Meanwhile there was excited buzzing and nervous laughter—the sound of the crowd after a fight on the field—and Sam rode it out for a few minutes. Then he said dryly, "You back to normal, Bert?"

Bert managed an angry laugh. "Sure. It's just that damned brother of mine; he—"

"Good," Sam interjected briskly. "I've got a few more things I want to say here about your legal responsibilities as employers. And you might want to pay special attention to this, Bert."

Bert scowled; everyone in the room knew of his recent troubles with the law, the law in this case being FIFRA, the Federal Insecticide, Fungicide, and Rodenticide Act. Claire, meanwhile, was slipping out the back door. She had watched enough amateur softball to know that some people could stand nose to nose and scream at each other and then sit down and drink a beer together five minutes later, but she wasn't one of them. Public displays of naked aggression upset her. And she suspected they upset Emil, too; it had taken something powerful to ignite him like that. Was he really so passionate about the plight of migrant workers? Or was this some deeper, more private sibling conflict, a grown-up version of Terry and Shannon on the back seat?

Should she go after him? She looked after him uncertainly. She had always felt protective toward him and would like to think that they were still friends; she had so few friends here. But after his behavior at the library, that seemed unlikely. Anyway, it was almost time for the tour, and she should really get down to the lab to play her role (sort of Madame Curie/flight attendant).

Not that she expected anyone to show up. The orchards and greenhouses had more popular appeal, and Claire herself, being new in town, wasn't as much of a draw as, say, Sam, or Ray, or other local boys. But a few people trickled in throughout the afternoon: most she knew by sight, some by name. Several were curious about the Rodriguez murder, and she patiently explained the protocol she followed in testing for resistance to pesticides and fungicides—a procedure that had provided crucial evidence in last year's case. Wayne Harris stopped by, and they talked about walnut blight.

"I've been thinking about your problem," she said. "Seems like the worst blight was on your outer rows of trees, and I'm wondering whether they could have been weakened by herbicide from your neighbor's field." This was a not uncommon source of accidental—or, occasionally, deliberate—damage to trees and fruit.

Harris frowned, then winched as the skin tightened above a healing cut on his cheekbone. The sternness of his tough, blunt-featured young face was usually softened by his molasses-thick Texas accent. But now his voice was hard.

"Well, if so, I'll kill the fucker," he said; then, "Sorry," apologizing for the obscenity. (This always made Claire, who had a mouth like a hockey player, want to smile.) "My profit ended up on the ground in July. All I'm gonna harvest is my costs."

Claire nodded sympathetically. As far as she could see, Wayne had done just what he was supposed to do in life: worked his butt off as a roustabout in the oil fields near Bakersfield, got married, worked his butt off, saved his money, had kids, worked his butt off, leased his small walnut ranch from Bert Yankovich to make the proverbial better life for his kids, worked his butt off.

And for what? He was as broke as a lazy man.

"I don't know that it has anything to do with herbicides," she said. "We'll watch it really carefully next year."

But farming wasn't like the lab. There was no control over the environment. Next year was a whole new ball game and a whole new set of variables: different weather conditions, different neighbors, different pests. They both knew that the mystery of this year's blight might never be solved, and in any case he would never recoup this year's losses.

"Well, I just had a little money come in," he mumbled, "and I got me some roofing work over the winter. Guess we'll git by."

He left, and she propped her elbows on the cool Formica counter and stared out the window at the tinder-dry hills. The sun shot through the cellophane tops of the tall burnished grass—wild oats, *Avena barbata*. Not native, Sam had told her, but introduced from Europe, it had spread as grazing had destroyed the indigenous bunch grasses, until it covered the hills of California from Oregon to Mexico. From a distance it looked as soft as fur, and once, when Claire had first come to Kaweah County, she had stopped her car, climbed a fence, and lain facedown on a hillside. The grass had been brittle and sharp.

She began to think about the conundrum of brothers. She had a brother—an older brother, Charles, who had taught her to fish and hunt and catch a baseball and then sort of slipped out from her life at puberty. But *two* brothers . . . that was something else. That was a relationship to be reckoned with. Take Bert and Emil (she wasn't quite ready to take Shannon and Terry). Bert was not unlike many of the more successful local growers, conducting his business in a way that he undoubtedly characterized as tough but fair and Claire thought of as unscrupulous and ruthless. Even Sam, who was much more sympathetic to agribusinessmen than she—though not as sympathetic as he was supposed to be—had called Bert a son of a bitch.

But Emil . . .

She remembered that very first encounter at the library, back in March or April, when she had known Emil only by his reputation and by his bumper stickers.

"Good book?" she had asked, glancing at *Desert Solitaire*; she was always on the lookout for kindred spirits.

"Abbey's my f-favorite w-writer," he had answered, making it through the *f* and the *w* on sheer willpower, and then, touchingly, "He's not afraid to be p-p-passionate."

Surprised and intrigued—it was the most original literary comment she had heard in Kaweah County—Claire had looked at him with interest. A potential friend, perhaps?

That afternoon he had lent her his own copy of *The Monkeywrench Gang*, pulling it from his car, where, she suspected, it normally resided permanently like a Bible. And subsequently she had made overtures of friendship whenever she saw him.

But it wasn't easy. She had had to cultivate him as patiently as he did his organic grapes.

At first talking to Emil was like hitting tennis balls off a cliff. Nothing came back. And when he did begin to respond, it was frustrating for both of them, because he was so hard to understand. Somehow Claire had thought of a stutter as one of those archaic childhood conditions that had disappeared in twentieth-century America, like diphtheria, but evidently she was wrong, or Emil had dropped through the net of speech pathologists and biofeedback training and other modern psychosociomedical miracles.

It was not simply a stutter. Emil's problem was farther up the line than that. Over the next few months she had had ample opportunity to analyze it and had decided that he somehow reversed the whole mechanics of speech, trying to produce sound on an intake rather than an exhalation of air. Every sentence became a gulp and a gasp. His own words smothered him.

And all the while he was watching her face. Often, mistaking her concentration and nervousness for impatience, he would disappear.

But one day, after a symposium at the station on organic fertilizers, Emil had shown up at her office and had begun to talk. About topsoil. Tons of it, blowing and washing away every year, he had said—stammering badly at first, then growing more fluent and angry, as if every grain were a dime out of his pocket. Turned out Emil had a lot to say about topsoil and sustainable agriculture. People were stewards of the land, not owners, he had said; they had no right to abuse it, or mine it, or despoil it.

"Or sell off every square inch of it to developers," Claire had added.

"R-r-right. Developing land is l-like t-trying to b-be a p-professional organ d-donor. You c-can only g-go so f-far!"

Remembering that remark now, she smiled.

But while she might like Emil for his politics and his intelligence and his humor, hers was a minority opinion. In Kaweah County, and particularly in the company of Kaweah County growers, Emil was a freak, a true bleeding-heart liberal in a county where the prevailing politics were slightly to the left of Gengis Khan; an ecoactivist among people who sported SIERRA CLUB: HIKE TO HELL! bumper stickers; an organic farmer where the dominant approach to insects and disease, in spite of Ray's evangelism on behalf of integrated pest management, was Spray-More; a vocal supporter of the Farm Workers Union and employer of unionized labor—this really rankled—when the prevailing attitude toward farm labor was an ugly mix of contempt, ignorance, and dependence, with an occasional dollop of paternalism.

Finally, when most grape growers in the area were doing pretty well, Emil had the dubious distinction of being about to go broke.

At least, that was the rumor. The thought occurred to her that Emil might have asked his brother for a loan and been refused; maybe that was the source of the rancor. She would have to ask Sam about *los hermanos* Yankovich. That would be a nice neutral topic.

Veils of blue smoke had begun to blow past her window. It was time for the barbecue.

"Thanks, Ray—ooh, watch it!" Claire said as Ray's string tie snaked toward the gooey sauce he had just slathered on the spareribs. He and Bob Higgenlooper were dispensing the charred meat, and she noted with relief that their butcher's aprons did not say "Pennwalt" or "DuPont," but merely "Kiss the Cook."

It was over one hundred degrees out here in the open field behind the station buildings; the distant hills wavered like mirages through the heat rising from the big steel drum barbecues. The younger crowd had stripped to tank tops and shorts, but the older people, raised in a more formal era, sweated it out, the men perhaps permitting themselves to remove their western-style jackets, the women, encased like bolsters in polyester dresses and nylon stockings, fanning themselves in the shade. Claire headed for the beer keg, searching the crowd for Sam and the boys or anyone else she knew.

"Well, howdy. Can I pump you a drink?"

She had nearly collided with Tom Martelli, who was making a beeline for the keg from the opposite direction.

"I didn't know you harbored an interest in integrated pest management," she said.

He opened his blue eyes very wide. "I harbor an interest in free beer and ribs," he said, patting his stomach. "Anyway, this is a major social event in the county. Sort of like a Harvard tea party." He grinned at her. They had a running joke about the gentility of her New England upbringing: she would describe being mugged on the MTA or robbed at gunpoint in her lab at MIT, and he would continue to talk about tea parties and ladies' deportment. Which was about as accurate a picture of Cambridge as it was of this bucolic paradise, where bodies seemed to appear in canals at regular intervals—

"Tom," she said suddenly, "what do you know about the kid who drowned in the Friant-Kern the other day? Is that your jurisdiction?" It was very hard to tell who was responsible for what around here.

"No, that's the county sheriff's. But I know one thing." He paused dramatically. "He didn't drown."

"What?"

"Nope. Ol' J.T.'s got a real mystery on his hands there. Coroner can't figure out what killed him. Looks like the official cause of death is gonna be 'heart failure.'"

"'Heart failure'! He was only nineteen!"

Tom shrugged. "It does happen. But 'heart failure' don't necessarily mean nothin' except the medical examiner couldn't find any other cause of death. There was no pulmonary edema—that's fluid in the lungs, to you. And no knife in the spleen, which is a bigger surprise."

"Why?"

"Well, evidently this boy used to like to drink at El Aguila. That's a bar—"

"I know, I *live* here, remember?"

"Right, but it ain't exactly a refined place. And witnesses said this kid had a fight with some unidentified individual the night he died. Some *huero*"—pronouncing it *gwer*-oh—"that means Anglo—who everybody recognized and nobody knew. I guess we all look alike to them. So I agree, I ain't real happy about 'heart failure.' I been following it, just in case."

Just in case county sheriff J. T. Cummings, that cretin, completely screwed up. Why the voters returned him to office term after term was another mystery; but Martelli had run against him one year and lost humiliatingly, so now he just sort of looked on in frustration.

"Did they ever—" Find his clothes, she meant to ask, but Tom cocked his head.

"Aw—that's Marie."

Now she heard it, the faintest of calls from the far end of the field. Amazing how couples became tuned to each other's frequencies—of voice, at least, if not of mind.

"I've gotta go, my in-laws are here," Tom was saying. "Why don't you come over and join us?"

"Oh, no . . . thanks, but I better find Sam and the boys. Thanks anyway. See you later." She watched him walk away, feeling slightly forlorn, then turned and scanned the crowd once again.

There, beyond the barbecues—there was Sam's dark head.

And next to it, Linda Nelson's blond curls. He was bending down to hear her while the kids—Sam's two, plus Linda's sons, Douggie and Kevin—chased each other in a circle around them.

They all looked as if they belonged together; they looked like a goddamn Norman Rockwell painting. Ordinarily Claire somehow managed to feel superior to women such as Linda, but in occasional moments of insight her elaborate defenses cracked. Why hadn't Sam married Linda long ago? They had been lovers on and off for years, before Claire; Linda was pretty and blond, she liked children, she was intelligent and sweet-tempered. While she, Claire . . . She caught sight of her reflection in the lab's windows. Bird's-nest hair, bony face, lanky frame: a scrawny, plain, mean-spirited bitch, she thought morosely, and the kids' presence seemed to be really bringing out her nastiest qualities.

She finished her beer and walked slowly back inside and down to the lab, too absorbed in self-loathing to see Sam waving at her.

She must love him, she thought, closing the door behind her, if the despair she felt at the thought of losing him meant love. But she couldn't ignore their incompatibilities forever, could she? Should she? She suddenly wondered if she were seizing on the boys' visit as an occasion to drive him away. Sara, a compulsive and ingenious psychoanalyzer, would approve that convoluted interpretation.

Did she love Sam, did Sam love her—unsolved problems excited her, but problems without a solution made her physically ill. She cranked up the air-conditioning and read a journal.

Chapter 4

At six she left the lab by the front door, avoiding the lingering barbecuers, and headed home. She slowed before Riverdale and the road to Sam's, then realized she was not quite ready for another dinner *en famille*. Instead she turned off at the forest service station, where the fire danger, she noted, was already HIGH, and cut north along a gravel road marked "J26." She passed vineyards and open fields and orchards, but mostly she passed orange groves. This was orange country; not for nothing was the field station called Citrus Cove.

They were beautiful trees, oranges: pools of cool dark green in this baked landscape. (In fact, the French—perverse as always—had once grown them as ornamentals, treasuring their glossy foliage, symmetry, and sweet-smelling flowers. Evidently nobody had thought to try the leathery fruit.)

But this year acres of citrus were yellowed and brittle like old wallpaper, as if the grim reaper, that resourceful fellow, had spilled acid from a helicopter. There had been a rare hard frost for days in December, killing not only fruit but whole trees, whole orchards.

Since Claire now had a professional interest in death—of plants, at least—she tried to perceive the pattern of destruction. Cool air drained downhill, which was why the fragile citrus was planted on the slopes of the foothills; why the propellerlike air circulators whirled to keep the lethal chill from settling too long. But here in a hollow was a perfectly healthy tree; next to it a brown skeleton; beyond that a partly damaged tree with bare branches protruding from thick foliage like arms with the sleeves pushed up. Death looked random, but she knew it wasn't.

She just didn't have all the information.

Cutting through the groves, she turned at Bill's Backhoe and drove along progressively narrower and rougher dirt roads, heading north and east, then north once more. When she finally pulled off the road, it was at a point much like every other point: to her right a narrow irrigation ditch ran along the road, to her left a vineyard offered a little shade. But it was the open field beyond the ditch that had brought her here: a modest-size plot of alfalfa, golden in the late afternoon sun.

Only alfalfa wasn't golden. It was green, purple if allowed to flower. Those yellow blooms nodding there were in fact "fiddleneck," *Amsinckia intermedia*, an attractive little wildflower with coiled caterpillars ("cymes," according to Sam) of flowers ("inflorescences," op. cit.). And unfortunately the harmless-looking plant contained strong alkaloids poisonous to the stock this alfalfa had been planted to feed.

She got out of the car and slammed the door, waving away the ensuing explosion of dust. Then she strolled north along the ditch. A number of people were interested in biological control of fiddleneck, including herself and Allen Okamoto down at Riverside. Their backgrounds in mycology had led them to several pathogenic fungi that looked promising: *Entyloma seritonum*, for example.

Her task was to design an experiment to test it and to find an appropriate test site, and she was nervous about it. In the lab she was an ace, but this was her first field trial, and the outdoors was so messy! So unpredictable!

But this was a nice field—self-contained, smallish, but level and open, with what looked to be uniform drainage, sunlight, and heat. She'd have to find out who owned it and obtain his cooperation. Probably he'd agree: alfalfa was a good crop for an integrated pest management experiment, even among hardliners, because its profit margin was so low that it didn't pay to spray it with expensive herbicides.

She looked down to find that her good black suede loafers were now gray with fine alluvial silt and wondered for a moment if she should return to the car for her boots. Like the real farm advisers, she now routinely carried in her trunk boots, hat, jacket, a complete change of clothes, several gallons of water, shovel, Styrofoam cooler, and a field kit she automatically stuck in her pocket when she was working—gloves, knife for cutting samples, plastic bags for preserving same. But the damage was done, so she kept walking, sinking up to her ankles in the stuff. It was like moon dust.

She glanced at her watch, wondering if she had time to visit Wayne Harris's walnut grove, which was just up the road. Six-thirty. Not too late, but too hot; the temperature was still ninety plus. Just beyond the mountains sat tight white clouds like scoops of cottage cheese, as if the very air had curdled from the heat.

The canal on her right was surprisingly clean, and while she herself would never put as much as a toe in it, considering what it tended to pick up—microbes, pesticides, bodies—she could understand why all the local kids swam in these irrigation ditches during the sweltering Valley summers; why Hector Cedillo had decided to take a drunken midnight swim. In fact, someone else was swimming in this very canal, she saw—and stopped dead.

Not swimming.

Floating, face down, arms stretched wide, absolutely motionless. There was a stasis in the pose, a comfortableness, almost, that made her think the figure had floated there for a long time.

Oh, Jesus, not another one! Dazedly she walked toward it, slowly at first, then breaking into a half run. *CPR, why hadn't she ever gotten around to taking a CPR course? Junior Lifesaving, then. That was going way back . . . YWCA pool, reek of chlorine, that fat girl with the braids and the German name who had almost sent her to the bottom when she'd attempted a hair carry . . . um, victim's head to the side to clear the airways, whatever that involved; extend the chin, pinch the nostrils . . .*

All too soon she had reached the figure. It was a man—a young man, she thought—slightly built, wearing sport shirt and shorts and a rubber thong on his right foot. Only his right foot, she noted with the clarity of nightmare. His left was bare.

She sank to her knees and grasped him under the arms. He was heavier than she would have believed possible—the term dead weight suddenly acquired meaning—but worse, he was slippery. Her initial spurt of adrenaline enabled her to drag his torso onto the bank, but that was the easy part; and though she grabbed him by available handles—shorts, shirtsleeve, ankle, and yes, even hair—she couldn't manage to pull more than a third of him out of the water at any one time. After a few minutes of this intimate tussling, his thin, muscular body was as familiar as a lover's, but so cold, so inert, and stiff, like an inflated doll; he reminded her horribly of her dreams of Tony Rodriguez, who came to her periodically, smiling and slimy from the lake where they had found him. The conviction grew inside her that this man, too, was way beyond CPR and unobstructed airways. Finally, realizing there was no help for it, she slid into the ditch herself, where the now turbid water reached her waist, and gave a mighty heave.

And rolled him neatly onto the weedy bank.

She struggled out of the ditch and rested on all fours, gasping, arms trembling, clamping down on nausea. Airways? Nostrils? Hesitantly she turned him over, glancing at his face and then away. A young man, yes. Not as young as Tony Rodriguez had been; this man looked to be in his early thirties. And he looked very dead. But how could you tell? Should she begin mouth-to-mouth?

A new wave of nausea and a strong sense of futility sent her stumbling after help instead. She was tottering toward her car on perilous legs when she heard an approaching siren. A Chevy Blazer with a familiar black-and-white insignia skidded to a stop, and out stepped Tom Martelli.

"I know," he cut into her incoherent stammer, "a hysterical old lady reported it ten minutes ago. Let's go look at him. And what are you doing here, anyway?"

She explained, as they trotted back along the canal, where Tom crouched beside the still figure.

"Been dead for a while, I'd say," he remarked after a moment, and she felt enormous relief; there was nothing she could have done for him. "Not too long; just the beginning of rigor—though that could be the cool water. Where was he— just above the culvert?" She nodded. "Another drunk farmworker, I reckon." He paused, then added triumphantly, "And this one's *mine*!"

Oh, yes, she thought vaguely, this was probably inside Riverdale town limits. Once again she tried to study the man's face but had to look away immediately. Sunburned, she noticed. A farmworker? Maybe; that high-bridged nose and curly hair could be Mexican—or Armenian or Sicilian or all-American hybrid, for that matter. His shirt (she found she could manage to look at his shirt) was Central American—rows of parallel tucks down the front—but lots of Anglos favored that style, too.

But what was that blob of yellow over the pocket? She knelt beside Tom.

"You see a wallet?" Tom asked.

"No, but I think there are keys in his shorts," she said, remembering that small hard lump in his back pocket.

"Three bodies in canals in three weeks," Tom murmured thoughtfully. Now that one was his, they were all his, and he could allow himself to think about them. "Though the first, Perez, was just a straightforward drowning—you say this guy was *floatin'*?" he asked sharply as something struck him.

"Yes, facedown."

He began to mutter about feet tangling in weeds when Claire interrupted him. "Picked himself a dandelion," she said, point to the limp flower stuck in a buttonhole.

Tom fingered the shirt. "Yep," he said, eyes still far away.

"Only it's not really a dandelion."

"It's not?" He focused on the lapel.

"Uh-uh."

"Well, it sure as hell looks like one to me. What is it?"

"No idea," she said between teeth that chattered despite the lingering heat. "Sam would know. He's a better botanist than I am." Another siren was approaching rapidly.

"Mmm. I guess it might be important." Tom carefully extracted the sodden fragments from the buttonhole and placed them in a plastic bag.

The siren became deafening, and an ambulance pulled up behind the Blazer.

"We'll have to do a few things here; shouldn't take me more than half an hour. Why don't you go on in to my office?" Tom said, and Claire gratefully started once again for her car. "Oh, and phone Sam when you get there," Tom called after her. "Tell him to come on down before the evidence wilts."

Chapter 5

Claire and Tom stared solemnly at the bedraggled flower that lay precisely in the center of Martelli's vast mahogany desk like . . . like a patient anesthetized upon a table, thought Claire, vaguely remembering her Eliot. Something about memory and a geranium—no, that was another poem, and anyway this wasn't a geranium. Nor a dandelion, either; even she had realized that, though it looked like one, with its broad head of yellow ray flowers. Well, maybe a cross between a dandelion and a daisy. Flowers that looked something like this were so numerous that despairing botanists had created a new taxonomic category especially for them: God Damn Yellow Flowers.

However, this particular GDYF was a *Hulsea*. So Sam had stated firmly as soon as he saw it, and now, flanked by Claire and Tom, he was seated at the desk, his fat *California Flora* open beside him.

Claire watched over his shoulder while he followed the flora's key to the genus *Hulsea* with his forefinger. He read each of the dichotomous choices aloud.

"Stems more or less leafy/stems scapose." ("Scapose"? As a biologist she had had to take botany, of course, but she had always hated that pretentious Latinate gobbledygook. If she wanted to keep this job, however, she was going to have to override aesthetic reservations and give herself a crash refresher course.) "Stems leafy," he decided. "Plants viscid pubescent, not at all woolly/plants more or less woolly." He looked closely at the specimen. "Not at all woolly," he pronounced. "Heads solitary/heads in corymb." Whatever a

43

corymb was, this head was clearly splendidly solitary, and: "Solitary, four to six point five centimeters across," concurred Sam.

It was a short key. This last decision had led inexorably to a particular species of hulsea, and Sam turned the page and read its description. After a moment he gave a grunt of dissatisfaction and, flipping back to the key, ran through the choices again. As Claire and Tom stirred impatiently he pulled out a hand lens and a ruler and carefully examined the limp bit of vegetation, from time to time muttering, "Cespitose . . . one to four decameters . . . monocephalous . . ." He leaned over and sniffed. Finally he snapped the *Flora* shut and stood up.

"Where did you find this, did you say?" he asked.

"It was in the guy's buttonhole," Tom replied. "He had on a short-sleeved sport shirt, light blue. Also tan shorts and rubber sandals, what-do-you-call-'em, thongs. Well, one rubber thong."

Sam considered a moment, then said blandly, "Was he sunburned?"

Claire's jaw dropped, and after a moment Tom answered irritably, "Yeah. As a matter of fact, he was, Sherlock. Why do you ask?"

While Claire's mind raced with theories of, say, minute flakes of sunburned skin somehow adhering to scapose corymbs, Sam gestured toward the flower.

"Hulsea algida," he said modestly. "Alpine hulsea. That's what I thought when I first saw it, but the specimen's in bad shape, and anyway, it's a little late in the season. It's supposed to bloom in July, and we've already had a lot of hot weather, but it's definitely too tall for *Hulsea vestita,* and *heterochroma* is—"

"Dammit, what about the sunburn?" Tom interrupted fiercely. "Is this a . . . a rare tropical flower or something?"

"Well, no, it's not uncommon," Sam said cautiously, paused, then delivered the punch line. "Above ten thousand feet."

"Ten thousand feet?" exclaimed the others in gratifying chorus.

"Yes," he said smugly. "That's why it's 'alpine' hulsea; it

grows at very high altitudes, in the alpine fell fields. Mostly from Whitney northward, but I've seen it closer to home, up around Mineral King and in the Golden Trout Wilderness. But whoever he is, he sure didn't find it down here in the Valley. And as for the sunburn . . ."

"You get a hell of a sunburn at ten thousand feet," Claire interjected somewhat absently, remembering a painful episode from the previous summer.

She had been wondering what a Mexican farmworker would be doing at ten thousand feet and now was more certain than ever that this man—the third man—was not a Mexican farmworker. But then what was he? What kind of life had taken him from the exaltation of a high Sierra peak—and he had been exalted, he had picked himself this boutonniere—to a cold, lonely end in a ditch?

"How long ago did he pick this?" Martelli was asking Sam.

"I have no idea," Sam replied doubtfully. "I rarely pick flowers. Except to key them out, or press them as specimens."

"Dandelions fade fast," Claire supplied from childhood memory. "This one still looks pretty perky, considering."

"It's not a dandelion," Sam said sternly, as she knew he would.

"It was in water when we found it," remarked Martelli. "That might prolong its, uh, 'perkiness.' "

"Maybe," Sam said. "But really, there's no way of telling. Closest place he could have picked it is up near Mineral King. . . . When did he die? We can work backward from there—"

"You don't understand," Tom said. "I want to work *forward* from when the flower was picked, to figure when he died!"

"Won't the coroner—"

"Coroner's gonna have trouble with this one. The body was in cool water, which delays the onset of rigor mortis. And I can't for the life of me figure why he was floating in that canal."

"What do you mean?" asked a bewildered Claire.

"Drowning victims sink. At least, until they start to decompose; then they bob up again—'floaters,' we call 'em, full of these nasty gases—"

Claire wasn't impressed; biologists couldn't afford to be squeamish. "Are you saying he didn't drown?"

"Not necessarily. He could have been hung up in some weeds. All I'm sayin' is, both time and cause of death aren't exactly clear cut," he explained with a certain amount of satisfaction. "For the moment, I'm assuming that a) he did drown, and b) this happened sometime during the night, because that's when you're likeliest to get drunk and fall in an irrigation ditch—though there's a problem with that, too. If he was floating there all day, seems like somebody woulda found him before you did, Claire. But anyway . . . could this flower have been picked yesterday morning?"

Sam shrugged helplessly. "Maybe. That's pushing it."

"Okay. Let's say he was up near Mineral King. That would make a four- or five-hour hike out, and then another three hours to drive down the mountain. . . . What is it, Saturday? Say he breaks camp early Friday morning, picks himself this posy, hikes out to the trailhead, drives down—he could have been down here by late yesterday afternoon. Whoever he was."

Yes, Claire thought. Whoever he was.

"You know," Sam said, "if he was hiking in a Wilderness Area, he should have registered with the forest service. Why don't you talk to Andy Willis down at the Riverdale ranger station, see if there's anyone unaccounted for?"

"Good idea." He reached for the phone, and after a brief conversation he reported that fully a dozen people had checked in to backpack in the Golden Trout Wilderness Area over the previous weekend and hadn't yet signed out.

"This is peak season up there," he said. "We'll have to sift through these names, find out who's actually still up there, who just didn't bother to check in when they left, and who's actually missing. We may even have to wait for missing persons reports to trickle in. I'll pursue some other avenues, too, but we don't have a car and we don't have a wallet, so identification could take a while."

"What's 'a while'?" asked Claire.

"Days, if we're lucky. Weeks, if not."

Weeks? She might have to wait weeks to know the name of this man? That seemed intolerable!

She wanted to know his name.

It was partly an obsession with the act of naming that had driven her into science. Now, for example, if somebody brought her a fruit with a disease she couldn't identify, she suffered the equivalent of an itch between her shoulder blades until she named it, even if she couldn't cure it.

Well, she must make do with what information was available. "Tom, why did you think he was drunk?"

He took a minute to reply. "The coroner's report will tell us for sure. I'm just sort of assuming he was drunk, or sick, or *something*, because why else would a perfectly healthy, well-coordinated young man drown in a four-foot ditch? Especially if he was a hiker, for chrissake.

"Anyway," he continued, "that last guy they pulled out of a canal, uh"—here he glanced at a typewritten report—"Cedillo, Hector Cedillo, must have been lit up pretty good. Blood alcohol of point one five. Though the first guy, Perez, was sober," he muttered, shuffling papers.

" 'Course, I don't think this here guy was a farmworker," he added, confirming Claire's intuition. "He was dark complected, yeah, but something about the way he was dressed and—well, here, take a look at him."

And before Claire could react she was once again looking at the face of the dead man.

Back at the canal she had felt shy, even a little superstitious, about staring at him; somehow it was easier to look at a photo. The face was not terrible or distorted, only a little swollen as if from sleep—in fact, it had the peaceful anonymity of sleep. All in all an ordinary, pleasant, familiar kind of face; couple of days' growth of beard from the trip to the mountains, and that sunburn: the end of his nose looked very red even in the bad color snapshot, and Claire caught herself thinking crazily, He's going to be sore tomorrow. Then she felt slightly sick.

"Never saw him before," Sam said in a businesslike tone, handing the picture back to Martelli, but Claire knew he had been disturbed by the photo. He had had nightmares about drowning ever since Vietnam, and now they could have nightmares together.

"Okay. Thanks for your help," said Martelli. Meanwhile Sam, obviously, was examining the plastic bag that had contained the specimen.

"What's this?" he said to himself, pulling what looked like a second short segment of stem out of the plastic bag. He looked at it with his lens. "It's the stem of another hulsea," he announced. "He must have had two, originally."

"Really? Maybe it just broke off the other one."

"Uh-uh. I told you, they're monocephalous. One head per stem," he graciously elaborated. "So he must have lost the other flower somewhere."

"Anywhere between here and ten thousand feet," Tom muttered, but dutifully made a note. Hesitantly Claire asked the question that was really on her mind.

"Tom, don't you think three drownings in three weeks is stretching the bounds of coincidence a little far?" (In fact it seemed perverse, a black joke, that *anyone* would *drown* in this place, where every drop of water was tracked like plutonium. You would really have to work at drowning here. It was like the old story, probably apocryphal, of how the very first two cars registered in the whole state of Missouri, or Arkansas, or Kansas, or wherever, smashed bang into each other.)

"You're wondering if the deaths could be related. Sure. Obviously. But sometimes we get these little flurries—"

"But if this man's cause of death is also 'heart failure'—"

"Then we've got a real mystery on our hands. A real mystery," he repeated hopefully. "Though he looks kinda peaceful," nodding at the photograph. "Like most drowning victims I've seen, at least the ones that ain't been in the water long. But that guy Cedillo"—he lowered his voice portentously; Tom liked melodrama—"well, Ricky—Enrique Santiago, you know, my other officer—has a buddy who's a county deputy, and he was there when they pulled him out of the water. And he said that from the expression on the kid's face he died pretty hard. Ricky said he looked terrified— scared to death, in fact." He laughed a little. "You won't find that in the coroner's report. It ain't scientific."

They rode back up the hill in silence, each lost in private meditations. Claire was thinking about the man in the canal and about the line between conscious and not conscious: so incomprehensible, so subtle, yet absolute. Every night we cross it, she thought; every morning we return. And then, once and only once, like the man in the canal, we don't come back.

Then we've got a real mystery on our hands.... What was that? Oh, Martelli, talking about Cedillo. But there seemed to be no mystery about how the man in the canal had died. She understood that: he had tried to breathe water instead of air, and our lungs forgot that trick long ago.

The only thing she didn't understand was why he was in the canal in the first place. And who he was; he had slipped over the line nameless.

After they turned into Sam's driveway they sat for a moment in the dark. She picked up his hand and ran her fingers along the ridge of his knuckles; his skin was dry and slightly rough. He pulled her as close as the Toyota's bucket seats would allow—wanting, like her, she thought, to confirm that they lived, to overlay the memory of cold, stiff limbs with warm, responsive ones. They climbed the stairs, arms wound around each other. Sam opened the door, then stooped to kiss her.

"Just a minute," he said, standing. "I have to go call Linda and make sure the kids are all right." And he disappeared into the kitchen.

Claire walked back out onto the porch, letting the screen door slam. Of course he should check on the kids. Of course. It was perfectly natural. Only did he have to pick that exact moment to do it?

Dust, fine as talcum, rose to her nostrils on the evening breeze, and for an instant she had a piercing memory of the smell of wet sidewalks after a thunder shower. If only it would rain, maybe these knots of unhappiness would melt.... Fat chance. It wasn't going to rain for months and months. She was going to have to find some other resolution.

She heard Sam behind her.

"Claire," he said cautiously, "are you angry?"

"No. Yes. You just saw the kids three hours ago. You know they're all right."

"I worry about them. And seeing that guy tonight . . . it sort of upset me, I guess. Made me realize how fragile they are."

"It upset me, too." And I'm fragile, too, she thought, but didn't say it.

"Oh."

After a moment he came up behind her and put his arms around her. "Look, I'm sorry. Maybe my timing wasn't very good. Come into the house now. Please."

They went into the house, but for Claire the mood had passed and she took little pleasure in sex. At three in the morning she awoke in a cold sweat, heart pounding. Some dream had propelled her to consciousness, but all that remained was terror and the sense of her own death, waiting. Sam flung an arm over her and murmured a few comforting syllables, but she lay awake for a long time, staring up at the dark.

Chapter 6

The Sunday morning sun filled a square of light on the bedroom floor. Soon the little house would begin to heat up; soon, perhaps, the man in the canal would rise up to haunt her once more. But right now, at seven A.M., it was delightfully cool and the fears of the night were forgotten.

Sam disappeared into the kitchen and presently appeared, naked, carrying two cups of coffee. Claire propped herself up on one elbow and watched him with pleasure; it was wonderful not to have to jump out of bed and cover themselves for the sake of the children, who had slept over at Linda's.

"Thanks," she said, accepting a cup and smiling at him. His black hair stuck straight up like porcupine quills (Cherokee hair, she thought of it, because Sam, like every other Oklahoman she had ever met, laid claim to being one thirty-second Cherokee. No more, no less.) He hadn't yet stuck his glasses on his face, and for a change she could see his eyes. Under their dark, level brows they were the clear warm brown of the coffee. *"El tiene los ojos morenos,"* she murmured, remembering her Spanish exercises.

"Moreno? What about him?"

"Who?" she said, confused.

"Ruben Moreno. Isn't that what you just said?"

"No, actually, I was referring to the color of your eyes. Ruben Moreno . . . didn't Emil mention him when he was berating Bert yesterday?"

"That's the man."

"Emil was pretty angry about him."

51

"Yeah, well, Emil's an angry guy. He's Bert's brother, after all."

Emil, an angry guy? Her gentle, timorous Emil?

"Anyway, about Moreno," he continued. "He's a *contratista*, a labor contractor."

"Oh." A pause. "And what does that mean? What does he do?"

"Contractors in general? Or Moreno?"

"Yes," she said, meaning "both."

"Well. Labor contractors provide labor, just like it sounds. They hire people, supervise 'em, fire 'em, pay 'em. And sometimes they act as coyotes, running a sort of underground railroad, carting undocumented workers up from Mexico and points south—a kind of do-it-yourself *bracero* program. Lots of room for abuse there."

"Moreno was a coyote?"

"Was. I hear he's gone legit. Working for Bert Yankovich, hiring for a cannery. But even if Moreno's retired as a coyote, he's still a sleazy character. You hear a lot of stories about Ruben. And most of these contractors, they treat their people badly. Workers hired by labor contractors make less than half of what direct hires make."

Claire sipped her coffee and waited passively to receive information. When Sam slipped into didactic mode he tended to tell her a little bit more than she wanted to know. More *and* less.

"See, around here agribusiness is getting more and more bureaucratized, like any other industry," he said. "Like General Motors. Owners and managers and workers—they're all separate outfits now. The actual owners might be the actual growers, like Bert, or they might be a bunch of dentists from Long Beach looking for a tax shelter."

A handful of worried-looking men in white, stumbling through an orchard, looking for shelter: the image made her snicker. Sam looked at her in bewilderment, then continued.

"Anyway, owners often turn the actual operations over to management firms—guys with ag degrees, usually—and *they* hire a labor contractor to supply the workers. The contractor has to assure the manager that his crew is uncontaminated, you know, one hundred percent union free. Otherwise, the owners just fire the managers and hire another firm. So the contractors are a major stumbling block to organizing workers. And Emil . . . well, Emil still longs for the glory days of the UFW. He still wants to walk on his knees from Delano to Sacramento, right behind César." He grinned.

"You think he's a crackpot," she said severely.

"No. Ah, no. It's easy to make fun of Emil, but I'm all for unionized farm labor; I think everybody should make a living wage . . . and his basic plan isn't that farfetched. Organic farming—no, what does he call it, 'sustainable agriculture'— is a noble goal—hell," he interrupted himself, "in spite of what Bert thinks, organic produce is becoming marketable. It might even be the wave of the future. You know, I'm running that trial on organic peaches—"

"I know. Incidentally," she added casually, "when are you wrapping that up?"

"Next week. I'll finish harvesting by the end of the week. But back to Emil—he's over his head. He's inexperienced and undercapitalized, and he hasn't made himself any friends. He's pretty screwed up."

"Unconventional," she countered. "And shy."

"It's more than that. I don't think Emil survived his childhood," he said cryptically, and she thought about that.

After that day at the station she and Emil had met a few times at Katy's Koffee Kup for koffee (it was simply truth in advertising for Katy to give the sludge she served its very own name), to talk. Small talk, shop talk, really—breakthroughs in biological pest control, or drip irrigation versus check-and-furrow, or optimal pruning techniques for grapevines. Politics, too. By Cambridge standards Claire was a slightly left-of-center liberal, but she had quickly learned to take nothing for granted out here. Perfectly nice people diverged radically from what she thought of as the norm even on what seemed like bedrock issues, like the Environmental Protection Act, or a woman's right to control her body, or prayer in the schools (especially prayer in the schools). She and Sam were usually in agreement, but even Sam surprised her sometimes.

But Emil was way ahead of her. Emil had thought hard about labor problems, water rights, land use, overgrazing, deforestation, and free trade, and she had no doubt that his positions were absolutely progressive and politically correct. Under other circumstances this might have been doctrinaire and tiresome—well, it *was*, occasionally—but mostly it was like cool rain in the desert.

Sam had teased her about her "dates," but they both knew that this was no flirtation—knew, somehow, that Emil was presexual. (Claire had wondered about this, of course, just as she wondered about everyone's sexuality. Not that she wanted to sleep with every man she liked; the speculation had little to do with lust. It was pure curiosity. Sex was at once such essential and such privileged information, and she was a woman who craved information.)

And then one day, after a dissertation on the GATT, Emil had suddenly said, "Have y-you noticed that I d-don't stutter with y-you as much as I d-did?"

There was something about his tone that had made her stomach tighten even as she'd answered, "Yes. I had noticed you seemed more relaxed."

"It's b-because I f-feel so c-c-comfortable with you. I f-feel like I've known you all my life."

Oh, shit, she'd thought. She'd better be careful.

She'd known dozens of Emils throughout her career in science: intellectually sophisticated but emotionally unformed, lonely, and vulnerable.

Was she doing something dangerous, something wrong, in pursuing this friendship?

But he was pleasant, stimulating company, and she *liked* him. Surely that was worthwhile and worth nurturing. And he'd told her himself that his stutter was better!

Sam was still talking. "You know," he said in apparent non sequitur, "if I ever caught anybody hitting my kids, I think I'd kill him."

"Hitting the kids?" she repeated, dumbfounded. "You think Chuck is hitting the kids?"

"Oh, no, no, Debby has more sense than that, she'd never let anything like that go on. . . ." His voice trailed off. Then he said, "I'm thinking of trying to get the boys for longer. Maybe a couple of months, every summer."

Claire closed her eyes. It's not that the idea had never crossed her mind; she had known that it was what Sam wanted. Maybe Debby wouldn't agree to it. But that was a slim hope. The divorce had been amicable, as these things go; it was a reasonable request; Debby was by all accounts a reasonable woman. . . .

"What makes you think this is such a wonderful place for kids?" she asked, keeping her voice calm. "The Valley is full of toxic chemicals. Fresno County's water has the highest level—"

"Of DBCP in the state. You're preaching to the choir here, Claire. But that's the Valley. The air and water are pretty good up in the foothills—"

"The pollution levels in the Valley in summer are as bad as in L.A., and the ozone levels are worse at higher—"

"Altitudes. Claire, I want them here."

Yes. That was the important thing. Sam carried the mysterious conviction that he had failed everyone who had ever depended on him, so obviously he wasn't going to let this happen with his kids.

Resignedly she said, "Well, I can see how it's a good idea from your point of view. But I'm not sure what *I* would do."

"What do you mean?"

"Look, Sam, I'm just dead weight"—she stopped abruptly and chose another phrase—"excess baggage, when the boys are here. I'm irrelevant to them, I'm an irritant to you—"

"That's not true!" he interrupted angrily, but Claire continued as if he hadn't spoken.

"And since our relationship is the primary reason I remain here, if *it's* shot to hell, well—why would I stay?" she concluded defiantly.

"I thought you wanted the farm adviser job!"

"I haven't decided."

"So in other words," he said after a moment, "you're asking me to choose between you and them."

"No, of course not." What kind of monster would do that? "It's just that— Oh, shit, Sam," she said, "why didn't you marry Linda Nelson? Things would be a whole lot simpler."

It was meant as a sort of mournful joke, but Sam reacted violently.

"Goddamn it!" He slammed down the coffee cup so that the hot liquid sloshed across the patchwork quilt his mother had brought from Oklahoma. "Every time we have an argument you say the same two things! 'Why didn't you marry Linda?' " he mimicked. " 'I'm going back to Cambridge!' Well, I didn't marry Linda," he continued with exaggerated patience, "because I didn't love Linda, I loved you, God help me. And if you want to go back to MIT, then for Christ's sake go—only don't use it as a threat to keep me in line!"

He rolled out of bed and wordlessly pulled on his clothes, then said in a normal voice, "I'm going to get the boys. There's a softball game at three, if you want to come." And he was gone.

Claire sat in bed, angry and confused. Even in absentia the kids had managed to sabotage a moment of intimacy between her and Sam and had forced her to present herself as a selfish bitch—a persona, she admitted, that certainly had elements of truth. Yet Sam had said he loved her, and she wanted to believe him.

But it was a damned irrational kind of love. She had always been attracted to style and had set great store in *opinions:* on books, movies, music, art. Sam thought such preoccupations more or less trivial, kind of a harmless hobby, like knitting or building models. The qualities he claimed to admire were *moral*—goodness of heart, generosity, integrity, that sort of thing. So either they were lying to themselves about what they wanted, or what they wanted was not what they needed, or their relationship was essentially one of convenience—or Eros had lashed out wildly and at random, as the little tyke was rumored to do.

Eventually she bestirred herself, read the Sunday paper without much comprehension, and set up her makeshift darkroom in the bathroom, where she printed a roll of old negatives and hung the contact sheets up to dry.

At two o'clock she had relaxed enough to close up shop and drive down to the softball game—partly as a peace offering to Sam, partly because she genuinely liked baseball. It was the only team sport she really understood, and she liked sitting on the blankets with the wives and kids cheering their husbands and daddies to victory; it was one of the few times she felt connected to the community.

She stepped onto the porch, paused a moment, then succumbed to neurosis, walked back in, and dialed the phone.

"Did you identify that guy yet?" she asked when Tom Martelli answered.

"What guy?"

This time she didn't give him the satisfaction of an exasperated response, and eventually he said, "Oh. The fellow you found? Nope, not yet."

Silence. "Any leads?" she finally said.

"Well, we've narrowed it down to two names. B. Robbins and J. Levine. Might be we'll know by tomorrow."

"Call me—"

"As soon as we know. I got the picture by now, you want to know who he was. How come you're so interested, anyhow?"

"I . . . I *found* him!" she sputtered, feeling her reasons must be self-evident.

"And that makes you responsible for him?"

"Well, it certainly makes me interested in him!"

"Why?"

"Look, you may find dead people all the time, but I hardly ever do—"

"Hardly ever?" he echoed mockingly.

"Well, okay, never. I never find dead people, okay?" she retorted, absurdly defensive. Tom and Sam both had the habit of pulling rank on her when it came to life's grim realities. "And I never even *see* dead people; it's not part of my daily experience. I mean, these days you have to be some sort of a *professional*—a doctor, or a nurse, or a policeman—to deal with death. So this was pretty profound for me. . . ."

Martelli cleared his throat impatiently. Personally she thought this was a very interesting topic, one she could have pursued with Emil or maybe even Sam. But not Tom. For Tom, conversation was one of two things: direct exchange of information or verbal competition disguised as banter. "I want to know his name, that's all. I'll feel like something is resolved when I know who he was."

A pause. "I'll let you know," he said, his inflection like a shrug.

"Okay," she breathed, and headed for the game.

The VFW field was on the northeast side of Parkerville, and she soon found herself slightly lost, bumping along a dusty street called Walker Road in the Mexican section of town. It was a neighborhood of trailers, decrepit motels, and tiny, ramshackle wood-frame houses. Small houses and big cars: Monte Carlos, Galaxies, Malibus, Cutlasses, all twenty years old, but they could, with constant coaxing, haul six or seven men to the fields.

She was late for the game, but even on the best of days Walker Road was not a route for impatient drivers, and on weekends it was barely a thoroughfare at all. More like a long, narrow park as people crossed nonchalantly in front of her or stood talking directly in the center of the road. Kids played tag, and the big cars crouched on either side, hoods in air—some snout to snout, as if in weird acts of mating— while their keepers tended then. A pair of legs protruded from beneath a blue Le Mans like the remains of lunch.

And it was here, on a hot Sunday in August at 2:55 P.M., to that avowed agnostic, secular humanist, and skeptical scientist Claire Sharples, that the Virgin of Guadalupe appeared.

It was just beyond a white Chevy Impala that She materialized: the *mestiza* Madonna of a million murals and dashboards, of the *café con leche* skin, luminous black eyes, and lustrous hair, a woman of such astonishing beauty, such radiance, that she shone brighter than her glowing corolla. A small brown infant peered from the cradle of her arms.

It was a trick of dust and sunlight, of course. In a moment the vision resolved itself into a remarkably pretty but definitely mortal woman in faded jeans and flame-colored tank top, holding a very ordinary baby. Nevertheless Claire shivered, and it seemed to her the woman's dark eyes followed her slow passage all the way down Walker Road.

She arrived at the game just in time to see Sam make a spectacular diving catch in center field, roll to his feet, coil himself, and whip the ball all the way to home, beating out the runner by a half step.

Now here was another thing she failed to understand. On

the rare occasion when Sam talked about his childhood, he implied that he had been a misfit, withdrawn, unathletic—a Shannon, not a Terry—all of which seemed to make sense. Yet he turned out to be an excellent ball player. So what was she supposed to believe? Sometimes Sam was like Mexican radio: she got a word here, a word there, but never enough to draw accurate conclusions.

"What's the score?" she asked the boys after they had stopped hopping up and down.

"Four–three, them. Bottom of the fourth. Two down," said Shannon economically.

"Dad tripled in the second," Terry added.

"Left-fielder should have had it," Shannon remarked judiciously.

The next batter popped out to retire the side, and Sam came walking over to them, rubbing his elbow.

"Nice play," said Claire. "Are you okay?"

"Yeah." He shrugged. "You missed my fabulous hit in the second—and there's no way," he continued slowly and emphatically, looking hard at Shannon, "no way that ball could have been caught. They were lucky to hold me to a triple. And turn your cap around! That bill is there for a reason! Either that or put on sunscreen. You too, Terry."

Shannon looked stubborn and moved the bill about ninety-seven degrees toward the front of his head.

"Oh! I called Tom before I left," Claire said, "and he said they're close to identifying the—that man," she finished guardedly, thinking of the kids.

"Oh?" He looked at her with every appearance of intelligent interest but immediately began shouting to his teammate at the plate. "Big stick, Johnnie! Big stick, now! Sorry, go on," returning his attention to her.

"Yes, he said they'd ruled out all but a couple—"

"Sam, you're up next!" someone called.

"Sorry," he said again, and trotted away. It was just as well; Claire had realized that she didn't want to discuss this subject around Shannon and Terry.

The first two men had gotten on base, and now the fielders, remembering Sam's wallop, moved out.

"Dad's gonna lay down a bunt," Shannon said confidently,

and sure enough, Sam squared off to meet the first pitch head on. The ball dropped three feet in front of the plate and he took off like a rocket, arms and legs pumping. He crossed first a nanosecond after the ball *thunk*ed into the first baseman's glove.

"Why didn't you whomp it, Dad?" Terry asked in disappointed tones as Sam came limping toward them. (Claire resisted the urge to ask him again if he was okay.) "Why didn't you hit a home run?"

"It was a sacrifice play, dummy," said Shannon scornfully.

"What's that?"

Sam rested his hand lightly on Terry's head. "Well, a sacrifice is when you do something . . . hard, or not much fun, because it helps other people." For some reason Claire felt herself redden. "For example, in this case I bunted even though I knew I probably wouldn't get on base myself. If I had hit the ball hard, it would have been more fun for me, but I might have hit into a double play or flied out. This way I advanced the runners."

This gave both Terry and Claire something to think about during the remainder of the game, which Sam's team lost seven to four.

That night after Sam had anointed himself with Ben-Gay and hobbled to bed, she mentioned her trip to Los Angeles on Monday. "I can do some work on the *Entyloma* project and see Sara and Steve—you remember the Ashes—"

"You're leaving tomorrow?" Sam inquired, like a dunderhead.

"Yes, tomorrow," she repeated patiently. "I just told you. I'm going to see Allen Okamoto at Riverside—"

"Oh, right." A long, thoughtful pause. "And you're coming back Wednesday?"

"Wednesday night."

"Before dinner?"

"No, late," she said, wondering why a man who hadn't been able to remember what day she was leaving was now so interested in the details of her timetable. "I might stay over 'til Thursday morning."

"Mmm." Another pause. "We've really got to move Peterson away from shortstop," he announced presently, and with resignation she listened to yet another play-by-play analysis, another scheme for improving the team by stealing key players from other teams.

She was just starting to nod off when she heard Sam say, "Listen. I want to apologize for this morning."

"*You* want to apologize?"

"Yeah, well, explain, anyway. About the boys. It's just that—" He halted, then went on rapidly, "It's just that I really love them, and I hardly know them. I feel so distant from them. Just about the time we're starting to relax with each other, to connect, maybe, it's time for them to leave—"

"Sam, please!" she interrupted. "Of course you want to spend time with your children! If anyone should apologize, it's me." She traced the line of stitching along one square of the quilt. Finally she said, "I know I'm a selfish person. By nature or nurture or . . . or choice, I guess. It's a quality I've cultivated, to be able to succeed in my career—well, never mind, I don't want to excuse it. But I can't pretend to be something I'm not, because it doesn't work, and I end up resentful."

"Why do you have to make everything so complicated?" he complained.

"Because it is complicated!" she flashed. "You're not just trying to find a new first baseman here, Sam!"

He didn't argue. He just looked depressed.

Chapter 7

On Monday she stopped in at the lab to collect her notes for Allen, picked up the phone to call Tom, then turned away resolutely. Just as she was locking the door behind her, the phone rang.

It was Martelli.

"You know where Sam is, by any chance? He's not in his office."

"Out in the field somewhere, I guess," she said.

"Well, tell him to give me a call. I got some news from Andy Willis."

"Tom!" she half yelled with irritation, just catching him before he hung up. "Tell me! I'm involved in this, too, remember?"

"Oh. Yeah. Well, B. Robbins showed up."

"Who?"

"B. Robbins. One of the last two backpackers who hadn't checked in on time."

"Oh. Right," she said. "Was he all right?"

"She. Betty," scoring a point against the feminist. "Yeah, she was fine. Just lost track of the time, Andy said. Sounds like a real space case. But anyway, we called the L.A. number the other guy, Jonathan Levine, had given, and talked to his roommate. And sure enough Levine hasn't come home yet. The roommate didn't think anything about it; said they didn't keep tabs on each other and that he figured Levine met someone. A girl, I guess he meant."

"Did you find out where he worked?"

"Well, I'm coming to that. Seems he's a reporter, for a

newspaper in L.A. I talked to the editor this morning, but he said Levine was on vacation, that he didn't have regular hours anyway, and it wasn't unusual for them not to hear from him for weeks at a time."

"Oh." A pause, then, "Tom—why don't you just send a photo of the dead man down to L.A. and see if they identify him?"

"I did. Faxed it this morning."

She waited. She was beginning to feel as though Tom had suckered her into a surreal chess game. "And . . . ?" she prodded.

"He just called. The editor, I mean. He identified the photo as Levine."

"Jesus, Tom!" she exploded. "Why didn't you just say that in the first place!"

"Well, you're a scientist," he said in hurt tones, clearly enjoying this whole conversation, "I thought you might be interested in the process of how we gather evidence and draw conclusions—"

"What paper?" she interrupted, seizing the offensive.

"What?"

"Newspaper. What newspaper did Jonathan Levine write for?"

"Oh, some little rag I never heard of. The *L.A. Free Press.*"

"The *Free Press*? What would somebody from a newspaper like that be doing up here?" she asked, then immediately imagined a scenario in which Levine was working on a hot story and was killed because of it. Somehow.

"Hiking in the Sierras, like half of Los Angeles," Tom said in a bored voice.

"You don't think he was working on a story?"

"A *story?*" he said incredulously. "You think there's such a shortage of events in L.A. that some poor fool has to come to Parkerville for a *story?*"

"Um, maybe not." *PARKERVILLE, GATEWAY TO THE HIGH COUNTRY* proclaimed a sign at the city limits; places like Parkerville had to advertise what they were on the way to rather than what they were. "Did the coroner's report come in yet?"

The inevitable pause, then, "Not completely, no. Preliminary conclusion is accidental drowning. . . ."

"But . . . ," she prodded.

"Oh, there's just some difficulty with establishing time of death, because of the body bein' in cold water. Like I predicted. Tell Sam to call me, okay?"

Jonathan Levine.

It was a familiar name, a nice middle-class Jewish name. She had known one other Jonathan Levine in her life, in third or fourth grade. She hadn't known him well; he had transferred to private school in fifth grade, and she had never seen him again. But people from that time in her life had become archetypes, the stuff of dreams, and she remembered him perfectly. Bookish, shy, slightly built—the kind of little boy, in short, who might have grown into a wiry reporter for an alternative paper.

So Levine's name and the fact that he worked for Sara's newspaper and the liberties she had taken with his person in hauling him out of the water and the memory of little Jonnie all amplified the odd sense of familiarity she had felt in Tom's office. It was as if he were indeed an old friend—an old friend about whom she somehow had developed amnesia.

And how would an old friend come to his end facedown in an irrigation canal? No, not even a canal; the Friant-Kern, where what's-his-name, Cedillo, had been found, *that* was a canal—part of the Central Valley Project, broad, with steep smooth concrete sides. Dangerous. This was just a . . . a little muddy ditch, in the middle of nowhere.

He had *not* been working on a story, he had *not* been murdered. He had simply fallen into a ditch. It didn't make a lot of sense, but then accidents didn't, by definition.

She loaded her car, checked her supplies, and headed south.

It's hard not to be excited at the start of a journey, even when you're perplexed, even when it's 100 in the shade and 110 on the front seat of a Toyota. Claire's exhilaration lasted until Bakersfield. For many miles she had distracted herself in meditations upon Sam and Jonathan Levine, her life in general; in singing and composing imaginary photographs; in counting the number of new signs that read "Regarding This Property"; and, finally, in simply enjoying the Valley's roadside colors. Alkali white, cool gray green (jimsonweed, turkey mullein), rust (curly dock), all against the omnipresent pale gold of dry grass: by eastern standards these were the subtle colors of autumn or early winter, but here they were the dead-summer palette of dormancy, estivation.

But at Bakersfield, that aggregation of oil fields, equipment yards, fast-food chains, and truckers' motels, she hit the interstate, and the cars started cruising by with their windows rolled *up*. Cars full of smug-looking people lolling about. Air-conditioned cars.

She opened her thermos and took a swig of tepid water and, after a moment's hesitation, let it trickle onto her forehead. Why the hell didn't she buy a new car? She could certainly swing it—not a BMW or a Mercedes, but another Toyota, say. Or a Mazda. With air-conditioning, of course. Or—how about a little pickup? Now that was an idea! She and Sam could haul, oh, lots of things—

Wait a minute, a *pickup truck*? What was happening to her? Next she'd be shopping for a gun rack! It was a good thing she was about to get a dose of cosmopolitan culture; she was starting to lose her sense of values! She poured more water on her head.

Farther south, and the Tehachapis were a hazy ridge dead ahead. Vineyards here, and cotton—cotton all the way to the Temblor range, the western border of the Valley—and, where the land was unirrigated, ragged eucalyptus, smoky salt cedars, a bright median border of oleander, and tumbleweed, rolled up against wire fences. Immigrants all, even the tumbleweed, which had come from Russia. Sometimes it seemed to her that everything here had been grafted on, even the weeds. Take that cinder-block Baptist church out in the bare field off to her left. There was nothing indigenous about it; it could have been in Des Moines or Teaneck. Only there it would have been softened by the green of encroaching grass, maples maybe, ialanthus certainly. But these arid lands (she took a drink of water) were completely unforgiving. Put up an ugly building here and it sat like an unhealing scar, never transformed, never accepted.

She poured more water on her head.

Up the Grapevine, through the pass, and onto the high plateau of the Tehachapis. At four thousand feet the air cooled somewhat and with it her temper. Now this was beautiful country, in its stripped-down way: real southwest highlands of juniper, piñon, and sage, plus the occasional colony of knobbly Joshua trees that had crept over from the Mojave like the phalanx of some very slow, very weird invading army. Once she saw a small wetland where a stand of the star-topped rushes called *tule* twinkled at her as she passed. There were jagged ridges split by rough gray seams like vertebrae, then deep canyons. Ridges. More canyons. Ridges, along which new housing crept like impetigo, and then the long descent, the sky ahead deepening to an ominous maroon, the air thickening like rancid grease—

And then she was in it, in the L.A. basin, threading the tangles of over/underpasses, looking down on an endless darkling plain of suburbia, of ornamental shrubs, rooftops, palm trees, and the occasional clot of taller buildings on the horizon. Then, finally, off the freeway, onto surface streets, and into Sara's neighborhood, still to her eyes blandly suburban. Stopped at a red light, she looked to her right and saw a thin, barefoot black man, regal in green-striped bedspread, gesturing to an empty sidewalk.

No, she was wrong. This was the big city after all.

Sara and Steve's house, which was near UCLA and had cost the earth, was unprepossessing and tiny. But it was filled with pleasing ethnic doodads, it had a lovely garden, and the air was delicious. Sara, who was small, round, and pretty, was currently also tanned and very chic, so the first thing they did was go look at the Pacific Ocean, and the next thing they did was go shopping. Claire had to keep a tight rein on herself. Could she really wear that leather skirt to the next field station open house? What would happen to those boots after one day of foothill dust? She compromised between need and want, and meanwhile she and Sara chatted in a comradely fashion, retesting the somewhat tenuous bonds of their friendship.

Late in the afternoon they drove to the *Free Press* office, where Sara had to drop off her week's copy—and where Claire planned to interrogate the editor about Jonathan Levine. Heading east, they left the Ashes' tiny homogeneous neighborhood for a very different part of town. Stacks of rackety bungalows climbed steep hills on either side of her; brightly colored signs shouted urgently and incomprehensibly from every direction: *RAID Es Efectivo Contra Cucarachas; Mercado Mexicana; Silvia y Chocolate— Restaurante Cubana; Carnicería Salvadoreña*—Claire felt that she had wandered across a border.

The office itself was perched above a Vietnamese noodle house and reeked of boiled beef from the tenants below and perpetual hysteria from its own deadlines. Standing at the center of the chaos was a man with dark glasses, thinning hair, and small goatee. This latter-day beatnik was Bernie Perlmutter, the editor in chief, with whom Sara deposited Claire, then left to talk to a friend.

Perlmutter made the halfhearted small talk of a busy but gracious man, his distracted eyes scanning the room for problems requiring his intervention, until Claire said, "I was sorry to hear about Jonathan Levine."

He started. "You knew Jon?"

"No, I . . . I found him."

There was a moment of shocked silence as they both digested this statement. "But he seemed like someone I could have been friends with," she added lamely.

Someone called, "Hey, Bernie, take a look at the proofs for this cover," and Perlmutter turned to confer with a young woman with stiff orange hair.

"This yellow looks like dog shit," he said plaintively. "Can't we do something about it?"

"I thought dog shit was what we were after," Orange Hair mumbled. "Okay, I'll fool with it."

Perlmutter turned back to Claire. "Sorry. Barely controlled panic here, as usual. Jon . . . yeah, you would have liked Jon. Most people did, once they got past his pertinacity."

Claire looked at him blankly. Then, "obstinacy," she said.

"Right. A terrible attribute in an ex-spouse and a sine qua non in a journalist, and Jon was a very promising journalist.

Wrote about environmental issues, mostly. Broke a big story here about pollution in Santa Monica Bay. Won us an award, actually. I can't believe this happened. Was he . . . I mean . . . how . . . how did he look?"

"Very peaceful," she said, remembering that sealed, secret face.

"I understand he was up in the mountains right before he was killed."

"Yes."

"That's good." He nodded soberly. "He was a real Sierra Club type. Rock climbing, canoeing, hiking—"

Levine was beginning to emerge as a very heroic figure. Seeker after truth. Lover of nature. Protector of the planet. "Was he from L.A.?"

"No. I don't . . . didn't know much about him; he was very private. I think he had gone to UCLA, and was from back east—"

"What?" she interrupted. "Where?"

"I don't know," he answered, furrowing his brow. "New England somewhere, maybe. Vermont, New Hampshire . . . why?"

"Oh, well, it's crazy, it's just that . . . when I was growing up in western Massachusetts, I knew a kid named Jon Levine. I'm sure it's not the same guy, it's a common name—"

"Stranger things have happened," Perlmutter said, stooping to paw through a file drawer. "I once ran into my fifth-grade teacher from P.S. 101 in the men's room at Victoria Station. . . . Here! Here's his personnel file. Let's see what we've got. . . . Mmm, not much," he said, straightening. "Address: Fifty-four Gayley—that's near UCLA. Health insurance: Kaiser. Next of kin: Lucille Levine, mother, Albany, New York."

Right over the state line from Massachusetts, thought Claire. Still, probably just a coincidence. "So I gather he was up in, uh, my part of the world"—clearing her throat—"my part of the world, on vacation," she said with a slight interrogative lift.

"Well, partly. He said he was going to do a little hiking, and I guess he did. And maybe some whitewater rafting—"

He stopped suddenly, as if that phrase, with its promise of explosive life and hilarity, had reminded him of the reality of absolute stillness and dark water. Claire winced in sympathy.

"But he was working on a story, too," Perlmutter continued.

"He *was*?" Hmm. Maybe she would scoop Martelli.

"Oh, yeah. He was always working on something."

"What was the story?"

"No idea," he said. "All I know is that he called me, oh, last week, and told me he'd have something interesting for me when he got back. But Parkerville . . ." He shook his head. "Hell, I don't even know where it is!"

Claire was thinking furiously, *environment, pesticides, air pollution, logging in the southern Sierras, degradation of watershed,* when she heard Perlmutter say, "But I told all this to your sheriff, you know. Marconi, is that his name?"

"Martelli," she corrected automatically. "You did?"

"Yeah, this morning. On the phone."

There was a long silence while Claire replayed the morning's conversation with Tom. Could he have *forgotten* to tell her?

Tom had never forgotten anything in his life, except maybe his wife's birthday. He had denied that Levine was working on a story. He had lied to her. But why?

"—and that's about all I can tell you about Jon," Perlmutter was saying. "Except that he was always trying to get me to do something strenuous and dangerous. Like go down the Kern River on a rubber raft." He laughed, rubbed his paunch protectively. "Jesus. I'd always say 'Jon, let's just take a taxi!' I'm a New Yorker, you know?"

He looked at her with a kind of appeal, as if asking her, a complete stranger, for some sort of absolution. Then someone yelled, "Hey, Bernie!" He gave himself a little shake and said briskly, "Well, I've got to get back to work. Nice meeting you—and thanks for telling me about Jon." He turned away, then halted suddenly.

"You know, Jon was an athletic guy, and he could take care of himself. I'd really like to know how this happened."

"Me too." And I'd like to ask Tom Martelli one or two questions, she added silently.

Perlmutter stared at her for a moment and stepped back into the daily maelstrom.

Sara returned and they made their way back down the narrow stairs and onto the freeway again.

"What did you and Bernie talk about? He never has a minute to spare for me."

"Um . . . nothing, really. He must have wanted a break." It was funny, she wanted to ask about Levine, but she could imagine perfectly Sara's melodramatic, almost prurient reaction to the news of his death, and she just couldn't face it right now. She didn't want to dine out on Jonathan Levine.

It didn't matter what she wanted, however. Sara said, "Oh. Well, I heard some awful news. Really terrible," and paused portentously.

Claire responded dutifully and listened to the story of a young reporter who had accidentally drowned over the weekend, somewhere north of Los Angeles—fortunately Sara was vague about the geography, so Claire retained her secret. "Did you know him?" she asked.

Not really, Sara admitted. She had met him once or twice, didn't know anything about him. But still, it had unnerved her; she wasn't sure she could drive.

Luckily it was rush hour and she didn't have to drive, just sit behind the wheel and endure. They inched their way toward the west side. "I hope Stephen and Jeff aren't already waiting for us," Sara muttered at one point.

All the world called Sara's husband "Steve" except Sara, who always referred to him as "Stephen" in a very special voice. But—

"Who's Jeff?" Claire asked, and Sara looked slightly uncomfortable.

"Oh, he's a friend of Stephen's," she said brightly. "They swim together."

"Oh."

"I thought it might be nice if we all went out to dinner."

"Oh."

"You looked really terrific in that silk blouse you bought today."

Claire snapped to attention. "Sara, what are you doing?" she said sharply. She realized her friends had disliked Sam.

But would they stoop to fixing her up at the first possible moment?

"What do you mean?" she returned, all injured innocence. "He's a good friend, that's all!"

Claire settled back and watched the lines of palm trees slide past each other; these L.A. palms were impossibly tall and thin, all at exactly the same height and all canted alike, as if suspended from their buoyant heads like aquarium plants. Okay, maybe she was wrong about Sara's machinations. But this Jeff person wasn't going to get more than basic small talk, of the How-long-have-you-been-in-California variety, out of her. . . . Then she began composing an opening salvo to fire at Tom.

They did arrive home eventually, and Claire, refusing to examine her own motives, changed into her new blouse, which was stone-washed silk of a sort of sea-foam green and brought out her eyes, Sara had said. She returned to the sound of male voices in the living room and ran to receive an affectionate embrace from Steve, who looked happy and trim, having gained an inch or two of chest and lost an inch or two of waist and, alas, of hair.

"Claire Sharples, Jeff Green," Steve said, and she turned to meet his companion.

And swallowed hard.

Green was a knockout. He could only be described by what your English teacher used to call "active verbs": his hazel eyes danced, his thick hair sprang from his smooth forehead, his magnificent body radiated energy, his copper skin glowed with a perfect lifeguard's tan. Well, hell, he probably *was* a lifeguard. Sara had said he was a swimmer, and nobody that pretty could have brains, too—

"Jeff teaches history at UCLA," Steve announced.

Uh-oh.

"And just got tenure," Sara added proudly, with a sidelong glance at Claire. "We're celebrating."

"Congratulations," Claire managed to say. "That's a major accomplishment."

Jeff gave her a dazzling smile. "It's a miracle, considering my politics."

"Jeff's a real firebrand," Steve cut in. "The sixties redux."

"Conviction didn't go out with the Nehru jacket," Jeff snorted good-naturedly.

Oh, Christ. A politically correct professor of history with the body of a lifeguard. Damn Sara anyway. Maybe he was gay.

She realized she had been staring at him wordlessly for several seconds and said the first thing that popped into her head.

"So . . . how long have you been in California?"

Sara and Steve looked at her as if she had lost her mind and Jeff seemed a little puzzled, but he smiled warmly, as though she had made the wittiest remark in the world.

"All my life," he said.

At Jeff's suggestion they ate at a Korean restaurant with grills built right into the tables, and while Steve, Sara, and Claire reminisced about people he didn't know, he patiently and expertly plied his chopsticks to keep them supplied with thin slices of broiled meat. Then they all talked about movies, to which Sara contributed many articulate opinions in complete sentences that would appear in her next review, Jeff a leftist critique, and Claire the monotonous repetition that she hadn't seen it. Then on to Central America, support for the arts, and defense spending.

Inevitably the conversation turned to what they missed about the East Coast.

"Non-Hollywood movies," said Sara. "Of course."

"Walking," said Steve. "And I don't mean race walking around a track. Just walking to get where you're going."

"Talking," his wife added. "Talking fast, like your head is exploding. Conversation with my friends at home is like being hit by a fire hose! I love it!"

"Seasons," said Steve. "Except winter." ("Ah, you have to take all four," admonished Jeff.)

"Acres of lawn, and old houses."

"Those little white road signs on back roads."

"Good Italian food."

They continued sentimentally in this vein until Jeff put up his hand and said, "Listen, I've heard all this before—except the part about the fire hose—and all I can say is, California, love it or leave it." He turned to Claire, who had been silent during the exchange. "How about you, Claire?" he asked. "What do you miss?"

Claire was in fact feeling rather fatigued, which was odd, since this was her dream evening—enhanced, even, by the exciting presence of Jeff. But she seemed to have lost her facility for recreational talking. She made an effort and said, "Lakes. Clear, green lakes you can swim across." Not rivers, she thought. Rivers were narrow and congested and muddy. Like canals.

Jeff's eyes brightened, if that was possible, as he asked, "Do you like to swim?"

"Mmm. It's always been my idea of peace, and freedom."

"Sounds like a political party," he said, and she laughed at the lame joke. "Yeah, it's wonderful," he agreed. "Maybe next time you're here we can swim together. You'd like the UCLA pool—it's as big as a lake."

Maybe it was the prospect of swimming with Jeff Green, which made her feel a little light-headed; maybe it was the wine; maybe it was because she felt she had so far failed to distinguish herself in the conversation. In any case, Claire suddenly found herself doing something inexcusable.

"You know that guy from the *Free Press* who drowned? I found his body," she blurted. Then she literally slapped her hand over her mouth, but not before Steve had said excitedly, "What guy?" and Sara had exclaimed, "Claire!" in tones of unspeakable horror. "How did it happen?" she demanded while Steve repeated plaintively, "What guy?"

"Sweetie, I told you. Jon Levine, the reporter," Sara said impatiently, then returned her attention to Claire. "What happened?"

"Oh, you know," she said feebly. "I just . . . found him. Saw him floating in an irrigation canal." She was deeply ashamed; she had done exactly what she had condemned Sara for, exploited a tragedy for pure gossip value. It was despicable.

Jeff at least had the sensitivity to stay out of the whole exchange. In fact, he had become utterly quiet ever since she had dropped her bombshell. But Sara was irrepressible.

"Claire, that's just incredible! Did you . . . I mean, had he already . . . you know . . . died, when you found him?"

"Yes. Look, Sara, let's just drop it, okay? We can talk about it later, if you want. I feel very bad for mentioning it here."

Sara, who was essentially a good-hearted person, saw that Claire was genuinely upset and clamped down on her curiosity, and Steve followed her example. They all sat in silence for a moment—if Claire had wanted to trump the conversation, she had certainly done so—and soon, with mutual comments about sudden weariness and early morning commitments, they headed for the Ashes' car.

Jeff was driven to Westwood. He had been subdued since the restaurant, compounding Claire's profound regret over her lapse of judgment, but when they pulled up in front of his apartment he paused on the sidewalk, leaned through the back window, and took her hand between his own. "It's been a pleasure," he said quietly. "I really meant what I said about taking you swimming. When do you think you'll get down here again?"

"I don't know," she said, pleased and surprised. "In a couple of weeks, maybe."

"Wonderful. Just call me." He pulled a card from his wallet and very, very delicately tapped it into the breast pocket of her silk shirt. No one else could have gotten away with it. It sent her basal temperature soaring about five degrees.

"Bye," he said to the group at large, and bounded up the stairs.

She spent Tuesday at UC Riverside with Allen Okamoto, talking about biological control of fiddleneck. They needed something cheap and effective, but not *too* effective; the goal was to contain, not eradicate, and like any proposal to tamper with the natural equilibrium, the project required delicacy and precision. No one wanted to wipe out fiddleneck, a perfectly pleasant little flower, or set in motion some concatenating ecological disaster.

Entyloma looked promising. It was a leaf smut that attacked members of fiddleneck's family, *Boraginaceae*, but left alfalfa unscathed. Being a smut, however, it was an "obligate parasite" and grew only on the leaves of its specific host—became, in fact, part of the leaf. So it couldn't be grown in the laboratory. Allen would have to find an infected population in the wild.

But by afternoon it was obvious that in her eagerness to escape Kaweah County she had jumped the gun: neither she nor Allen had really done their homework to talk very productively. So after dinner with the Okamotos, and oaths of renewed enthusiasm for *Entyloma seritonum*, she set out for home again, a day early.

Home? Yes, it felt like home. She hardly winced at the superheated blast of air that greeted her when she coasted down the Grapevine into the Valley; she gazed with a certain perverse pleasure at the ugly landscape softening in the twilight and, upon stopping for gas, found herself smiling indulgently at a grumpy-looking father herding two small children to the bathroom and back.

The interesting subject of Jeff Green occupied her as she drove up Highway 99. Jeff, who was everything people up here were not: witty and smart—no, Sam was smart; *hip*, then—and politically correct and a snappy dresser. Jeff would never deliver a monologue on sedges or . . . or topsoil, to a reluctant audience, though he would listen with polite attention were someone else to do so.

Exactly. That was the problem. What was Jeff Green so passionate—to use Emil's word—about that he was willing to bore people? His politics? Then why was he living the relatively posh life of the tenured academic? Why was he swimming in the UCLA pool every day, working on his tan? And goddamn it, why did he look like that? A man that beautiful was bound to be a narcissistic jerk—

Oh, wait, there was nothing wrong with Jeff. Absolutely nothing wrong. . . .

Nothing at all. In fact, anything potentially offensive in the way of looks or manners or attire had been banished from his person. He was a sort of regression to the mean, whereas Sam, and Sam's long bony body and haphazard clothes, were definitely an acquired taste, like the stripped-down landscape she was passing through. They made quite a pair, the two of them, she thought, smiling: Sam with his collarbone like a coat hanger and pelvis like a keel, and she . . . she wasn't much better; between them there was hardly a soft place to lay one's head.

Sam's guilt, Emil's torment . . . she had outgrown Jeff's sunny virtues, she told herself; she had developed a taste for the maimed and the mysterious.

Which brought her to Jon Levine.

What story had he been working on, and why had Tom misled her?

And—she suddenly realized—if he had misled her about this, had he told her the truth about the coroner's report? Well. She would ask him in the morning.

By the time she drove into the driveway at nine, she was eager to see Sam and even looking forward to seeing the boys, sort of.

But the Valiant was gone, the house dark and the sink full of soggy pizza crusts and swollen, starfishlike creatures clustered around the drain that gave her a momentary jolt until she realized they were the sepals of tomatoes. Well, at least they got some vitamin C, she thought, swabbing the sink and blotting a line of ants with a sponge. She assumed they had all gone off to the latest Schwarzenegger blockbuster, until she saw the note by the phone.

"Monday 9 AM. Claire—took the boys up to Quaking Aspen to fish for a couple of days. We may be back before you—if not, Thursday morning at the latest. Love, S."

It was the wordiest missive she had ever received from him, and she took no pleasure from the fact. She was disappointed and angry. Here she had been working herself up about him since Bakersfield—and he was off somewhere with the boys! Typical!

Still, another day or two of solitude, that wasn't so bad; she would enjoy that. She would get up very early tomorrow and stop by her test plot of alfalfa—maybe stop by Wayne's walnut grove, too—and spend all day thinking about the project, so that when she saw Allen again she would be prepared. Not that she was in any hurry to visit L.A. again. Why should she be?

And, oh, yes, she would call Tom Martelli.

Monday's paper had been tossed unread on the coffee

table. She broke the string and scanned the front page, and a headline at the bottom caught her eye.

MYSTERY SURROUNDS CANAL DEATH, it said. "The mystery has deepened in the case of a man whose nude body was recently discovered in the Friant-Kern. It was originally believed that the victim, 19-year-old Hector Cedillo, drowned in the canal, but the county coroner has established the cause of death as heart failure. Authorities speculate that Cedillo may have stripped to swim in the canal, and that the shock of the cold water aggravated an existing heart condition. Cedillo's blood-alcohol level indicated he was intoxicated, authorities say."

So Martelli had told the truth about that, at least. But did "heart failure" mean heart failure, or did it mean "We don't know what the hell killed this ol' boy?"

Chapter 8

By seven A.M. Wednesday the house was already beginning
to creak with the gathering heat, and Claire enviously imagined Sam and the kids, still shivering in their plaid wool
shirts, waiting for the first rays of sun to shoot through the
tall firs. Sam was probably pumping up the camp stove to
make cocoa. . . .

Ah, well. She pumped herself up, for another visit to her
alfalfa field (this time, she hoped, body free), and started
down the hill. But along about Riverdale she started reviewing a dream about Jeff Green, and the Toyota's automatic
pilot seized the helm, turning south and heading toward the
station, as always. After a couple of miles Claire emerged
from her fog, realized her mistake, and began to make her
way on surface streets north through Parkerville.

She crossed the slough where the river ran out. The river
had always run out; that is, it had never made it to the ocean,
but once upon a time, before Prosperity Dam, it had at least
formed a shallow lake some miles to the west. Now there
was only this channel, clogged like a diseased artery with
what she had once taken for bamboo, until Sam had delivered a lecture on the subject of *Arundo donax*, giant reed
grass. This "invasive alien"—a racist term, she claimed, but
Sam had merely blinked—provided reeds for saxophones.
But since it achieved heights upward of three meters and
grew two feet a week, or a day, or an hour, she couldn't quite
remember, a single plant could have supplied all the high
school bands west of the Rockies. And that meant a lot of
leftover *Arundo*. Its rhizomes crawled under the ground and

up it sprang, like dragon's teeth, forming thickets so dense that nothing else could breathe, not willows nor birds nor fish. Even the tires and major appliances and brown plaid sofas that inevitably found their way to the channel bottom disappeared under *Arundo*. Burn it, it came back threefold; hack at it, it liked it; it grew in streambeds and roadsides and on dry slopes. It was *Über*-plant. One day there would be nothing but *Arundo*.

And on the northern bank of the slough another invasion had taken place, as the quaint prewar bungalows fell to rows of gimcrack duplexes that would last maybe twenty years before they too were nudged down into the sludge. Well, people had to live somewhere, Claire supposed, as she tried to keep the mountains to her right and turned another corner—

And saw Sam's car, parked on the street.

She did a double take, checked the license plate, and wondered for the briefest of instants what it was doing there; and then the realization exploded like a cerebral hemorrhage. That was Linda Nelson's house.

Then and there her brain stopped. But her hands and feet worked moronically, and she continued to move along like Wile E. Coyote tearing past a cliff's rim, buoyed by ignorance until he looks down. When *she* looked down she was maybe a mile away. She pulled over to the curb and tried to think of a reason other than the obvious one for Sam to be parked in front of an old girlfriend's house at seven-thirty in the morning on a day when she was supposed to be out of town. Something to do with the kids, maybe? But all she could hear was Sam's voice—*"Wednesday night? Thursday morning? When exactly are you coming back?"*—and the pulse in her throat, thrumming like a hummingbird.

Shakily she retraced her mindless path, parked across the street, and stared without comprehension at the old blue car and then at the house behind it, with its pathetic fake half timbering, its yellowing grass, its battered backboard in the driveway. An Edward Hopper house, dingy, utterly ordinary, yet full of terrifying portent. After a moment she opened her glove compartment and found an unsent postcard from last year's vacation to Yosemite. "Back from LA," she scrawled. "Call me at the office. Claire."

That nonchalant missive would give him something to think about. Only it gave her something to think about, too. The glossy photo of Half Dome was poised above Sam's windshield wiper while she asked herself if she was really still going to look at fiddleneck at this moment—fiddleneck, while her life burned?

Well, what else could she do? Lurk in her car and wait for them to appear? Peek through the bedroom window? Telephone anonymously? At the moment her past seemed to collapse into one long sequence of being left. Surely, after all that practice, she could achieve some grace, some wit, some style; could take control instead of standing like a great wounded buffalo with imploring eyes. But first she had to get out of this claustrophobic warren of condos, find some open road, drive somewhere . . .

She took corners too fast and at random. This was a new, a western, idea: driving as spiritual analgesia. In Boston, where therapeutic driving would have been a joke, she had walked; by the end of her breakup with Phil she had probably walked to Albuquerque without ever leaving the greater Boston metropolitan area. But out here the severity of a personal crisis could be measured in gallons of gas; you just pointed yourself in an arbitrary direction, fixed your eyes on the horizon, and mashed that pedal to the metal until you banged into some major geographical barrier—ocean, mountain range—that put human vicissitudes into perspective. Or crossed an international border, ditto. If you didn't feel better by Canada you were in trouble.

So she needed a highway. Any highway. She turned east, north, east—and was totally, hopelessly lost. Her throat tightened with panic and despair.

No, wait. These trailers and *mercados* . . . the VFW field . . . wasn't this . . . yes! This was Walker Road! There was the white Impala of blessed memory, still up on blocks! And beyond it . . .

Beyond it was the slightly potbellied, indubitably secular figure of Tom Martelli. He was standing by a black-and-white Chevy Blazer, and as she slowed to gawk he stepped into the street and flagged her down.

"Howdy," he said. "Out of your territory, aren't you?"

"I'm a little lost," she replied in a quavery old-lady's voice she hardly recognized. Tom leaned on the window and looked at her curiously. Tom. There was something she was supposed to ask Tom. . . .

"You all right?"

"I—" Tell all, part of her urged. Cry, if possible. Warm waves of sympathy will wash away the pain. . . . She cleared her throat and her mind and sat up straight. No. Wit and grace, those were her watchwords. And anyway, Sam's best friend was hardly an appropriate confidante. "Yes, fine," she said in a near normal voice. "But this isn't your jurisdiction, is it?"

"Not ordinarily. But Jonathan Levine is my case. And he was living here when he died."

"*Here?*" She took in the derelict motel behind him, unnamed except for a perpetual VACANCY sign.

"Yep. He'd rented a room in this place for the last three weeks. The forensics people finished here yesterday, but Ricky and I were going to have one last look around before we pack up his effects."

At that moment Deputy Enrique Santiago stepped down from the Blazer. A dark-eyed man in his late twenties with a dashing Zapata mustache, Santiago managed to look muscular and trim in the blue uniform that on Tom was congenitally rumpled. "Tom," he said, "message just came through. Injury accident at Fourth and Willow."

"Shit!" Martelli thought a moment. "Okay, you go on, I'll finish up here. Come back soon as you can, I could use another pair of eyes."

Claire, meanwhile, was staring hard at the VACANCY, trying to imagine either of the Levines—little Jonnie or Jonathan, they were becoming conflated in her mind—in this place.

It was a terrible thing to think, but rural poverty often had a picturesque quality that its urban counterpart lacked. This motel, for example, was almost charming. It was a horseshoe of three detached blocks: three units per side, two at the end. A halfhearted coat of mocha paint was peeling away from the Spam-colored stucco underneath, and the wooden porches sagged and buckled; in fact, there wasn't a right angle to be seen. But a huge cottonwood nearly filled the courtyard and hung halfway over the street, and the whole complex reminded Claire, who in spite of everything retained romantic ideas about the Golden West, of a run-down old ranch bunkhouse.

"Tom," she said on impulse, "could I come in and see his room?"

"You! Why?"

He was looking at her strangely, and she realized her voice was still high and a little hysterical from Sam. She took a deep breath and tried to sound casual.

"I'm interested in this guy. Because I found him, I guess." Tom still looked mulish, and suddenly she resented the hell out of him for making her feel morbid and defensive, for making her flatten her voice.

And anger kick-started her brain; she remembered what it was she had to say to Tom. "I thought seeing his room might give me a hint about what story he was working on when he died."

This failed to provoke objection, guilty start, or even sheepish grin. He regarded her meditatively, as if the subject of Levine's purpose in Parkerville had never been broached. "Well. I guess it can't hurt. But don't touch nothin'."

A yellow police line had been set up around the middle unit of the right-hand block—unit number seven—and Tom and Claire ducked under it. Claire felt the stares of the women and children who had gathered in a nearby yard. They were curious, but not curious enough to come closer. Their interactions with the police had not been pleasant.

Tom fumbled with the key for a moment, then the door swung open.

Number seven, like numbers one through six, presumably, was not furnished with color TV, or water bed, or air conditioner, or Sanitized strip across the toilet. Sour smelling and incredibly hot, it contained a sagging double bed under a chenille bedspread, three tables, two lamps, and a molded green plastic chair. On the ceiling, directly over the bed, was a huge water stain shaped approximately like Minnesota.

There was nothing picturesque about number seven.

"Whew," said Tom, wrinkling his nose, "seems like the newspaper could've sprung for better than this."

"It's a small paper," Claire said dully; she had suddenly remembered Sam, and her enthusiasm for the room had vanished abruptly. But even in the midst of her apathy she eyed the expensive-looking REI pack leaning against the wall. Seems like Jonathan Levine could have sprung for better himself.

Tom headed for the closet while she examined the box of reading material neatly packed up by the police. Magazines on top: *The New Yorker, The Nation, Science.* It might have been her own bedside table. Newspapers: the *Los Angeles Times; The New York Times;* and, of course, the *L.A. Free Press.* Books: a hiking guide to the Sierras; *Huelga!,* which was a hagiography of César Chávez; a publication of the California Institute of Rural Studies on Mixtec Indian farm laborers; Carey McWilliams's *Factories in the Field.* She suddenly felt real grief for Levine's loss. They obviously shared interests, including a fascination with farmworkers—and she had to hand it to him, he had solved the problem of breaking into that society simply by moving into it. A reporter's trick.

"What the hell was he doing here?" muttered Tom.

"From his reading material I'd guess he was doing a story on farm labor." She prodded one last time. "Bernie—you know, his editor—said he was researching a story up here. As he *told you when you called.*"

At that casual "Bernie," he shot her a surprised look, but all he said was, "Yeah, but why was he *here*? He could have done research from the Holiday Inn."

"Not the same. Anyway, the Holiday Inn is a terrible place."

"I think it's nice!" he protested. "They have this honeymooners' special—three days for ninety dollars. Continental breakfast, swimming pool, the works. Marie and I have done that a couple of times when we wanted to get away from the kids." Claire listened in disbelief, and he recalled himself to the present. "And it seems like you could interview farmworkers without living like one."

"Yes, but maybe," said Claire, "maybe he *wanted* to live like one."

"What?"

"Yes. You know, César Chávez, the whole farmworkers' movement, those were exciting times. Righteous." Maybe he wanted to walk on his knees from Delano to Sacramento, she thought: maybe that was the story. A sort of memorial to Chávez. FARMWORKERS TODAY: DID HE MAKE A DIFFERENCE? Something like that. "A liberal Anglo like Levine might see the lives of people here as kind of, um, romantic."

"Romantic!" Tom snorted.

"Yeah. Simpler. Purer. Not so much urban angst, or . . . or deception."

"Well, I don't know about *angst*—never have known exactly what that was—but I'll tell you what. A few days in this motel, and this life wouldn't look so romantic, I guarantee you. And this is a pretty *good* place, as these things go." He stared at her. "You seem to know this guy pretty well."

"No," she said, still looking through the books. "I mean, he reminds me of this boy I knew when I was nine. By the way, did you ever find out where he was from?"

"Yep," he said. "Someplace in New York. Sichen—Cheniss—"

"Schenectady?" she guessed, remembering the mother in Albany.

"Yeah, that was it."

"You're sure." God help her, she even wondered if he was telling the truth about *this*. "Not Massachusetts."

"Nope. Sicheneckatty. At least, that's where he lived before he came out here. I don't know where he grew up."

"Oh. Could you find out for me?" Not that it mattered; he had been somebody's little Jonnie, and his life ended too soon, and badly.

Tom shrugged. "You can ask his mother when she comes for the body."

They returned to their respective piles. "What's this?" she asked presently. She had come to two pieces of paper sealed in a plastic bag.

She unfolded the first. It was a spray notification handbill, announcing that a field was to be sprayed on July 1 and would be safe for reentry on August 1.

The other was a scrap of lined paper, torn from a pad.

Scrawled on it in a left-hander's back-slanting script were two phone numbers, Los Angeles and Sacramento by their area codes.

"Hey!" he scolded reflexively. "Don't mess with that stuff!" Then, in a normal voice, "Um, they were in a book. That book on top."

Factories in the Field. "Are they important?"

"Damned if I know. The notice is a standard one; maybe he just picked it up somewhere and was using it to mark his place. And I assume he was saving the other for the numbers. I'll call them eventually. But mostly I'm interested in it 'cause of the paper."

She looked at it. "It's just ordinary spiral notebook paper. From a steno pad."

"Right. Only at first we didn't find a steno pad, or a notebook. No paper, nowhere, not until we found his car— Oh, did I tell you we found his car? New Honda. Parked by a walnut grove along the Alta-Woodbury Road. 'Bout a mile from where the body was found, but that canal runs by there, all right. Still, if that's where he went in he floated a hell of a long way," he muttered.

"So you did find a notebook in the car?" she prompted.

"Yep. In the trunk. Brand-new steno pad. Matches this paper. Only one sheet missing. I counted," he said, and the obsessiveness of this act startled her enough to lift her mental fog of misery for a moment.

Counting sheets of paper in a pad . . . sealing random scraps of paper in plastic bags . . . *forensics people.* That's what Tom had said when she'd first arrived, "forensics people."

"Tom . . . you lied about the coroner's report, too. This wasn't an accidental drowning, was it?"

But for some reason the word *drowning* summoned a new wave of grief. *Sam—oh, Jesus, what was going to happen with Sam?* The pain coursed through her veins as if a tourniquet had been loosened. She sat down abruptly on the flaccid bed and covered her eyes with her hands.

Thus distracted, she missed the gratifying experience of seeing Tom finally look uncomfortable. "It was a drowning, no doubt about it," he said. "There were traces of sand and weed in his lungs."

He stopped. Claire looked up and waited. Eventually he said, "But there was a contusion on the victim's jaw—I noticed that right away, don't know if I mentioned it."

"No."

"Oh. Well, seems he'd also suffered a blow to the head. Concussion. And there were bruises on his wrists and on the back of his neck. Oh, yeah, and some scratches on his nose."

He took a breath. Now that he was divulging, he was divulging all. "And we found some interesting tire tracks about thirty feet from his car—big tires, probably a good-size pickup. And deep, like some vehicle had been waiting, and sort of spun out when it pulled away. 'Course, I can't prove that."

He stopped, approached the climax reluctantly, haltingly, as if climbing up his own sentence hand over hand. "So I think . . . what may have happened . . . well, what I think is that somebody was waiting for him there. Somebody who held his hands behind him and pushed his head down in the ditch." With relief he lapsed into police syntax. "At present I am regarding Levine's death as a probable homicide."

Claire merely nodded. Jonathan Levine had been murdered, Sam was sleeping with another woman. At the moment both seemed equally monstrous and equally inevitable.

"Oh, and they're puttin' his time of death way later than I guessed," he added, fluent again. "Even with the cold water, medical examiner reckons he'd only been dead maybe six hours when you found him, which means he died Saturday around noon."

This was way more detail than Claire required, but Martelli was on a confessional roll. "Personally, I wish he'd put that back some, but he's diggin' in his heels, won't go farther than twelve hours, or six in the morning. Which logistically is a problem for me. See, we figured he came straight from the mountains where he picked that flower, without changing his clothes, right? So we're talking a seven-hour trip, at least. . . . He'd have to leave mighty early to arrive in time to die by noon, and he'd have to've left in the middle of the *night* to get here by early morning. I think he came down the day before, and was killed sometime during the night or real early morning. Just makes more sense. So I'm negotiatin'—"

Claire was only approximately following this timetable and had had enough. "Tom," she interrupted, "why did you lie to me about Levine?"

"I didn't exactly lie—"

"You exactly lied."

Long silence this time. "You seemed too interested in this guy," he said eventually. "I had the idea that you might want to get involved in the investigation if you knew it was murder."

"And if I had?" she asked coolly. "You seemed fairly grateful for my participation when Tony Rodriguez was killed."

"That was different. That was you *and* Sam—now don't get on your women's lib high horse," he said rapidly, fending off outrage. "There is a difference between you and Sam—"

"Obviously. He's a man," she said acidly, and Tom threw his hands up in exasperation.

"He was a *soldier*!" he said. "He knows how to take care of himself. I mean, did you enjoy getting chased and run off the road and shot at last summer?"

Actually, it had been rather exciting. In retrospect. "No, but I wasn't hurt—"

"Luck. Pure, blind luck—"

"And this isn't that kind of situation—"

"How the hell do you know?" he demanded. "You thought about what happened here, Claire? I mean, really thought about it? This ain't . . . ain't okra weevils or pistachio smut! Somebody seems to have put a knee in this fellow's back and held his head under the water for a long, long time."

Okay. She did think about it. That peaceful face had been a lie. Little Jon Levine, all grown up, had died thrashing and scrabbling and gasping for air. Just like a fight on the playground in Pittsfield, Mass., or Schenectady, New York, what did it matter . . . only the recess bell had never rung.

"That indicates what you might call a certain disregard for human life," Martelli was saying. "You ain't trained to deal

with this, and I won't be responsible for you being involved!"

"All right. But there was no reason to lie to me."

"I thought there was. You're a strong-willed woman."

She? Strong-willed? Had he been talking to Sam?

Had Sam been talking to him?

Did Tom know all about Linda?

Was *everyone* deceiving her about *everything*?

They were walking out into the morning, blinking in the
harsh sun, as Sam rose to the surface again like a—a
"floater." My God, she thought, it's still morning. How will I
get through a whole day? And the next, and the next?

The crowd, now grouped tentatively around the dead Impala, was close enough to resolve itself into two men, six
small children in cheap, bright clothes, and two girls, eight or
nine years old, who seemed to be caring for them. Suddenly
the door to number six banged open and a young woman
stepped out to regard her.

It was the Madonna of Walker Street.

Claire caught her breath once again at the woman's beauty
and thought, Well. So this was Jonathan Levine's next-door
neighbor.

Their eyes met for a moment. The gaze was cool, intelligent, and a little puzzled. Hardly what one expected from a
madonna.

Tom didn't seem to notice the woman. "Listen, you tell
Sam—"

But she never had to deal with this potentially awkward
request. Out on Walker Road a gleaming black van with
opaque windows like nictitating membranes was cruising
slowly by. It rolled to a stop in front of the Impala, and
Claire noticed that the crowd moved back about three steps.
After a long moment a window descended gradually, revealing life within, and waves of Brut rolled toward them. Sleek
and kempt as his vehicle, the driver leaned out, gave Claire a
cursory look of appraisal. His eyes moved to Levine's neighbor and lingered there. Finally he turned to Martelli with a
huge smile.

"Nothing wrong with my people here, I hope, Chief
Martelli," Ruben Moreno said.

He had a curious voice, a sort of husky alto, quite androgynous (Claire realized that Moreno would probably have slit her throat for that adjective, once she had explained it to him).

"No, no, this has nothing to do with you, Moreno," Tom said grumpily.

"Glad to hear it. We like to stay on good terms with the authorities." He gave Tom a friendly wave and began to drive off.

" 'My people,' " Tom repeated disgustedly but without much heat. "Jesus, what a prick."

The van stopped about twenty yards up the street. Moreno leaned out the window once again and called back in Spanish in that high, hoarse voice, *"¡Señora Perez, recuerdes lo que te dije!"* Then he pulled away at a stately pace.

Remember what I told you, Claire translated uncertainly. The Madonna—Señora Perez—stared after him, eyebrows drawn together in thought, or something harder.

At the station a pile of pink telephone slips was stacked on her desk: "8:55. Sam. Call him at home." "9:30. Sam. Call when you get in." "9:45. Sam. Pls return his call." "10:00. Sam. No msg." Fuck him, she thought viciously, he can bloody well come and find me—

At that moment he walked through the door.

Any faint hope that she might have misjudged the situation vanished when she saw his stricken face. His dearly beloved, treacherous face. For a moment she actually felt *sorry* for him. After an interval of terrible silence he said, "You got back from L.A. early."

"Yes. Sorry."

"We got back early, too. Shannon felt sick when we started up the mountain, so we stopped at Douggie and Kevin's and spent the night—"

"On the couch?"

"What?" he said, startled.

"I said, did you spend the night on the couch?"

He looked at the floor. She waited—waited, for an apology, an explanation, an excuse, a promise—anything that would cool the core of hot anguish hissing inside her.

Nothing happened. It was a hell in which normal time had been suspended.

Finally Claire, suffocating with misery, broke the silence. "Was this the only time?" she blurted, hating herself, but at least it was a simple question, allowing for a simple "yes" that would spring them both from this trap of mute agony.

He shifted uncomfortably, and she drew in her breath. "No?" she said incredulously. "*No?* Jesus Christ, Sam, what have you been doing to me?"

"I didn't want this. I didn't plan it."

"Of course you planned it! The minute I told you I was going out of town the gears started whirring!" And when was the *last* time? That conference in Sacramento?

"I didn't plan it," he repeated stolidly, though he wouldn't meet her eyes. "It just . . . happened."

"Oh, you were helplessly swept along before the torrent of your passion!" she said with what was supposed to be stinging sarcasm, but her voice shook. "Is that supposed to make me feel better?"

"I can't make you feel better." And that was the first true thing he had said all day.

She was suddenly cold. This was bad. No contrition, no explanation—this was as bad as it could be, this was not just a fling, this was—

This was Sam leaving her.

Her knees buckled under her, and she collapsed on a stool. "Why?" she croaked.

He leaned against the counter and studied a beaker. "I don't know if I can explain," he said. "I . . . it's not that I don't care for you. . . ."

Cared for her. That was good, right? So—

"Then why?" she asked again, dazed. If she could just *understand* this, maybe it wouldn't hurt so much.

There was another long silence. "It's the boys, Claire," he said finally. "It's my boys. Right now they mean more to me than anything else, and I want to make a home for them, and a life."

"And that excludes me?" She stood up and walked toward the window, automatically registering the familiar flash of color outside: the peaches, glowing on their branches.

"Isn't that what you've been telling me? That you don't want to be a mother?"

Whirling to face him again: "Jesus, Sam, I've been trying—"

"You don't have to try. You don't have to be what you aren't. I respect your decision, and I admire you for knowing yourself well enough, and for being honest enough, to tell me."

Oh, yeah, respect and admiration. Mighty cold comfort. It was dawning on her that he was serious, that he was talking about ending their relationship not for another woman, or his career—bad reasons, terrible reasons, to be sure, but reasons she could understand—but for his *kids*. It had never occurred to her that such a thing was possible.

"I don't believe this," she said numbly.

"Claire, I'm sorry—"

"No!" she shouted suddenly, pounding the zinc-topped table. "I mean that literally! I do not believe this!"

"Claire, listen—"

"You're lying to me! This is all an elaborate con! You wanted to sleep with Linda, and the rest of this is bullshit!"

"What are you talking about—"

"People don't leave people they love over things like this!" Her voice had risen shrilly.

"'Things like this,'" he repeated. "You mean 'children.' Yes, they do, Claire. Grown-ups do."

Oh, God, she thought, deflating instantly, he's right. I'm a self-centered adolescent—I know it, and evidently he knows it, too. If only I had tried harder with the kids; tried to like them, tried to make them like me—

Wait a minute. Why was *she* feeling guilty? He was the one who had lied and—and cheated, in the parlance of the damn country music he was addicted to—and generally acted like a weasel!

"Look," she said evenly, "fatherhood may be an honorable estate, but it doesn't excuse you from all decent behavior. I mean, we should have *talked* about this!"

"We did."

"No! Not . . . not explicitly. Not honestly. It never seemed real—" She stopped, realizing her misstep, and Sam pressed his advantage.

"Real? The fact that I have children doesn't seem real to you?"

"No, it doesn't," she answered defiantly. "Not yet. And please don't take that tone of gentle reproof, it makes me want to smash your nose in!" She took a deep breath. "It's perfectly true that I have no experience of children, and I need some help and some time to ... to take them in. So if I'm competing against Linda in the Natural Aptitude for Motherhood stakes, well, I'm going to lose. But it's hardly a fair contest; I didn't even sign up for that event! It wasn't required when we began this relationship. You changed the rules."

"The situation changed."

"*You* changed the *situation*!" she shouted. "Don't talk as if this were an act of God!" The blood throbbed ominously in her temples. Grace and wit, she thought, what happened to grace and wit? Urgently she tried to think of something that embodied one or the other, and when nothing presented itself, she aimed for clearheadedness instead.

"Okay," she said calmly, sinking to the stool again. Her mind was bearing down on her explosive feelings, creating a precarious and very temporary control—like stomping on the brakes and the accelerator at the same time. "Okay. If I understand you, you've decided, unilaterally, that the most important thing to you is your children, that I can't participate in your life with them, and that Linda can." She paused, inviting protests or denials. None came.

"Well, it seems to me ... it seems to me ... Goddamn it, Sam!" she screeched, as the brakes gave out abruptly. "You should have talked to me about this! I deserved that much, at least! I mean, you didn't confide in me, you deceived me and ... and betrayed me!" Melodramatic, but there it was. "It's like you weren't—like our relationship wasn't—worth much after all! So if this is how it ends, so be it," she finished recklessly—

And halted, appalled. Her mouth had run her into a showdown that her head would very much have liked to avoid. Hopelessly she looked at Sam, knowing full well that he would never back down, that real men didn't ever admit they'd done wrong. They might cheat on their girlfriends and generally behave like rodents, but their honor drew the line at apology—

"You're right," he said. "I'm sorry."

Silence. "What?"

"I said, I'm sorry. Of course I should have talked to you, but I was . . . well, I was afraid you'd be angry. So angry you'd leave me." He laughed shortly. "Obviously I haven't thought this out too well, because I really don't want you to leave me."

"Then what do you want?"

"I want . . ." He trailed off, and she silently completed the thought: He wants it all, of course. The boys; me for company and sex; Linda for mothering. And sex. Why not?

A new surge of anger carried her over the next conversational shoal. "I need to think about this. Can we talk after work? At your house?"

"My house?"

"Yes, you know, the house where you live. I'll need to pick up a few things."

"Pick up . . . Where are you going?" he asked, disconcerted—to her immense gratification.

"I don't know." She remembered her cozy Riverdale bungalow, whose lease had lapsed in March. *Don't be in such a goddamned hurry to give up your own place; here endeth the first lesson.*

"Look, you don't have to move. I can—"

"Sleep at Linda's?" she finished venomously. "Thanks. You do what you want, but I'm not staying at your house."

"But where will you go?"

"I don't know," she said again. "Some motel, probably. Look, just leave, will you?" she said urgently as her will slipped away and the first forlorn wounded buffalo appeared on the ridge, its moist eyes imploring and helpless.

He left—probably, she thought bitterly, to put in a healthy and productive day's work. As for her, all she could do was lock her door and lie facedown on the floor, as if standing upright were altogether too foolhardy and unpredictable. Cheek pressed into cold linoleum, lungs filled with purifying fumes of Lysol, she considered the future. L.A., and Sara's smug sympathy? She shuddered. Back to Cambridge, then. But she had come fleeing heartbreak in Cambridge; was she once again to be hounded across the continent by faithless love?

Never had she imagined that her relationship with Sam would end like this. Never. If she had thought about it at all, she might have assumed—well, frankly, she might have guessed that she'd leave *him*, for another job or another climate. Or, simply, another man. Because yes, okay, there was a certain exaggerated interest in Jeff Green. But if this was poetic justice for a few harmless fantasies, it was harsh poetry indeed—

Sam, deceitful! Sam, nursing his private agenda, planning this campaign of lies! It was beyond belief. It took her breath away. He, whom she had thought honest to the point of maddening self-righteousness; he, whom she had believed to be laconic, not secretive. . . .

Well, she had taken his silence for consent. That was her fault, she supposed.

If only she had had time to prepare; if only this hadn't happened so suddenly. . . . But no, nothing prepared you for those time-stopping moments when the terrible dichotomies of life revealed themselves. Yes or no, true or false, guilty or not guilty, it is or it isn't. *Yes, it's malignant; I'm sorry, but he's dead; no, I don't love you anymore*—

Still, this was not yet one of those moments, she told herself; Sam didn't even know his own mind. And she could not think about it while her heart throbbed like an amputated limb. One day, one night at a time, then. And tonight—

Yes, tonight.

Not for the first time she wished she had managed to make more friends in Kaweah County. There was Cathy Bakaitis, but she was out of town, and Tom and Marie, but they evidently were Sam's friends. A motel, then, as she had told Sam.

Parkerville had two "good" motels. The Wagonwheel Inn was funky, pleasant, and out of the question because Linda worked there. The Holiday Inn was a Holiday Inn, and not even a particularly clean one. She had stayed at many such places on business trips, and even then, full of purpose and confidence, she'd found them depressing. Now she might blow her brains out in the bubblegum-scented bathroom— perhaps the very suite where Tom and Marie spent their blissful honeymooners' weekends.

She thought for a moment, then pushed herself up to hands and knees and crawled to her desk. She pulled down the phone, dialed Tom Martelli's office.

"Tom? I think I left my sunglasses in Levine's motel room. Can I get back in there?"

Chapter 9

Claire was wilting under the scowl of the manager, a hugely fat woman whose tiny glittering eyes took in the Toyota parked outside, the expensive (by any global standard) clothes, the white face.

"Why you want to live here for?"

"I just broke up with my, uh, my husband, and I need a place to stay for a little while."

"I like to rent by the month," said Mrs. Avila impassively, to appeal to universal sisterhood having failed to move her.

"Your signs says by the day or week. Look, I can pay you two weeks in advance. Cash."

Eyelids up a micron. "The police been working there."

"They're finished. I just spoke with the police chief on the phone. He said he told you that this morning."

"Why you want number seven? I got another unit vacant. I gotta clean number seven." And tear up the floorboards, thought Claire, to discover the secret of its allure for all these strange gringos.

"I can wait, I don't need to move in till tonight. I . . . I'd feel more at home there. I knew the man who rented it before." C'mon, lady, don't make me beg. This was a crazy idea to begin with.

Mrs. Avila heaved a giant sigh and reached upward, testing the tensile limits of her rayon housedress. Then she dangled a key with her left hand and held out her right, palm up.

Back up the walk, past the cottonwood, conscious of the eyes following her—frankly curious, the children's; suspicious and faintly hostile, the adults'. A curtain flicked in the window of number six as she passed, and she nearly knocked over a spindly bean plant in a pot on the porch. There were several plants, in fact; they all were chlorotic and sickly.

The momentary triumph she had felt at besting Señora Avila was flattened by the hot, stale wind that rushed out of number seven when she opened the door, and she surveyed her new home with dismay. What had she been thinking? She should forfeit her deposit, save her sanity, and check in at the Holiday Inn. Maybe Jonathan Levine could live in this little hotbox of a room; he had a reason (whatever that was). But she was already depressed, emotionally fragile, and this place . . .

It looked all the more grim for having been stripped of Levine's few possessions. His "effects," she amended; odd word, that, as if the only effect the dead had on life lay in the *things*, the objects, they left behind. When that was the least of it, she thought, fingering the bedspread, then wandering toward the bathroom.

Objects could be poignant and incredibly evocative, of course. Almost anything; even . . . even a clothes hanger. She had paused by the closet and was looking at the six or seven skeletal wire hangers, pathetic, somehow, in their emptiness. This morning they presumably had held Jonathan's clothes. She hadn't noticed. What would he have worn, besides chino shorts and that blue Central American shirt?

Jeans, probably, she thought, and cotton knit sport shirts. From L. L. Bean; he'd probably been a New Englander, after all. Slowly she took down a hanger and perched on the edge of the bed, regarding it abstractedly. He had sported his little yellow flower, so he had been too rushed even to change out of his hiking clothes, that morning—or night, if Tom was right. Why? What was his assignation, there by the canal in the middle of nowhere? A woman? The Madon—Señora Perez? "Señora"; she was married. Reason for secrecy, and God knew the woman herself was reason to hurry, but—surely he would have changed, and showered, for her?

Not a woman, then. Someone else. The wire form revolved in her hands, and she stared at it, as if through a window onto Jonathan Levine's last night on earth. She seemed to see him driving along a rutted dirt road as the moon rose over the vineyards. He was searching. . . .

He was searching the blackness on either side of the road for . . . something, someone . . . and cursing, because he was tired. Exhausted, in fact; he'd hiked out of Mineral King that morning and torn down the mountain to make this meeting, and his feet hurt—and he was sunburned, she remembered suddenly. *He reached up ruefully to rub his blistered nose, and brush the soft petals of the flower in his buttonhole, and smile in the dark, remembering the stony field high above the tree line where he'd picked it.*

A stranger in these lands, he'd be following directions (Whose directions? part of her whispered), *half-lost, turning down those damn roads that bisected vineyard after vineyard, grove after grove. They were all exactly alike to a newcomer, so he'd be looking for a landmark of some sort. Maybe . . . a light?*

A muted clink interrupted her trance, and she looked up to see the silhouette of a woman standing in the doorway, the late afternoon sun streaming around her like solar flares. Her arms were flung out in fierce jubilance; she was Boadicea, or Liberty Leading the Troops, and she wielded a staff and a shield—

"Excuse me, miss," said Boadicea. She stepped forward, and the staff became a mop and bucket, the shield a baby, resting peacefully on her shoulder. "La Avila, she tell me to clean up this room. I can come back later."

It took Claire a moment to realize that this was her mild Madonna, her neighbor. Number six. Señora Perez. What was it about the woman—or, more likely, about Claire—that imbued her with such mythical presence?

"Oh, oh no, that's fine, I'm just leaving," Claire stammered, scrambling to her feet. This, *this* woman was going to clean her room? "Uh, look, you don't really have to do that—"

"I clean all the apartments. It's my job," she said, sweeping past Claire toward the bathroom and calling over her shoulder. "*¡Ven, mijita!*" A little girl of about three suddenly materialized and trotted across the room to grasp the shirttail of her mother, who meanwhile had efficiently transferred the baby to her left arm, propped the mop against a wall, and begun filling the sink—all before Claire could make a move to help.

Embarrassed to stand idly while Señora Perez worked, Claire gathered herself to leave. The rush of water stopped, and she turned to see the woman regarding her, not unfriendly. "You gonna live here?" she asked Claire in her lilting accent.

"Um, yes. For a little while."

"You with the police?"

"No!" Scotch that rumor, if there was to be any chance of friendship. Or information, if that was what she was here for.

Eyebrows contracted skeptically, and Claire noticed a tiny beauty spot centered exactly between them—like a *bindi*, the mark that upper-caste Indian woman applied. Wasn't that also the location of the pineal gland? The third eye? And one of the chakras, if you believed in that kind of thing?

Which Claire didn't, particularly.

She examined the woman covertly. She *was* a sort of miracle: a miracle of what the species could occasionally do, a paradigm. She was tall—almost as tall as Claire, who was five nine—but not rangy like Claire: she had long, elegant limbs, and breasts, and a waist, and hips. Her face with its strong Indian bones wasn't exactly pretty; in fact it was almost severe, but softened by a full mouth with bee-stung upper lip, and skin that would have the velvet feel of African violets, and a delicately chiseled nose, so unlike Claire's own shapeless schnozz, which had been a torment to her in adolescence. . . .

"I saw you with that Chief Martelli this morning," the woman was saying.

Claire came out of her aesthetic trance. "That was just . . . I was helping him. I was sort of a friend of the man who lived here." God, she was beginning to believe this herself.

"Why you want to live here for?" Señora Perez asked reasonably.

Claire hesitated. Finally she said, "I need a place to stay for a little while. My husband left me," choosing the same near truth she had offered Señora Avila. But this time the words drew the pain up in her like blood into a syringe, and she had to blink and turn her head for a moment.

"Ah." The woman's face cleared. "I know. My husband, he . . . he died—" She stumbled over the word but forged ahead. "Three weeks ago."

"Oh." Claire's gaze moved to the baby and then to the little girl watching her from behind the curve of her mother's hip. "Oh. I'm so sorry."

Tears glistened, but she managed a shrug. "The men. Seem like they always leave, one way or another."

Gratitude for this gritty philosophy overcame Claire's shyness. "My name is Claire," she said, on impulse sticking out her hand.

The woman regarded it blankly for a moment. Uncertainly she wiped her free hand on her jeans and began to offer it, then reconsidered and rested it on her little girl's head. "Luz," she said, pronouncing it "loose." "Luz Perez. And this is Ana, and this"—looking fondly at the baby—"is Juanito. Juan junior."

"Mucho gusto," Claire said carefully, then exclaimed suddenly, "Whoa! Juan *junior*? Your husband's name was Juan Perez?" she asked, trying to keep the inappropriate excitement out of her voice.

Puzzled nod.

"Did he . . . how did he die? If you don't want to talk about it, I understand," she added hastily.

"He drownded," Luz replied flatly. "In a irrigation canal." For a minute Claire thought that was all she was going to say. But no; she was telling her story.

"They say he was drunk. That *cabrón* Ruben Moreno say he saw my Juan drunk and es—estag—estagging—"

"Staggering?"

"Sí, estaggering around the vineyard after lunch, at noon. At noon! Juan never drink when he was working! He was a good husband, he work hard, he didn't go for other women—"

Well, he wouldn't, thought Claire.

"—or spend his money on *cerveza*—" The words were coming faster, wilder now. "He wasn't drunk, he was *sick*!

He got the flu for a month, but he can't take time off from work; he had to keep going, to feed his family, so he get more sick, more sick, and . . . and I guess he just pass out and fall in the water," she ended in a small voice.

"Did anyone see him fall in?"

"No. They find him about two o'clock, and come and tell me." The words caught in her throat, and she began to cry in earnest, collapsing onto the hard green chair.

Had Jonathan Levine known about this? Claire wondered, intrigued in spite of her sympathy. Was this his story? Now was obviously not the time to ask these questions, with Luz sobbing and Ana and Juanito beginning to wail in close harmony. Claire sat on the bed and tentatively laid her hand on the woman's shoulder.

"I'm sorry, Mrs. Perez. Luz. I shouldn't have asked you about your husband; I didn't mean to upset you."

"It's all right. I cry for him and I pray for him, what else can I do?" She looked up at Claire with huge, brimming eyes. "But it's so sudden, you know? I keep thinking, if I have some time to get ready . . . but that's crazy," she said, shaking her head, and Claire started at hearing her own thoughts about Sam echoed so precisely.

And why should that surprise her? It was a common reaction to tragedy.

Because it hadn't occurred to her that she could identify with this woman, that's why. She had been so fascinated by her appearance that she had been watching her talk instead of listening to what she was saying. Which was what men did to beautiful women all the time.

"I've got to go," she said, suddenly ashamed. "Please don't worry about cleaning the room."

"I got to," Luz said tonelessly. "I got to feed these kids somehow." She paused. "You'll like it here. This is a good place, a real good place."

Good place? Claire echoed to herself, looking around her. Well, it depended on what you were used to. "Thanks," she said.

She found the pay phone by Señora Avila's office and called Martelli.

"Howdy," he said, extraordinarily genial to atone for past sins. "You find your sunglasses?"

"My what? Oh, my *sunglasses!* Right, right, yes, I found them, thanks. And in fact I got to talking with Levine's ex-neighbor, the woman in number six. The one Ruben Moreno talked to."

"Oh, *that* neighbor!" he said energetically. He had noticed her all right.

"Well, guess whose widow she is."

"I give up."

"Juan Perez!" Silence. "You know, the guy who drowned? Before Cedillo? The first guy."

"And . . . ?"

"That could have been what Levine was investigating!" she said impatiently.

"Mmm. Interesting idea." She preened for a moment. " 'Cept there was nothing to investigate. I read you that report myself: Perez drowned."

"So did Levine!"

"Yeah, but there were no signs of . . . of foul play, with Perez. He just fell in the canal and drowned. Like he was drunk, maybe."

"*Was* he drunk?"

"No," he admitted. "I don't believe so. As I remember, though, his wife said he'd been real sick." A pause. "I s'pose Levine could've been interested in him as an example of the hardships of the farmworker's life. But the death itself was an accident, Claire. Drop it."

"Okra weevils," she quoted sourly.

"What?"

"Nothing. Forget it."

She stumped back to her room, which Luz had vacated, and sat down on the hard green chair. From long personal experience of good ideas casually dismissed (or occasionally appropriated) by senior scientists, she knew there was only one way to deal with Martelli: be right, and gently and persistently beat him over the head with her conclusions until he came around. So she set out to be right.

Assume Jon's murder was connected with a story he was investigating. (There were other possible explanations—jealous suitor of Luz, say, or some x factor from his past—but this seemed to be a good working hypothesis.) And assume further that the story had to do with farmworkers, that that's why he'd stayed in number seven.

First, what about that story might have got Levine into trouble?

And second, who would he have agreed to meet in a walnut grove in the middle of the night . . . or at the crack of dawn. . . . Damn! She wished she'd paid more attention to Tom's dissertation on time of death.

Well, leave that for later, and concentrate on the first question.

Into her mind came the image of Ruben Moreno, cruising by the Vacancy Motel. Moreno, looking murderous at the open house. Moreno, leering at Luz; Moreno, the reputedly reformed *coyote*, the *contratista* about whom you "heard a lot," according to what's-his-name. Sam. Abuses by labor contractors might make a great story, and Moreno certainly seemed like a villain.

And speaking of villains, there was Bert Yankovich, and speaking of Bert, there was pesticide abuse, César's last crusade. What if, for example, Levine had found out about Bert's spraying of CONKWEST and was threatening exposure (an exposure of an exposure)? Another great story! Maybe she should call Perlmutter and take over Levine's position—

No, she chastised herself. She was no Levine, no whitewater rafter; she had no intention of putting herself in harm's way by meeting questionable "sources" in remote places. She would simply keep her eyes and ears and mind open, would study the problem in the way she studied . . . okra weevils, pass on the information to Tom Martelli, firmly and politely—and make him do his fucking job!

It *did* occur to her briefly that staying at number seven was not the most cautious of decisions, but she didn't dwell on it. Nor did she plan to tell Martelli, of course.

Underpants, bra, socks, jeans, linen pants—
"Claire!"

—blue top, striped top, bathing suit, T-shirt, sleeveless dress—

"Claire, for God's sake! Wait a minute!"

—toothbrush, toothpaste, soap, shampoo—

"Claire!" Sam grabbed her by the upper arm. "Let's talk about this for a minute! You said you were coming up to talk."

"I changed my mind." Her eyes were fixed on her suitcase and her mind on her task and if her concentration wavered—if she looked into his eyes—she was lost.

"You're being childish," he said angrily.

"Childish!" she exploded, violently shaking off his arm; then, after a moment, she repeated the word. "Childish. As in: naive. Trusting."

It was a good rejoinder; he started a sentence, broke off helplessly. Yet the truth was she *was* being childish, and she knew it. But all afternoon her anger and hurt had simmered—and her humiliation. Especially that. Sexual humiliation: the idea that he might prefer someone else in bed to her—to *her*!—represented so intimate, so fundamental a rejection that she could barely stand to think about it. And humiliation at her own gullibility: she felt like a sucker. A dupe. Sam had persuaded her that what he lacked in social graces was more than compensated for by his moral superiority, and she had bought it—

Well. She had persuaded herself. She had wanted to believe that *she* was the complicated one; that Sam was simple and pure-hearted. She had wanted to justify the compromise she made: the absence of amenities like . . . like conversation, and shared interests, and common culture, in exchange for his alleged virtue.

And surprise, surprise, he was just an ordinary guy, with ordinary failings and subordinary communication skills.

Hairbrush, hair ties . . . oh, magazines. *The Nation, The New Yorker, California Agriculture*—

"At least tell me where you're going!"

—photo album. "No." She straightened, took a deep breath, and turned in his general direction, focusing on a spot about a foot above his right shoulder. "Please, Sam. Just let me do this one thing. Let me pretend that *I'm* walking out on

you." She marched through the living room, where Shannon and Terry were absorbed in TV. Did they know what was going on? Did they care? When they glanced up at her their faces were distracted, indifferent. Still . . . "I'll see you guys soon, okay?" she managed to get out. "Bye."

"Bye," they muttered, eyes returning immediately to the screen. But Terry looked after her as she banged out the front door.

Sam trailed behind. At the bottom of the steps she halted and looked back at him. "Don't worry," she said, addressing the hummingbird feeder six inches to his left. "I'll be at the lab. You'll see me every day." Oh, God, yes, seeing the ex at the office; a special circle of hell reserved for modern lovers. "We'll talk, if that's what you want. Right now I'm too angry." That was good, she thought, sliding herself into the Toyota; high marks for adultness, admitting you were angry. All in all, one of her better leavetakings.

She flicked the rearview mirror to its "night" position so she couldn't see him watching her from the porch and spun out of the driveway.

By the time she came to the highway the day's hot sustaining wrath had given way to evening's slow melancholy, and she rolled to a stop, literally unable to think of what to do next. She turned on the radio—the classical station—and turned it off again. Opera. She liked opera, but in her present tender state the sound of people shrieking at each other in a foreign language was intolerable.

Across this vacuum flashed a long-forgotten sentence from the women's bathroom wall in Al's Taproom, Pittsfield, MA: THE BEST WAY TO GET OVER A MAN IS TO GET UNDER ANOTHER ONE.

Since this was a dangerous remedy, and possibly what had involved her with Sam in the first place, it was probably just as well that her options for such solace were limited. There was Jeff Green, but she hadn't laid the groundwork there, and he was some two hundred miles away.

"Just as well," she said out loud, and repeated it several times, like a mantra.

It was sheerly out of curiosity, therefore, that she pulled across the intersection into a parking lot and opened her glove compartment. She retrieved her map of L.A. and located West-wood. Three hours to Los Angeles, say, then another forty min-utes . . .

She pulled herself up short. What was she thinking? She didn't even know the guy! No, her reliable, time-tested treat-ment for heartbreak was work. Rev up that overtrained brain and solve a problem, by God.

But work was now contaminated by Sam. Damn! It was ex-actly what had happened with Phil at MIT! First time tragedy, second time farce.

Only it didn't feel like farce.

But at least it *felt*, she thought, suddenly remembering Jon Levine. I hurt, therefore I am. Levine felt nothing. Why? What, or who, had he been investigating?

She was having trouble stuffing her map of Los Angeles back into the glove compartment. Exasperated, she unloaded items one by one; the problem seemed to be this paperback-size packet . . . which proved to be, in fact, a paperback, *The Monkeywrench Gang*.

And that started her thinking. When she was doing prelimi-nary research for a project, she didn't begin at the library, she began on the telephone. She talked to experts, like Allen Okamoto. And who would qualify as Kaweah County's most conspicuous liberal authority on local environmental and labor controversies?

And who would be nice to talk to right now, as a friend (a friend who didn't seem to be speaking to her, but nevertheless a friend)?

She started the engine and headed west (noting that the fire danger was now VERY HIGH; what was the next superlative? BALLISTIC?), then south along the foothills, then east toward Tierra Buena, finally coming to a stop on a low ridge below Teapot Hill.

Chapter 10

The building she looked down on might have been a mid-western farmhouse—except for the palm trees. Ink black against the creamy orange sky, exotic, outrageous, these oversize feather dusters were date palms—or *Phoenix dactylifera*, if you were Sam. (And damn it, why was the entire state of California mediated through Sam? Why had she let that happen?) The darkness below the palms was the jungle of cactus, roses, and orange, grapefruit, lemon, and peach trees that often shaded these old Valley houses—two of every kind, as if the original farmer had meant to create a sort of sampler of Paradise. Towering over all was the old pumphouse, enclosed to resemble a watchtower or a church steeple—which in a way it was, water being the sacred stuff that made everything possible, from this showy little oasis to all the riches of the wide San Joaquin.

While the night deepened and a light came on in one room, Claire's misgivings about her reception by her "target" (somehow she thought of this as a kind of raid) sharpened. But surely she could heal the rift, regain his affection, she thought uncertainly.... Finally she brought herself to start the engine, roll down the long dirt road, creep up the front steps, and knock on the door. Her pulse was racing.

Silence. She knew someone was there; someone had turned on that light. She knocked again. Movement within; footsteps approaching the door and stopping.

"It's Claire," she called in a tremulous voice.

The door swung open. "I was in the neighborhood and I thought I'd drop by," she said.

For a moment there was no reaction; then, "I g-guess you'd b-better come on in," said Emil Yankovich.

She stepped across the threshold and into the past. She had never been inside Emil's place, but Sam had told her that it had belonged to a farmer who had died a few years ago at a ripe old age. Emil had bought it lock, stock, and barrel from the bank and not changed a thing, apparently; aside from a pocket calculator on a low rosewood table, next to what looked like a stack of bills, the room was exactly as it must have been in the old man's prime, say, 1938: massive over-stuffed chairs, mauve patterned rug, fringed lampshades, cabinet radio that might have received the clarion tones of FDR.

It was probably total indifference to his surroundings that allowed Emil to live in this mausoleum, but as Claire followed her silent, not to say reluctant, host, she had the fanci-ful notion that something weirder was at work. As if to test her hypothesis, she paused by the mantel and lifted one of a half dozen faded photographs.

"Your grandfather?" she asked, and Emil shook his head.

"No idea who any of 'em are," he said brusquely. "They w-were here when I moved in." After a moment he spoke again, as if in answer to a question. "No. I have n-n-no wish to mem-mem-mem—"

He stopped, and she kept her face absolutely neutral. Any hint of frustration or sympathy would, she knew, silence him. "Memorialize my own family," he finished carefully. It was as she had thought, then: along with the rug and the bookshelves and the lamps, Emil had bought himself a whole new family tree. But one photo was set apart from the others. She lifted it from a massive mahogany sideboard and studied the slender woman in a gingham housedress, hair upswept in severe forties-style pompadour, holding a jolly baby. Above the too bright, conventional smile that split her thin face, her eyes were troubled—and familiar. Emil's eyes.

"My mother," he said unnecessarily.

"She was beautiful." Somehow she knew a woman with that tragic face should be referred to in the past tense, and sure enough, Emil replied, "She died when I was a k-kid." Then he continued before she could respond.

"Look, I d-don't want to be rude, b-but I'm real t-tired." His voice issued wearily from the recesses of his venerable sofa, and she looked at him carefully. He did indeed look exhausted.

Emil was not unattractive—that is, it was hard to tell much about the face under the beard, but he had a big, strong, competent body like his brother's, and really nice brown eyes, expressive and intelligent, and right now there were dark circles under those eyes. Maybe he was sick; there was a nasty summer flu going around.

"D-did you come out here f-for some reason?" he was saying. "Because it's not a g-good t-time for me."

"Oh, sorry!" she said, flushing. "I'm sorry to impose, I was just on my way to, ah, to somewhere else, and I thought I'd stop by." She took a breath. "Though there was something. I was sort of wondering whether a man named Jonathan Levine had ever talked to you."

"Who?"

"Jon Levine. He was a reporter for an L.A. newspaper who was staying up here for a while—"

"You mean the g-guy they found in the c-canal?" he said, struggling upright. "No, I never t-talked to him! No! Why w-w-would you think I did?"

There was such alarm in his voice that she backed off immediately. "It's nothing, Emil, I only thought that he might have interviewed you because your politics were similar, and because you know a lot about local issues. . . ." Soothe and flatter, she thought, hearing herself; who says I don't have maternal reflexes?

"Well, he didn't," he said, subsiding and resting his head in his hands.

After a moment she asked timidly, "Emil. Are you feeling all right?"

"F-fine. I'm fine. I just need some sleep," he said with a certain finality.

"Oh. Okay, then. Well. I'll just be on my way." And she scuttled out the door—quickly, to spare herself the humilia-

tion of confirming that Emil had no intention of apologizing
or of preventing her from leaving.

Not my week to connect with men, she thought with
phony flippancy as she headed for Parkerville. Possibly not
my decade; only time will tell. But it was strange about Emil.
He had seemed surprisingly disturbed at the mention of
Jonathan Levine. Was that natural? And so hostile toward
her of late, though unfortunately that was no mystery.

Because the last time she and Emil had met at Katy's, he
had told her he loved her.

He had been talking about . . . manure, she seemed to remember: sheep versus cow versus horse. Urgently, of course;
now that he would talk to her at all, his words poured forth
like a flash flood, as if he had to get them all out before his
traitor throat closed up again. And truth to tell, her attention
was wandering somewhat. Not that she wasn't interested, not
that he wouldn't let her speak—he was always fascinated by
her response. But Emil would *only* talk about the very abstract or the very mundane: lofty theories of social organiza-
tion, or cow shit. Never feelings, never personal history, and
occasionally she wearied.

So she had been studying the displays of "Barbed Wire
through the Ages" and local cattle brands (ancient 4-H projects of Katy's kids, Claire figured) that adorned the walls
and half eavesdropping on the next table. Two old boys in
their fifties wearing cowboy hats and checked shirts, with the
seamed faces and softening bellies of retired farmers, were
shooting the breeze. What would it be? she wondered. Car-
buretors? Backhoes? Pumps, she had decided; it was always
pumps—

"—get me one of them new Laserjet two-D printers," one
of them was saying.

"Yeah, I been thinkin' 'bout that. First I'm gonna upgrade
my operatin' system, though."

"Good idea. How much RAM you got on that puppy, anyway?"

". . . love you," she had heard, and jumped.

"What?"

Emil's face—or at least his forehead and nose, which was

all she could see around the beard—was red, but he had met her eye. "I'm sorry," he told her. "I don't know any other way than to say it right out."

But what exactly had he said? "What do you mean?" she asked cautiously.

"I . . . you . . . you're the m-most wonderful p-person I've ever met. You know me b-better than anyone ever has, except my m-mother." She could see his jaw tighten as his stutter clamped down on him again.

Oh, shit. He *had* said it. She, know him better than anyone? The sad thing was, it was probably true—and she didn't know him at all.

"Emil," she had begun gently, "I care very much about—"

"No!" His mouth worked a moment, then he seemed to will it to relax. "You don't have to say anything. I don't expect anything from you. I know you're with Sam, and even if you weren't, I'm not—I can't . . ." His voice had trailed off. "I just had to t-tell you, that's all."

And that had been the end of the evening. And the end of the friendship, she thought now with real regret; if it had been up to her, they would have continued, but she wasn't the one whose defenses had been breached.

They had met once more at the station, and he had seemed comfortable. But judging from his behavior at the library, and at the open house, and again tonight, there must have been a delayed reaction. Obviously Emil was miserable because of her, and she would respect that.

Just to delay her "homecoming" to the Vacancy, she took a detour through downtown Parkerville. As she stopped at the light at Main and Olive a crude neon bird of prey flashed at her, and prudently she reached to lock her passenger door. Imagine Tom thinking she didn't know El Aguila, when it made the front page of the *Sentinel* every other week. Brawls, drugs, prostitution . . . it filled a lot of local needs.

As the light turned, a couple of men emerged from the doorway and swayed unsteadily on the curb. The neon eagle flapped its wings and lit their faces for a moment, and she felt a start of recognition. Not really surprising, she thought, and filed the moment away.

Back on Walker Road the smell of refried beans lingered in the air, churning her stomach with hunger, and, piling injury on to multiple insult, number seven was stifling. She opened the bathroom window and the door, hoping the cross-ventilation would cool the room, and stepped dispiritedly out onto the front porch. A moment later a screen door banged, and Luz and a man and woman (brother? sister? some relation, certainly) settled on their stoop.

Claire considered withdrawing. But her room was so unappealing, and darkness was enclosing them and buffering them, and anyway, for all the notice the group gave her, they might have been across the courtyard instead of five feet away. So she walked to the far end of the porch, where number eight was currently vacant. She leaned against the post, looked out at the street.

Families were all very well, but why did they have to be so *exclusive*? This group to her right was wrapped tight in a semipermeable membrane that admitted only offspring—Ana and two older boys, who ran whooping in the street but checked in periodically at home base—or emissaries from other family units. With no family to define her, she had no status in this place, she was invisible, and suddenly she understood Emil's attempt to buy himself out of that isolation with his fading photographs of strangers.

A baby's cries drifted across the courtyard and then subsided. The continuo of light coughing and sniffing that underlay her neighbors' conversation made the rapid Spanish quite incomprehensible to her, but she could feel their eyes turn in her direction from time to time. Suddenly the group broke rank, as Luz stood and walked toward her.

"Claire," she said, "how you like—"

The screech of tires that interrupted this invitation sent kids scattering and brought parents to their feet; Luz's friend—brother?—advanced with clenched fists, halted, and moved backward when he saw the big black van stopped smack in the middle of the road. Footsteps crunched in gravel, someone approached; and then the Vacancy's dim lights picked out the features of Ruben Moreno.

"Buenas noches," he said, his soft voice belying the arrogance of his arrival; then he stopped short and took in

Claire's pale face. "Good evening, miss. You a friend of Chief Martelli's, right?"

She nodded.

"You living here now?"

Again she nodded, reluctant to be engaged in conversation. There was nothing she liked about this man, not his reputation or his manner or his after-shave or the sudden silence he evoked in her neighbors—or what he might have done to Jonathan Levine. He looked at her hard for a minute or two, then turned back to Luz and her friends/relatives and began to speak to them in Spanish.

It seemed that after all she was doomed to hear opera tonight—worse, opera in the dark, in which you rely on pitch and dynamics instead of gesture, and there's every likelihood of misinterpretion. First there was an antiphonal section between Moreno and Luz, in which his remarks were increasingly long and insinuating and hers increasingly monosyllabic. Suddenly her voice soared angrily and Moreno's became harsher. Not louder—that husky voice seemed incapable of greater volume, and Claire wondered if Moreno had once been jabbed in the throat by one of "his people." Immediately the other two jumped in, in placating duet. There was a long silence; then Moreno spoke, calmly this time, and walked slowly back to his car.

The group burst out agitatedly, circling their wagons and shutting her out once more, and after a moment Claire retired to her marginally cooler room, shut the door behind her, and began to sort through the things she had brought from Sam's house.

The magazines she stowed on the bedside table, exactly where Jonathan had piled his. There was no other logical place. As she lifted the oversize, ungainly photo album, wondering what had possessed her to bring it, a whole packet of ancient black-and-whites that had been shoved between the pages slipped out and spilled across the floor. Cursing, she gathered them up, vowing to mount and label everything in the album, someday, even these . . . these . . .

These elementary school class photos. Quickly she sorted through them. Miss Cook, kindergarten . . . Mr. Helms, sixth grade . . . Miss Quick, second . . . Mrs. Hampton, fourth.

There he was. In the first row, because he was short (Claire, of course, was the keystone of the back row, as she had been until tenth grade, when the boys had caught up). She studied the big, dark eyes in the fragile face, the curly hair, the shy smile: it was not impossible. The nose was smaller and less aquiline, but noses sometimes transformed themselves around puberty. Jonnie Levine could be Jonathan Levine.

She scanned the other faces. Christine Labourdette, Marian Phinney, Tommy Johnston, Melanie—um, Hagopian, Melanie Hagopian . . . To her amazement, she was able to name all but three of the children in the photo. And after four minutes of concentration she retrieved them, too.

Funny that these kids still lurked in her subconscious, even showing up in dreams from time to time. She felt an intense longing to know what had become of each and every one—wanted a documentary, like Michael Apted's *28 Up*, that would telescope their lives into five-minute segments.

She resumed unpacking.

As she draped her clothes over the hangers, a strange feeling of déjà vu overcame her: the lift of her arm to this closet in this squalid, steamy room was intensely familiar, as if she had done it dozens of times before. But it's not me, she thought suddenly; it's Jonathan. Jonathan Levine. I'm living his life. I'm using his closet, talking to his neighbor, staring at his walls. . . . If I looked in the bathroom mirror, who would look back at me? She sat on the bed and remembered his pleasant face, eyes closed, features smoothed.

Once again she saw that last night.

That night. He'd be looking for a light . . . no, lights, plural: headlights, to be exact. The headlights of the pickup that Tom had said was waiting for him at the intersection.

So . . . he'd finally seen their steady glow and, relieved, pulled off onto the narrow verge, his own lights picking out the tall weeds and glancing off the black water of the canal. He'd eased himself out of his car with much stretching and mock groaning after the long drive, probably locking his car behind him, even out in the middle of nowhere—he was a city boy—then he'd walked across the road to the pickup, halted by the driver's side, leaned in, and . . .

And what? Kissed her? Punched him in the face? Said "Howdy"?

Who was driving the damn pickup?

Her vision faltered as she tried desperately to see the face of the driver. Instead the image of another face—tanned, untroubled, welcoming—pulled her off the bed and set her marching automatonlike down to unit number one, the manager's office. Señora Avila (or La Avila, as Luz so felicitously called her, like a diva) was nowhere to be seen; the babble of a TV in a back room hinted at her whereabouts. But there in the corner was what her cunning subconscious had sought: the pay phone.

"Swimming? Tomorrow?" Jeff Green's voice was surprised but cordial. And also a little cautious; Claire had the distinct impression that he wasn't alone and suddenly thought to look at her watch. Oh, Jesus, it was eleven-thirty! No wonder he was surprised. And had company. "Sure, of course," Jeff was saying. "I teach till five tomorrow. How about if I meet you at the pool at six. You know where it is?"

"I'll find it," she said, regretting the call mightily even as she hung up.

Funny, she thought, flopping facedown on her bed again, that she had felt compelled to call Jeff an instant after imagining Jonathan Levine's last hours. Then she dismissed the idea—tried, in fact, to think of nothing at all, especially the heat.

She was awakened around four A.M. by her neighbors in number six, leaving for the fields. Awakened, too, was the black despair over Sam that had crouched motionless all night like a patient spider. Now it began to creep along her limbs and up her spinal column toward her brain. Dumbly, helplessly, she waited, until the back of her neck prickled with what felt like panic or returning circulation, and she knew pain was seconds away. Quickly she turned her attention to the noise next door and began to count voices: one adult male; two women, one of whom sounded like Luz; one baby crying—Juanito; one small child—Ana?—and several older kids whose ages and sexes she couldn't sort out.

That made six or seven humans in a motel room that crowded her. Impossible; she must have miscounted. She closed her eyes and began to count again . . . and fell asleep.

At seven she woke again and dressed, discovering in the process that she had forgotten to pack any decent shoes and the belt to her linen pants (so much for being chic for Jeff Green). Her adult neighbors were gone, all but Luz, sitting on the front porch between the peppers with Juanito on her lap.

Claire flinched and regarded her warily: what would her own fervid imagination project onto the poor woman this morning? Juno? Astarte? Mother Teresa? But no, Luz was what she was, a young Latina woman diapering her baby. Very young, Claire realized now that she saw her clearly; she couldn't have been more than twenty-one or -two.

"Buenos días."

"Buenos días," Luz replied, flashing a smile. "You trying to learn Spanish like Juanito, no?"

"Juanito?" Claire repeated, looking with confusion at the baby, and Luz laughed merrily.

"Oh, not my Juanito! Jon, your friend. That's what I call him, 'Juanito.' "

"Oh." Claire laughed, too. "How was his Spanish?"

"Lousy! I always have to translate for him, when he ask questions."

"Questions? What kinds of questions did he ask?" Again she subdued the eagerness in her voice and made ready to back off at the first sign of discomfort or evasion.

But Luz responded easily. "Oh, all kinds—like, where we work, how much we make, how much for rent, where we cook, what we eat, do we like our work, do we like the *contratistas,* the labor contractors . . . at first I think he might be trying to recruit for the union, you know, for César, and some people here think he is with the Migra, they won't talk to him. But finally I think he really is what he say, a reporter."

Claire had to head for work and put in a few token hours before leaving for Los Angeles, but work meant Sam, and

Sam meant a queasy amalgam of feverish anticipation and cold fear ... and she couldn't, she really couldn't pass up this opportunity, she told herself. That this woman was willing to talk frankly to her was amazing and probably transient, the product of grief and loneliness and sleepiness. She knew this because she was herself grieving and lonely and sleepy. Also very curious. About Jonathan, about Luz, and Jonathan and Luz.

Had Jonathan stayed in number seven simply because of Luz Perez?

"Did you get to know him at all? Jonathan, I mean?" she asked.

"Well, I translate for him, like I said. ... At first I say I can't, I'm too busy, and then he offer to pay me, but I don't want to take his money till I know what he want. 'Cause Juan just die, and I ... I think this Juanito like me, you know?" she said matter-of-factly, a person for whom this was an inevitable hazard, like death and taxes. "So the only thing is, I let him buy groceries for us once. Because the kids, they were hungry." She paused, then asked hesitantly, "Is it true what they say, that Juanito—Jon—he drownded?"

Claire nodded.

She crossed herself. "Just like my Juan," she whispered, tears sparkling in her eyes.

"And Hector Cedillo," Claire added without thinking.

"¿Quién? O, Hector, sí. He was a friend of my husband's cousin."

While Claire wondered if this was significant, then decided no, many people here would be related to each other somehow—that's why they ended up here instead of someplace else—Luz gave Juanito a bottle.

"It's bad, very bad, all these young men." She shook her head. "Who will be next?"

Next? It hadn't occurred to Claire, but now that she thought about it, yes, One, two, three did seem to imply four, even if the connection wasn't apparent.

And if three was murder, not accident, did that say something about one and two?

She reserved the idea for later. She had to go to work. ... "Luz, how many people live in your apartment?"

she asked. Now she was definitely stalling. But she had peered through the doorway of number six, and unless it somehow concealed an attic or basement, it was an exact replica of number seven, down, or up, to the waterstained ceiling. Except that the floor was padded wall to wall with mattresses.

"*Pues*, it was four: my husband's sister—how you say, my sister-in-law?—and her husband, and their two kids. Juan and me and Ana and Juanito lived in number three. It was a real good place, the best we've had—when we first come up we lived in a room that didn't have no floor, or water, or toilet," she added, perhaps seeing incredulity on Claire's face. "But we both get laid off at the packing house after the freeze—I have to quit anyway, 'cause of the baby, but we was counting on that work for Juan until the apricots come in. So Dolores and Martín, they say we can move in with them till spring. And then Juan died, and I got no money to move. So we got seven."

She shifted the baby, and the corners of her mouth turned down ruefully. "Too many, no? But I can't find no work right now. Everybody's picking grapes, and it take practice. My Juan, he made good money with the grapes, and Dolores and Martín, too, it's good work for them. But I tried, and I can't make no money at it. Besides, who'll watch my kids? So right now I clean rooms for La Avila and I work sometimes at Contessa." (This, Claire knew, was the tomato cannery.) "Ruben Moreno, he's the *contratista* there, he say he can get me steady work—"

She stopped short, and Claire, remembering last night, wondered what duties "steady work" might include. Was extortion of sexual favors part of Moreno's unsavory reputation? It was straight out of Victorian melodrama. Sam would know—Oh, Jesus, Sam, work, she couldn't put it off any longer. It was eight-thirty. But she was starving; she would have to stop for a doughnut somewhere. . . .

"Oh, I was wondering—how do you cook?" she asked, in her desperation deploying one last delaying tactic.

Luz pointed to a charcoal grill just inside the door. "There's a oven down at the manager's office if we need it. And a refrigerator, but I try not to use it. People take your stuff," she said indignantly. "We should help each other, not steal from each other—¿Ay, Ana mijita, qué haces?" And in an instant she had run across the yard to separate Ana from an evil-looking scrap of rusty metal, pausing only to shove Juanito into Claire's unready arms.

Claire looked down at the baby. The baby looked up at Claire with unblinking, wary eyes, and for a moment she hoped . . . But no. Babies can smell fear. Within seconds the eyes had scrunched shut, the pink mouth opened, the little face crumpled into a tragic mask of inconsolable grief and rage. Juanito began to bawl.

She cringed. Was she doing something wrong? Surely not. She had held babies before, it really wasn't that complex mechanically. No, it was just that she was giving off cold, spinsterish, and generally bad vibes; she had flunked the simplest task of maternal aptitude—

"He just want Mama," Luz said, retrieving him and hoisting him to her shoulder, where the crying stopped magically; and then, curiously, "You got kids?"

"No," said Claire, thinking that this must be obvious.

"Why not?"

Why not. She thought of a dozen things: of her heroes Rachel Carson and geneticist Barbara McClintock, laboring in solitude; of her once ambitious hopes for her own career; of her unhappy, thwarted mother; of her own need for privacy, her short temper and lack of patience; of Sam and Shannon and Terry . . . and shrugged at the impossibility of communicating any of this in small talk.

"Just never wanted them, I guess," she said.

Luz's face was polite and uncomprehending, and Claire, being out of excuses, set off for work.

Like most dreaded events, the day was both better and worse than she expected. Unfortunately, the areas in which it was better were entirely trivial, whereas it was worse in ways she hadn't even thought to fear. A conversation with Ray that might have elicited uncomfortable questions, for example, went off smoothly: she told him she would be out of town for a day or two, and he didn't ask why; she requested that during her absence he get help from Sam in determining the owner of her alfalfa field, and he didn't want to know why she didn't ask Sam herself.

Sam, however . . .

At first it looked good. She had fantasized that he would appear, solicitous and contrite, at the laboratory door as soon as she arrived, and she would be cool and aloof, willing to be wooed but in no way eager. And in fact he was downstairs waiting for her when she finished talking to Ray. But as soon as she saw his anxious face she knew she would be betrayed by tenderness and hope.

They exchanged tentative hellos. "How are you?" he asked.

"Fine."

"*Where* are you? I mean, where have you been staying?"

"I'm . . . I'd rather not say." Even in her weakening condition it seemed obscurely important that she keep her life at the Vacancy unknown, private. The sudden memory of Luz wiping little Ana's nose made her feel strangely comforted, and she surprised herself by saying, "How are Shannon and Terry?"

Sam looked as startled as she felt. "They're okay. Terry keeps asking about you. He misses you."

"He does?" She was nearly undone by this, and when Sam added, "I miss you, too," her knees buckled under her. "Oh, God, Sam—" For a moment she was too giddy with relief to continue. The phrases clamored to be heard: *I miss you so much I can't breathe; I'll come back, we'll forget all about this.* . . . But underneath them a new voice, a suspicious voice spawned in the last few days, asked: Why hadn't *he* said these things? Surely "Please come back" would logically follow "I miss you, too."

So what she actually said was, "I'd like to stop by your house to pick up a few more things. Tonight." (What about Jeff? Oh, forget Jeff!) "We could talk then."

And Sam squirmed. Visibly. "Tonight?" he echoed. "Uh, tonight . . . tonight's not good." Just that: "not good." "How about tomorrow?"

"Got a date?" she asked mildly, and as she watched him redden the floor fell away from under her. Well, at least he hadn't lied (he could have, so easily—a movie with the boys, a meeting), and at least she had not opened her heart, she had maintained her dignity. Thank God for something; thank God for bitterness, and mistrust, and scar tissue. . . .

"I don't know," she said with a passable attempt at brusqueness, "I may be busy tomorrow." And, oh yes, thank God for Jeff. "But I'll try. Tomorrow, after dinner. Say eight-thirty."

She left for Los Angeles at two, and the drive, formerly an adventure, was now a torment. Today, when she looked closely, decay and death marked the journey. Frost and drought and long-horned Australian borer beetle had blasted the eucalyptus. Sun and dust had faded the gay pink olean-der. The balls of deracinated tumbleweed pressed themselves against the wire fences like prisoners, and the crimped Pleitos Hills at the base of the Grapevine, whose wrinkles and folds usually fascinated her, merely made her rub her own corrugated brow and remember that *pleitos* were "quarrels."

There was a new sign in front of an apparently thriving citrus ranch that said "For Sale. 50 Acres. Zoned Commercial," with the craven addendum "Will Build to Suit." This provoked her usual meditation on the metastasis of suburbia and the future of American agriculture. It happened so fast! Day one: neat rows of trees, a "Regarding This Property" sign; day two: 'dozers snarling, trees in bare ruined choirs on the ground; day three: neat rows of houses with banners flying—ORANGE GROVE ACRES! LUXURY HOMES ON QUARTER-ACRE LOTS!!—productive land lost forever. How long before every acre of California's arable land was developed and they all bought all their produce from Mexico?

By the time she reached the San Diego Freeway her stomach was in spasm and her chest hurt from anxiety and smog.

Chapter 11

"Tierra Buena!" Claire squeaked in disbelief. "You're from *Tierra Buena*?"

They were sitting on Jeff's Haitian cotton sofa directly under a Georgia O'Keeffe poster, while Coltrane's ballads swung softly in the background. Many laps had been swum that afternoon—tirelessly by Jeff, halfheartedly by Claire—in the crowded UCLA pool that for all its vastness was more Cuisinart than New England lake, and ravenous appetites had been created. Thereafter, in Jeff's airy apartment, mussels in marinara sauce and tomatoes and basil with balsamic vinegar and French bread and peaches with cream and marsala had been eaten, voraciously; wine had been drunk, liberally; and espresso was brewing.

It was impossible to believe that Tierra Buena, which was ten miles down the road from Riverdale and made it look like Biarritz, had produced this experience.

"Well, I don't tell that to just anybody, but . . . yeah," he said, looking around at the evidence of his life. "I suppose my politics are just about the only part of my background I haven't jettisoned. And some people might argue that." A shadow of a frown passed across his face.

"How did the Valley produce a . . . a leftist?" (She had been going to say "*yuppie*.") "I hardly ever meet a Democrat!"

He laughed. "Believe it or not, I got it from my father, probably the county's last unrepentant New Dealer. A closet socialist, actually. He came out from Arkansas in 1938. . . ."

As Claire listened in astonishment, his unaccented Pan-

California voice described a background almost identical to Sam's. How could that be? Were people arbitrarily divided at birth, regardless of circumstance, into those who stayed planted and those who cut themselves off at the roots? The provincial and the cosmopolitan? If so, Sam was unquestionably the former and she and Jeff the latter, and maybe that was why she felt an affinity for Jeff that was missing from her relationship with Sam.

Because they talked so easily, she and Jeff, so wittily, each catching the other's references, tone, and jokes. They talked about their work, their relationships, their favorite writers, California, politics. They traded academic horror stories: advisers who regularly stole their students' ideas, postdocs who cracked under pressure, collegial rivalries that hardened into hatred. But subject matter was almost incidental to the strong undercurrent of flirtation, and to Claire this was excitingly familiar. This was how civilized people . . . courted.

The CD ended, and the silence became unbearably charged.

"I'll put on some more music," Claire offered with something like relief, and sorted through his impeccable collection, "Do you ever listen to country?" she said, selecting Duke Ellington.

"No, I have to say that's one thing I've never learned to appreciate."

More high marks for Jeff, she thought, as the rhythms of "In a Mellotone" filled the room. Anyway, she certainly couldn't cheat on Sam while Merle Haggard was singing.

Cheat on Sam? What was the matter with her? Right now, perhaps at this very *moment*, Sam was with Linda Nelson . . . She left this thought unfinished and gazed through narrowed blinds at the street below, her view bisected by a single tall palm tree in front of the apartment. A flash of gold on the windowsill caught her eye, and she bent to identify it: an earring, a gold hoop for a pierced ear.

"Well, you're certainly the best thing to come out of Tierra Buena," she said lightly, returning to the sofa and to an earlier, less dangerous mode of small talk. "Except Judy Schottweiler, who was Southern San Joaquin Valley Olive Queen this year."

"I know. My parents send me newspaper clippings. They grow olives themselves. And speaking of orchards," he continued, neatly changing the subject, "what about the groves of academe? Do you miss them?"

She leaned back against the sofa. "Oh, I miss some things. I miss the people—some of the people," she corrected, remembering Phil, that cad, and Mulcahey, her tyrant of an adviser. "And . . . well, most of my work now is pretty empirical, you know" (assuming an exaggerated hick accent), "'Hey, maybe this will work!' 'Hell, yes, let's give her try!' I miss solving tough intellectual puzzles."

"So what stops you from coming back?"

"Got an hour?"

"Got all night." He settled back and put his arm across the sofa behind her. She noticed that his ears were definitely not pierced, and she noticed that she had probably drunk a little too much Cabernet. A small, hard object pressed into her right thigh, and she shifted her weight and brought up . . . another earring, an amethyst in a silver setting. Reflexively she touched her earlobe; no, certainly not hers. She was wearing long beaded loops.

By now the Ellington band was In a Sentimental Mood, and Jeff's right arm slipped around her shoulders. He set down his wineglass with a certain deliberation; she found herself mesmerized by the beautifully articulated muscles of his brown forearm. When she looked up his face was very close to hers.

Well, why not? she thought. Why not the off-white apartment and the miniblinds and the art on the walls and the stimulating conversation? This was what she had come for, wasn't it?

Jeff brushed her cheek and started to say something. Instead he kissed her.

Usually that moment, the actual instant when fantasy became fact, terrified her. What led up to it and what came after were fine, but during the transition Claire could never sort out her feelings, couldn't distinguish between sexual arousal and sheer panic, and this had led to some bad mistakes. And this time there were the additional confounding variables of grief and confusion and anger over Sam.

So she repeated the kiss for experimental purposes (science demands replicability). Yes. Sexual arousal, no doubt about it.

So, very soon, the choice had to be made: the bedroom or the lonely interstate and her sweltering room. Claire's body was casting an enthusiastic vote for the former, but her mind and her heart each got a vote, too, and she suspected they just weren't up to it.

But then there was Jeff, my God . . .

The point of swimming on your first date, as California discovered long ago, is that you got to pretty thoroughly check each other out. Claire had already experienced a moment of revelation when Jeff had lifted himself out of the pool in one fluid motion and stood before her, dripping; had already gaped at that luxuriant flesh, so unlike Sam's pared-down frame. If ever he stopped swimming, he might run to fat. But of course he would never stop swimming; he would always have those perfect pecs, lats, abs, glutes—she had had to stop herself in midinventory. But it was hard not to regard him as a gorgeous object, hard not to feel like Cro-Magnon confronted by smooth *Homo sapiens*.

And his face, with its long sharp Irish nose, prominent jaw, wide, expressive mouth, and that unconscious habit of raising one eyebrow when he spoke that completely charmed her—it was a wonderful face, and just because 98 percent of people on the planet would have agreed was no reason to deny it. She had maligned him: he was no regression to the mean. He was nowhere near the mean, he was off the chart.

In short, he was a god, and she was no goddess. Why didn't he simply mate with the UCLA women's swim team—those glorious eighteen-year-olds she'd seen in the locker room, with their flawless golden skin, broad shoulders, tight boys' buttocks, and long legs—and improve the gene pool?

Well, where did she think the earrings came from? Still, he had had plenty of time to observe Claire's lanky charms, and presumably she had made the cut. That was comfort for her wounded pride.

And maybe that's all she could handle right now.

"Jeff," she said, struggling upright, "maybe I'm being presumptuous here, but—did you want to go to bed with me?"

"Yes, actually," he said, deadpan. "I've been thinking about it."

"Me too. But I can't."

He waited politely.

"See, I . . . I'm in a relationship that seems to be unraveling," she said haltingly, trying to pump blood back up into her brain. "It's either going to unravel completely, or it's going to knit itself up in some way that I can't imagine, but right now I'm in a sort of limbo, and I'm not concentrating very well." (That was a lie; she could concentrate with supernatural intensity on the curl of Jeff's mouth, the light stubble from his jawline down along his throat, the weight of his hand on her leg.) "I'm afraid I'll screw up, you know? I might be acting out of anger at Sam. It wouldn't matter if I didn't like you, but I do. So . . . I can't."

"You're sure?" Jeff asked, and she nodded dolefully.

"Okay," he said with a nice balance of regret and good nature. "I hope you work things out, if that's what you want— but if you don't, you hop a fast freight south!" For once Arkansas echoed in his voice, and she smiled and kissed him. This was nearly fatal, but presently there was a reluctant readjustment, as hands were removed from legs thighs breasts etcetera, hormones resorbed or, more likely, left to circulate toxically, thermostats set down from foreplay to cuddling.

Eventually she settled in the crook of his arm. "When was the last time you were in Tierra Buena?" There was something reliably anaphrodisiac about Tierra Buena.

"March," he replied, smoothing her hair. "For my father's birthday. Why?"

"I don't know. Just wondered if you ever got up that way."

"Not if I can help it. Anyway, you're unavailable," he said, assuming she was proposing a tryst.

"For now."

"Ah, don't torture me!" he said with a mock groan. Then, curiously, "Where are you staying, if not with—what's his name—Sam?"

She laughed.

"What?" he said.

"Oh, it's crazy, that's all. I'm staying in this fleabag motel for migrant workers. In Jonathan Levine's old room."

His lazy stroking stopped abruptly. "Who?" he asked in a voice whose casualness would have deceived her from across the table, but not with her head on his chest, where she could hear his heart rate explode, *thud-thud-thud*, like a marathoner toiling up Heartbreak Hill. And he definitely wasn't moving; in fact, he was perfectly still—as still as he had been, come to think of it, when she had first mentioned Levine to Sara and Steve at dinner.

"Jonathan Levine," she repeated cautiously. "The reporter for the *Free Press* who drowned in Parkerville last week. I talked about it at dinner the other night."

"Oh, right." He pulled himself into a sitting position, so that she had to do the same to remain at eye level. "Why are you staying in his room? Seems pretty morbid."

"I suppose it could be. I just needed a . . . a halfway house, and I knew this place was vacant. It's strange, I know; I really can't explain it." Or won't.

He yawned elaborately and draped an arm behind his head, automatically pushing back at the elbow as swimmers do, to stretch the triceps. Covertly she observed his biceps swell like a weight lifter's. Strong arms.

Arms that could overpower a wiry but small man and press his head into muddy water.

This crazed notion was suppressed almost before it formed; good God, even if Jeff and Jonathan had, coincidentally, *known* each other (and as Perlmutter had said, stranger things had happened), the state was full of men who could have overpowered Levine—athletes, bodybuilders, men like Bert Yankovich, or Emil, with their big farmers' bodies . . . even Sam, if he had taken Levine by surprise.

"You didn't by any chance *know* Levine, did you?" she asked.

"Know him? How would I? But," he said, breathing into her ear, "I can think of better approaches to convalescence."

So can I, she thought. So *did* I. But I'm not going to start this again.

"Jeff"—tensing—"I have to go."

"Go?" he said, startled. "Go where?"

"Go home," she said. "Back to Parkerville."

"Now? It's eleven-thirty, Claire, you can't drive up there now! Stay here," he said reasonably. "I'll take the couch."

But Claire was suddenly beyond reason. Days of deceit, doubt, and vague suspicions had just taken their toll, and she wanted home, wherever that was; wherever people and events meant exactly what they appeared to mean. The Vacancy, say, with Luz and Ana and Juanito. "No, I . . . I've got to be at work early in the morning. I'll stop at a motel if I'm tired."

She was on her feet, gathering up a few clothes that had been shed in the course of the evening, when she sensed Jeff behind her. Two heavy hands dropped on her shoulders. "This doesn't make sense; you're too tired. Stay here and leave early in the morning."

"No!" she exclaimed, pulling away and turning to face him.

Now some people believe that Man was once smaller and weaker than Woman, but that in olden times, in the glory days of matriarchy and goddess worship, our foremothers became greedy and for their own sexual pleasure began to select for the hunk factor in their males. Who of course turned on their mistresses like pit bulls as soon as they were able.

Bad paleohistory, maybe, but good myth, for it captures the paradox of desire and fear that men's sheer physical strength can evoke in women. In Claire, for example, who had delighted in Jeff's body all day and now regarded his magnificence with panic. What had made her think all that power was for her, that is, *for* her? He could do anything *to* her he wanted: rape her, or hurt her, or even . . . even drown her in the bathtub; and certainly he could prevent her from leaving. The fact that he didn't was mere fragile social convention, like stopping at a red light.

But of course most people do stop at red lights. And in fact Jeff pulled on his shirt and said, "Well, all right. But let me make you some coffee—and you have to swear that you'll stop at a motel as soon as you get tired. Bakersfield at the latest."

She promised, touched by his earnestness. At midnight

there was a caffeinated kiss under a lone palm tree, the slam of a car door, the gurgle of an engine, and Claire was off. In her rearview mirror she saw Jeff standing under a streetlight next to the palm, waving to her, diminishing.

The L.A. jazz station faded out in the mountains north of the city, and by some sadistic coincidence of stratospheric conditions all she could find was a country station out of Bakersfield. Either it was Thursday Night Cheatin' Hour or infidelity always constituted 90 percent of the genre's thematic content, but in any event singer after singer was about to cheat on his woman, or, had cheated on his woman and she had thrown him out, or, she hadn't thrown him out but had made his life a living hell, or, he was sending her a roomful of roses so she wouldn't throw him out. Occasionally a gal would tell what it was like to be cheated on: how, goddamn it, she'd love him forever if she wanted to, or how she (the singer) had his memory and his class ring, but she (She) had him. . . .

No wonder, Claire mused, taking in this chronicle of the perfidy of little *m* man and thinking about Sam. No wonder. A lifetime of country-western radio would certainly influence your views on the relations between the sexes.

The miles rolled by, the cheatin' went on. She came to the top of the Grapevine and looked down the pass, where a long, living, shimmering line of southbound headlights plunged down into the Valley and stretched out to the horizon, or where the horizon must be; as she descended, the air became moist and stagnant, smelling, somehow, of wet dog. Soon she realized that she was zipping through Bakersfield and that she had listened to this music with complete absorption for two solid hours.

Should she stop at the Oildale Motel 6, which was coming up fast? It was two A.M., and she had promised Jeff, but she was still alert, and home was only an hour away. So she grabbed a quick cup of coffee at Perko's and kept driving, harmonizing to songs whose choruses she could anticipate after half a verse. The predictability didn't seem to diminish her enjoyment.

A Dr. Pepper at the all-night Mini-Mart in Tierra Buena;

she thought longingly of Jeff and Jeff's bed. Her reasons for refusing it seemed completely obscure. Maybe she should call his parents and ask to crash for the night. She giggled and staggered back to the car.

At three-thirty A.M. she made her way along the front of the motel, stumbling with fatigue and nearly knocking over Luz's peppers, catching herself so that she wouldn't awaken her neighbors, who would have to leave for the fields in less than an hour. The last part of the drive had been a grim game of stay awake, reminding herself to stay between the lines long after she had forgotten their significance, reminding herself to keep her eyes open, reminding herself to remind herself . . . Someone in number six—Martín, probably—was snoring so loudly, she could hear him through the door. It was a friendly, peaceful sound, and as she fished for her key she wondered if Jonathan Levine had come to feel this incongruous relief, this sense of homecoming, about the squalid little room.

Her keys clattered noisily to the porch. She winced and stooped to find them while fumbling in the dark for the doorknob, at which point it became clear that she didn't need her key. The door was open.

Claire was not the kind to leave a front door unlocked, much less open. But there was always a first time, and lots of people had the key to this room—*La Avila*, and Luz herself, for that matter—and the lock was so flimsy the door could have blown open and anyway, she was incredibly tired, she didn't want to have to think about this. She just wanted to go to sleep. Still, she stepped inside with as much wariness as her clumsy limbs would allow and ducked as she turned on the light.

A perfunctory inventory showed everything seemingly in order, her meager possessions present and accounted for. Gratefully she flopped onto the bed, thought a moment, hauled herself up to prop the plastic chair under the doorknob in case the door wasn't latching properly, and collapsed on the bed again, pleased with herself. But sleep wouldn't come; she was still buzzed and vibrating with the road. So after a moment she switched on her light and felt for *The New Yorker*, which she had left by the bed the night before.

It was gone.

Absurdly, this disturbed her far more than the open door. Anything could have happened to the door, but each night for nearly thirty years she had laid a book or a magazine on the floor in exactly the same position before falling asleep, and today somebody had moved it. Maybe it *was* only the manager, or Luz, but somebody definitely had been in her room during the day—

Bong!

The metallic thud rang out from the general direction of the closet, and Claire froze, suddenly completely alert. She knew exactly what it was. She had heard it at least once a day since moving to number seven. It was the unholy clang the cheap metal shower stall produced when you so much as brushed it with an elbow, which was impossible to avoid in a three-by-three area.

Someone was in the bathroom.

Instinctively she flung out her arm and cut off the light and for a moment lay rigid, heart pumping as Jeff's had just hours ago. Then she gathered herself and lunged for the front door—and yelped with the excruciating pain of ramming her foot against the chair she had wedged there. Oh, yes, she had prudently trapped herself inside her own room with her intruder.

In the slapstick interlude that ensued, she succeeded in jamming the chair even more firmly between the doorknob and the floor. Any instant she would hear the heavy footstep, feel the hand on the shoulder (*and why did that seem familiar?*) or around the throat . . . but finally a wrought-iron leg snapped off in her hand. Feverishly she swept away the whole ugly, useless piece of shit, plunged through the door, and found herself sprawled at the feet of Martín, who had been awakened by her struggles and was standing outside in his underwear.

He gazed down at her, annoyed, bewildered, and sleepy. *"¿Qué pasa?"*

"Oh, Martín," she gasped, *"hay . . . hay algo*—no, damn, *alguien . . . "* Her Spanish was leaking away, following the usual last-hired-first-fired rule of information retention under stress. *"En mi cama,* no, I mean *baño, en mi baño . . . "* Luckily Luz appeared behind him, clutching her robe around her.

"Luz," she shouted over the baby's wail, "there's somebody in my room! In the bathroom!"

Actually Martín understood this perfectly well. *"¡Ladrón!"* he hissed, doubled over in a brief coughing fit, then crept stealthily along the walk and into her room. He nearly stumbled over the chair, that assemblage of the devil, but recovered and scooped up the leg to use as a weapon. Then he moved toward the back of the dark apartment, followed at a discreet distance by Claire, while Luz watched from the doorway.

But he reached the bathroom entirely without incident or mysterious noises and after a pause flipped on the light. Straightening, he said calmly, *"No hay nadie,"* affirming Claire's worst fears, worse even than robbery or mayhem: humiliation. There was no one there at all. She had imagined it; she, a hysterical female, had confirmed Martín's macho cosmology—

He said something else she didn't understand. Luz moved timidly past her into the bathroom, then called, "The window is broke. Martín thinks he broke the window when he leave." Claire rushed to join them and saw the jagged teeth of glass that were all that remained of her high bathroom window. Thank God, she thought; thank God both that he had been here and that he had left.

By that window? Measured with the eye, it seemed so small. Surely only a child could pass through it, or a slender woman—not a grown man with a grown man's shoulders, like Martín, or . . . or Jeff Green . . .

Jeff Green? Jeff Green was two hundred–some miles to the south, sleeping the sleep of the just, or at least the perfect.

But was he? He had assumed, after all, that she would spend the night on the road somewhere—had made her swear to this, in fact. If he had left right after her, in his Porsche or whatever he drove, and hauled ass and hadn't stopped anywhere, he could certainly have beaten her up here.

But he didn't even know where "here" was. All she had told him was that it was the same crummy motel that Jonathan Levine had lived in—

Exactly. And if he had known Jonathan Levine—despite his denial—he might have known about the motel. Especially if he had killed him and broken in tonight to . . . to recover some sort of incriminating evidence, like Jonathan's notebook. Or to stop Claire's investigation—to stop Claire altogether, maybe. Just in case sweet talk and sex appeal might not work. After all, what else could explain his interest in her? Come to think of it, wasn't it immediately after her first mention of Levine that his flirtation had shifted into overdrive?

Oh, this was insane, this was too transparent even for her! She felt guilty about lusting after Jeff, so he was a murderer. Her confidence and her trust in men were at their nadir, so his interest in her was a sinister lie. Why shouldn't he be attracted to her, goddamn it? A much likelier burglar was that small, sturdy villain Ruben Moreno.

If Jeff had squeezed through that window, he had long ugly scratches in that satin skin. And how would he explain that to the next Earring?

She supposed she should report the break-in to Martelli in the morning—

In the morning! she interrupted herself. It *was* morning; Christ, it was five A.M. and she still hadn't slept! She hustled Luz and Martín out of her room, thanking them incoherently, closed the bathroom door and piled the wreckage of the chair against it, and more or less passed out on the bed.

Chapter 12

Some hours later she made for the bathroom, stumbled over chair fragments, and just managed to resist the impulse to hurl them at the wall: given their malevolent karma, they would probably rip through the wallboard between her and number six (FREAK ACCIDENT KILLS SLEEPING BABY IN EAST PARKERVILLE), and actually the pause reminded her to wear shoes and thus avert a tragic encounter with the shards of glass on the bathroom floor.

Still half-asleep, she shuffled down to the pay phone and called Tom Martelli, who was more confused than interested to hear that someone had broken into her room.

"You mean Sam's bedroom?"

Oh. Right. "Uh, no," she said uncomfortably, "my motel room. I'm not living at Sam's right now; I'm staying at that motel on Walker Road where Jonathan Levine lived." Pause. "In his room, actually."

Dead air at the other end of the line; she had finally managed to stump Tom Martelli. "In Levine's room," he said eventually, choosing to ignore the first half of her speech.

"Yeah, well, you know, it was vacant. . . ." She trailed off, then added defensively, "You said you were done with the room!"

"Oh, we're done with it, it's not illegal." Another long silence; then, keeping his voice level as though talking to a dangerous lunatic, he said, "Look, I appreciate your, um, enthusiasm, but I thought we had agreed that you weren't to get involved in this. So why don't you go on home."

Home? Where was that? "Actually, I sort of like it here.

That is, the room's awful, but I like my neighbors. And I think they might know something about Levine. So are you going to come over and investigate?"

"That's Parkerville police jurisdiction. Why call me?" he said icily.

"Because Levine was your case!"

"Levine? Why should this have anything to do with him? Prob'ly just a straight robbery. You're a likely target over there. Stand out like a sore thumb—a rich white sore thumb, which is another reason to go back home. But you call Wiggins at Parkerville police. He's a good man," he said dismissively.

"Tom!" She caught him just as he was hanging up. "Those phone numbers Levine jotted down. Did you check them out?"

"Yep," he replied, then continued reluctantly. "The L.A. number belongs to a Dr. Lucy McAdams at the UCLA School of Public Health. The other one is, uh"—rustling papers—"Gary Wilson. He's with the state attorney general's office. I haven't been able to get hold of either one. I'm waitin' on them to call me back."

"Oh. What *is* happening with the case?"

There was the familiar evasive silence. Then, "Nothing much," he admitted. "The LAPD are looking into his life down there."

The pulse drummed in her ears. "Anything look likely?"

"A couple leads, nothing definite. By the way," he added with audible effort, "if you happen to run across any helpful information during the very short time before you move out of Walker Road, I hope you'll pass it on to me."

"Sure, of course," she said distractedly, and hung up, too rattled even to enjoy the small triumph. *Leads in L.A.*

She was walking to her room after an inconclusive talk with La Avila about fixing the window when a flash of red on the front lawn caught her eye. She turned toward it—and stopped cold.

There, under the big cottonwood, sprawled facedown in the utter abandon of exhaustion—assume it was exhaustion—was a body: a woman, hair tied back in the bright red bandanna she had noticed.

Slowly, reluctantly, dazed by *déjá vu*, she moved toward the figure.

"Sh-h-h!" hissed someone behind her. She gasped and jumped. The voice had issued from number six. . . .

Luz, stacking mattresses. "It's Dolores," she whispered. "She's too sick to go to work, she got the flu."

"Lot of it going around," Claire remarked, light-headed with relief. Flu was not nearly so irreversible as . . . what she had been thinking.

"*Sí*, everybody here got the flu. 'Farmworkers' Flu,' Jonathan called it. But Dolores, she might lose her job if she don't show up, but she just can't go. I gotta take her to *la clínica*, but Martín's car don't work," indicating the white Impala that Claire had long since come to think of as sculpture, not vehicle.

"I could take her."

"*¿De veras?*" asked Luz.

"Sure. Where is it?"

"Alma. But we have to go after lunch; they got well-baby in the morning. And today is my day at the cannery."

"I can swing by and get you. I'll come by for Dolores at one." That meant she would put in a scant three hours at work—but then Ray hadn't been expecting her at all. And the trip to the clinic would occupy her mind, maybe keep her from obsessively rehearsing tonight's confrontation with Sam, for a few hours anyway. . . .

As she backed up she knocked over a tomato, but Luz caught it in mid arc.

"Sorry," Claire said, "I keep doing that."

"Is my fault. Everybody laugh at my 'garden,'" Luz said.

"No, no. I think it's a great idea!"

"At home, *en México*, my family always have big garden. *Frijoles*, tomatoes, peppers, *maíz*, everything. So when I first come up with Juan, I plant in front of our room. But then we have to move right away, and I have to leave my plants—so this time I put everything in *macetas*, how you say . . ."

"Pots."

"Oh, like for cooking. In pahts," repeated Luz carefully. Claire thought what a comical word it was. "So when I

move, they move. Only I don't think they look so happy."
She looked down ruefully at her crop.

"I think they need bigger pots," said Claire.

"I think they want to be in ground. They not want to be in pahts, and move all the time."

At the station Claire checked the big board, where everyone more or less accurately recorded their day's agenda, and saw with relief that Sam was out in the field all day. Ray, however, she found in his office.

"Didn't expect you back till tomorrow," he said.

"My plans didn't quite work out."

"Mmm. Well, 'fraid I've got some bad news for you. You know that alfalfa field you were interested in?"

"Yes?"

"It belongs to Bert Yankovich."

"Oh, no!" she exclaimed. Bert would never cooperate with any sort of government functionary (her) messing around with his crop for experimental purposes—not after that pesticide disaster with his vineyard.

"Actually, it's not as bad as it might be. Old Bert might be feeling a bit more gracious after yesterday— Oh, that's right," he broke off, seeing Claire's puzzlement, "you didn't hear. He's appealing those charges, and County's backing down a little."

"What?"

"Yes, they called yesterday with the results of their repeat testing. And except for the specific area they tested initially—the easternmost rows of vines—the darn thing's clean! So they don't know what to think."

"You mean Bert was actually falsely accused for once in his life?"

He chuckled. "Maybe so. Doesn't seem fair, does it? Poor Mac Healy had to call him to relay the information and listen to him gloat for five minutes. Seems that anonymous tip was a bum steer." He paused. "I'd like to know how that all happened, come to think of it. Maybe Sam should call what's-her-name, Catherine Bakaitis, at County Ag—"

"No," Claire said quickly, protecting her turf, "I'll call her. We're friends."

As she flicked through her Rolodex for Cathy's number,

the thought struck her: That was *Bert*'s field. She had found Levine floating by Bert Yankovich's alfalfa field.

On the other hand, Tom had said the body might have floated a long way. And if Bert hadn't sprayed CONKWEST after all, he didn't have an obvious motive for killing Levine.

Which would leave Moreno, and "leads in L.A."

Cathy was back from her vacation. They spent ten minutes catching each other up on current events, personal and professional; on plain old gossip; and on gleeful jokes at the expense of the patriarchy of Kaweah County. Then Claire said, "I understand you got some bad information regarding Bert Yankovich's vineyard."

Cathy groaned. "Oh, you heard about it. Then I guess everyone in the whole damned county knows."

"I move in peculiar circles," Claire reassured her.

"Well, *some* people," her friend said edgily, "took the incident as evidence of the unfitness of me personally, and of my whole gender, for the illustrious position of ag commissioner. I mean, I wasn't even *here*, I was in Tahoe, and I didn't want the bloody job in the first place, I'd just as soon be back in Berkeley—"

"I know. But what did happen?"

"Oh, those dickheads who did the testing," she said wearily. "Instead of taking some random sample of the vineyard, they only did the two rows right next to the road—"

"The ones that were easiest to get to," Claire interjected.

"Exactly! So it turns out that they were the only rows that had been contaminated. The rest of the field was clean!"

"That's weird," Claire said thoughtfully. "Where did you get your information?"

"Anonymous call."

"I know, but . . . young? Old? Male? Female?"

"Male, I think. I didn't actually take the call, I was gone. Charlie Padgett took it, and now *he's* gone. Won't be back till the thirty-first, I think."

"Did he say anything else about the caller?"

"Well, like I say, I wasn't here. But I did hear one second-hand crack. I heard that Charlie said the caller didn't have much of a future in that line of work."

"What did that mean?" Claire asked, bewildered.

"Hell, I don't know. The caller *was* a lousy whistle-blower; he blew the whistle on the wrong field. But Charlie didn't know that at the time. I'll talk to him when he comes back, if you want."

"Yes. In fact, tell him to call me. See you soon."

Claire left the problem of Bert's grapes and turned to the problem of Bert's alfalfa. Damn! He *would* be the owner! Of all the alfalfa fields in all the world ... Still, there were other fields, that was important to remember. She had just taken a liking to that one, had begun to design her experimental plots with it in mind. Maybe she would pay old Bert a visit this afternoon and test the waters. At this hour he was out working, but she left an obsequious message on his machine, telling him she'd like to drop by. "I have to stop by the Contessa cannery and take a friend to the family clinic in Alma, but I should be able to meet you at five," she said, overexplaining in her nervousness.

After a moment she picked up the phone again and dialed Steve Ashe at UCLA.

He listened to her in silence, then broke in, perplexed. "What's all this about, Claire? I don't understand—"

"It's crazy, Steve. It's probably nothing, but humor me. Can you do it?"

"Well, I feel sort of funny sneaking around, but ... sure. Sure, I guess so, for you. If you want discretion, though, it's going to take me a few days."

"That's fine!" she said eagerly; she wouldn't have to think about it for a day or two. "Oh, and Steve—" She stopped, wondering how to express this. "Um, since discretion *is* important ..."

"Don't tell Sara, right?" He laughed. "I can't promise anything. We both know that when it comes to secrets, my wife has the scruples of the *Enquirer* and the guile of Woodward and Bernstein—or vice versa."

At one she stopped by the motel to pick up a gray-faced Dolores, who had Ana and Juanito in tow as well as her sons, Francisco and Mario. These last were a surprise, since they were big boys and could take care of themselves, and there was barely room in the car for them. But they crammed themselves in and drove west along 170, turning south through the fields and along the railroad tracks till they came to the Contessa Tomato Cannery. (A sign depicting a busty Neopolitan beauty said "CONTESSA—Valley Sweet!") Claire scanned the parking lot for Luz and spotted a familiar glossy obsidian van at the far end of the lot, separated from the funkier vehicles of the employees by a moat of asphalt. Ruben Moreno's car.

But no Luz. Claire walked toward the corner of the factory, where a handful of workers was offloading crate after crate of scarlet plum tomatoes, dumping them onto a belt that moved them through a sort of car wash. She accosted a young man and said simply, "Luz Perez?"

"I think I seed her near the grab," he said, glancing over his shoulder nervously and edging away.

The "grab"? Imitating his involuntary look, she saw the tomatoes emerge dripping from their bath and move up a gravity-defying conveyor belt. The grab, she concluded, dragging the innocent fruit inexorably toward their collective fate. If she followed their odyssey, she might come to Luz. She stepped inside the building.

It was like falling down a rabbit hole.

The hot white light of the San Joaquin vanished, leaving her abruptly blind. So her first impression was smell, the overpowering, queasy, sweaty smell of a million stewed tomatoes. Then came the sound, a great deafening cacophony of clanking and hissing and vaguely digestive noises. Her vision cleared, and she goggled at a maze of pipes. Nearby, two men in hard hats pored over clipboards and peered at machinery, ignoring her completely.

Once again she looked to the tomatoes themselves to make sense of this chaos. Here they came, through a high opening in the wall behind her, riding the "grab" and spilling into a tank to be steamed and mashed. Farther down the line a fat man in a *chef*'s hat, honest to God, poured a bucket of—oregano? basil?—into a vat of percolating pulp. Beyond that the pipes disappeared through the wall; following, she entered a small, brightly lit room filled with stainless steel.

Here were the guts of the place. Here the actual canning was done. Nozzles oozed obscenely; cans whirled and clicked into place with cheerful idiocy; the floor, slimy with tomato blood, was ceaselessly hosed off by silent workers who, smocked and sexless, their hair tucked into shower caps, resembled deranged OR nurses. It was a scene out of *Naked Lunch.*

Claire stared hard at the figures: they were all female, but none of them, she determined, was Luz, though even Luz would have disappeared in that garb. "Luz Perez?" she shouted.

There was no sign that they had heard, and she shouted again, straining hoarsely above the din. Finally one of the women looked up.

"Right sack."

Claire must have shown her confusion, because the woman repeated herself.

"Bright stack," she said, possibly, this time, and jerked a thumb toward a door on the far side of the canning room.

Feeling more than ever like Alice, Claire stepped through . . .

. . . and found herself in a cavernous, cool warehouse, surround by twenty-foot stacks of unlabeled aluminum cans. They gleamed dully in the dim light. Ah. "Bright stacks," she muttered, noting the offhand poetry of technical jargon.

After the racket of the factory, the warehouse was eerily quiet. Her footsteps echoed as she wandered forlornly down one aisle and up another, calling, "Luz . . . Luz . . ." like a faint night bird, until she had almost forgotten what the point was.

Suddenly there was a scrape and a rumble, and something moved into position to block the light dead ahead. She squinted and saw a huge fanged thing facing her; it took a moment to realize that it was a forklift and that it was bearing down on her like a bull in a chute.

She resisted the urge to run, instead pressing herself against the stacks. The machine and its rider, whose face was in shadow, whizzed past, coming within about a foot of her.

Okay. Luz or no Luz, she had had enough of the Contessa's Valley Sweetness. But now she was completely disoriented, could not even find the door to the canning room, which in her memory had become an oasis of light and humanity. Through the stacks she moved, first at a purposeful walk, then breaking into a panicky trot.

Behind her she heard the whir of the forklift again and whirled to see it barreling toward her once more. This time it was clutching a stack of cans wrapped tightly with transparent plastic—bound and shrouded, like a spider's prey. Spooked, she backed away.

Surely the lift wasn't actually *following* her, she thought as the driver bore down. He was just going about his business, ignoring her as had all the humans in this place (she couldn't help looking down at her arm as if to confirm that she was still visible). There was no reason for him to chase her.... Desperately she searched for daylight. The forklift was close enough to touch when she bolted and ran for the far side of the warehouse.

Abruptly the building disgorged her into the parking lot, not a hundred feet from where she had entered.

A knot of workers was standing to her left, staring at her. No, not at her, beyond her. She looked over her shoulder to the far end of the lot, where Moreno's van was parked. Just then the side door slid open and a figure emerged. Not Moreno's natty self, no: a woman, who paused, dazzled by the light, then adjusted her clothing and walked toward the crowd. For a dreadful moment Claire thought it was Luz. But as she approached, Claire saw that she was even younger than Luz—no more than seventeen, probably, very pretty. She was expressionless. The crowd parted to let her pass; she paused again to fish in her pocket and brought out a shower cap. Then she disappeared inside the building.

Claire looked at the faces around her—averted, ashamed, maybe, but eyes glittering with a kind of suppressed excitement—and thought incredulously, *Here?* In the *parking lot?* At *lunchtime?*

A whistle blew. *"Bueno,"* somebody shouted, "break's over. Back to work."

People wandered back inside the cannery, and suddenly she saw Luz, who was still staring at the van, waiting. Claire watched to see if Moreno would appear, but no, the engine started and the car moved away. When she looked back, Luz's face was grim and maybe a little frightened.

Quickly Claire turned her head. She didn't want Luz to look frightened; she wanted her magnificent, fearless.

Later, in the converted storefront that was *La Clínica Familiar*, Claire wanted to ask two questions. One was whether Moreno indeed had sex with his female workers in his van and, if so, whether they were willing partners. But when she looked around at Luz and Dolores and the young mothers and not so old grandmothers and nurses and female doctors—at this place, in short, in which women were so central—it was hard to imagine a world in which they were mere afterthoughts, snacks. So she asked the more outrageous question instead. "Luz—can you think of any reason someone would chase me with a forklift?"

"Forklift" was a hard one and required some enthusiastic pantomime, but when Luz understood she looked bewildered. "Chase you? No," she said. "Except . . ."

"What?"

"Well, the men there, they are mean to the women sometimes. *¿Cómo se dice?* Tease? Yes, tease them."

What an opening. "Like Ruben Moreno?"

Her face shut down.

"Luz, does Ruben . . . does he make the women . . ." Desperately she searched for the comprehensible euphemism.

Dolores said something to Luz, who answered her, then spoke slowly to Claire. "He make the women go with him sometimes, yes."

"Does he threaten them?" Luz looked blank, so she amplified, "Say he'll take their jobs away if they don't, um, go with him?"

No answer. Then, *"Sí,"* she said reluctantly.

"You know that's illegal. He could go to jail—"

She stopped when she saw a look that she imagined to be pure contempt; just the briefest narrowing of the eyes that said, to Claire's tender liberal conscience, Look, lady, you don't have to hose off tomato pulp ten hours a day to feed your kids—you don't even *have* kids, you unnatural bitch—so don't tell me what's illegal!

But she couldn't quite drop it. "I could help," she said faintly.

Luz was expressionless.

"You once told me you should all help each other," Claire added, and left it at that, because after all, what did she know?

Hours later, late for her appointment with Bert, Claire tore up 170 toward the lake. After an eternity of sitting in the *clínica*, Dolores had seen a doctor, but then they had to wait for Francisco and Mario, who as it happened had come along not for the ride, but to see the nurse themselves. During the winter the migrant education people had discovered "something wrong with their blood," and on further questioning Claire deduced that this was anemia, due, astonishingly, to malnutrition. Not too much junk food, just not enough food, period.

"Nobody had nothing to eat," Luz declared cheerfully. "Because of the cold."

Claire had thought a moment. "You mean because the freeze killed the citrus crop?"

"*Sí.* Nobody had no work till March. No work, no food."

But finally Luz had persuaded her to leave them there, claiming they could all get a ride home from Dolores's friend's cousin. This is not a First World life, she now thought as she turned north toward Bert's house. Dickensian factory, kids hungry and anemic, parents always sick—in fact, only Luz seemed to be immune from the "farmworkers' flu."

What wimpy microorganism was a match for the radiant Luz?

She skidded to a stop just past the driveway, backed up carefully, and pulled in.

Chapter 13

Bert Yankovich's house stood at the crest of a high, bare hill overlooking Lake Prosperity, which was a State Water Project reservoir and possibly the ugliest body of water in California. But then it was an ugly house: a sprawling structure of pink-and-white brick and no particular architecture, its primary function was to impress. Even its total absence of landscaping seemed deliberate, as if a visitor unmoved by all else would at least be awed by the thought of Bert's air-conditioning bills.

There were two cars in the drive: a spotless white Lincoln Continental and Bert's real working vehicle, a new but grimy Ford truck. Two cars ought to add up to one human being in residence, she thought hopefully, ringing the doorbell.

And once again waited humbly for a Yankovich to decide whether to admit her to his home. It was getting a little old. And it was hot out here! She pressed the doorbell again.

Sometime after the third ring, Bert Yankovich condescended to open the door to her. He loomed in the dark hallway like a brooding grizzly and wordlessly motioned her into the living room. For a moment she was dazzled—by the light from the picture window that gave onto the lake and by the room itself, which contrasted devastatingly with the cannery and the dirty clinic and was white, all white, and lavish. Obviously the fantasy of the ex–Mrs. Yankovich (who, if rumor be true, was currently living in Fresno with her daughters on meager alimony). Claire wondered who kept it in its pristine condition, had a brief, bizarre vision of Bert pushing a vacuum around, and dismissed it immediately. She would bet he never used this room, that he had a lair somewhere with a wide-screen TV and a pile of empties.

"So," he rumbled, "I understand from Ray that you want me to let you use my land for . . . scientific inquiry." The last phrase was weighted with something, sarcasm probably.

"That's right," she answered. "Did he tell you which area I'm interested in? It's maybe twenty acres, right off J29 by an irrigation ditch—"

"I know the field," he broke in. "I got some vineyards there, too. It's where they found that guy floatin'." He paused. "Come to think of it, you found his body, didn't you? That got anything to do with why you want this particular field?"

"No, that's why I found the body. I was looking at the alfalfa."

He grunted skeptically. "Okay. What's in this for me?"

Bottom line. "Well, we can't pay you, if that's what you mean. But you'd be one of the first to know if this biological agent is effective in controlling fiddleneck. And of course you'd get an acknowledgment in the article—"

"Article?" he repeated sharply.

"Yes, we'd publish our findings in a journal. *California Agriculture,* something like that."

"Oh, yeah. I seen that one. That's a pretty good magazine." He looked meditatively out the window, and she followed his gaze to the lake—where the after-work crowd kited around in speedboats and tried to convince themselves they were having fun—and then up: up the steep yellow slope where crows circled; up to its crown of fedora gray granite; up to the blue tip of a mountain peeking behind it. So cool, she thought wistfully. Even ten miles up 170 where Sam was it would be five degrees cooler—

"I suppose you'll spray the smut in spring, before the basidiospores germinate," Bert was, incredibly, saying.

She gaped, then rallied. "Uh, yes, the basidiospores are more infectious, of course, but we'd work with the *Entyloma* in its teliospore phase, before it produces the basidiosp—"

"How're you gonna prevent the control plots from being contaminated by spores blowin' over?"

"Uh, well, that's—that's a good question." He meant to

rattle her, and he was succeeding; she had expected to be interrogated, but not quite at this level of expertise. "But I think we can address it if we separate the treatment and control areas adequately. . . ."

Floundering like an undergrad in an oral exam, she trailed to a halt. Bert grinned. "I got an ag degree from Davis," he said. "Did you know that?"

"Yes, I—"

"I was good at that stuff, too," he continued a little defiantly.

"Evidently," she muttered.

"Would have liked to go on. But my dad died"—here he looked at a photo on the wall of a beetle-browed old man who scowled back at him—"and I had to take over the business. Thought I might go back to school once Emil come up. But Emil . . ." He made a harsh, wet noise in his throat, then fixed her with a baleful eye. "Somethin' wrong?"

She had been staring. "No . . . no, of course not. That's . . . I'm sorry . . . ," she stammered. She was struggling, really struggling, to integrate this information. Bert, a frustrated academic! Emil, she could see, but Bert!

Oh, but why not Bert? God knew—*she* knew—that hers was not a profession of unworldly, gentle scholars, that there were angry, belligerent, even violent professors.

"As I was saying about my brother," Bert resumed. "Emil never learned you gotta pay for everything in this life. Sooner or later, you got to pay."

Right, she thought, listening to the rasp of his voice, and sometimes you get billed forty years later for something you didn't know you'd bought. Like lung cancer.

"And he don't take care of things. Seems to think somebody should take care of him. He's like his mother there."

She felt a flash of resentment on behalf of that worn-out woman in Emil's photograph. Taken care of? Hardly.

"Me, I learned from my father," he was saying. "A pragmatist. He taught me what the world is like: eat or be et. I aim to be the bear, not the bait. Tell you what," he continued, switching gears from redneck philosopher to successful businessman, "you write out the details of your proposal for me, and I'll consider it."

"That's . . . very kind of you, Mr. Yankovich, uh, Bert. I'll
get it to you right away. And thank you!"

"I ain't promising nothin'," he said, double-clutching
down to yokel again to deliver this classic valediction.

"Right, of course. Thanks again for your time."

Either elation or nerves made her hands shake so that she
had trouble with the ignition key. Well, she had bearded the
lion (was that attaching or detaching the beard? Detaching,
probably, like scalping), and Bert was one formidable dude
all right. But he was human, he had his vanities, and this
project might appeal to them. In fact, she just might persuade
him to cooperate. She started the car.

Even now, at six-thirty, the temperature hovered in the
upper nineties, and those blue mountains beckoned. She
headed east on 170 (where the fire danger was now EX-
TREME), figuring she could at least cool herself for a while
on the river before she had to make her way to Sam's. Past
the lake, then, the sun on the hot asphalt making sky-colored
stripes that slithered off into the yellow grass as she neared
them; past Riverdale and the turnoff to Sam's; and across the
river at the east end of town. The road followed the north
side of the V-shaped canyon all the way up to the river's
source, the Great Western Divide, and for a moment Claire's
imagination climbed and veered right on up with it.

But not today, she thought regretfully, pulling off at a
turnout about five miles up from town and walking over to
the edge.

Two hundred dizzying yards straight below her the river
ran lightly over flat rocks, collected in green pools, and tum-
bled down stairways of smooth stone. And while from up
here the plunge looked impossibly steep, locals knew how to
find the narrow ledge of path that led down through the
dense chaparral.

Well, she knew how to find the path, so *she* must be a
local. She considered this conclusion for a moment, then
started down.

The trail was no cinch, reflecting a switchbacks-are-for-
sissies attitude. It tended to crumble away from under the
feet, and she clutched at a prickly chamise, coming away

with nothing but needles, and then at a more substantial man-zanita. She loved the manzanitas—their blood red trunks, smooth as lava; their snaky thickets of bare red branches and bright gray-green coins of leaves. *Perfectly adapted to an arid environment,* droned someone's familiar didactic voice in her head. *The waxy leaves reduce transpiration and grow vertically, turned so as to be parallel to the sun's rays. . . .*

A nice trick, that, presenting an edge to pain instead of taking it broadside.

After ten minutes of scrambling and slipping and scraping between elephantine boulders, Claire was at the water. In an-other minute she had hopped her way onto a tabletop of granite in the middle of the river.

A short way downstream where the sun still hit a shallow pool, a group of Latino teenagers splashed and shrieked, the boys making precipitous, slippery leaps from boulder to boulder pulling themselves back and forth across the water in the little handcart that hung suspended from a cable. But her part of the river was already in shadow, and the breeze picked up and came in low and cool across the water, finally lifting the heat's oppression (*com*pression it was, really, like a huge hand squeezing air out of the lungs). She lay on her back and drifted into the mental meandering that leads to creative breakthrough or obsessive gridlock.

Sam's house, 8:32 P.M. Boys come rushing to greet her and throw arms around her. Sam acknowledges he has mis-judged her maternal qualities and apologizes for cheatin' with Linda. She graciously accepts apology and promises to try to forge better relationship with Shannon and Terry. Does not mention Jeff Green. Sam embraces her and—

She sat up straight and cut short this fantasy, sternly ad-monishing herself not to get her hopes up. *I have no control over my hopes,* answered a mournful voice, and she lay back down.

Okay. Don't think about Sam. Levine, what was he work-ing on? Pesticides? Labor contractors? The death of Juan Perez? (Though Tom was right, that appeared to have been a simple accidental drowning, no mystery there.)

No, the *mysterious* death, other than Levine's own, was Cedillo's heart attack. But that, unfortunately, wouldn't work: Levine had been high in the mountains when Cedillo was killed—the forest service and his "dandelion" testified to that—and had himself died immediately thereafter.

Then there was Ruben Moreno. The indictable offenses kept mounting. How about extorting sex from female workers in the parking lot of the cannery? Jesus, there was a subject for an exposé! Someone needed to question Luz more expertly than she had done and talk to Moreno—

And check his arms for scratches. Because whoever had exited her bathroom window last night had certainly raked himself along the broken glass, leaving blood and DNA and fibers and other forensic riches.

Damn, why hadn't Martelli come when she'd called him this morning? Despite what he'd said, she was sure this wasn't a simple robbery attempt. Someone had been looking for something or trying to intimidate her.

She should call the Parkerville police from Sam's. How big was that window, anyway? Maybe one by two; that made the hypotenuse . . . um . . . one forty-four, plus, oh, say, six hundred; take the square root . . . Well, something less than thirty inches, anyway. And her own shoulders, measured now by the accurate unit of a hand's width, spanned less than twenty inches, though of course they had depth, too, but *she* could probably make it, and Luz, and Ruben, of course. And Jonathan Levine, he was small—

Jonathan Levine?

The idea rose up out of the ether to arrest her headlong stream of consciousness. Jonathan Levine was dead: she herself had grappled for a half hour with his lifeless body; his poor mother was coming to claim him. Yet Claire's mental momentum was such that she was unable to prevent herself from imagining Levine—restless spirit, poltergeist, zombie, whatever—creeping into her room, and she shivered with a superstitious frisson.

Or maybe just the cold wind. For it was suddenly seven-thirty; the sun was setting directly down the canyon, the teenagers were gone, and it was time to leave.

She hopped onto a small boulder and teetered there a moment, avoiding a tangle of nettles and scarlet monkey flower on the upriver side. As she made her way across the cause-

way of slick rocks toward shore, she decided with shaky
bravado that number seven was a perfect site for ghostly vis-
itation. Violent death; victim returns to significant place;
tries desperately to communicate with new occupant through
visions, trancelike states, etc. Well, dammit, he'd have to be
more explicit—

Something moved in the brush on the far side of the river.

It was probably only a deer come to drink at sundown, but
suddenly it occurred to her that a woman who had been chased
by a forklift (possibly) and had surprised a burglar (definitely)
probably should not be hiking down an isolated trail in the
mountains. But she hadn't thought of the trail as isolated: it was
familiar, it was just off the highway . . .

Just off the highway in Flatland, perhaps. But in a three-
dimensional world she was far below the road and completely
alone. Or maybe not. The brush crackled again.

Panicked, she leapt for the last stone, and her right foot
slipped and she went hurtling through space to land with bone-
jarring force on the river bank.

For a moment she simply crouched on hands and knees,
stunned with the impact and gasping with a sensation too over-
whelming to name. Then it resolved itself into *pain*—pain so
intense all she could do was sit and rock back and forth and
curse.

In a minute or two she was able to take inventory. Bleeding
left elbow and knee: that was nothing, just a few more addi-
tions to the archipelago of scars that bore witness to a lifetime
of not watching where she was going. But this intolerable throb
somewhere below her right shin—that was a problem. In another minute she wiggled her foot very cautiously. Everything
seemed to work. Okay, maybe it was only a bad sprain; she had
sprained that ankle, her right, once before (stepped into a hole
while thinking about something else). She stood up slowly, balancing on one leg; then she put a little weight on her right
foot—

Oh, God! With a cry she crumpled to the ground again, tears
of agony and frustration filling her eyes. She had better prepare
herself for a long, cold night by the river; she would never
make it back up that joke of a trail on a bad leg. In the morning
her ankle would be better, and/or other hikers would be down.

Sam himself might come looking for her; after all, her car was
parked right off 170, where anyone could see it—

Anyone at all. She hoped again that what she had heard was
a deer. Anyway, Sam would just assume she had snubbed him.
And she didn't want him to rescue her, it was too humiliating.
"Well, kids, once again Dale Evans has been captured by out-
laws, and Roy has to rescue her"; or "Once again, kids, just as
Sheila and Lance are running from the villains, Sheila sprains
her ankle because she's wearing these ridiculous little high-
heeled sandals, and Lance has to sweep her up in his brawny
arms and run for two. . . . " From an early age Claire had determined to be rescuer, not rescuee. She stood again and tried her
right foot.

The pain was excruciating, but either she was prepared for it
or it was a little less than before. In fact, maybe if she soaked
her ankle in the river for a while and then had something for
support . . . She laid her foot, sneaker and all, in the cool water,
and the relief was immediate and miraculous. While she sat she
looked around for a likely stick and found a long pole of alder,
which she worked at with the buck knife she had automatically
grabbed from the trunk. At least she had provided herself with
a weapon, she thought sardonically, though if she had grabbed
her boots instead, she might have saved her ankle.

By now it was eight and really getting dark. Reluctantly she
pulled her foot from the water—it was mercifully numb—
grasped her walking stick, and began.

At first she listened for noise behind her. But ten yards up
the trail the feeling returned to her ankle with a vengeance,
flashing messages of fire to her brain that overrode any other
thought: *Stop! Lie down! What are you doing to me?* She
started to sing to drown them out, but all she could remember
were country songs from—last night? Was it only last night? "
. . . I can hear that jukebox moanin' from the corner of the
bar . . . " she hummed, then decided she needed all her concentration for the epic journey ahead of her.

So she inched upward at no more than desert tortoise speed.
Even so, halfway up, the trail caved in under her and she scrab-
bled desperately at the loose talus, at the last possible moment
catching hold of a protruding root. She watched her stick
bounce down the canyon and hit hard. After that she gave up

all pretense of walking upright and dropped to a crawl; this hurt her wounded knee but was a hell of a lot more secure.

About fifty yards from the top the path became a narrow artery between huge granite boulders. Here she could swing herself from rock to rock with her arms and relieve all pressure from her bad leg. With the pain momentarily relieved, she suddenly remembered that she was supposed to be listening for a pursuer, and she paused. Silence, except for the roar of the river below.

If she had been less worried about spectral or human threats, she might have been more alert to the real dangers of the trail. Like placing her hands where she couldn't see them.

But as it was, she allowed herself to relax, to think about the end: a few more boulders *(lift, swing),* then perhaps ten yards of steep trail *(lift, swing),* and then, then, the Holy Grail, a stucco-colored Tercel. *Lift, swing; lift, swing; lift—*

Sssssssssssss!

Claire froze in midswing, more alert than she had ever been in her life. Genetically wired circuits were going off like alarms all through her body: *so close! where was it, where? There!* In the shadows, on a ledge a few feet in front of her shoulder—a ledge that would have been her next handhold.

It was too dark to see the diamonds or the rattles but there was no mistaking him, coiled, his wicked wedge-shaped head aimed at her like a dart. A death machine. Well, that was unfair; he had just crawled peacefully out on the cool rocks to enjoy the sunset, and she had come crashing clumsily along. Nonetheless if she had had the artillery and the skill she would have blown him in two, no question about it.

But she didn't. She had a small dull-bladed knife. So now what? Ordinarily she would have simply backed up and taken a detour. But ordinarily she wasn't crippled, and ordinarily the only available detour wasn't through thin air. Maybe if she stood there quietly he would just . . . slink away?

She stood there quietly for quite some time. The rattler showed no signs of slinking. Okay. The distance between them was about six feet, farther than she had thought in her initial primitive terror. Far enough for him not to feel threatened if she hobbled by, very slowly, thinking mellow thoughts? Was he

bluffing? More scared of her than she was of him? She sputtered with hysterical laughter.

She edged forward. He rattled again; her heart went into pal-
pitations, and she stood paralyzed for another five minutes, random morsels of information zizzing through her brain: *apply
lymph bands between the wound and the heart . . . keep victim
absolutely immobilized!* . . . Finally, beyond shame, she once
again dropped to all fours and crawled. This had the advantage
of putting her below his line of sight but was extremely painful
and meant that she couldn't move in a hurry if she had to. Now
she was directly under the ledge; now she was past him; and
now she was out of the rocks and safe.

Adrenaline kept her moving quite quickly. It was now very
dark, but here at least the path was relatively wide and level.
But without her stick she could proceed only by a combination
of hopping and shuffling and grabbing at branches and roots,
and once she fell and cried out in pain as her right leg doubled
under her. For several minutes she thought she was actually
going to have to stop right there, fifty feet from the end of the
trail. But eventually she struggled to her feet again and limped
on and at last came to her car.

Her car. She wanted to weep on its hood, embrace its steering wheel. How could she have considered parting with it? She
backed it out onto the highway, thankful her left leg, which had
to work the clutch, was intact, and wearily drove to Sam's.

Chapter 14

The house was lit and the blue Valiant parked in the driveway when she pulled in at nine-thirty. Grimacing in pain, she eased her foot off the accelerator, then sat like jelly, slumped against the side of the car with her eyes closed. From the porch, as from a great distance, she heard Sam's voice.

"I had just about figured you weren't coming," he called in that ghastly mix of relief and reproach we reserve for loved ones. Then, with real alarm when he saw she wasn't moving, "Claire? Are you all right? " In a moment he was at the car.

"I'm okay; I just sprained my ankle," she mumbled as he helped her out. For a few steps he supported her with his arm; then, clicking his tongue impatiently, he picked her up and carried her toward the house.

Lance and Sheila. All she could do was laugh.

"What?" he panted, staggering as he climbed the stairs and opened the screen door with his elbow.

"Nothing," she said, squirming so that they both nearly fell over. "Put me down, I can walk. Sort of."

"Yeah, right." He dumped her on the couch, propped her foot on the coffee table, and began to strip off her sneaker and sock, muttering something that sounded like "should have worn decent shoes."

"At least they aren't high-heeled sandals," she said feebly, getting a bewildered look. Meanwhile, Terry and Shannon emerged from the bathroom dressed in pajamas, their eyes as round as the cantaloupe that was slowly revealed to have taken the place of her ankle. "Hi," she said weakly.

"Jesus, Claire," Sam was exclaiming as he beheld the damage.

He leaned over as if he were going to kiss her, then abruptly drew back and looked away. "You really did yourself in."

"And I haven't even told you about the rattlesnake." Or the ghost, she thought, but said nothing.

"Rattlesnake!" said the small Coopers in chorus, their eyes growing even bigger. Claire began to enjoy herself.

"Oh, yes, we had sort of a Mexican stand-off," she said airily, then wondered if that was an ethnic slur. Sam opened his mouth, cleared his throat, then said merely, "I'll get some ice. We ought to have that X rayed," and walked to the kitchen.

The boys came and sat by her on the couch, gazing with awe at her foot. They smelled of shampoo and looked damp and sweet. She was too tired to think, so without thinking she reached out and smoothed Terry's hair, tucking it behind his ears. He accepted these attentions as the most natural thing in the world.

"Was it a big rattler?" he asked.

"About three feet long, I guess. It was hard to tell because he was all coiled up. I didn't count his rattles."

"They don't get a rattle for every year, like most people think," Shannon announced importantly. "They get one every time they mo—molt, which is two or three times a year."

"I didn't know that," Claire said. "Have you seen a rattler?"

"Yeah!" said Terry. "Up at Sequoia once. And we saw a bear, and Daddy—Dad—caught some fish and I helped clean them—"

"And there are marmots up there, they're these small rodents," broke in Shannon.

"Yeah, they're real fuzzy!" Terry said happily. Claire watched them in wonder, as if she had never seen them before.

Sam returned with ice wrapped in a towel. "Hey, it's late, you can tell her about it tomorrow." Tomorrow, she thought. Am I going to be here tomorrow? "You guys all set out there? Got a flashlight? Off you go, then. They're sleeping out back in a tent," he explained to Claire as the boys headed for the back door. He grinned. "Starting out there, anyway."

"Night, Dad," she heard, and, after a moment, with a certain amount of pleasure, "Night, Claire."

"Now," said Sam, when it was quiet, "what happened?"

When she got to the rattlesnake he shook his head, pursed his lips, and said irritatingly, "You've got to be careful when you're scrambling, you've got to look where you put your hands—"

"I was careful!" she snapped, somewhat truthfully. "Don't scold me; I'm not Shannon!"

"Okay, okay," he said pacifically. "It's just that snake bites are no joke."

No joke. For a moment she allowed herself to imagine lying there in the cold with poison coursing through her system. . . . How did snake venom work, anyway? Was it a neurotoxin or—

Neurotoxin.

Heart failure.

Flu.

"That *cabrón* Moreno said he was drunk. . . ."

Good God!

Sitting up very straight, she said slowly, "Sam. When you gave your talk at the open house the other day, you mentioned some signs of organophosphate exposure."

He looked puzzled but said readily, "Yeah, flulike symptoms, and . . . um, excessive tearing, dizziness, bradycardia—"

"Bradycardia!" she interrupted. "Abnormally slow heartbeat, right?"

"Right."

"Can that actually cause heart failure?"

"Well, possibly, in somebody with an underlying problem. There was a suspicious case last year, in Arvin." He was looking at her as if this were some kind of hypothermial rambling.

"I knew it!" She slapped her thigh in excitement, then yelped at the consequent pain.

"Maybe I'd better take you down to the ER tonight."

"Absolutely not," she replied adamantly. "It's just a bad sprain, I've had one before. . . . Listen, would you call Tom Martelli?"

He glanced at his watch and started to protest, but "Please, it's important!" she interrupted, and, responding to her barely contained hysteria, he humored her. In a moment he leaned out from the kitchen.

"Okay, I've got him. Now what?"

"Ask him if they did a cholinesterase test on Perez or Cedillo."

He stared at her, understanding dawning gradually, then disappeared again. " . . . a-s-e," she heard him say. "For pesticide poisoning."

There was a long silence, then, "I don't know," she heard. "She can't, she's immobilized. Just a minute." He leaned out again. "He thinks it's highly unlikely they were tested. Can the tests be done now?"

"I have no idea, he'll have to ask the coroner. All I know about it is what you told me." She hesitated. "I don't even know if they'll still have the tissue and blood samples, or if they'll have to exhume the bodies."

He conferred for a minute, then reappeared. "He says, how about Levine?"

"I suppose if they have samples of . . . whatever they need, they could test them. I doubt they'll find anything," she said, lolling back on the couch as if she could now die peacefully.

Sam came in and stood over her. "Tom wants you to stop by his office first thing tomorrow and tell him what's going on. And I'd like to know, too. I had no idea you were thinking about this. But that can also wait until tomorrow." He paused. "Why don't you come to bed?"

To bed? Here? Just like that, without having the Talk? And she was too tired to have the Talk.

"*Go* to bed, I mean," he mumbled, seeing her face. "To sleep. You must be exhausted. You can have the bedroom or the couch, whichever."

Still she hesitated. If would be so comforting to go to bed with Sam as if nothing had happened—Linda and Jeff and Jon Levine and Hector Cedillo and rattlesnakes and all the rest of it; as if the problems of two little people didn't amount to a hill of beans in this crazy world. (But of course Humphrey and Ingrid had spent a good hour and a half of memorable screen time examining those beans.)

"That's probably best. I am awfully tired," she said, thinking she would hate herself in the morning. "I'll take the couch," she added, not wanting to look at the familiar bedroom, at the water-stained flowered wallpaper, the heap of dirty clothes in the corner, the books scattered on the floor, the dusty clock radio tuned to the country station, the battered bed-and-dresser set from Sears that had been Sam's parents'.

Wordlessly he handed her a sleeping bag and retired, leaving her alone in the living room. Through the half-open door as through the wrong end of a telescope she could see him slumped on the bed, reading; after five minutes he still hadn't turned the page.

Served him right. She had won this round, she thought dispiritedly . . . a totally unsatisfying victory. In fact, all this manipulation and jockeying for advantage and exacting incremental revenge was proving to be singularly unrewarding. Why not simply tell him how she was feeling?

A revolutionary, an audacious idea.

"Sam," she called softly, and he looked up. "It's not that I don't want to go to bed with you," she said. "I do. Very much. Very much," she repeated with more fervor than she had intended. "It's just that I don't know what it would mean, and I guess I think it might mean more to me than to you, and I'm feeling pretty insecure right now." As she said it, it somehow became less true. "So first I want to talk about what's happening between us—"

The miniature figure in the other room opened its miniature mouth.

"No," she said, holding up a hand, "I really am too tired. Tomorrow, okay?"

"Okay," he repeated after a minute.

She lay back, feeling better than she had in days. After all, she had been perfectly honest with him about her fears and feelings *and* had managed to have the last word!

"Daddy . . . Daddy . . ."

Claire had been asleep for several hours when footsteps and a small voice awakened her. The light came on in the bedroom and Sam was up on his elbows, making groggy interrogative sounds. She could just see Terry standing in the darkness, rubbing his eyes.

"Daddy, are there rattlesnakes in the back yard?" she heard.

"No, sugar, there aren't. Do you want to sleep in here with me?"

"Yes."

"Do you want me to help you bring your blanket in?"

"Yes."

With a groan and a curse Sam pulled himself upright and shuffled toward the back door. Claire rolled over and went back to sleep.

Chapter 15

Tom's office was a corner of a cement block building he shared with the fire department and the California Highway Patrol. When Sam walked and Claire hobbled into his room, he was dividing his energies between a box of pineapple bran muffins and *The Pesticide Handbook.*

"Have a muffin—What the hell happened to you?" he said to Claire, who was leaning on Sam's grandfather's cane, an ornate affair of mahogany and gold plate.

"Nothing serious. So," she said, eyeing his reading material, "you know all about organophosphate poisoning?"

"Neurotoxin," he said with his mouth full. "Destroys cholinesterase, which ordinarily facilitates the breakdown of acet"—consulting his book—"acetylcholine, which is a neurotransmitter . . . whatever that means."

"Basically, it means the victim's nervous system goes crazy," Sam said, "whether said victim is leafhopper or human being. Everything fires at once—you know, convulsions, coma, death. But that's in acute cases. There's a whole range of symptoms associated with low-level exposure."

"Like slowed heartbeat," Claire interjected eagerly, "which can cause heart failure in some people."

"Heart failure," Tom repeated.

"Exactly," she said, fixing him with a meaningful glance. "And flulike symptoms. Everyone on Walker Road has flu—" Except Luz, she realized suddenly. And Luz didn't work in the fields. QED. "And I bet half of it isn't flu at all, it's chronic organophosphate poisoning." She needed to inform the clinic about this, so Dolores and the other workers could be

160

treated. . . . Suddenly she was really angry. Somebody was poisoning her friends!

"Walker Road?" Sam repeated.

She ignored him and continued, "And the early signs of acute poisoning can mimic drunkenness, and Juan Perez was seen staggering around the afternoon he died. Ruben Moreno assumed he was drunk, his wife says he was sick—"

"And you say he was exposed to a pesticide. We'll know for sure when the toxicologist's report comes through, but it makes sense," Martelli said. "I think it was making sense to Jonathan Levine, too."

"What do you mean?"

He finished the muffin and took a halfhearted swipe at the sticky ring around his mouth. "I finally reached one of the two phone numbers on the scrap of paper. The woman at the UCLA School of Public Health. Levine had called her to ask about the symptoms of exposure to pesticides, especially to organ—org—"

"Organophosphates?" Claire supplied, and he nodded. The farmworkers' flu, she thought triumphantly. Of course! *That* was Levine's story! Only . . .

"Would that have provided a motive for murder?" she asked, then suddenly remembered the CONKWEST in Bert's vineyard, which Martelli probably knew nothing about. It was really too bad that had been a hoax.

"Sam," Tom was saying thoughtfully, "you know that anonymous tip that came through? About the Yankovich vineyard?"

Incredible. He knew all about it.

"Suppose it was Levine," Martelli continued. "Would that be enough for a motive for murder?"

Sam frowned. "Well, use of a nonregistered pesticide could mean criminal charges, and it could certainly mean a lot of bad, maybe even ruinous, publicity for Bert. The Ricardo brothers, the guys who grew those contaminated watermelons last year, have gotten out of food crops entirely. But Levine couldn't have made the call. When it came through he was up in the mountains. And anyway, those charges didn't pan out."

"That's right." Tom sighed. "Well, even so, I'd like to know who tipped off the state."

"And maybe you should question Luz Perez about her husband," suggested Claire. Gentle persistence.

Tom looked at her resignedly. "I'll have Ricky talk to her this afternoon."

"Why not you?"

"Oh, they may not talk to Ricky, and they surely won't talk to me. El Cherife, they call me; think I'm gonna turn 'em in to the Migra. Hell, I got no interest in that. My own parents came over from Italy...."

His voice trailed off, and Claire thought about what unpredictable lessons people took from their lives. There was Tom, and Emil, but then there was Bert, also the child of immigrants and yet completely contemptuous of Mexicans and their culture.... Well, hell, this whole county was full of Arkies and Okies, "Joads" who had suffered fearfully at the hands of local landowners during the Depression—and now they were the landowners, and the bosses, and they were the worst bigots of the bunch! Some of them, she amended, thinking of Sam. And Jeff.

"Well, tell him to also ask her about what Moreno's been up to at the cannery," she said, and described yesterday's visit.

She heard Sam's breath hiss between his teeth. Martelli winced, but all he said was, "That's not exactly my jurisdiction, it's Cummings's. But he'd need to get somebody to testify to make a case. Would this Perez woman do it?"

"Maybe," said Claire, remembering Liberty Leading the Troops.

"Okay. Take care of that ankle."

"I will. And Tom—you'll tell me if there's any new information on Jonathan Levine?"

"Of course," he said irritably. "Hell, yes. Why wouldn't I?"

"What's this about Walker Road?" Sam asked as he helped her into the car.

"It's a street up in northeast Parkerville."

"*I* know where it is. Why do *you* know so much about it? You don't know Parkerville at all—" He halted as possibilities occurred to him.

"That's where I've been staying," she said reluctantly. "In an old motel."

"What?" He stared at her, then hit the brakes as he took a curve too fast. "Why? To make me feel guilty? You could have stayed with a friend, for Christ's sake!"

"I don't have any friends here."

"Well, whose fault is that? Anyway, you could have stayed at a better motel, at the very least! It's not like I threw you out on the sidewalk without any money—"

"I'm living there because I want to," she retorted. "And don't worry, nobody knows; no one will think badly of you!"

He cursed and swerved to avoid a chipmunk. After a moment they both spoke at once.

"Look, Claire, I—"

"We have to—"

They stopped short, and Claire said, "You first."

"Let me pull over so I don't kill us both. Accidentally," he added wryly, as if expecting to be done in with full deliberation during the ensuing conversation.

They pulled into the entrance of a dirt road and parked in the shade of a generous valley oak. Claire's hands were sweating and her foot throbbed, and she rummaged in her purse for aspirin so she wouldn't have to look at Sam.

"You were right," she heard him say. "You were right about the kids; we should have worked together on this problem with them. . . ."

He stopped. There was an edge to his voice that made her heart not leap in her breast; that made her think this was not a reconciliation, but a confession.

"I was right about your feelings for Linda, too," she said finally.

At first he didn't answer. Then he said, unhappily, "I hadn't realized how much I missed her. She's so—"

Womanly, and warm, and giving, and all the things you're not, she supplied, and snapped, "Please! Spare me the details!"

"I was just going to say that she seems to really need me. I've never been sure about you; you seem so self-sufficient."

A left-handed compliment, she supposed. And an exhortation not to make a scene? "I'm not," she said tersely, thinking, Christ, I hear your voice in my head all the time; every time I look around I hear your voice, explaining, interpreting . . . Sometimes I think I have to be alone so much because

I actually have no personality of my own, that I'm just a con-
duit for other people's voices. . . . "That should be obvious
after the last few days. Maybe my style is different from
Linda's, but I need you, too. Or . . . I don't know about need,
but I want you. I don't want to lose you."

He picked up her hand. "I don't want to lose you, either." A
pause. "I feel crazy."

If this was meant to elicit sympathy, it failed. "Oh, it's not
crazy to love two people," she said absently, thinking of Jeff
and not noticing Sam's startled expression. Of course she
didn't love Jeff; she was infatuated. But he scared her, too.

No, right now the only effective buffer between her and despair was the problem of Jonathan Levine. By thinking hard
about Levine she could—just—retain some poise.

Still Sam held on to her hand. "Give me some time to sort
this out."

"What else can I do?" she said. Then, to her surprise, she
began to cry—awkwardly, constrictedly, like someone new to
the experience. She covered her face with her free hand.

"Ah, God, Claire," Sam said, pulling her against him. At the
familiar smell of him and feel of his sharp collarbone she collapsed entirely, and sobbed without restraint.

But what am I doing? she thought after a moment. This is
the Stockholm syndrome, seeking comfort from the one who
caused the pain! And at that she drew a long, tremulous breath
and pushed away from him.

"I need to get more clothes," she muttered, not looking up.
"And my mail."

"You're going back there?" he said incredulously.
"To . . . to that motel?"

"It's where I live right now! It's where a lot of people live!"
she said defiantly, as if making some obscure political point.

"Why there?" he asked after a moment. "Why that motel?"

"Jonathan Levine lived there," she replied reluctantly.

"Jonath—you really *are* involved in this case! Why?"

"Yeah, I just sort of got sucked in," she said evasively. "I
feel he's someone I could have known—" She stopped suddenly. "Sam. Did Tom tell *you* that Levine was murdered?"

"Yeah."

"When?"

"I don't know," he said vaguely. "Before . . . "

"Before I found out about Linda?"

"Yeah, I guess so. Why?"

"That son of a bitch," she said. He had lied to her, then called Sam and told him the whole story. Beware of men in packs.

The remainder of the ride to Sam's ranked right up, or down, with the worst fifteen minutes of her life. At the house the boys had been drawing snakes all morning, and marmots, and stegosauruses, and Ninja Turtles, and B-52s, and Stealth bombers. They were eager to show her their efforts, having finally, it seemed, accepted her just as she was about to move out.

"Why are you leaving again?" asked Terry, when he saw her overnight bag.

"I have . . . uh . . . a research project"—she supposed Jonathan Levine was a sort of research project—"and I have to go somewhere to take care of it."

"Will you be back for dinner?"

"Not tonight, no."

"Will you be back before we go down to Mom's?"

"Um . . . I'll see you before you leave. Of course. Maybe we could go to the library," she said on impulse, then wondered how she would take the son to the library when she wasn't speaking to the father.

"Okay," Terry said cheerfully. "Bye."

She had to accept Sam's company once more for a ride to the emergency room, where she was judged to be sprained, not broken, and was wrapped and presented with crutches (which chafed her armpits and were soon discarded for the cane). After that she declared herself capable of independent living— which she was, just barely, as long as she didn't have to hit the brake pedal too hard—and headed home to number seven.

Luz greeted her warmly, wanting to know about her ankle, wanting to know where she had been last night. She had been worried, she said, especially after the break-in. "But I figure you were with your husband, no?"

Claire nodded glumly, and Luz flashed a dazzling smile. "*Bueno*. You two have peace again, maybe."

Before she had to answer this, or even think about it, Ricky, AKA Officer Enrique Santiago of the Riverdale police, arrived in an unmarked car. He strode up the walk toward number six with an air of professional competence and maybe just a hint of swagger, a confident man who was young and healthy and handsome, and knew it. And then he saw Luz.

His head snapped back as if he'd been hit in the face.

But Claire introduced him, and he managed to pull himself together, asking questions in what seemed to be a businesslike manner; since they spoke in Spanish, she wasn't sure. She drifted into her room—even hotter than before, because Martín had kindly tacked plywood over the bathroom window. Luz had cleaned up very thoroughly. So much for forensic evidence, she thought, and picked up a magazine and tried to read. But her mind whirled like a roulette wheel, men's names ticking over in time to the throb of her ankle: Sam. Jeff. Jonathan. Emil. Sam. Jeff. Jonathan. Emil. Sam. Jeff—

Jonathan. She arrested the cycle by falling asleep.

The moon was rising over the walnut grove as he drove along the rutted dirt road, searching the blackness on either side for the other vehicle. Damn this bastard anyway—why did they have to meet at night in the middle of nowhere? It had been a long and exhausting day; he was tired, he was sore, he was sunburned—he rubbed his nose ruefully—his feet hurt. And he wasn't looking forward to this interview at all.

He turned north, according to instructions, and suddenly saw the lights of a parked car about a hundred yards ahead, beyond an open field. He pulled off beside an irrigation canal and walked across the road. The lights went out.

"Get in," a muffled voice ordered, opening a door. He got in.

"So," he said after a long pause, "what have you got to say?"

They talked for twenty minutes, the other at first smooth and persuasive and then increasingly angry. He was acutely uncomfortable. His nose hurt. He scratched his chest where the flower irritated it. He wanted to go to bed. Finally he cut the other short.

"Look, this is pointless," he said. "You haven't told me any-

thing I don't already know, and you haven't changed my mind. If you've got something else to say, you know where to reach me." He opened the door, stepped out, and began walking toward his car.

He was fumbling with his keys—a city habit; it was ridiculous to have locked his car out here—when he heard the other door slam behind him. He whirled just as the headlights came on, blinding him. He called, shielding his useless eyes; he listened, but the soft dust of the road absorbed all sound—yet he was sure someone was approaching. Panic crept up the back of his neck.

Suddenly his left arm was wrenched behind him. Instantly he twisted away. But he was very tired and the other man was strong and angry and in a moment his other arm was behind him and he was being half dragged, half lifted toward the canal.

He was almost too shocked to resist. This can't be happening, he thought dimly, yet there was a kind of nightmarish familiarity about it that sapped his will, as if he had been waiting his whole life for this moment.

He was pushed remorselessly to his knees on the slippery canal bank—and then his head was being forced down, into the dark water.

Now he began to struggle.

Claire woke moaning, flailing the air, fighting her way up from sleep, and stumbled out onto the front porch to recover.

Usually she contemplated her dreams with a certain solemn awe. It amazed her that her own superrational mind could produce these works of art; that what she called thinking, that is, the planning, reasoning, defining, examining, figuring, deducing, inducing, and analyzing by which she made her living and otherwise operated day to day, was merely a ripple on a deep, murky pool. Let others consider their dreams random electrical perturbations; she took them very seriously.

But this—this didn't even feel like her own dream! Driving narrative, taut suspense, brutal climax—not at all her style, which tended toward the moody and pointless. In fact, this didn't seem like anybody's dream. It was too lucid. More like a memory. . . .

In which case she was asking herself to believe that someone was remembering his own death.

And not just "someone." Jonathan Levine, to be exact.

It was bad enough to hear Sam's voice in her head, but altogether unacceptable to dream someone else's dream, to . . . to channel Jonathan Levine! She tried and failed to produce a suitably skeptical noise.

In the cool night air the spasmodic beat of her heart quieted slowly, and soon she noticed soft voices off to her right. Luz and Enrique were sitting under the cottonwood in the dark, still talking. A long interrogation, she thought; and then Luz's clear laugh rang out, joined after a moment by Enrique's rich baritone.

Love is for the young and beautiful, thought Claire with knee-jerk cynicism, smiling anyway. The terror began to pass—but she slept in her car.

Chapter 16

On Sunday she went into the lab, partly for her own sanity, partly to atone for her recent flakiness. Boys, bodies, breakups, and Bert notwithstanding, her work must go forward.

Allen had found a small population of infected fiddleneck, which they hoped would neither die nor recover before the spring. This morning she sketched Bert's twenty acres with various designs for her experiment. First she divided the field into small plots of one yard square; then, remembering Bert's comment on the possibility of contamination of control plots by the spores, she added a surrounding buffer of twenty yards. She numbered the plots from west to east and used a random number table to select which plots would receive the treatment, such as the *Entyloma*. But even with randomization she must confirm that the test areas were comparable to the control plots on all relevant variables. "Soil type," she wrote. "Moisture. Sunlight. Drainage."

At eleven o'clock she looked at the phone and at her watch; too soon, she thought, church was just letting out—and then she caught herself.

Was she really going to do this?

Evidently, because at noon she lifted the receiver, replaced it almost immediately, picked up the Parkerville phone book, and flipped to the four-page Tierra Buena listings. Then she dialed Green, Leroy E. and Dora.

"Yes?"

It was an elderly woman's voice, slightly suspicious.

"Mrs. Green? My name is Carolyn . . . uh . . . Benedict"—

Arnold. Quisling. Brutus—"and I'm a friend of Jeff's from graduate school."

"Oh, yes." Warmer now and slightly interrogative.

"Well, I was just passing through on my way to Sequoia Park, and I wondered if Jeff were possibly in the area."

"Oh, no, honey, he's not, he's down in Los Angeles." Her Arkansas accent was very evident now.

"Oh," said Carolyn Benedict, in disappointed tones. "Well, maybe I can catch him on my way back. Does he get up here often?"

"Hardly ever, dear. He's very busy, you know. He hasn't been up to stay since March."

Simple declarative sentences that hinted at pride in Jeff's success, resentment that he didn't visit his parents, defensiveness at revealing this to a stranger—but Claire was unmoved by family dynamics. "Thank you, thank you, Mrs. Green," she said fervently—but Dora was engaged in a muffled conversation on the other end.

"Yes . . . yes . . . well, she don't care about that . . . all right, all right, I'll tell her" she heard, and then Mrs. Green came back on the line.

"My husband wanted me to tell you," she said with the chronic suppressed exasperation of forty years of marriage, "that Jeff was here a week ago. But that was only for one night; he was on his way to San Francisco, and he just stopped by. He hardly ever does that. Would you like his number in Los Angeles, dear?"

What I'd like to know is the date of that visit, whether he went out during the evening, whether his clothes were wet when he returned—and why he didn't tell me this when we were making out on his couch. "No thanks, I have it," she said brightly. "Just thought I might catch him. Bye."

She replaced the receiver very gently and nearly jumped out of her skin when it rang immediately.

It was Sam.

"Did you tell Terry you'd take him to the library?"

"Yes, as a matter of fact—"

"Well, he keeps talking about it.

"Really?" she said.

"Yeah. Should I tell him you can't do it?"

"No . . . no, I'd like to. I'm just surprised that he wants to go with me. How about next week sometime?"

"They're leaving next Friday," he said coldly.

"*What?*" Of course, they had to be back in Los Angeles right after Labor Day for the start of school. She had just forgotten it was so soon.

"—Labor Day," Sam was saying, and she interrupted him.

"Right, right, I know." She thought for a moment. "The main library is open until six tonight. Why don't I come by around three-thirty and pick him up? And Shannon, if he wants to go."

"How about me, if I want to go?"

"No." She relented and added, "I'd feel like I was being evaluated. We can talk afterward, if you want."

Shannon did want to go. But what both boys wanted most of all was to see her ankle again.

"You know, the swelling's gone down quite a bit," she warned as she sat on the front porch steps and unwrapped it. "It's not as spectacular as it was."

True enough, and they stared with undisguised disappointment at her bare ankle, only slightly thicker than normal.

"It looks sort of ordinary," Shannon said sadly.

"Sorry. It still hurts, though," she said in consolation, reswaddling the foot.

In the car Terry bragged, "If I'd seen that snake, he woulda been history!"

"If *I'd* seen him, he woulda been outta here!" Shannon countered.

"Woulda been toast!"

"Woulda been road kill!"

"Woulda been . . . woulda been . . . toad snot!" Terry yelped, inspired at the eleventh hour.

"*Toad snot!*" Claire exclaimed, and burst out laughing— which of course drove the boys into a frenzy of renewed, if inferior, efforts.

"Worm snot!"

"Worm shit!"

"Bat puke!"

"Cat piss!"

"Cow fart!"

"You fart!"

"No, *you* fart!" Shannon yelled, socking his brother . . . somewhere; Claire heard it land.

And now they were totally out of control, screaming and raining blows on each other on the back seat. What would Sam do? What would *Linda* do?

She bore it for as long as she could, then pulled over and stopped the car. Quietly but with great authority, she hoped, she explained that this was a dangerous road, that she couldn't drive with them screeching and fighting, that in any case they would have to be quiet in the library, that if they couldn't calm down, they wouldn't *go* to the library. There was an instant of silence during which she asked Terry about his Transformers.

The god of stepmothers and baby-sitters must have been watching over her, because it worked. They talked about Transformers for the rest of the journey. At the library Shannon played with the PC and then found biographies of baseball players, astronauts, Nazis, and other role models, while Terry hunted down books about dinosaurs. Claire introduced him to *The Shy Stegosaurus of Cripple Creek*. Both of them read to themselves on the way home.

I can see this can be done, I can see that, she thought. You just have to give yourself up to it. Sacrifice to advance the runners. Even I could do it for a few days, but—day after day? Week after week? How do people sustain it?

"How was it?" asked Sam, who met her at the front door.

"Fine. First they were monsters, then they were angels."

"In other words, totally typical." He smiled fondly.

There, she thought, seeing that smile, that's how he does it; that's what makes it tolerable; that's what I'm missing. He loves them. I don't. I could get to like them, but how do I know a priori that I could love them? Just because I love him, and he loves them? If A loves B and B loves C, then A loves C? Uh-uh.

Unconscious of these hardhearted thoughts, Sam sat down on the porch, his long legs spilling down the step, and patted the floor next to him.

"Sit with me for a minute."

She lowered herself slowly, as wary of his intentions as of her ankle.

"How's the leg?"

"Hurts. I don't know what I would have done without this, though," tapping his grandfather's cane on the step below.

"Still at the motel?"

"Still at the motel." They certainly were being cordial.

He nodded, started to speak, halted, began again. "Look. I've been thinking a lot about this," he said in a stifled voice. "About our conversation yesterday. About . . . about our relationship."

"Me too," she replied; he looked relieved and immediately relaxed, assuming she would take charge of the conversation, fill the silence as always. But after a week of fencing with Tom Martelli, she had learned how to wait. So she waited.

And waited.

She almost cracked, but she held on, and eventually he said reluctantly, "What have you been thinking?"

"You first," she said. "You introduced the subject."

"Oh. Well. Basically . . . basically, I've been thinking how much I miss you." Pause. Swallow. "And that I'd like you to come back."

"And Linda?" she asked after a moment, strangely detached.

"I guess I love Linda, too. But I'm willing to stop, uh, seeing her."

Seeing her. Going with him. So many euphemisms for a simple physical act. "But what about the boys?"

"Well, that's the problem, isn't it?" he said, becoming agitated. "I mean, I'm supposed to rank all these feelings. Like: I want you in my life, and that means losing Linda. Okay, I accept that. But if I have to choose between you and the boys . . . I have to choose them, Claire. But it's *you* who's set it up as a zero-sum game!"

"You mean you can't have everything you want."

"I can't have anything I want!" he exclaimed, then took a deep breath. "What I want is you, and the boys for as long as I can get them. And you have to tell me if that's a possible combination."

"What about them? Do they get to vote between me and Linda?"

"No," he said. "This is my decision. That's what I've figured out in the last day. Oh, Claire," he said, suddenly earnest, "they can *like* you! I've seen that! And you could like them if you'd give them a chance."

"I am starting to like them, Sam." It was true, she realized; now that she was less afraid of them, as long as she could curb their excesses she enjoyed their loony energy (this was probably the trick to coexisting with males of all ages). "They're nice—basically nice—funny kids. But I don't know if I can love them, and I don't think I have enough of a . . . a nurturing instinct, to be a parent *without* loving them."

"You could try," he mumbled.

"If I tried, it would be because I love *you.*"

There was a long silence. "And you don't love me enough," he said finally, and she didn't contradict him. Everything in her was screaming *Say yes, you moron! You want this man; a week ago you would have crawled on your belly to Bakersfield to hear this! Say yes, you'll come back, you'll love him, you'll love his kids! Just . . . say . . . yes!*

But she didn't. Instead she rose and made her way painfully down the steps and stood with her back to him, watching the evening creep up the hill.

"I love you, Sam. But I don't trust you." She took a breath. "I don't think you know what you want. I mean, only yesterday you told me how much you loved Linda. And now, just because I had a good day with the boys, you've switched allegiance. You don't seem to be behaving very rationally."

"Well, you'll have to do the analytical thinking for both of us."

"I will," she replied, ignoring the sarcasm. "I think there are two problems here."

"Only two?"

"Well, maybe three. Three major ones, anyway—"

"Do you have a written outline?"

"Look, I'm in pain here, too!" she flashed. "And this is the way I handle it, okay?"

He subsided, and after a moment she continued.

"Three problems. First is the kids. But the kids are academic until we consider problem number two, which is whether we are going to stay together. Now this isn't a question of love, per se; I know I love you, and you've said you love me—"

"I do."

"Okay. As a matter of fact, I believe you. But obviously *something* is wrong, and I think there are two issues: trust and compatibility. Well, actually, they're related, and they both have to do with understanding, so maybe *understanding* is the major point here. I mean, can we understand each other well enough to have confidence in each other? Can we make each other happy? Do we want the same things—"

"Which brings us back to the kids again. Maybe you need a flow chart—"

"Yes, but let's leave the kids for a minute—"

"I mean, maybe the kids aren't a major heading at all, maybe they're just an 'issue.'" His voice was rising. "And maybe the fact that I love you is a subissue—"

"Sam—"

"Or a footnote. Or—"

He suddenly broke off and took a long, ragged breath. When she turned around he was sitting in a posture of utter desolation, knees drawn up to his chest, face buried. She had never seen him look so disconsolate.

"Oh, God," she groaned, scrambling back up the stairs as far as his feet and wrapping her arms around his legs. "Oh, God, Sam, please don't be sad! We'll talk about this some more, we'll . . . we'll work something out, okay?"

Weasel words, "work something out"; the adult equivalent of "there, there." He didn't lift his head, but she thought he nodded, and after several minutes she released him and drove home.

Chapter 17

The damn phone was ringing as she struggled to unlock the lab door on Monday morning. The door swung open, she dropped her cane, picked up the cane, and dropped the keys; meanwhile her head was pounding from a miserable, sleepless night and the usual four A.M. wake-up call at the motel and the phone was shrilling like a cicada—only to cease, she knew, just as she made it to her desk.

"Hello?" she said breathlessly.

It was Tom Martelli. The medical examiner had done some tests on Perez and Cedillo. Was she interested?

Very interested indeed, she said, headache forgotten.

"Near as they can tell after all this time, Perez's cholin—cholinesterase level was about forty percent of normal. Typical of chronic exposure, the ME said: not low enough to kill him, but enough to make him sick. They haven't finished the cholinesterase on Cedillo yet, because they found something else that they're analyzing."

Wait. Prod. "What?"

"Traces of an organophosphate. On his skin."

"On his *skin*?"

"Yep. Mostly on his face, including inside his mouth and nostrils. Probably traces in his stomach, too, ME says."

"As if he had actually been sprayed," Claire said thoughtfully.

"Yep."

"Did they identify the pesticide?"

"Not yet. Tomorrow. Oh, and Cummings passed on another tidbit. Don't think it has much bearing on anything, but remember I said Cedillo had been fighting in a bar the night he was killed?"

"Yes?"

"Well, they finally ID'ed the other fella, the *huero*. Little bantam rooster of a guy, name of—"

"Wayne Harris."

"Yeah," he said, floored. "How'd you know?"

"Women's intuition," she said nastily, and let him hang there a moment. But she couldn't carry it off, she had to brag. "He's one of my clients. He had a cut under his eye, and I saw him in front of El Aguila one night. I just had a . . . a hunch, I guess you'd call it."

"A hunch," he repeated, half mocking. "Okay, Ms. Drew. Score one for you. But tell Harris to stick to his pistachios."

"Walnuts."

"Whatever. Bye."

"Oh! Tom!" she said, just catching him. "Levine's mother. When did you say she's coming?"

"Um—tomorrow, I think. Yeah. Tomorrow. Had a hell of a time with her; she wanted to take the body right away. Something about Jewish custom, they bury their people right away. But I explained about the autopsy and all, and she agreed to wait."

"Would you do me a big favor? Ask her where her son grew up?"

"Where . . . Oh. Right. You still thinking he might be your pal. Sure, I'll ask her. Bye."

She'd just begun to process this new data when the phone rang again.

"Finally!" Steve Ashe greeted her. "I've been calling your number at Sam's, and you're never there."

She could hear the question in his voice—a feeble flicker, no doubt, of the white-hot curiosity of his wife.

"Oh, hi, Steve. Sorry; I've just been incredibly bus—"

"I'm glad I caught you," he interrupted, uncharacteristically. "I tried to reach you yesterday. I really need to talk to you. What the hell is going on with Jeff Green and this guy Levine?"

Silence. Her watch—analog; she was a sentimentalist—seemed monstrously loud. "What do you mean?"

"I *mean*," he said, overemphatic with distress, "that per your request I started to ask around, very discreetly, to see if there was a connection, and the next thing I know Jeff is asking *me* about this Levine character, and about you, and the *next* thing I know the fucking *police* are here, questioning me and everyone in the UCLA History Department! That was Friday."

Tick. Tick. "So was there?"

"Was there what?"

"A connection."

This time the silence was on his end. "Ask him," he said finally. "I gave him your number at the lab. He's going to call you. Soon. Goddamn it, Claire," he burst out, "I feel like I betrayed my best friend!"

"Steve," she began, but he had hung up.

Now there was no question of working. But she couldn't leave, either; she had to wait for Jeff's call—which came in about two minutes; he must have been trying while she talked to Steve.

"Claire," he said without preamble, "I have to see you."

"I know."

"I can drive up this afternoon."

"No—no, there's nowhere we can talk. Let's meet halfway."

"Bakersfield, then," he said. "After work. You know Polly's House of Pies? It's on California, between a Ramada Inn and a Sir Lube."

Sir Lube? She giggled, then sobered immediately. "I'll find it. I have to talk to some growers this afternoon; and then it'll take me an hour and a half to get there."

"I can make it by six-thirty."

At seven she pulled into Polly's and looked for a sexy red sports car, then realized she was on the wrong tack entirely and searched for something sleek and environmentally correct. When she saw the new white Accord with ski rack and Amnesty International bumper sticker, she knew he was there.

The restaurant was crowded, but he'd found a corner table that was relatively secluded, and two green Beck's bottles suggested he'd been waiting for a while. He rose to greet her, stylish as a *GQ* cover in white pants and short-sleeved cocoa-colored shirt that set off the warm tones of his skin, and when he took her hand her heartbeat and respiration took off in a way that was totally inappropriate to the circumstances, said circumstances being 1) that she was in love with someone else; and 2) that he was just possibly a ruthless killer. (She had to remind herself of the latter, because she couldn't really believe it.)

As they settled, a noisy extended family seated themselves at the next table, and Jeff winced.

"I really need some privacy for this," he said. "Would you mind if we went next door to the motel? I rented a room in case this place was too crowded."

Despite everything, some insane part of her wanted very much to retire to a motel room with Jeff Green. But it was a part she managed to ignore.

"I'd rather not," she said, and he looked pained; in fact, as she became accustomed to the restaurant's dim light, she could see that he was a little less robust than formerly, his face fine drawn and pale—which made him seem, for the first time, vulnerable, and thus all the more attractive. They can always get to you through pity, she thought, remembering Sam, and waited stolidly for him to begin.

"I was . . . less than honest with you," he said, pitching his voice below the boisterous crowd next door. "About Jonathan Levine. I guess you know that."

"I know something, yes," she answered cautiously.

"We were friends once. Good friends. I had no idea that he'd been mur—" He stopped, apparently having trouble with the sentence. "That he'd died," he said finally, "until that night the four of us had dinner."

"Were you still friends?"

"No. We had a falling-out, some years ago," taking a sip of beer and clearing his throat.

"Jon and I were sort of allies as graduate students," he continued. "We were the two lone leftists in a very conservative Department of History. But there were some bad feelings over . . . an incident"——a woman, Claire deduced——"and somehow a harmless academic competition got out of control."

He stopped and took another drink of beer, while Claire's own graduate school experience and hyperactive imagination supplied narrative details: Jeff's star rising in the department while Jon's fell; Jeff, for whom everything came easy; Jeff, with his sharp, agile mind, his looks, his charm, his talent for cultivating the right people, despite his radical politics. (She remembered marveling at the half-gainers and twists and pikes he'd done off the high board at the pool the other day. Jeff was a man who always knew where he was in space.)

And Jon——

What had Jon been like? There were no hints from his pleasant, unremarkable face. A nice guy, Perlmutter had said, and a good journalist, but that was later. In grad school he might have been slower than Jeff: a plodder, perhaps, maybe even stubborn and truculent. Pertinacious. He might have made enemies.

And, in slightly paranoid fashion, might have fastened his resentment on Jeff.

"If Jon had spent a little more time on his own work," Jeff was saying with unconscious condescension, "and a little less attacking my papers, he might have done well. But he never finished his dissertation." Eventually Levine had had to leave school and had become a freelance journalist——never ceasing to dog his rival's footsteps. He was an investigative reporter, after all, and every time Jeff published a paper, Jon was ready with a letter to the editor, ferreting out sloppy research, minor errors, unsupported assertions, etc., etc. Not being the work of a reputable scholar, his charges were generally greeted with superior smirks.

"But it was still extremely annoying," Jeff concluded petulantly.

"A blight on your otherwise shining career," she remarked, and he had the good grace to grin. She was beginning to relax. This was a not unfamiliar story of graduate school——pathetic, but certainly not a motive for murder, at least not of Jon by Jeff. Jon was the man off balance, the man with the grudge, here.

Of course, the victor writes the psychiatric history, whispered a mocking voice. Because the thing was, she temporarily found herself completely on Jon's side. Jeff had begun to remind her of all the cocky, superbright boys of science who had, with superb self-confidence, elbowed past her over the years. She had hated them, she had competed with them, she had alternately detested and desired them.

Jeff might not be a murderer, but he was probably an asshole.

Their neighbors' noise level had risen several decibels, so that they had to strain to talk, and on impulse she said, "Let's go next door and continue this." So they grabbed their unfinished beers and walked across the parking lot to a room in the Ramada Inn.

Claire felt a little queasy as he slammed—but didn't lock— the door behind them and queasier still when he said, "There's a little more to this story." She positioned herself at the circular wood-grained table, next to the door, and Jeff sat across from her.

It seemed that the most serious incident in this long-standing feud had occurred in the past few months. ("I don't know where he found the time," Jeff commented dryly.) In a letter to the *American History Review*, Levine had claimed to have evidence that Jeff's newly published, well-received, and tenure-procuring book, a study of nineteenth-century working-class culture in San Francisco, contained serious factual errors—that Jeff had in fact deliberately misrepresented data from an unpublished thesis that would otherwise have contradicted his conclusions. This was threatening to cause quite a flap in the hermetic world of American Cultural History.

"Was it true?"

"No! Of course not!" he exclaimed. She could hear the echoes of his mother's exasperated tone. "It was a different interpretation, not a misrepresentation! I admit I'm sloppy sometimes, and I don't always cite sources as thoroughly as I might—as Jon has documented so assiduously—but I wouldn't bother to lie about data. I mean, it's just not worth it, it's all too petty." He paused, then continued more slowly, "That's not to say, however, that this couldn't have caused me some problems. Even an unfounded accusation can damage a reputation;

you know, 'If he wasn't guilty he wouldn't be here.' I was angry."

"How angry?"

"I guess that's what the Riverdale police will be asking me," he said grimly. "Not that angry, I assure you. Anyway, I would have been pretty stupid to do Jon any harm. Everyone in the History Department has known about our . . . our problems, for years."

"And yet you pretended to me that you didn't know Jonathan Levine," she said coldly, and realized she was angry, too. Guys like Jeff, these alpha males with their brains and their biceps and their industrial-strength testosterone and their Earrings, they ran the world. The consolation used to be that they dropped dead young of heart attacks, only now they were as fanatic about exercise and diet as they were about everything else, so they could just go on forever, fucking things up, fucking people over, just plain fucking—

"Yes, well, I apologize for that," he said, avoiding her gaze. "At first I was so shocked to hear about Jon that I couldn't say anything, and later . . . later, I don't know. Maybe I was afraid you'd think I was using you to get information about him."

"Which is exactly what I think."

"No, Claire!" He leaned forward across the table for emphasis. "I'd been looking forward to meeting you for months! Steve and Sara kept talking about you."

Oh, well, maybe he wasn't such a bad sort. But she was going to have to speak to Sara—

"And if I'd wanted to winkle something out of you, I would have, um, pumped you"—he pulled an unwilling smile out of her—"pumped you for information. But we didn't even talk about Levine. Right?"

"Right," she said reluctantly. "Do the police know you were up in Tierra Buena last week?"

She held her breath, but he answered immediately.

"I don't know. That was a fluke, it was just for a night, a Friday . . ." His voice trailed away, and she waited for him to ask how *she* knew. Instead, seeing her face, he exclaimed, "Friday night! Is that the night Jon was killed? Jesus Christ, I didn't realize that! Holy shit!"

He slumped down on his chair, looking defeated. So of

course she immediately reached to comfort him, then restrained herself. Presently he straightened and said, "I guess this reinforces my seismic theory of life."

"Your what?"

"Seismology as karma. You know how minor tremors can relieve pressure along a major fault? Well, I've wondered if a series of small unpleasant events reduced the likelihood of major catastrophe. All my life I've been incredibly lucky, and I've always sort of anticipated The Big One."

His grin neutralized any hint of pedantry, and she couldn't help smiling: she couldn't help liking him, Goddamn it. She made one more valiant effort to arrive at the truth.

"Would you take off your shirt?"

He looked startled, as well he might. But she had been eyeing his shoulders for some time now, was incapable of estimating their breadth, and this was the simplest solution.

"Sure," he said readily, "will you take off yours?"

"Maybe sometime. Not right now."

He shrugged, a man used to unorthodox requests of this nature, and unbuttoned his shirt. To avoid putting weight on her bad ankle, the most efficient way to examine him (she told herself) was to straddle his lap, facing him and balancing against his thighs.

"This is nice," he said lightly, eyes closed, arms hanging loosely at his sides as she ran her hands over his shoulders and back. "Sort of a dominatrix mode. You don't by any chance have some stiletto heels?"

"Just steel-toed work boots."

"They'll do."

His shoulders were smooth as the trunk of a manzanita. Whatever else he might have done, he hadn't struggled through her bathroom window, and there was no reason whatsoever to continue doing this, except severe sexual intoxication. Mustering reserves of sobriety, she dismounted and pulled away from him. "Thanks," she gasped.

He looked at her curiously, but all he said was, "Anytime."

They walked together out to the parking lot and paused by the Accord. "You may not believe this," Jeff said, "but I was really sorry to hear Jon had died. I liked Jon; the enmity was entirely on his side."

"Even though he had appointed himself your judge?"

He grimaced. "Maybe I need that. Maybe I need a conscience." He slid onto the front seat. "You'll plead my case with Tom Martelli?"

"I'll tell him what you told me."

He nodded, satisfied, and started the engine.

"Oh. Jeff," she said, leaning on the car door, "that initial disagreement, the one that began the friction between the two of you. Was that about a woman, by any chance?"

"A woman? Oh, no." He paused. "Actually, it may have been about me," revving the motor. "Jon was gay, you know." And he headed south.

Just north of Bakersfield she left the lights of the highway for a two-lane road and a moonless night, and suddenly she had the dislocating sensation of driving through a blizzard. But it was only flurries of insects that flew up into her headlights and smacked wetly against the windshield like flakes; only bare salt-colored earth that gleamed like snowdrifts along the shoulder.

A sharp spasm of longing cramped her heart: to be in the woods in winter, the snow falling silently, sifting into slow white drifts. She suddenly remembered a photograph of herself at age seven or eight—Terry's age, little Jonnie's age—standing knee deep in snow, a goofy hat with flaps on her head and a grin of pure happiness on her face. It was before her father had gotten sick, and he had taken the picture, no doubt darting forward and backward with his light meter until he was satisfied. They had walked along Buttermilk Creek for one whole afternoon, just the two of them, together. She hadn't thought about that for years.

It snowed in the Sierras, but it was a sort of theme-park winter that you visited rather than inhabited, always knowing you could leave. And how could she live without real winter, without its purifying cold? It was encoded into every cell of her body.

How could she ever have believed she could live here?

She must resolve her affairs—Sam, Levine—and leave.

But the air was heavy and warm and smelled of sweet grass, and after a while the moment faded.

She resumed thinking about Jeff.

Another hour of brooding and driving brought her into Parkerville, but no closer to the truth about him. She could see that he might be savage if threatened. He sure as hell wasn't going back to Tierra Buena to grow olives, and she could just barely believe that if he had unexpectedly run into Jon on a Kaweah County back road and they had decided to duke it out, man style . . . Jeff was a powerful man, and the fact that she liked him seemed to weigh against him, if anything. Her standards tended to be aesthetic, not moral, and clearly she was no judge of veracity. Look at Sam. And Tom. Yes, she could imagine a deadly collision of Jeff's anger and resentment and Jon's thwarted ambition and envy and maybe even unrequited passion—

Unrequited passion. Because Jon had been gay; taking this in required a refocusing—nothing major, just a subtle shift in the way she imagined him. In some ways it underscored their weird spiritual affinity—they even lusted after the same man!—and it sure as hell made her speculate about Jeff's own sexual history.

Could Jeff be gay? Was that evening in his apartment merely a brilliant performance aimed at derailing her interest in Levine? At this point she felt that as a matter of principle she should believe anyone capable of anything, but in fact she couldn't. Jeff had desired her, she was certain of that. Still, times being what they were, she was glad she hadn't let her hormones overwhelm her judgment.

But could Jon's sexual identity have any bearing on his death?

Well, it did seem to remove a romantic interest in Luz and consequent jealous boyfriend as a scenario. Did it introduce a motive as well?

Her thoughts turned to that ostentatious womanizer Ruben Moreno. Too ostentatious, perhaps? Maybe, but surely even in a macho culture and a benighted region, fear of exposure as a homosexual no longer represented a motive for murder.

She pulled up in front of the motel at about eleven and saw that Santiago's car was once again parked in front. Looks like Luz has a date, she thought.

A date. As she walked toward number seven, it seemed to

her that there was also something significant about tomorrow's date. August 30 . . . oh, yes. Charlie Padgett would be back from vacation the next day, the thirty-first; she could ask him about the famous anonymous call.

Somehow the prospect made her uneasy.

Chapter 18

"Good morning," she said, and Sam looked up from his newspaper.

"Hi," he returned, and they both smiled at each other, tentatively, wanting to resume diplomatic relations, or at least to declare a cease-fire. But with so much unresolved it was difficult to begin a conversation, so there was a long period of fidgety silence before Claire said:

"This guy Charlie Padgett from County Ag is supposed to call me tomorrow. I want to know if he can identify the person who tipped them off about Bert."

"That should be interesting!" he returned heartily, thankful for the neutral topic.

"Yeah. Though I've been thinking, and I find myself reluctantly agreeing with Ray. The logic of Bert having sprayed his own vineyard—and only two rows of that vineyard—with CONKWEST *after* it had been picked, still defeats me. I hate to say it, but Bert's right, it reeks of a setup."

"Setup!" Sam scoffed. "Who would set up Bert?" Then his face changed, and his mouth snapped shut.

Lost in concentration, Claire didn't notice. "I don't know," she said. "A farmworker, maybe? Trying to avenge mistreatment by Boss Yankovich?"

"Sort of a Rube Goldberg vengeance. Likely to misfire—which it did."

"True. Anyway, maybe the mystery caller's identity will be revealed."

Sam looked away and changed the subject. "Terry's ready

for *Son of Shy Stegosaurus*. You know, he and Shannon had a good time at the library the other day."

"Guess I passed the audition, huh?" she said tartly. "I'm really grateful."

She regretted the barb immediately, but too late; he slammed the desk with his palm. "That's not what I meant!"

"Sorry," she said. Her subconscious evidently hadn't heard about the truce and was still fighting guerrilla actions in the jungle. "I really am sorry, Sam. I . . . you know, I'm still pretty angry, and it's just going to erupt from time to time—"

"Erupt! Oh, no, one thing about you, you never erupt! You just sort of *slice* when I'm not looking, and next thing I know my head's been separated from my body!"

"You're sure it's your *head* you're worried about?" she flashed, stung by his injustice: here she had apologized, had actually admitted fault, and he had simply taken advantage of her weakness! They glared at each other; the arms dealers rubbed their hands in glee as the troops massed along the border.

But after a moment she exhaled slowly and said, "Okay. That's probably true. I can't promise not to slice, but I'll try to be more, um, straightforward." She even managed a conciliatory smile.

There was a brief silence. "Yeah. Okay. Me too," he mumbled.

"I really would like to see the kids again before they leave," she heard herself say, and realized it was true. "Um . . . how about this afternoon?"

"Sure! I—they'd like that."

"Good." She halted at the door. "Oh, by the way. When are you wrapping up your trials on the peaches?"

"Should finish with the yield counts Thursday."

"Thursday."

"Right."

"Then we can eat the fruit."

"Right."

At lunchtime she forced herself to call Bert on his cellular phone and arranged to meet him at his field at five. She had to describe the *Entyloma* project to him and get his approval; this was science biz, and the show must go on. Or, as Sam had once said, "I have to work with these people. Some I like, some I don't."

She had also rescheduled the pugnacious Wayne Harris, who had reported ominous-looking leaves on his walnuts, for this afternoon. So she took a quick drive up toward Alma to take a look, stopping first to replenish her cooler with sodas and ice. On the way to Wayne's orchard she knocked off two Sprites and was still thirsty. It might be the dust—harvest time was a particularly dusty time of year, especially when the mechanical shakers moved like madmen through the nut groves.

Or it might be the weather. All day the air had felt heavy and sultry, and off to the south a band of dark had moved steadily northward as if someone were pulling a window shade from the horizon, until now it covered about a third of the sky. The leading edge was the translucent iron gray of a frozen lake, but behind it came thick, sheenless clouds thinned to tissue at the margins. At home—by which she meant, this time, New England—they would have meant afternoon storm. Here, she wasn't so sure.

For some reason the shoulder along this stretch of the Alta-Woodbury Road was piled to a height of about two feet, as if to repel some very small or very demoralized attackers. The white earth sparkled with what she took for mica, then realized was in fact shards of generations of smashed beer bottles. She pulled off directly across from Harris's orchard, figuring she'd examine his trees as she walked up his drive, but halfway across the road she remembered her clipboard lying on the front seat and turned back.

But she had parked so close to the shoulder that to open the passenger door she had to climb up and around, and her feet sank deep into the soft, glittering earth, and her bad ankle turned under her, and the next thing she knew she was slipping backward toward the irrigation ditch behind her. Cursing, she windmilled her arms and recovered, retrieved her right shoe, which had been sucked off her foot, shook the dirt from it . . . and remembered. Tom had said Levine's car was found along this road.

Levine had gone into the water somewhere close by. This water.

She stared down at the unprepossessing little ditch for a moment, then staggered across the road, shoe in hand. Harris was watching her, grinning. Leaning against his truck and tapping a Marlboro out of a pack, he looked for all the world like an ad for Levi's, or maybe Rodeo—A Man's Cologne.

They walked to the last row of trees, Claire struggling to regain her poise and her shoe, and he pulled down a branch whose leaves were abnormally small and mottled with yellow. "There's more," he said. "And they're all on the outer rows. Just like the blight."

"I better send Jim over," Claire said finally. "But offhand it looks more like a nutritional problem to me. Like maybe these rows didn't get fertilized as thoroughly as the others."

"Yep, that's possible," he admitted. "But I want to make sure nobody's been sprayin' me with some shit when I ain't looking. 'Cause I sure as hell don't want another year like this one."

At two she left Harris and headed for Sam's. She was drenched with sweat and thought she was a little feverish and for a vertiginous moment wondered if she had caught a dose of "the farmworkers' flu" from Dolores.

Then she shrugged it off, deciding it was probably the weather. The black cloud had advanced another two degrees while she had talked to Wayne, and the wind had picked up, whipping leaves against her windshield from the boxcar-size truck packed with grapes rattling along in front of her.

When she turned her attention back to the earth, she was about to pass Tom's office, and in an instant the ugly subject she had evaded all day pushed forward. Jeff— Oh, God, Jeff. She had to talk to Tom about him. Could she tell his story in such a way as to diffuse Tom's suspicions—that is, could *she* lie to *Tom*? Tom was alarmingly shrewd.

Without knowing exactly what she planned to do, she zipped past the turnoff to Sam's and pulled up in front of the police station. But the Blazer was gone, and although she knocked loud and long, nobody responded. Relieved at her reprieve, she headed back to Sam's—only to see Tom barreling by, honking and waving. She almost turned around and followed him back to the station, but she was already late for Sam's, so in one of those fateful moments she had contemplated the previous week, she decided to keep driving.

No blue Valiant in Sam's driveway, but he pulled in shortly after she had arrived. Shannon and Terry burst from the car, and he followed, carrying a paper bag from Toys 'Я' Us.

"What's that?"

"You'll see," he said darkly, disappearing into the house after the boys. The slam of the screen door actually filled her eyes with tears. That sound that had jarred her nerves daily for almost a year; that sound that would no longer be part of her daily experience. . . .

But she had to get a place of her own, of that she was certain. There was too much she didn't know or trust about Sam. They had moved too fast. Understanding, that was the essential problem, or, no, maybe it was communication, maybe communication was the source of understanding. But how about empathy; was communication even possible without empath—

"Yow!" she exclaimed as something hit her with a certain force just under her right breast. A scarlet stain spread across her favorite white T-shirt, the one with silk-screened cowgirls of the thirties, and for a moment she was speechless with anger and confusion and a little fear. Had she been shot? Then where was the pain? And why was Shannon smirking at her from the front porch?

"Hey, remember what we said—no squirting unsuspecting bystanders!" Sam had reemerged from the cabin, still clutching the paper bag, and now he trotted down to examine her shirt. "It's like invisible ink, it disappears," he said. "Supposedly. *Ow!"* He slapped the back of his neck where a splotch of kelly green had just blossomed, and Claire started to laugh.

"Little bastards," he muttered. "They *swore* they wouldn't do this! They've been begging for these things for weeks! *Ouch!"* His arm dripped scarlet, and he backed slowly away from his eldest son. "Now Shannon, I'm unarmed! Remember what we agreed?" Shannon advanced steadily, his eyes cold and merciless, his pudgy hands clutching the very real looking Uzi (Oozy?). Sam's back was against the porch now. "Shannon, I'm warning you . . ."

Suddenly his hand darted into the sack. "Hah!" he cried, pulling out a little water pistol and zapping Shannon with a bolt of blue right on the chin.

Listening to Shannon's loud shrieks of delight and indignation and Sam's triumphant yells, Claire thought tolerantly, Boys and their squirt guns; I won't even bother to consider the Freudian implic—*ouch!*

A direct hit to her rear end; she whirled to see Terry chortling not ten feet behind her.

"Catch!" yelled Sam, tossing her another pistol—an old-fashioned low-tech model of yellow plastic. Instinctively she fired at Terry and caught her persecutor on his right shoulder. And then it was full-scale war.

The adults were outgunned—their little pistols had a range of about half that of the Super-Zappers (that's what they were called, evidently)—but the boys shot at each other more often than at Claire and Sam, so their attention was divided. Even Claire found the action exhilarating and, after the initial shock, refreshing—it was a little like rain—but then she landed on her ankle, which exploded with pain. She hobbled to the porch steps, closely pursued by a manic Terry, who was screaming, "No prisoners no quarter no prisoners no quarter!" until Sam intervened.

"Okay, enough. Back yard," he said. Terry quieted when he saw that Claire was really hurt and chased Shannon to the back of the house.

Claire looked down ruefully at her multicolored shirt—red and green and blue where she had taken some friendly fire (her own, for all she knew). Sam stood in front of her.

"Your leg okay?"

"It's much better, but it's not up to this. I thought the boys and I would have a poignant, dignified afternoon."

He laughed and knelt, gently feeling her ankle. "Dignified? Maybe in ten years. Yeah, it's swollen." The warmth from his hand eased the pain and radiated up her leg. She closed her eyes. When she opened them again he was regarding her thoughtfully. "Your face is blue," he said.

His head was thrown back to look up at her, and his absurd Adam's apple was in relief—sharp, conical, and, at the moment, green. Without thinking she leaned down and ran her tongue around it. "I wonder if this stuff is toxic," she murmured.

"Can't be," he said after a moment. "The FDA protects us."

He bent forward and began to lick the line of blue along her throat, and then, suddenly, he was half kneeling between her legs, pressing hard against her while she grabbed the back of his shirt and started to tug it over his head—

All of a sudden he yelped and straightened, and a chorus of snickers erupted around them.

His own son had Super-Zapped him between his bare shoulder blades.

Caught thus in flagrante and halfway between anger and embarrassment, the adults scrambled to their feet, Claire flushing under her blue to a no doubt becoming magenta. Terry and Shannon were doubled over in giggles, which eventually spread to their elders.

"I have to go anyway," Claire said when she caught her breath. "I have to go meet Bert Yankovich." She paused. "Listen, what are the boys doing tomorrow?"

"Thought I'd take 'em with me on some field calls," he said. "Why?"

"Well, why don't you bring them by the lab?" she said recklessly. "They might enjoy it. Especially Shannon."

"Really?" he said, surprised. "Great! And I'll catch you later!" It was a promise and a mock threat.

"Bye, kids! I'll see you tomorrow!" she called merrily, and started down the hill feeling giddy and feverish. But it was frequently the case that her mood descended with altitude, as if every pound per square inch pressed down on the top of her head like a heavy thumb. So at fifteen hundred feet she thought, *Will* Sam "catch" me? At thirteen hundred, Do I even want him to? They certainly had wanted it thirty minutes ago, but that was in the grip of battle lust. . . . And finally, when she reached the highway, Will my shirt ever be white again? (The colors had faded but were still visible.)

Thus did her spirits descend like a zeppelin with a slow leak. A low rumbling, which she took for a flat, only deepened her depression. Great, she thought resignedly, the perfect end to a perfect afternoon . . . Then she realized it was thunder. The sheet of black was now nearly overhead, parked neatly at the Kaweah County border. Tropical storm, she decided, feeling an obligatory pang of concern for local growers, and then she nearly whooped aloud. Rain for dinner!

Chapter 19

There was no sign of Bert's pickup when she pulled up by the alfalfa field. It wouldn't be the first time she had been stood up on a field call, but it was just past five and he might very well show. Remembering the soft silt along this road, she opened her trunk and changed into boots, wincing a little at the throb of her right foot as she stuffed it into stiff leather. Automatically she pocketed her field kit and grabbed her cane.

She surveyed the scene—cautiously, for she had suddenly recalled that this was her first actual visit since she'd found Levine's body *(Don't look at the canal)*, her previous attempt having been short-circuited by a disastrous cruise through a certain neighborhood in North Parkerville *(Don't think about Linda)*. To kill time, and memory, she turned away from the irrigation ditch, toward the rows of grapevines on the near side. This wasn't much better *(Hector Cedillo had died in a vineyard)*, but the vines themselves were interesting enough that she was soon distracted, and she started walking along a dry furrow.

The mountains were beginning to emerge. No matter how "hazy" (read smoggy) the day—and despite the oncoming rain, today had been opaque—around this time the long rays of sunset threw the Sierra into relief, a kind of benediction. But even obscured, the mountains defined the immediate landscape because they determined the movement of water. Pour a bucketful onto apparently level land and watch where it went: that was west. Rivers flowed west.

So, too, Claire now moved west, between two rows of rococo curling tendrils and strongly veined dull green leaves that were just beginning to brown and fray at the edges. Between the rows wild lettuce had bolted, sending up brittle scaffolding that towered over her, and in the heavy, expectant air the vines had an almost hallucinatory clarity. She wondered again if she was sick. Or poisoned.

The field had been picked, but one bunch of luscious purple fruit glowed from the depths of the vines, and she stepped onto the central berm and stretched out her hand. Given what she now knew about pesticides, a snack in the field was ill advised, so it was just as well that she was diverted by another mutter of thunder. Just as she was wondering whether she should go on home, wherever that was, and reschedule her meeting, a pickup rocked to a stop behind the Toyota, and Bert stepped out.

"Howdy," she called. "Hope you got your crop in!"

"Don't think the rain'll amount to much," he replied, approaching the vineyard. She moved to meet him, then stopped at the crackle of paper underfoot. Curious, she lowered herself with her cane and retrieved it. It was an aging notification of spray date and safe entry date: this vineyard had been sprayed July 1 and therefore was declared safe to enter thirty days later, August 1 blah blah blah—

It was the same handbill that Levine had used as a bookmark.

Did that mean anything other than that Levine had been in this vineyard at some time?

"Whatcha got there?" asked Bert, who had strolled up beside her.

"Just an old spray warning," she said, balling the handbill to toss away. It was unexpectedly stiff, and she uncrumpled it and examined it.

Yes, she was right. It was actually two flyers, one stapled on top of another. She pried them apart. Underneath was an identical notice, except that the dates were different: July and August *10*," not 1.

"Funny," she remarked, "they must have got the date wrong." Or, more likely, the spraying had been rescheduled, and they had changed the dates. . . .

She stared at the handbills again, temporarily forgetting

Bert's presence. What if this were no innocent mix-up? What if someone had deliberately backdated these notices, so he could harvest his crop sooner? Before, for example, a freak storm blew up from the tropics?

That would be a serious matter, she thought, slowly folding the notices and pocketing them. That would endanger workers' health. The thirty-day waiting period was probably too short anyway, and sending someone in a field before whatever-it-was—MONITOR, HAZARD, ARMAGEDDON—had broken down was irresponsible at best, criminal at worst.

Was *this* why Levine had saved the handbill? Had he discovered that someone had been altering spray dates and exposing laborers to high levels of pesticides? The farmworkers' flu . . .

And wait—August first.

Juan Perez had died on August first.

Had Levine linked the death of his neighbor's husband to the illegal backdating? In fact, had Perez died *here*? Who owned this vineyard?

The sound of a throat being cleared brought her back to the present. Bert was standing patiently. His face seemed to bulge and shift shape while she watched. She pressed the back of her hand against her forehead; it was clammy.

"Sorry, Bert, I—"

Bert! The unlovely blurt of a name was a revelation. *Bert* owned this vineyard, just as he owned the alfalfa field next to it! He had told her so the day she had visited him!

Then it was Bert who had lied about his spray dates, Bert who had sent Juan Perez into his death on August 1, Bert whom Levine had confronted that night in the walnut grove up the road . . . and Bert's huge hands that had closed around Levine's neck and held his head underwater. Abruptly she was reliving that nightmare of helplessness.

All this time Bert simply waited, in itself out of character, a curious expression on his face. He's watching me, she thought suddenly; he's waiting to see if this registers, if I figure it out. And when I do . . . what? The canal?

"Um, Bert," she said shakily, "I'm not feeling very well. I wonder if we could reschedule this for another day."

"Sure," he said politely. *(Politely? Bert?)* "Can I give you a ride anywhere?"

"Oh . . . no, you go on. I'll be okay."

"You better let me take you," he said insistently. "Your color's not so good."

I'm probably still blue, she realized with a touch of hysteria. "No—really. I'll be fine."

But Bert was not to be put off. He moved forward and clamped a hand around her upper arm. "I'll take you."

"Okay," she said, "maybe that's a good idea. Thanks." His eyes narrowed at the sudden acquiescence. "It's just my . . . my sunglasses!" she exclaimed. "I dropped my sunglasses at the end of the row. Hang on a minute while I get them." He appeared to look at her suspiciously, to look at her cane, to look at the cars parked a good one hundred yards behind them, and then (so it seemed to her) to decide there was no way she could escape.

"Sure. Go on."

She hobbled with exaggerated slowness down the row, rounded the corner, crouched, and waited.

After two minutes she heard an uncertain "Claire?" and peered cautiously through the curtain of leaves. Bert had begun to stalk purposefully down the row of vines just to the north of her. "You okay?" Her heartbeat took off and she pressed herself back, into the thick foliage. At that moment Bert called her name again.

He was moving closer and closer, calling her name—softly, menacingly—and then he was only ten feet away; any moment he would see her huddled there. A flock of crows seeking fruit swirled aimlessly above the vines, then lit in one quick movement like smoke sucked in.

The psychedelic vines reached for her, curled around her. A monstrously loud crack sounded just behind her ear, and she jumped. Then something bounced off her nose, and for a moment she thought she had been Super-Zapped again, only this time for real. . . . But it was just a raindrop. Now scattered drops fell lightly around her, rattling the leaves and triggering little explosions of dust where they hit the ground. A drop beaded up on the soft powder right by her foot, and she stared at it, mesmerized.

Suddenly Bert was directly opposite her, with only the lattice of grapevines between them. In a moment he would round the corner and see her there. She stared through her frame of grape leaves at those huge, murderous hands. . . .

I'm ba-a-ack, Jonathan seemed to whisper to her fevered consciousness.

"No!" she heard herself yell. "Not again!" And with berserker strength she rammed her cane through the vines, tangling his legs.

He fell heavily. By then she was around the end of the row, beating him on his back and arms with the cane, inspired by a fury maybe not wholly her own. "You son of a bitch!" she sobbed. "You son of a bitch!"

A gallant ambush, but doomed, given the relative difference in strength, size, experience, and aggression—even allowing for the supernatural on Claire's side. She landed a couple of solid but hardly disabling blows before Bert, with humiliating effortlessness, grabbed her stick, wrenched it away from her, and clambered to his feet. His face was dangerously red, his sides heaved, he positively trembled with pure fury.

"You son of a bitch," she panted, "you killed Jon Levine."

"You're insane," he growled between gritted teeth and twisted her arm behind her. "You must be sicker'n I thought!"

For a moment her righteous rage was suspended, and she saw her fear and suspicion rationally for the sheer speculation it was. But then the mists closed again. And in any case, whether or not Bert had killed Jon Levine, it seemed that he might kill *her,* or certainly hurt her. Because now she had made Bert mad, and when Bert was mad anything could happen. Anything. Right now he was cursing her and gripping her arm so tightly it seemed he penetrated the bone, and she whimpered in pain. *The knife,* a voice whispered. *Use your knife.* And suddenly she remembered her buck knife, slipped carelessly into her back pocket a few moments ago. If she could just reach it with her left hand . . .

She did. While Bert continued to rave, she snaked her arm behind her back, unsnapped the sheath, and grasped the handle. . . . *Now stick it in his fat gut,* the voice said—and she balked.

And then it was too late. His eyes widened for a moment, then he grabbed her left wrist and whipped her arm down sharply across his knee. The knife flew through the air, her eyes filled with tears, and she cried out. But the knee had given her an idea. Was she strong enough to bring her own knee up into his groin—

"Claire?"

They both heard it. Bert whirled, and then she heard something else—the rustle of footsteps in dry leaf litter.

"Need a wrestling partner, Bert?" a familiar voice drawled. "I could find you a better match." And Tom Martelli strolled forward, followed by Enrique and another man she recognized as a forensics expert who'd worked on poor old Larry McKeever's car last year.

Bert seized the offensive. "Martelli, this crazy female attacked me for no reason," he said. "Started pounding me with that cane. It's a wonder my skull ain't broke."

Martelli looked at her. "That right?"

"Yes, I did hit him—but it wasn't for no reason. I was afraid he was going to hurt me because I discovered . . . that is, I realized," she faltered. "I think he killed Jonathan Levine," she finished.

"Really," Martelli answered with what was probably sarcasm. She tried to mount a defense, but suddenly all she wanted to do was nap. Barring that, she simply sat down right where she was, in the still dry dirt (Bert had called it: the rain had already stopped), turned her head aside—and threw up.

Santiago stared at her in dismay. "Sorry. I'm all right," she mumbled, embarrassed, but actually feeling a little better—except for the throb in her arm and her wrist and her ankle.

Tom shot an appraising glance in her direction. "I got a few questions for you." (*He* had a few questions for *her*? How the hell had he managed to show up in the middle of nowhere at the crucial moment?) "But they can wait till tomorrow. You don't look too good," he added, peering at her in the waning light. "Why don't you go home? And if you want to lodge a formal complaint against Ms. Sharples"—turning to Bert—"I'll be happy to take it. Right after we finish with your truck."

"My *truck*!" Bert growled.

"Yes!" Claire exclaimed, reviving. "Jon and Bert sat and talked in his truck before Bert killed him!"

"You keep your hands off my truck!" Bert was saying.

Martelli ignored him. "How do you know?" he asked her.

I dreamed it. "It . . . it just must have happened that way."

"Mmm. Morrie, what do you think?" he called to the forensics person, a big sandy-haired, shambling man who was circling Bert's pickup warily, as if it might suddenly roar to life.

"I think it would be a hell of a lot easier in daylight. He's already been driving the damn thing for two weeks, right? So one more night won't make any difference."

Martelli nodded. "Agreed. Drive it on in to Riverdale. And Morrie—wear gloves!" Morrie looked at him sourly and he chuckled.

Bert was unaccustomed to being snubbed, and now he exploded. "Martelli, you bastard, you got no right—"

"I got a warrant, Bert," Tom said mildly, holding it up like a flimsy cross before a vampire. "You know, you really ought to watch that temper. It's going to get you into trouble one of these days. Back off!" he said with sudden sharpness, and turned to Claire.

"Since I can't help but notice that you're still here, why don't you go ahead and tell me how you did come to conclude that Mr. Yankovich here killed Mr. Levine?"

In reply she tossed him the wad of folded flyers and prepared to explain their significance.

"Mmmm," he grunted. "Backdated. And it's the same one Levine had. This here is Bert's vineyard, too," he added, thereby short-circuiting two-thirds of her explanation.

She was duly impressed, not to say mystified, but said merely, "Yes. And I think . . . thought . . . Jonathan Levine knew, and threatened Bert with exposure, and Bert killed him."

"What the hell—" Bert said, and Tom motioned to Santiago, who herded him to the Blazer where he couldn't overhear.

"You thought that purely on the basis of these?" Tom asked.

"Well . . ." No need to mention dreams and/or hallucinations. "Yes."

"I mean, Bert didn't *say* anything, while you were whanging on him? Nothing incriminating?"

"Um . . ." She searched her memory. Bert hadn't said anything that wouldn't be expected from a man defending himself from a sudden, pointless attack. "Not that I remember, no."

Tom looked at her for a moment. Then, "Shee-it!" he said disgustedly, and fell silent.

Luckily Claire couldn't feel more chastened on this subject than she already did, so after a moment she ventured, "But why did you come out here? To the vineyard?"

"Oh. Well, I was looking for you, actually. I wanted to tell you that I talked with Gary Wilson, the second person on Levine's scrap of paper—"

"The man in the state attorney general's office," she said.

"Right. And he remembered Levine's call. Said Levine had asked him about the penalties for backdating spray notification."

"Oh!" That's why Martelli had understood the implications of the flyers so quickly. She felt relieved. But he still hadn't really answered her question—

"I passed you on the road a couple of hours ago," Martelli was saying. "Looked like you were headed up to Sam's. But Sam said you were coming out here to meet Bert, so I just thought I'd cruise out here, too."

All the way out here, with a storm coming, just to pass on this information? And with a warrant? She glanced at him sharply; he must have had his suspicions about Bert, too. But he looked as bland as ever.

"What *are* the penalties?" she asked.

"That can wait," he said. "Let's get out of here before we get poured on—and before Bert's truck gets a bath. Go on home now," he told her. "I'll call you tomorrow."

She headed slowly for her car but after two steps remembered Sam's cane and her buck knife. A few moments of searching, and she spotted the cane at the end of the row of vines: a ray of sunset had escaped from under the sheet of clouds and glinted on its embossed head. It did Sam's grandfather proud today, she thought; it gave a scoundrel a sound thrashing.

Because he was certainly a scoundrel if he had backdated those notices. He just might not be a murderer.

There was no sign of her knife, though; that was her penalty for drawing it in anger. Bert must have knocked it clear into Kern County when he thought she was going to eviscerate him, which of course she would never have done. . . .

Would she?

She might have, she realized with astonishment. She had been so sure that he had murdered Jonathan Levine and was about to do the same to her . . . but now she wondered if she had needed a couple of aspirin instead of a knife.

No one could call it cozy, perhaps, but the Vacancy did have that humblest of comforts, familiarity. In one practiced, balletic movement Claire opened the door of number seven, stepped back to let the fetid air roll out, and squatted on the front porch. She tried to ignore the dull throb of her head.

She suddenly realized that she had been hearing soft snuffling off to her right for some time. In the dark she could just make out a dim form in front of number six.

"Luz?" she called, but the sobbing stopped, and the figure rose and disappeared through the door.

Her own febrile dreams sputtered through a troubled night, but Jonathan Levine did not expropriate her unconscious. Did that mean (she wondered groggily at four when she woke)— did that mean that Levine had been killed by Bert, and his spirit was therefore now at peace? Or, more rationally, that deep down she *believed* his murderer had been found, and therefore *she* was at peace?

Outside, although it was still pitch dark, people emerged from doorways in a parody of suburbia: jeans with bandannas stuffed in the pocket and shirts with sleeves torn out and straw cowboy hats, instead of three-piece suits; paper lunch sacks instead of attaché cases. Martín had a cap that said "Ortega's Bait and Beer"; Dolores's hair was done in two braids, country fashion, and tucked under a red kerchief.

Claire wondered if she had been to the clinic to be treated for organophosphate exposure. "Dolores," she called, then paused to compose the sentence in baby talk. "Um . . . ¿Has visitado la clínica otra vez?"

Dolores looked quickly at Martín, then answered politely,

"Sí, me dieron medicina y me siento mejor. Gracias," and walked toward the road, where a battered pickup was idling.

They gave me medicine and I feel better, Claire translated, suddenly certain that she was lying. But why? Then she realized that if Dolores were diagnosed with pesticide poisoning, they would yank her from the fields. No work, no food, as Luz had said so succinctly. But surely she would get workman's comp . . . or would she, if she were undocumented? Sam would know—

Cursing silently, she squelched the thought. There were sources of information other than Sam! There was Luz, for example, who had just stepped onto the porch and was handing what looked like a fried egg wrapped in a tortilla to Martín. He too headed for the pickup, now stuffed with four or five people.

She approached Luz, then halted uncertainly. In the graying light her neighbor's face was old and haggard, and Claire suddenly remembered last night's quiet sobbing.

"Is . . . is anything wrong?" she asked timidly, but at that moment a baby began to cry, and Luz rushed into number six.

In the faint hope of a few hours of sleep snatched before work, Claire had just withdrawn to her room when she heard her name.

Luz stood in the doorway, clutching Juanito and looking drawn and desperate.

"Claire . . . I don't know what should I do," she said in a strained voice.

"Luz! For God's sake, what's wrong? Come on in, sit down!" She indicated the chair that was no more. "Oh. Let's go outside, it's cooler anyway." They perched on the edge of the porch, and Claire again said, "Now. What's wrong?"

"It's Enrique."

"Enrique?" she repeated in surprise. Santiago had seemed like a solution, not a problem.

"*Sí.* He want me to talk about Ruben Moreno and the girls at Contessa. He say they can put Ruben in jail for es . . . esexual harass," she said carefully.

"Well, that's true. If he's threatening women to get them to sleep . . . to go with him, that's illegal."

"But I lose my job for talking about this."

"They can't fire you for testif—" She stopped, realizing that maybe they couldn't fire her, but they could probably deport her. Or did Luz have papers? She had no idea; it had never seemed to matter.

"—I lose my job," Luz was saying, as if Claire hadn't spoken, "and maybe I don't get another one, people think I make trouble, and then how I take care of Juanito and Ana? *¿Ay, Juan,"* she said brokenly, *"porqué me abandonaste?"*

Why did you leave me? The primal cry of the bereaved. Claire laid a tentative hand on her shoulder. "Luz, I can't tell you what to do. But you know what Ruben is doing is wrong. He's hurting these girls. What if Ana were all grown up, and he was doing this to her?"

A low blow, and she regretted it; Luz's face crumpled, and she dug the knuckles of her fist into her forehead in anguish. Still Claire pressed on, almost against her will, as if condemned to make the politically correct argument regardless of pity and personal feelings.

"There are lawyers who will take your case for free," she said. "And Ricky—Enrique and I can help you. But it's up to you to decide," she ended, mouthing the platitude with a certain distaste.

"I think I decide to go back to Mexico," Luz muttered without looking up.

When Claire left for work, for once her mind was full of someone else's problems.

Chapter 20

As Claire turned south toward the station, the sun cleared the crest of Slate Mountain and stabbed her left eye, and at that moment she remembered that the kids were coming to the lab. She also recalled that several people at work commuted up and down the snaky curves of Highway 170. If she were to stay here in Kaweah County, maybe it was time to ascend to the mountains.

Her lab was like a high-tech garage sale, filled with a confusion of glassware (beakers, racks of test tubes), arcane machinery (gas spectrometer, microscope), and computers, not to mention sprays of leaves, branches, and fruit—yet when Sam and the boys showed up at ten, both kids were immediately drawn as if by tractor beam to the half-hidden collection of bags of almonds, growing or not growing fungus.

"Eeeuw," said Terry, opening one, "gross!"

"What are they?" asked a fascinated Shannon.

"Almonds," said Claire. "I'm checking to see which ones have a disease. I put them in the bags with a little damp paper and wait to see if a fungus grows on them."

"Cool! What's in these?" pointing to the rack of water blanks.

"Water."

"That's all? Just water?"

"Yep."

"Why do you have it in these test tubes?"

"Well, it's distilled water, and it's all measured out in case I have to dilute something. . . ." She wondered if she were talking over Shannon's head (Terry had already wandered off and was looking through the microscope) and looked around for an illustration. "For example—go open the refrigerator and look on the bottom shelf. See those peaches?" Peaches! she thought suddenly. Shannon nodded. "See how they have soft brown spots? Well, that's a disease, a mold."

This brought Terry back. "Eeeuw, gross!" he said again.

"And if I want to study the mold, I wash the fruit to get the spores—those are sort of little seeds of mold—and I mix them with the water in the test tubes. Then I spread it on these petri dishes with a little food, and watch the mold grow. See?" She pulled out a petri dish that was covered with colonies of *Monolinea laxa*.

"Cool!" said Shannon again. So the visit was a success.

"Thanks," Sam said quietly as they headed out the door.

"My pleasure."

He lingered a moment. "Oh," he said suddenly, "did Tom get hold of you yesterday? What was that all about?"

"I'll tell you later."

"When?" he pressed. "Can you come up tonight?"

She hesitated. They both wanted to consummate what had begun yesterday afternoon, she knew. But that wouldn't solve anything.

But hell, life was short.

"Yes. Sure," she said. "After dinner."

"Okay. I'll take the kids to . . . they can play with friends," he said, and kissed her on the forehead before she could react. So the boys went out to visit some growers, and Claire remained to count moldy almonds . . . and contact Charlie Padgett about the mysterious phone call.

But before she knuckled down, she had some outstanding business. She marched upstairs and into the station orchards, past the grapes and kiwis and solarized soil and pistachios and oranges, and stopped at the peaches. Against the still gray skies they glowed with their own incandescence.

The crop was noticeably more sparse. Sam and his associates had harvested fruit from the two groups, the organic and conventional—but not all the fruit; that was the beauty of sampling. She strolled slowly and deliberately past the trees, teasing herself, considering a fruit and then rejecting it. She was seeking out the biggest, ripest peach, the perfect peach, the archetypal peach, the Platonic ideal of peach. Finally she wrapped her hand around a heavy down-covered globe and pulled. No insect damage; no soft areas of brown rot; good heft; good color, modulating from a delicate apricot to a deep burgundy . . . yes, a worthy fruit. She rinsed it under the spigot and bit.

Ah, God. It was orgasmic. It was everything she had imagined—and so few things were. The sweet juices spurted into her mouth and ran down her chin. She ate another, pocketed a third, and returned just in time to catch the telephone.

True to his word, Tom Martelli was calling her.

Now obviously, what she wanted to know about was Bert, but "Phosthion," he said the moment he heard her voice.

"What?"

"That's what Cedillo had been sprayed with. Phosthion."

"Huh. That's CONKWEST."

"Yeah. Isn't that what Bert was cited for—spraying CONKWEST on his grapes?"

"Well, yes, but I imagine that's just a coincidence. It's a widely used pesticide, for cotton and . . . and soy, I think. Just not approved for grapes. I mean, Cedillo wasn't actually found in that vineyard, was he?"

"Naw. Not too far away, but not right in the vineyard."

"That's what I thought. So I wouldn't make too much of the Bert connection." But bodies can be moved, she thought. Or move, if they're in flowing water, like Levine. And Cedillo wasn't working with cotton or soy; this was the grape harvest, and he was picking grapes like everyone at the Vacancy. She was subtly misdirecting Tom, and she wondered why.

"What's the story with Bert?" she said.

"His lawyer told him to keep his mouth shut, which he mainly did. But he did allow as how posting those spray notices would have been Ruben Moreno's job. Anyway, I told him not to leave town."

"What about the truck?"

"Ah, that's gonna have to wait till tomorrow, I'm afraid. Morrie's called away on another case, and I really need him to examine it."

"Mmm. By the way, what *did* this Wilson fellow at the attorney general's office tell Jon Levine?"

"Told him the spray date violation wasn't his jurisdiction, it was County Ag's."

"Oh." She thought for a moment. "He must have said something else to you, or you wouldn't have come tearing after me when you heard I was with Bert. With a warrant for his truck," she added.

"You're right," he admitted. "He told me enough to make me think that somebody just might want to silence Levine. Wilson said the fine for a violation like this is probably a couple of thousand dollars, but the county ag commissioner's got some discretion and could consider this one violation—or could count one violation per worker."

The previous ag commissioner wouldn't have done it. But Cathy might do just that. "So if Bert had a crew of ten in there, that would be a sizable chunk of change, even for Bert," Claire said.

"Right. And then there's Perez," Martelli continued. "If he *did* drown because of chronic poisoning, well, Wilson told me that then it becomes a case for the attorney general. And then we're talking criminal charges—manslaughter, maybe. And sky's-the-limit damages. And—"

"I'm beginning to get the picture," interrupted Claire. "We're talking motive to shut Levine up."

"Right. Now I reckon if Bert *did* kill Levine—and I ain't sayin' he did—it was because he just . . . lost his temper. This fellow threatened him and made him real, real angry, like you did yesterday, and that ain't a good idea. Say they happened to run into each other—"

"No," said Claire. "Bert arranged to meet him."

"How the hell do you know?" Martelli demanded hotly. "You keep making these statements. Like yesterday: 'They sat in his truck and talked.' I mean, if I could come up with *one* piece of evidence that linked the two of them—say, that put Levine in Bert's truck—then I might be able to construct a fairly strong circumstantial case against Bert. So if you know anything I don't—"

He waited, but there was nothing she could say. Dreams

were not admissible in a court of law or a scientific journal, and that was a good thing.

"What about Levine's wallet?" Claire asked suddenly.

"What about it?"

"Well, doesn't the fact that it was missing make this look a little more premeditated?"

"Nope. Just looks like Bert covering his ass after the fact. Lifting the wallet to delay identification—though he should have disposed of the car, if he was going to be thorough." He paused. "Well, maybe we'll find something tomorrow," he said sadly. "And if not . . ."

Claire finished the sentence silently for him. If not, then a closer examination of Ruben Moreno . . . and "leads in L.A."

She really had to tell him what she knew about Jeff Green. After all, it was a chance to trump him. But somehow that idea brought her no pleasure.

Wayne Harris called to cancel his afternoon appointment with her and Jim, so Claire had an entire unstructured afternoon. Her work lay in piles and bags and petri dishes before her, demanding her attention, but instead she opened the top drawer of her desk, pulled out a battered paperback, and began to read. At three she decided Charlie Padgett was not going to call her unsolicited about the anonymous tip, so she laid aside *The Monkeywrench Gang* and called him. But he was out.

In fact, he was out until after Labor Day, the receptionist told her.

"After Labor Day!" she repeated incredulously. She couldn't possibly wait a week to solve this problem!

Well, maybe she could solve it without him.

Padgett's remark that Cathy had passed on—that the caller had "no future in this line of work—" must mean something. If by "line of work" Charlie had meant whistle-blowing on pesticide abusers, then he was right. Because the caller had certainly screwed up this time: Bert's vineyard was clean, except for the mysterious contamination on the east side, and that could just be an artifact—

But Padgett hadn't known the vineyard was clean when he made the comment. So by "line of work" he must have

meant "making anonymous phone calls." And that might indicate the caller wasn't intelligible on the phone—heavy accent, say (remembering her hypothesis of the vengeful
farmworker).

Or it might mean that the caller wasn't very anonymous,
that there was something identifiable about his voice.

She consciously relaxed the tightening in her stomach
while she thought carefully about this.

She knew . . . oh, several people with very distinctive
voices. Ruben Moreno, for example, who might have had
some reason to accuse his boss. Maybe to distract attention
from some perfidious schemes of his own.

Yes, maybe Ruben Moreno. But she had to face it: there
was one person in Kaweah County who had a most unusual,
most distinctive voice.

And if Bert had been set up, as he claimed, as she herself
suspected, the probable culprit—the *obvious* culprit, how
could she have been so stupid?—was the man who had that
voice. Who had tipped off County. Who carried a grudge
against Bert. Who had sprayed CONKWEST to "monkeywrench" him.

Who had killed Hector Cedillo.

Emil Yankovich.

"No," she said faintly; then, *"No!"* she yelled, slamming
her fist on the counter and rattling the glassware. "No, no,
no, goddamn it!"

Not Emil. Not gentle, principled Emil.

Wait a minute, she thought, sitting up straighter. She had
murder on the brain. Couldn't this have been a tragic accident? Emil had been spraying, presumably to, well, frame his
brother, and Cedillo had been there, for whatever reason.
Maybe even hiding, so of course Emil had no way of knowing of his presence. If he had read later about the death of a
young farmworker from heart failure, he would not have
connected it with his midnight foray.

The clothes. Her conscience interrupted this sophistry:
what about Cedillo's clothes?

What *about* his clothes? Would Cedillo have stripped because he was feeling sick? It didn't make sense.

What made sense was that the sprayer, knowing the

clothes were saturated with CONKWEST, had removed them. Which ruled out his—the sprayer's—okay, *Emil's* complete unawareness of Cedillo's existence.

But not the possibility of an unhappy accident, she thought hopefully. Maybe Cedillo *had* been hiding in the vineyard and trapped by the spray, and Emil had discovered him too late, removed his clothes to try to save him . . . or to destroy the evidence.

It was no use; she couldn't get at the truth by sitting in her office and speculating. She could imagine a tragic accident; she could also imagine—just—a murder. If Emil were surprised, if he lashed out in an instinctive moment of self-preservation . . . he was Bert's brother, as everyone kept remarking so tediously.

Oh, she should just drop this bomb in Martelli's lap and let him deal with it. But she suspected that in the eyes of the law the difference between accident and manslaughter was fuzzy in this case. Causing a death while committing a felony was murder. Now maybe spraying CONKWEST wasn't exactly a felony, but—something very bad would happen to Emil, there was no doubt about it. And she couldn't bear it.

Forty minutes later she had once again invaded Emil's sanctuary.

The solitary light was on when she walked up the front steps and tapped lightly.

"Emil?" she called cautiously, pushing open the door. The living room was empty. "Emil?" she called again as she moved into the next room and turned on the light. She was in the kitchen, also of 1930s vintage, except for the refrigerator and the toaster-oven on the counter. Beside her was an old-fashioned white enameled kitchen table, and in the center of the table was a note in Emil's inhumanly perfect script: "Claire, this is not because of you. I didn't mean for it to happen. I guess blood will tell after all."

She read it at first without comprehension. Then "God, no," she whispered.

What would he do to himself? Was she in time? Where would he be? The bathroom? Heart beating hard, she slowly climbed the stairs, leaning heavily on the banister. She turned on the light in the first room she came to, shutting her eyes for a moment; when she opened them it was indeed the bathroom. But it was empty: no one sprawled across the cold tiled floor or floating in a bathtub of stained water.

Sweating now—it was bad enough to find a body; it was worse to search for one—she moved from bedroom to bedroom, each perfectly preserved, each immaculate, empty. Finally she came to what, from neat stacks of books and other signs of habitation, must have been Emil's room, though it too was perfectly in period, the UFW poster on the wall exactly resembling the old NRA eagle. And it too was empty.

She limped to the window and looked down on the backyard. It was not quite pitch dark; a light glinted off Emil's Volvo, which was parked behind the house, and after a moment she saw that it came from the bottom floor of the pumphouse, where the door was ajar. She stared at this for a moment, then hopped down the stairs, through the kitchen and the pantry, and into the yard.

Moving cautiously, she slipped through the pumphouse door and found herself in a jumble of sacks, boxes, hand tools, and broken machinery: as in most of these old structures, the area beneath the cistern had been converted to an equipment shed.

"Emil?" she said hoarsely, squinting around the half-lit room, trying to make sense of the shapes yet afraid of what she might find. The shed smelled strongly of fertilizer and something else she couldn't identify.

Suddenly her heart thudded. There, my God, hanging from the roof beams . . . Oh. Overalls. But what about there, in that dark corner? Just some sacks, or . . . ? She approached warily, stepping between the hoes and the buckets and the clippers and the bags of manure; it was strange that as neat a housekeeper as Emil could operate in this chaos.

So intent was she on that far corner that when she tripped over something and looked down at the floor, it was several seconds before she understood what she was seeing and another second before her annoyance changed to horror.

A sound between a whimper and a moan escaped her. She clamped both hands over her mouth and stumbled out into the yard, taking in great gasps of cool night air. After a few moments she made her way back into the pumphouse.

Emil was lying on his left side. In his agony he had pulled down a rack of long-handled tools that lay across him like pickup sticks, from which one claw of a hand protruded. Just beyond it lay a white plastic jug, the red letters just visible: CONK—

What she could see of his face was no longer the face of her friend.

Some atavistic impulse to comfort, to compose those contorted features, made her bend and tentatively reach toward him. Then she drew away, partly from aversion, partly because she remembered that toxic doses of this stuff could be absorbed even through the skin. But it seemed too cruel to leave him untouched, untended. . . . She should . . . she should cover him, she thought wildly, looking around her for a blanket. No, that was crazy—she should call Sam—no, not Sam, an ambulance! Maybe he wasn't dead, she thought with a surge of insane hope and looked again at the figure.

The spilled pesticide was a dark shadow under the left side of his face. She wouldn't have expected it to be that dark. It must be the dim lighting in the pumphouse that made it look red, she thought. It must be the light that made the stain look as if it were still spreading, oozing from the underside of his face. Against her will she imagined the thick liquid soaking into his beard. . . .

His beard. Suddenly she squatted and peered gingerly under the clutter of tools. Even in the bad light she could tell that the face was clean-shaven.

The man lying on the pumphouse floor was not Emil Yankovich. It was Bert.

And he was breathing.

Chapter 21

The shock cleared the haze from her head. Immediately she saw that the jug of CONKWEST was securely closed and that the liquid on the floor was just what it appeared to be, blood. She began to pull the tools off Bert's body, thought better of it, and ran to call the paramedics instead.

Was there even a telephone in this anachronism of a house? She passed through the kitchen, paused by the table, and instinctively stuffed Emil's note in her pocket. A phone, yes, next to the radio; she dialed 911 and managed to explain the situation with some lucidity.

"What should I do for him?"

"A head injury, ma'am? Don't move him, just keep him warm. Ambulance'll be coming from Parkerville; it'll take 'em a good twenty minutes, I'm afraid."

She hung up and fought the powerful urge to call Sam. She just had the bad habit of calling him when she was in trouble. But no; when you were in trouble, and white, you called the police. She dialed Tom's number.

"Please let him be there," she breathed. The phone rang four times, then gave way to the static of an answering machine. "This is the Riverdale Police Station," came Tom's creaky voice. "Office hours are—"

Shit! She left an incoherent message that included Emil's telephone number and sat numbly for a moment. Keep him warm, she thought, and rose to search for a blanket, then jumped when the phone rang.

"Tom?"

"No, it's Sam."

214

"Sam," she repeated in wonder. "How did you—"

"Tom just called. He'll be there soon, he walked in while you were leaving a message. Where are you? What happened?"

Her voice was so shaky that it took him a moment to understand her. Then he said, "Jesus Christ. So Emil finally did it."

"I'm sure Bert started it," she said—and only then did she realize that she, too, was assuming that the brothers had fought.

"No doubt," Sam agreed. "Where is Emil?"

"I don't know," she said distractedly, "but I've got to go find a blanket for Bert."

"Do you want me to come over?"

Yes. "No . . . no, not if Tom's on his way."

There was a pause. "Listen, look out for Emil, okay? Who knows what sort of shape he's in."

"I know, and I'm worried. He might be hurt."

"That's not what I meant." And he rang off.

She fetched a blanket from Emil's room, limped back to the pumphouse, and spread it over Bert, first stooping to remove the remaining jumble from his back. His breathing was a faint rasp, but steady, and she sat and listened while Emil's note rattled around her brain like a nickel in a washing machine.

Suicide note, confession, or both? She had assumed it was a suicide note and an expression of remorse for Cedillo's death, and that still seemed to make the most sense. She pulled out the note and looked again at what he had said, considered each of the sentences.

"Claire, this has nothing to do with you." He had known that she, in her simple egocentric way, would assume he had killed himself for unrequited love.

"I didn't mean for it to happen." All right, spraying Cedillo was an accident or a reflex; she could believe that.

And finally, "Blood will tell."

Now personally, she didn't believe in "blood." In matters of nature and nurture, she came down firmly on the side of nurture until proven otherwise.

But Emil believed in blood and its thick, dark secrets. He

wouldn't have tried so hard to scrape his family off at the doorstep if he hadn't; he felt the sludge of genetic rage surging through his veins, and it disgusted him. So when he had stumbled on Cedillo Sunday night and had turned the nozzle on him, he'd thought his doom had come upon him.

But if it was a suicide note, how had Bert come to be lying here, breathing laboriously?

And where was Emil?

Bert sighed, and then there was a sudden suspended silence. She drew in her own breath for what seemed like minutes—and then he began again, inhale, exhale, inhale, exhale, the rhythm of life. Damn, where was the fucking ambulance? She listened for a siren but instead heard something else: a car starting.

In an instant she was on her feet and scrambling toward the house. The Volvo's engine was idling roughly, but it wasn't moving. And someone was sitting behind the wheel.

"Emil?" she called, approaching cautiously. At ten feet she saw that it was indeed Emil. "Are you all right?" She approached the inert figure with dread. But suddenly his hands moved on the steering wheel, and she breathed again.

Before he might drive off, she slipped onto the front seat beside him, leaving the door ajar so she could see by the overhead light.

"Are you all right?" she asked again. Rain was beginning to splatter lightly on the windshield. He turned his face toward her, and his eyes, in shadow, were like empty sockets. "Did you call the police?" he said dully.

"I called an ambulance."

Something about the silence that followed made her add, "He's alive, Emil. You know that, don't you? Bert's alive!"

A long silence this time, as if he hadn't understood, then "Oh, my God," he whispered. "I hit him so hard I thought— Oh, my God." And he began to shake like the old Volvo. She put an arm around his shoulders as if to warm him.

"Did you fight?"

"Yes. And I hit him with a shovel," still shivering.

"Did he attack you?"

"He had a pitchfork—"

"Then you were defending yourself!"

He looked at her as if she were crazy. "I hit him with a shovel," he repeated.

"Yes," she said patiently, "but he started it. And you didn't kill him." Not yet, anyway, she thought, remembering that ragged breathing.

He didn't answer for a long time. "Maybe not," he said finally. "But I killed somebody."

"I know," she said, and he started.

"You know?"

"That's why I came over. You sprayed Bert's vineyard, didn't you? And made the anonymous call? And Hector Cedillo was in the vineyard, and you sprayed him by accident—"

"Not accident," he corrected her, and wiped his mouth with the back of his hand. "Reflex. I have the reflexes of a killer."

Blood will tell. "What happened to his clothes?"

"He went into convulsions," he said, looking out the window. "It was hor-horrible—"

Some part of her noted that this was the first time he had stuttered. It was as if he were at last too exhausted to manage those superfluous syllables.

"And when he stopped I pulled off his clothes. I thought it might help him; they were saturated with the phosthion. But it was too late, I could see that. I was in—worked in, a hospital once, and I know when p-p-people are . . . gone."

"And then?" she prompted, hearing the rise and fall of a siren, still very faint.

"I . . . I guess I panicked. No, that's a lie. I was thinking very clearly. I du-dumped him in the canal and p-p-put his clothes in my t-t-trunk, to burn. Along with all my p-p-protective gear—Christ, I must have looked like a Martian, I must have scared that p-poor k-kid to death—" His breath caught in a sob, and it took him a moment to recover. "I just w-wanted the whole thing to g-go away," he said. "To p-pretend it never happened. But it d-didn't g-go away, it just g-got worse and w-worse, and f-f-finally—"

He stopped just as she thought he was going to strangle on the sentence. The sirens were closer. "Emil," she said urgently, "they'll be here soon. Tell me exactly what happened with Bert."

He lolled back against the seat, accepting the comfort of her arm. "He f-figured out that I sprayed his vineyard. S-Same way you d-did, I guess. He came over a few hours ago and f-found the C-CONKWEST in the p-p-pumphouse—"

"You left the CONKWEST lying around? Emil, why didn't you dump it?"

"I c-can't d-dump it," he said stubbornly, looking for an instant like the old Emil, "it's a p-poison, they should never m-make it. Besides, I . . . I thought I might need it again."

She let this pass for the moment. "Okay. Then what?"

"He s-started screaming at m-me, just like always, and h-he p-picked up the p-pitchfork. I thought he was g-gonna k-kill me. . . . It's f-funny, I think I c-could kill myself, b-but I couldn't let Bert do it for me. Like I said, reflexes."

"Is that what your note meant?" she asked. "Were you going to kill yourself tonight?"

He hesitated, then gave a single jerky nod.

"With the CONKWEST?" she guessed, and he nodded again.

Her hand crept up to cover her mouth. "Jesus Christ, Emil!"

"P-poetic j-justice," he said grimly.

The siren was very close now. Emil sat up and reached listlessly for the gearshift, but she laid her hand on top of his. "Stay here."

"I don't want t-to s-see him when they t-take him away," he said.

"Okay. But stay here. Everything will be all right, Emil. Really. We'll just explain to Tom Martelli that Bert attacked you; everybody knows about Bert's temper—"

"It's not only Bert."

"You mean Cedillo? But there's no reason anybody has to know about that," she said on impulse, and then realized this might be true. "Go in the house and wait. Promise me?" she said, reaching to shut off the motor.

Emil was limp, without volition. She had to open his door, grasp him by the arm, and lead him into the living room, where he slumped beneath the photos of strangers.

The paramedics pulled into the driveway, and she walked with them back to the pumphouse, where Bert was still wheezing. Fearfully she saw them turn him over, saw the dreadful wound revealed. "I hit him so hard," Emil had said. Jesus, he had hit him like a mortar shell! The whole left side of Bert's face, from temple to jaw, was crushed. Shards of bone gleamed whitely in the bloody mess, like the pit of a smashed mango.

"How is he?" she asked timidly, flinching at the absurdity of her own question, because clearly he was not good.

"Ugly but lucky," said the redheaded paramedic. "The blow was probably low enough so there's no brain damage. You know what happened here?"

"I . . . I'm not sure. I found him—"

"Because somebody sure as hell knocked him upside the head," he continued. "With a blunt instrument. Maybe that shovel. You know who?"

"No . . ."

"Well, miss, we've gotta get the patient to Mercy Hospital real quick, but under the circumstances we're required to call the county sheriff. And I'm afraid I have to ask you to stick around to answer his questions."

She had known they would call Cummings. Thank God Martelli would be there, too.

"Of course," she said. He was looking unhappy, as if he had just realized that this tall, strapping woman was herself perfectly capable of having knocked the victim upside the head with a shovel. What was to say she would stay around?

But just then Martelli pulled up, and the medic's face cleared.

"Christ!" Tom said, looking at Bert's ruined face roll by on the gurney. "He going to be all right?"

"Maybe," said the redhead, shoving Bert into the back of the ambulance.

"Emil finally whack him?" Tom asked Claire as the ambulance peeled out of the drive.

"Yes," she said, "but Bert started it."

"Don't doubt that for a minute. Where is ol' Emil?"

"In the house," she said, hoping this was true.

It was. Emil was sitting obediently in the mauve chair where she had left him, staring at nothing. She and Martelli plopped themselves onto the sofa, and Tom's questions began.

In a barely audible voice Emil allowed as how he and his brother had indeed fought; that Bert had threatened him with a pitchfork, and he had defended himself, very effectively, with the shovel.

"What was the fight about?" asked Tom.

"Since when did Bert need a reason to start a fight?" said Claire, intervening swiftly. She had been anticipating this moment and had settled on a course of action. To lie. She, a scientist, whose highest allegiance was to the truth, was going to . . . withhold data. Because otherwise Emil—

Emil! What about Hector Cedillo? she thought suddenly. Didn't he deserve the truth?

As the ship's clock on the mantel ticked off the seconds, she thought about this. She made herself fully imagine Cedillo, just a kid, really—much like the joyous kids at the river the other night.

What did the dead deserve? If truth, then she was wrong to lie, and she would bear that responsibility—

All of this moral wrangling was for naught, however, because Emil was talking. "Oh, he had a reason," he was saying. "He found out I sprayed his vineyard with an illegal pesticide and turned him in to the county."

Shit! Of course she couldn't protect Emil! Of course he was bound to sabotage any effort to obscure the truth! He wanted to pay for Bert, and for Hector Cedillo. Most especially for Hector Cedillo, although he hadn't said anything about him so far.

"That why that jug of CONKWEST was lying in your pumphouse?" asked Martelli, and she realized further that, Emil's self-destructive impulses aside, she could never have prevented Tom from ferreting out the truth.

This was obscurely comforting.

A siren she had been hearing subconsciously for some time suddenly became staggeringly shrill and then died away; tires squealed in the driveway, lights flashed, car doors slammed, a radio crackled, boots thudded. Authority had arrived, in the persons of J. T. Cummings himself, sheriff of Kaweah County, man of few words and fewer ideas, and a weasel-faced deputy.

He stopped dead when he saw Tom.

"Martelli, what the fuck are you doin' here?" he demanded. Claire was interested to note that at night, without his mirrored sunglasses, he was drained of most of his menace and stood revealed as the pink, plump, unprepossessing man he was.

"Keep your shirt on, J.T., I ain't movin' in on you. I'm just here as a friend of Ms. Sharples. She found Bert."

"Yeah, Bert," Cummings said more calmly. "Bert's been seriously hurt, I understand. You know anything about your brother's injuries, Mr. Yankovich?"

Impassively Emil recited his story once again, not omitting, needless to say, the cause of the fight. At this Cummings looked confused: was the spraying of pesticide a crime requiring action on his part? He defaulted to the familiar. "I'm gonna have to arrest you for assault, Mr. Yankovich."

"But it was self-defense!" Claire protested while Emil simply stood and walked over to the deputy.

"Maybe," said Cummings. "But we got to question him just the same. Oh, and Miss Sharp," he added as the three men headed out the door, "stick around Parkerville. I may want to ask you a couple of questions, too."

Claire turned to Martelli. "Will Emil have to spend the night in jail?"

"Prob'ly. He'll be arraigned and judge'll set bail."

"So I could bail him out tomorrow."

"Yup."

She fingered the note in her pocket. "Will they watch him pretty carefully? I mean, so he can't hurt himself?"

"Not all that carefully, truth be told. Things . . . happen, sometimes. Why, you want me to tell Cummings to put a special suicide watch on him?"

"Yes."

He looked at her curiously.

"Well, you know," she said hurriedly, "Emil's not the

most stable guy at the best of times, and he was pretty distraught over Bert; I think he feels incredible guilt—"

"Over Bert? Or over Hector Cedillo? Okay, I'll tell J.T.," he said, and ran to catch the sheriff, leaving her gaping.

"How did you know about Cedillo?" she asked when he returned.

"It's obvious. Whoever sprayed that vineyard sprayed Cedillo. He was covered with CONKWEST; he was found in a ditch about a quarter mile from that field—"

"It was an accident."

"That could be, but I'm gonna have to tell J.T." He stared across the room, looking for a moment as blank as Emil, but Claire knew it was illusion. "For a peaceful man, Emil's created a fair amount of mayhem," he said presently. "Cedillo, Bert . . . wonder what else he got himself into?"

"What do you mean?"

"Well, I was just thinking. Emil sprayed this vineyard, and killed Hector Cedillo in the process. Now let's suppose somebody saw him do it—and threatened to expose him." He was picking up speed now. "And let's say Emil—shut him up. And now feels real bad about it."

Claire was puzzled—somehow this didn't sound quite right. "Just exactly what are we talking about here, Tom?" she asked.

Tom looked at her with a strange light in his eyes. "Jonathan Levine," he answered. "We're talking about the murder of Jonathan Levine."

"B-but Tom," Claire stammered when she recovered, "it's impossible! Emil *couldn't* have killed Lev—"

"Why not?"

"Well, because," she began desperately, "because—because Levine was in the mountains on Sunday night. He couldn't have seen the vineyard being sprayed!"

"How do you know it was sprayed on Sunday?" Tom asked sharply. "It probably could have happened any time over the weekend. Right? I mean, I called Cathy Bakaitis today, and according to her, the pickers finished on Thursday and the caller—Emil—phoned late on Friday, knowing nobody would get around to investigating 'til the following Monday. He sprayed over the weekend—"

"To avoid exposing anyone," she interrupted.

"Maybe," conceded Tom. "In any case, Levine could have seen him, say, Saturday the thirteenth when he was leaving town. Or"—as a thought hit him—"the truth is, we don't know when Levine left town!"

"But the ranger station . . . ," began Claire.

"Oh, yeah, he signed *in* to enter the wilderness area Saturday. But I just realized that don't mean he actually *did* enter on Saturday. All we know is his exit date, because of that damn dandelion. I mean 'hussy.'"

"Hulsea."

"Whatever. We figured he couldn't've *left* the mountains later than the following Friday, because the flower was still pretty fresh, but we don't know for sure when he went up."

Claire was speechless. It was like some sort of remorseless karma or bad Hitchcock: Emil would be convicted of Levine's murder, too. . . .

"But what about Bert?" she said suddenly. "Yesterday you thought that Bert was the likely suspect! Just because he got his face smashed in and looks pathetic—"

"It ain't that," he said. "Bert's still the likeliest candidate, I'd say. But there's a couple of weaknesses in that case. Motive—"

"The backdating."

"Yeah, right. But that coulda been just a . . . a typo. Or even if it was deliberate, we don't know that it was Bert that done it."

"Who else?"

"Moreno. He's his labor contractor. He might've exercised a little personal initiative. Plus, we got no physical evidence linking Levine to Bert."

"You're searching Bert's truck tomorrow, though."

"Right. But I gotta tell you that after two weeks, I don't hold out much hope of us finding anything. And the main problem: timing."

"Timing?"

"Yep. If the ME is right that Levine died at noon, well, we all know where Bert was at noon on Saturday."

"At the open house," she said after a minute.

And so was Ruben Moreno.

"Right. And even if we push the time of death back to six A.M., we have to be willin' to believe that Bert showed up at the open house, slick as you please, just a couple hours after committing a brutal murder. Which I for one doubt he could've pulled off."

"But weren't you thinking Levine might have died earlier?" she asked, straining to remember the details of a conversation in the motel that she hadn't paid attention to in the first place.

"Right, and I might get another pathologist to back me up. Nevertheless, it's a problem."

She was staring despondently at the floor when a familiar hand touched her arm and a familiar voice spoke her name. She whirled to see Sam, followed by Enrique Santiago.

They regarded each other warily for a moment, and Tom, having drawn the correct inference from Claire's move to the motel, strolled tactfully toward the kitchen. He motioned for Santiago to follow him.

"What are you doing here?" she asked Sam.

"Well, after I talked to Tom, Ricky got on the phone to tell me exactly what happened with you and Bert yesterday, which you neglected to mention—"

"There wasn't time this morning—"

"Never mind, never mind, I didn't mean it as an accusation. I just meant that I started to get a little worried about what might be going on out here." He paused. "Are you mad at me for coming?"

"No. No, actually, I'm glad to see you. To tell you the truth, the last two days have pretty much done me in. In fact—" She hesitated. "In fact, would you mind . . . that is, could I stay at your house tonight? On the couch, I mean. I'm really wrung out."

She asked this with more diffidence than she actually felt; after all, she was a plucky damsel in distress, for Christ's sake. Sam was enough of a cowboy to respond to that, surely; he had come all the way out to Emil's on the off chance she might be in trouble.

But he took so long in answering that she thought he was going to refuse.

"Sure," he said finally, "of course. The kids'll be there, but I can sleep on the porch—if that's what you want. I have to pick them up at Linda's, though." He uttered the name with a hint of defiance.

"Fine. I'll wait in your car."

"Oh," he said. "*Your* car, actually. I rode over with Ricky."

Chapter 22

While Sam trotted into Linda's she sat looking straight ahead, trying not to think about how familiar this must be to him: the dip of the cracked concrete walk under his feet, the chlorine smell of the arborvitae, the rattle of the aluminum screen door—and beyond, hidden to her, the chipped tile of a bathroom, the hall light switch that his hand found even in the dark . . . Against her will, her imagination entered the bedroom and lingered there.

And lingered, and lingered . . . It was a good half hour before he returned, a drowsy Terry buried in his shoulder and Shannon following sleepily behind.

"Sorry," he said, hoarse with spent emotion, "there was a little bit of a scene." She looked at him curiously but said nothing.

By the time they had arrived at Sam's both boys were asleep. Sam carried them one by one into the living room and tucked them into the sofa bed. Then, in unspoken agreement, they drifted out to the porch. Claire was longing to know what had happened with Linda, longing for Sam, wondering whether they would make love tonight, or ever. But of course there was too much to talk about to attend to these trivial matters. Above all, there was Emil.

"It was all because of Bert's vineyard," she began. "See, Emil sprayed it to set up Bert. . . . " She trailed off, suddenly remembering Sam's expression the other morning when she had talked about Bert being set up. "You knew, didn't you."

"Not really. But it sort of had to be."

226

Unless you were in deep denial or deep idiocy. "Did you know about the farmworker?"

"What farmworker?"

"Remember Hector Cedillo, the second guy they found in a canal? Right before Levine?"

"Yeah?"

"Um . . . he was in the vineyard when Emil sprayed."

"Oh," he said after a long pause, and Claire answered fiercely:

"If you say 'Well, sure, he's Bert's brother,' I'll sock you! It was an accident!"

This was a somewhat untenable argument in light of what gentle Emil had done to Bert, but she made it anyway. Duly warned, Sam said nothing except, "Is he in jail?"

"Yes. Tom says I can bail him out tomorrow."

"Let me know if you need money."

"Okay." She paused. "Uh, Sam . . . how exactly do you bail someone out?"

He laughed and said, "I'll come with you. Don't worry, it's easy. Now tell me what happened yesterday with Bert."

She gave a terse narrative.

"You pulled a knife on Bert?" he interrupted. "You're lucky to be breathing! Whatever possessed you?"

"Funny you should use that word," she muttered, and paused. "Sam," she said finally, "have you ever imagined that someone was talking to you? Someone who couldn't . . . someone who wasn't . . ." She took a breath, said, "Say, someone who had died," and winced, waiting for the mockery.

But in fact he answered her seriously. "Well, not exactly, if I catch your meaning. But my father died when I was fifteen—"

"I know," she said dryly. She had lived with the guy for a year, she did know the basic biography. If he had told her the truth. . . .

"Right. Well, anyway, for a long time afterward—I'm talkin' years—there'd be some situation where I'd know exactly what he would have said. I mean *exactly*. He was so damn predictable, and he had these all-purpose Okie phrases he'd trot out for every occasion."

"Like what?"

"Oh, like . . ." He halted, searching his memory. "Like, 'Might as well, too wet to plow, too windy to haul rocks.'" (Except that what he actually said was something like, "Motts wayil, too wayit tuh playoh, too wandy tuh hawul rocks.") Claire couldn't offhand imagine a single situation for which this was appropriate. But she let Sam finish.

"He used to say that all the time. So for a long time after he died I'd find myself sort of waiting to hear it, and I'd be expecting it so . . . with such certainty, that sometimes it seemed like I *had* heard it. That the kind of thing you mean?" he finished, looking at her.

"Well, not quite. . . ." She found it almost impossible to proceed.

"This got something to do with what happened with Bert?" he said with unexpected shrewdness, and she nodded. Then, realizing he couldn't see her in the dark, she cleared her throat and said, "Yes."

He waited.

"It's very weird," she said. "It's Jon Levine. At first . . . at first he just seemed sort of familiar. I don't know, it's a common name; I knew a little boy with the same name when I was a kid. But then I moved into his room, in the motel, and . . . and the whole thing escalated: I started imagining his death, and dreaming about it, and then it seemed like I was having *his* dreams. I swear, Sam, it was like he was trying to contact me! And then, yesterday at the vineyard, I *was* almost possessed. I mean I heard his voice in my head telling me that Bert had killed him, telling me to use my knife—" She stopped, horrified.

"Was that the only reason you were afraid of Bert? Because you heard this voice?"

"Oh, no," she said. "It was the backdated notices."

"Oh, right. Ricky told me." He laid a comforting hand on her arm. "Doesn't sound crazy to me. Seems pretty plausible. Downright clever, even; Martelli has his suspicions about Bert, I think—"

"No!" she cried, breaking away from his grip. "Those notices weren't nearly enough data to convict Bert! Much less knife him!" She took a breath. "Sam, I'm a rational woman, I make my living on logic. But yesterday I was . . . dreaming with my eyes open, I couldn't trust the evidence of my senses. It scares me!" She shivered. "And the worse thing— what makes it all really suspect—is that I think I *wanted* it to be Bert who killed Levine."

"Why?"

"So it wouldn't be . . . anybody else."

He let this pass. After a moment he said, "Well, I wouldn't worry too much about it. I'd guess you had a low-grade fever." He paused. "Plus a touch of posttraumatic stress syndrome."

"What?"

"Yeah, sure. It's not just an artifact of Vietnam, you know; any kind of trauma can leave you sort of unhinged. And did you ever find a dead body before Levine? You ever even *seen* someone dead?"

"Um . . . well, no, actually—except Manny, last year, and I didn't really look at him, there was so much else going on. But I saw my father while he was dying! That was worse!" she said, absurdly defensive; Sam, baiting the effete laboratory scientist again. "Anyway, you saw me after I found Levine. I wasn't that shaken. I was a hell of a lot more traumatized by—" She stopped.

"By what?"

"By Linda," she said.

"Oh. Well, okay, that too. What happened between us—"

"What you did," she said, correcting his neutral syntax, but it was done without heat.

"What . . . I . . . did," he repeated reluctantly, "was traumatic, especially coming on top of that first encounter with death, which I'd guess rattled you more than you realized. I stand by my original diagnosis." He gave her arm a tentative squeeze. "I mean, you were pretty rocked by Tony Rodriguez's death last year."

"That's true, my subsequent behavior was erratic. I fell in love with you!"

He managed a laugh. Meanwhile, she relaxed a little and thought, Yes, he was probably right: she wasn't possessed, she was just . . . upset. Suffering posttraumatic stress syndrome, if you wanted to call it that. What a relief. Only why did Sam have to be so comforting, so sweetly reasonable, just as they were breaking up?

Happily, she was distracted from this question by a faint buzzing, like wings brushing a screen. It grew louder and more distinct, and eventually she understood that it was raining again.

"Ah," they both said simultaneously, releasing breath they hadn't known they were holding. Then they scrambled backward under the eaves and watched it pelt down on the drive.

After a while Sam let his hand slide down her arm and come to rest idly on her thigh. In a few moments she felt it tighten—subtly, very subtly—and suddenly she was faint with desire. She laid her hand lightly just above his knee; as formal as a quadrille, the movements of old lovers, and presently, at the ordained time, she turned toward him.

"Are we—" she began, but at the same moment he had swung toward her.

"Shhh!" he said fiercely, covering her mouth with his own and pulling her onto his lap. In one arena, at least, they were in perfect agreement.

At any moment she might have said, "What exactly is the meaning of this? What implications for the future does it hold?" But in fact neither of them spoke; they were hungry for each other, and words were treacherous. Any syllable might blow them apart again. Even afterward they lay together wordlessly for a long time, occasionally shifting and resettling on the wooden floor. Eventually they slipped inside, past the boys and into bed.

The soft mattress and cool sheets were delicious, and she turned on her side and stared out the bedroom window. This view was the best thing about his cabin, and she knew she would miss it terribly: the hill sloping sharply toward the river, and, on moonlit nights, the inky shadows of oaks. But tonight was moonless. The storm had retreated for the moment, and to the east above the mountains the stars glittered as if the film of the centuries had been rolled back, leaving the sky transparent as glass, primordial. Emil must dream about skies like this, she thought.

"But it can't ever be the way it was," she murmured, meaning both life and Emil's life. Sam, assuming she was talking about them, said, "I know. But we'll work something out."

There, there, she thought wryly, but shook her head and said simply, "Emil."

"Oh." And then, after a moment, softly, "He's a poor tortured soul."

She looked at him sharply, but there was no irony intended. Occasionally these phrases from a Baptist childhood strayed into his conversation—and in fact it was as good a summing up as any.

Out of habit she woke at four, listening for the sounds of her neighbors. Instead she heard someone breathing two inches from her ear and jolted awake. But slowly she oriented herself, gazed at Sam (who was sleeping hard, mouth slightly open), then slid back into sleep herself.

It was nearly nine before she woke again, this time to shrill birdcalls under her window. After a few seconds she realized that they were children's voices. Still drugged with sleep, she tottered into the living room, where Sam was slouched on the sofa, reading a journal.

"You're not at work."

"No. After last night I couldn't ask Linda to baby-sit, and besides, it's their last day. I figured I'd just hang out, see if you wanted to hang out, too." He leered and slid his hands up her bare legs.

She was too groggy to respond. "I have to see about Emil. I have to get him out of jail."

"Relax," he said, pulling her onto his lap, "it's all taken care of. I bailed him out this morning while you were snoring. Figure of speech," he added.

"How did he seem?"

"Emil? As good as he ever seems. I gave him a ride out to his place."

"He's out there alone?" she said, scrambling off his lap.

"Yes. Claire, for God's sake, he's perfectly all right—"

"All right? Last night he was about to kill himself—"

"So he claimed—"

"And a night in the county jail couldn't have improved his morale! I'm going to call him. Um"—squeezing his hand—

"let's take a rain check. If that's an expression you use out here."

"It is, and it means putting something off for a very long time," he said grumpily, but he let her go.

But Sam was right, Emil sounded fine. "It's g-good t-to have it all out in the open," he said. "And I t-talked t-to my brother this m-morning. He's g-going to b-be okay, after s-some reconstructive s-surgery."

Tough old grizzly, thought Claire, and made Emil promise to meet her at Katy's for dinner. She hung up, greatly reassured.

But she wondered if he would be quite so cheery if he knew Tom Martelli suspected him of the murder of Jon Levine.

"Tell me again what the problems are with the case against Bert," she said loudly to Martelli an hour later. They were sitting in his office, and the volunteer firefighters had chosen this moment to gun all the engines of all the trucks simultaneously, for God only knew what purpose. Boredom, probably.

His shoulders lifted and dropped with the inevitable, but for the moment inaudible, sigh, and he ticked off the points on his fingers. "One," he yelled as the engines whined toward meltdown, "time of death. That's somewhat open to argument. Two. No witnesses, no physical evidence to link him and Levine. Three. We don't know for sure that he did change the dates on those notices. And if he didn't, he wouldn't have been scared by Levine's threat of an exposé."

"And you think Ruben Moreno would know the truth."

"Might."

"But you don't think he'd want to tell you about it."

"Not particularly, no. Not unless we had some leverage. . . ." He trailed off and looked thoughtful. The engines ceased, leaving a silence as profound and intrusive as the noise. Claire waited. And listened.

"Absolutely not," she said presently. "It's too dangerous for her."

"I can protect her—"

"From the INS?" she challenged.

"No," he admitted after a moment. "But do you know for sure she's undocumented?"

"I just assume so. Everyone else down there seems to be."

"Well, find out, if you can. 'Cause I can't keep her from being deported, but I can probably take care of her otherwise."

"I'll ask her," Claire said finally. "But if she says no, that's it. I'm not going to pressure her."

Two hours later she was talking to Tom from the pay phone at the Vacancy. "She does have papers," she said. "She and Juan applied under amnesty. But she says she'll only do it if I come too."

"*She* says? Or *you* say?" asked Tom. Claire was mute. "Okay," he said grudgingly, "maybe that could even work to our advantage."

"And you have to swear you can protect her. Don't lie to me to *handle* me again."

"Handle you?" he repeated.

"Manipulate me. Swear it."

"I swear."

The sky had cleared after last night's rain, and the wind was blowing hard in East Parkerville, a tidy middle-class neighborhood where Moreno had a tidy suburban house. Tom trotted up the stairs and knocked on the front door, and from the car Claire could smell warm tortillas. Through a window she caught a glimpse of the family sitting down to lunch: Mama, attractive and plump; son, on summer break from Cal State Fresno; two pretty daughters; and Papa Ruben, successful and respectable. Just as Tom had described it, a charming family establishment that he was willing to pull down on Moreno's head.

She couldn't feel too bad about that. Because Ruben was a thug. Oh, sure, he had been a farmworker himself, once, but had "advanced" in time-honored fashion, by stomping on the bodies of his countrymen—and -women. Kiss up, kick down, as Sam used to say in the service. Anyway, in the light of recent revelations regarding Ruben's sexual appetite, Claire was suddenly a little worried about those pretty daughters—but no.

No, Ruben was devoted to his family and to his hard-won respectability, Tom had said.

. That's why this might work, Tom had said.

"Sorry to barge in," she heard him tell Moreno's wife, "but I'm afraid I have to talk to your husband. It's very important."

The woman looked frightened, and Moreno came blustering out. "What is this, Martelli?" he said in his seared voice. "Can't a man eat in peace?"

"Ruben, I've got something to say to you that you may not want your family to hear."

Ruben shut up, and Claire and Luz Perez sat in the parked Blazer and watched Tom disappear through the front door.

Later he told Claire what had transpired in Ruben's spotless living room, which had reminded him, he said, of his dentist's waiting room, except for a few homey touches like the golden oak home entertainment center.

He had picked up a copy of *Family Circle* from the coffee table and leafed through it. "Ruben," he'd said, perusing a recipe for quick and easy tuna casserole, "there's a rumor making the rounds about you and some of the female workers at Contessa."

Ruben's big chair squeaked.

"Some of these women," Martelli continued quite loudly, "claim you, um, forced your attentions on them—"

"For Christ's sake, keep your voice down!" Moreno whispered fiercely. "It's a goddamn lie," he added.

Glancing through "Ten New Cool and Airy Summer Hair Styles," Martelli said, "Well, several women are willing to testify that it's the truth."

"I don't believe you," Ruben said with superb self-assurance. "That's a bluff, Martelli. You got nobody." It was then, Tom told Claire later, that he went to the living room window and waved.

Claire and Luz scrambled out of the car, and in a moment they were walking into Ruben Moreno's hall, Claire in the lead.

"*¡Tú!*" Moreno exclaimed as they entered, and he moved swiftly to block Luz's way. "*¿Eres loca, mujer? ¿Entiendes lo que haces aquí?*"

Tom grabbed Moreno's arm, but not before Luz had taken a step backward. Claire felt a sick wave of fear for her, and guilt. Do you understand what you're doing? Moreno had asked Luz, but he might as well have directed the question to Claire. Did she understand what she was doing to her friend, what risks she had persuaded her to take? Could Martelli in fact protect Luz from the repercussions of Ruben's fury?

"Goddamned bitch," Moreno said under his breath, retreating into the living room. He turned his head in a slow circle, taking in his forty-inch color screen with the statue of the Virgin of Guadalupe on top (she had graced stranger, and humbler, altars), his Sony VCR, his Onkyo CD player, his La-Z-Boy, his good life. Finally his gaze came to rest on Tom.

"Let's say I could make you a deal, Martelli," he said, ignoring the women.

"What sort of deal?"

"Say I could give you a piece of information. And you could forget about these ugly rumors." Here he shot a poisonous glance at Luz and Claire.

"What kind of information?"

"Good information. Stuff nobody knows but me."

"About . . . ?"

"About Bert Yankovich."

Martelli closed the magazine. "Something might be worked out." Only a polygraph would have known he was excited.

Ruben struggled visibly to decide who he was more afraid of, Bert or Tom. Claire watched without sympathy. "Well?" Tom prompted after a minute.

And then Moreno told him what Bert had done: altered the spray dates so the grapes could be picked sooner. "Just a little change," he said, "from August tenth to August first. No big deal."

Claire's legs went weak with relief. Luz was having trouble following the conversation and was staring at her anxiously, and she nodded violently; at least Luz's ordeal was for real information.

"August first," Martelli repeated; then, abruptly, "Tell me about Juan Perez."

Luz hissed.

"Who?" Moreno seemed genuinely perplexed.

"Mrs. Perez's late husband," Tom said, gesturing toward Luz. "Fellow who died of pesticide poisoning a few weeks ago. August first, actually—right after you sent him into Bert Yankovich's vineyard."

"That was no poisoning, that was a drowning!" Moreno said immediately; he knew who Perez was all right. "Son of a bitch got drunk and fell in a ditch! Ask her!" pointing at Luz. "Everybody knew that, even that gringo at the motel—" He came to a dead stop.

"That gringo . . . you mean Jonathan Levine?" Martelli asked. Claire was holding her breath.

Silence. Then a muttered, "Yeah."

"Did he ask you about Perez?" Tom pressed. "About whether the vineyard had been sprayed recently?"

"Yeah. And I told him I didn't know, he'd have to talk to Yankovich," Moreno said sullenly.

"And did he?"

"Did he what?"

"Did Levine talk to Bert?" Martelli said very slowly. His limited patience was wearing down.

"How the hell should I know? Ask Bert!"

"So you don't know anything about it."

"Not a thing," he said, leaning back in his chair.

It was at this point that Claire saw Luz close her eyes and lean against the wall as if she were going to faint. In an instant Claire had her arm around her shoulders. Tom acknowledged them with raised eyebrows as they moved toward the door.

As the screen banged behind them, Luz was shaking her head and muttering something in Spanish that sounded like a prayer.

"No more," she finally said in English. "I'm sorry. I can't do this no more. You tell the *cherife* he find some other lady."

"Of course, Luz," Claire said, swallowing her disappointment. What about prosecuting Moreno? "Thank you very much for coming here today. Oh, I think I locked the car; we'll have to wait until Tom's done—"

"I just walk home."

"But—"

"I just walk," she repeated, and set off down the street. Once again the black clouds crept up from Los Angeles.

"So when Perez went into Bert's field on the first," Claire said twenty minutes later as she and Tom drove toward his office, "it was still contaminated with . . . with MONITOR, probably, I think that's what these guys use for leafhoppers. And if Juan Perez was already ill from chronic exposure to organophosphates, another whopping dose could have made him acutely sick. Sick enough to stumble into the canal and not be able to pull himself out."

"Yep," said Tom, "that's what Ruben figured, afterward." He paused, then said sotto voce, "Funny he picked Juan Perez to go in that day. A little, what-do-you-call-it, David and Bathsheba action, maybe. Anyway"—resuming—"Ruben knew Jonathan Levine had been questioning Mrs. Perez—Luz, is that her name?—and her friends. He was afraid that one of Levine's informants had noticed the dates had been changed. Of course, *Ruben* was the one who actually made the changes on the notices, on Bert's say-so; he finally let that slip. Anyway, he was afraid that Levine might have made the connection with Perez's death—"

"He did make the connection," Claire interrupted. "That's what the spray notice in our—his motel room was about, and those two phone calls."

"I reckon so. And Ruben warned Bert that this reporter was gonna come gunning for him. Bert got pretty worried about you, too, by the way," he said in an aside. "I mean, why would you rent that same filthy little place? Too much of a coincidence. He sent Moreno to check out your room while you were gone and look for anything Levine might have left behind—"

"Like a notebook," she said, and Tom nodded. "Only the notebook was in the car. So it *was* Moreno in my room," she finished.

"Yeah. Scratches all over his shoulders. I checked, last thing."

"And how about the forklift at the cannery?"

"What forklift?"

"At the cannery. I told you, the other day. . . ." She trailed off.

"Forgot to ask him. What?" seeing her puzzled expression.

"Tom, that day I told you about the forklift, you said sexual harassment didn't fall under your jurisdiction."

"Not my jurisdiction at all," Martelli said blandly. "Guess Ruben didn't know that, though."

"But she'll be all right? She won't lose her job?"

"I'll do everything I can. If it comes down to it, I'll make Ricky marry her. Shouldn't be too hard."

It was like old times, like none of this crazy shit had happened, sitting with Emil in the tacky, friendly atmosphere of Katy's. When they had settled at their favorite table, under the Lazy S—the table at which Emil had declared his love—Claire said, "How are you?"

"I'm okay," Emil said wonderingly, and in truth he looked better than he had in weeks. "You know, C-Claire, maybe it w-was j-just the d-drugs, b-but when I t-talked to Bert this morning he was almost f-friendly. As if I finally won his respect." He laughed.

She was silent for a moment. "I guess you finally did something he could understand."

"Yeah. T-treachery and b-brutality. W-welcome t-to the f-family. Thanks, C-Cora," he said as the owner brought them their orders. Cora, a short, barrel-shaped woman, always wore tight jeans, cowboy boots, and a Johnny Mack Brown–style cowboy shirt. Nobody seemed to notice that she looked ridiculous, least of all her.

"I can't stay long, I have to be at Tom Martelli's," Claire said, and paused. "They're searching your brother's truck," she added, realizing he would have to know sometime.

"Why?"

"The death of Jonathan Levine," she said. She was whispering in order to stay below the hearing of the two silent young men at the next table, then realized this was unnecessary. Covered in white dust (fertilizer? plaster?), they nursed their beers and looked off into space with the apathetic stares of complete exhaustion.

Emil winced, but that was all.

"You knew, then?" she said in a normal voice.

"D-didn't know. W-wondered. After that n-night you asked m-me about him."

"Well, it's still just a hypothesis, but a strong one."

He pushed his chicken-fried steak across the plate. "C-call m-me when you know s-something," he said.

"I will. And I'll try to come over tomorrow if I can," she said, standing. "And please, Emil, call me if you start to feel . . . sad, or scared, or overwhelmed. Promise?"

He nodded dumbly and gripped her hand, and she felt a surge of tenderness that could only be called maternal.

Too bad I can't muster that with any consistency for actual children, she thought as she headed for Martelli's.

By seven a group had converged in Martelli's: Enrique, Sam, Claire, Tom, of course, and Morrie, who had spent part of the afternoon comparing the casts of the tracks Martelli had found near Levine's car with Bert's tires.

"No good," he said, coming in from the parking lot and wiping his hands on his overalls. "Son of a bitch has four brand-new tires. Must've bought 'em in the last week."

"Huh," said Tom. "If I were a suspicious man, I might start to wonder at the timing. People do buy new tires every now and then, but Ricky, let's find out where he bought these, see if they remember something. Like, the old ones were in good shape, or he didn't ask to save the best for a spare—anything that looks like he was in a god-awful hurry to get rid of those tires."

Enrique nodded. Everyone drifted out into the lot where Bert's pickup sat, squat and businesslike. In a precise reprise of yesterday, the sky had darkened and a few raindrops hit the ground. The smell of wet pavement made Claire want to swoon.

The men moved toward the truck; after all, they were to search it in the dark. "Might be fingerprints on the door handle on the passenger side," Santiago said.

Tom grunted. "Well, we might get lucky. Dust it, Morrie. Claire, hit the light switch by the back door."

It was like an exhumation, standing in the pool of sulfur-

colored light while the flotsam and jetsam of Bert's life was
disinterred. Debris of meals snatched on the run, receipts,
cigarette butts, gum wrappers, empty Coke cans . . . there
were odd bits of herbiage, which Tom dutifully placed in
plastic bags and handed to Sam.

They peeled up the floor mats and found more caked mud,
seventy-two cents in change, and a torn newspaper. Tom
rocked back on his heels and said, "We're going to have to
take out these seats. Do we have a socket wrench?"

"I've got one in my toolbox," Claire said proudly, "in my
trunk—"

"Of course we've got a socket wrench," Enrique interrupted indignantly, heading inside. Then followed a period
of unholy clanking and swearing, and eventually Bert's front
passenger seat was sitting in the drive twenty feet to the right
of the truck. Tom pawed through the trash that had lodged
beneath it. Finally he stood up, shoulders drooping.

"Nothing there," he said woodenly.

Nothing there. Nothing to tie Bert to Levine; nothing to
help Emil or Jeff.

Sam walked to the beached seat and turned it over. "Wait
a minute," he called over his shoulder. "Bring a flashlight
here, will you?"

Tom moved toward him, followed closely by Claire.

"Here," he said, kneeling and directing their beams to a
wad of newspaper that had become wedged between the seat
support and the cushion. Tenderly he extracted it.

It was a much creased portion of the *Parkerville Sentinel.*
Claire caught a fragment of date: June 15. Sam opened it
slowly and with great care, like a magician, and the last un-
folding revealed a fragile, faded object of yellow and green.
It looked very much like a dandelion, except that it was in
two dimensions instead of three.

There was a long silence. Then, *"Hulsea algida,"* Sam
breathed.

They all stood around in the dark for a long time, getting
bitten by mosquitoes and listening to Sam convince them of
the significance of this discovery. Even when he again explained the concept of "monocephalous"—"one head per
stem," he enunciated carefully—and described the habitat of

alpine hulsea, Santiago looked unimpressed, and Claire felt compelled to say, "I'm afraid a jury may be skeptical, too."

"But it's a perfect specimen!" Sam protested quaintly. "Herbarium quality! Trapped between all those layers of newspaper, under the seat—it was like a plant press!"

"That's what you did to the first flower, right?" asked Tom. "The one we found on Levine? Pressed it?"

"Yep."

Martelli was thinking. "Sam," he said suddenly, "can you swear that this is the same plant as the other one?"

"Same genus and species? Sure."

"No, I mean the *very same* plant! Oh," he said remembering. "It wasn't the same plant. They each have only one flower."

Sam beamed in approval and nodded vigorously. "Monocephalous!" he cried. But Claire shared Martelli's thoughts and also his frustration. Bert could claim *he* had gone hiking in the high country and picked his own hulsea. However unlikely that might seem.

"But it would have come from nearby," Martelli continued. "I mean, most likely. So it would be sort of a . . . a cousin, or a sister. Right? And is there any way to prove that? DNA or something?"

"Well, that's a very interesting question," Sam said. "Let me think about it for a moment." Tom waited in apparent indifference. But when, after about a minute, Sam said, "No. You can't prove it," he jammed his balled fist against his leg.

"What about isozyme analyis?" Claire protested. "Or DNA? Or—what do they call it—RAPDs?"

"Rapids?" Tom repeated.

"Random amplified polymorphic DNA," Sam answered. "It's just a technique for analyzing DNA—"

"I know, I've read about it. They're using it in forensics. So what's the problem?"

"Well, you'd have to talk to a geneticist for a really definitive answer," said Sam. "But I imagine that this is exactly the same as with forensic analysis in your line of work: comparison of DNA could confirm that these two flowers came from the same plant. But we can't prove that they merely came from the same *population*—that they were, say, growing side by side. If they were clones, or even if this were a rare plant, and someone had genotyped all known populations, it might be possible. But that's not the case. Sorry."

"It's probably okay," Tom said after a moment. "We'll just have to rely on common sense instead of technology. No one's going to believe that Bert took a little vacation in the mountains and picked himself a dandelion—hulsea, Sam, I know, I know—especially when we know when it had to have been picked, give or take twelve hours, and I'd bet we can establish Bert's whereabouts during that whole time. So," he finished, brightening, "I'd say this puts Levine in Bert's truck!"

Chapter 23

Claire was familiar with the emotion that should accompany the solution of a difficult problem, and vague uneasiness, which was what she was feeling, was not it. But she shrugged it off. Bert had murdered Jon. It made sense (didn'. it?); it was satisfying (wasn't it?); she had felt it in the vineyard, and by God, she had been right.

"Well," Tom was saying briskly, "guess I'll go pay Bert a visit, first thing tomorrow. Absolutely not," he added, anticipating Claire's request, "even if it was okay with me, the hospital wouldn't allow it. He's in serious condition, you know. If he wasn't so mean, he'd prob'ly be dead."

The kids were across the street at the Mini-Mart being baby-sat by Super Mario Brothers and Helen, who owned the place. At present Linda's was not an option.

"Good thing they're leaving tomorrow," Sam said with grim humor. "If I'd pissed her off at the beginning of the visit, I don't know what I would have done."

Claire started to point out the obvious: if he hadn't slept with Linda in the first place, he wouldn't have had to piss her off at all, but she restrained herself heroically. There would be plenty of time for more sniping and recriminations; tonight they should concentrate on saying good-bye to the boys.

But of course what the boys wanted to do was to 1) buy a pizza; and 2) watch a video. So that was what they did, Claire assuaging her conscience by making a salad, which she and Sam ate.

"When are you driving them down tomorrow?" she asked,

stabbing a chunk of red bell pepper from Sam's bowl, where he had methodically lined them up around the rim.

"In the afternoon. Here, have 'em all, they upset my stomach. Debby wants to take them shopping for school clothes over the weekend."

The peppers? thought Claire for an instant, then said, "I'm sorry they're leaving."

It was half sincere and half merely polite, but he called her on it. "Why?"

"Well, I'll sort of miss them, I guess. But mostly because I know it makes you sad."

"You bet it makes me sad!" he said tightly. "I mean, they'll be gone and you'll be gone! That is"—shooting her a glance under lowered lids—"if you're still planning to move out."

"Yes."

"But *why*?" He slammed down his fork. "Is it just to punish me?"

She tried to consider this calmly. "No," she said finally, pushing her salad away. "At least I don't think so. I just believe it will be easier for us both to figure out what we really want if we have a little distance. You have to decide about Linda, and the kids, and me—I know, you said you already came to a decision, but that was under duress—"

"Everything I do is under duress," he muttered, but she kept on as if she hadn't heard.

"And I have to decide about you, and about staying in Kaweah County. And when I'm living with you, everything I know about this place is refracted through you. It's not really your fault—"

"But I have to pay for it."

"We both have to pay for it, if that's the way you want to put it!" She took a breath. "If I'm going to stay out here, I have to make it my own somehow. I mean, even after living in that awful motel for two weeks I feel more like myself. And more at home."

He was silent. "So we're talking about a temporary move," he said finally.

"Maybe," she conceded, to make them both feel better.

The boys fell asleep in front of the TV—so much for quality time—and she moved into the bedroom, where, she saw, Sam had finally put a bolt on the door. Something glinted on the windowsill: it was only a screw left over from the carpentry, but it reminded her of the earrings in Jeff's perfect-as-a-stage-set apartment—

Jeff!

"Sam, I'm sorry, I have to make a phone call. I'll try not to wake the kids," she said breathlessly, and slipped into the kitchen.

Jeff was out. Jeff would be out a lot, she realized, as she tied herself in syntactic knots attempting to compose a message for his machine that was comforting but cryptic, in case anyone else happened to be listening. Finally she ended, "Oh, call me. I'll tell you all about it. Call me at . . . " She paused. Home is where you receive phone calls. "At the lab." Then she added, "I'll see you soon."

"Revenge?" Sam inquired pleasantly when she returned.

"Revenge?"

"Yeah. For the time I left you standing here to go call Linda."

"I hadn't even thought of that. No, it was just some-one . . . someone who'll be very relieved that Jonathan's murderer was caught." She could feel his curiosity; no doubt he'd heard the whole strained monologue, but that was all the explanation he was going to get right now. At least Jeff knew he was off the hook. . . .

Hook. It made her think about the locked trunk of Jon's car, and his notebook, sitting there until Tom had found it. Yet Bert had sent Moreno to squeeze through her bedroom window in search of the notes. Why hadn't he looked in the car? It would have been easy enough to do; Jon's keys had been in his pocket.

Maybe Bert had been too angry to think clearly.

But he had had the presence of mind to remove Jon's wal-let—presuming there was a wallet—to delay identification. And if he *really* was serious about preventing identification, why not dispose of the car? As it turned out, Martelli had iden-tified Levine through other channels, but once he found the car all they had to do was trace the plates. . . . What had Tom said were the weaknesses of the case against Bert? No physical evi-dence. Well, now they had the hulsea. Time of death. What was the problem with time of death, again? Too late, that was it. Levine hadn't died until noon. . . .

She jumped as Sam closed the door, clanging the bolt shut with a certain flourish. He began to remove her shirt. "This won't change the situation," she said sternly, helping him with an uncooperative button.

"Yeah."

"I'm still moving out. And we still have a whole lot to work out between us."

"I'm ready to start working right this minute."

"I mean it, Sam!"

"I know you do," he said, suddenly somber. "But can't we talk about it later?"

She sat for a moment. Then, "Absolutely," she said, kissing the hollow of his throat and banishing time and thought, for a little while, at least.

But eventually it was later. And for a change it was Sam who broke the silence.

"And tomorrow night?" he asked.

"What?"

"Tomorrow night. Where will you be? Here? The motel?"

The temperature had dropped, and she reached for her shirt. "Not the motel," she said. "I suppose my mission there is accomplished. I'll tell La Avila—"

"La Avila?"

"The landlady. That's what Luz calls her—"

"Luz?"

"Luz Perez. My neighbor. Juan Perez's widow."

"Oh. Right."

Right, she echoed, so you don't know anything about my life on Walker Road. I didn't know anything about yours, and we were living here, together, in the very same house! She pulled on her socks.

"Here, then?" he pressed.

"Just till I get a place in town. Or the mountains. Probably the mountains."

"Oh," he said in a small voice, and she turned on him, angry yet guilty at disappointing him "Look, I told you that! And great sex doesn't change anything!"

"It's more than great sex."

"Well, great—whatever happens when we make love. It's as if that's the only time the energy manages to cross the gap between us. And when it does, whammo! arc, ignition, combustion . . . it's exciting all right, but it isn't exactly a reliable power supply. You can't plug your toaster into it."

He laughed. She could always make him laugh. "Maybe we could improve the flow of current," he said.

"Maybe we could. I'd like to try—Sam, I'd really like to try," she said, rubbing her thumb down his cheek. "But I can't live here again. Not yet."

At eight the next morning Claire and Shannon and Terry finished their Cheerios, and the boys eyed their Zappers longingly while Sam began the long process of gathering their belongings.

"You need me?" Claire offered halfheartedly.

"No, I think I got it— Shannon, put that thing down! Not at the table! Yeah, okay, you can both take them outside, but just for a little while, then you've got to help me pack. Christ, Debby's gonna kill me when they show up with those things! Terry, where's your glove? Oh, here it is—"

"When are you leaving?" she asked.

"Around three, I think."

"Okay. I've got a lot to do today, but I'll be back by then."

As if it were already a poorly recalled episode from her past, the Vacancy looked derelict and unfamiliar. At first Claire thought it was just the strange unmodulated light from the still gray skies, but then she realized what was different. The white Impala had disappeared from the curb. And Dolores and Martín were out, of course, working in the fields, but to her disappointment even Luz and her kids were gone.

Only La Avila was in her lair. Claire checked out, firmly denying accusations that she owed another week's rent, and then loaded her car. It took her all of twenty minutes to erase all traces of her occupancy from number seven. Clothes on the back seat, books on the floor . . .

Just as she was composing a note in primitive Spanish for Luz, a deep *chockita-chockita-chockita* drew her attention to the street. The Impala pulled up, backfired, wheezed, and shook, and Luz staggered out with kids and groceries.

"You got it running!" Claire greeted her.

"*Sí*, Martín finally get the part he need. Enrique help him—he say this car *es un clásico.*"

The car in question was still in spasm, and they both took a moment to laugh at men and their wheels. Then Luz saw the empty closet through the open door of number seven, and her smile faded.

"You leaving?"

Claire nodded.

"Back to husband?"

She nodded again, thought of qualifying it, didn't.

"Good," said Luz, without expression. "You belong with him."

Meaning I don't belong here, thought Claire, and it seemed that they stared at each other across a chasm of class, language, possibilities.

"I suppose so," she said, "but I'll miss this place."

Luz sniffed. "This is not a good place," she said. "This is a place for poor people."

Before her filter of liberal guilt could snap into place, Claire retorted, "It's a very good place! It's where my friend Luz Perez lives!"

A slow smile from Luz. Claire dug in her purse and found a card. "This is my number at work. Call me if you ever need . . . anything, okay? Like a ride somewhere—just in case El Clásico stops working."

Luz grinned and gave her something in return. "I find somebody to press against Ruben Moreno," she said.

"'Press against . . . ,'" Claire repeated, dazed by riotous visions. "Oh. To press *charges*?"

"*Sí*, press charges. Claudia, that girl you see at Contessa. She don't have no kids yet, to worry about. And then maybe I . . . maybe I say something, and maybe some other ladies."

"Oh, I'm glad. That's very brave."

Luz made a face and shrugged, cutting her short. "It's Enrique," she claimed. "He keep talking to me."

Poor Luz seemed to be doomed to be harassed, one way or another. "How is Enrique? Are you two . . . ?" She let the question dangle delicately.

"Es muy temprano," Luz said, shaking her head. "And I'm very sad for Juan."

It's very early, Claire translated wistfully. For her and Sam it seemed so late.

The baby had begun to wail, and it was time for Claire to go. "Good-bye," she said. Luz's eyes were suddenly filled with tears—for Juan, no doubt—and so were hers. She laid a hand on Juanito's hot little head and called "Adios" to Ana. Luz hesitated, then stuck out her hand bashfully, but Claire grabbed her in a quick embrace. "I'll visit you," she said fiercely, and ran for the car, not wanting to see the polite disbelief on her neighbor's face.

When Claire squinted into her rearview mirror, she seemed to see a sort of punk Madonna, standing by the Impala, surrounded by grocery bags and holding a baby. But when she blinked away tears and opened her eyes, it was Luz, looking exactly like herself.

"While She Was Out," the pink slip on her desk informed her, Tom Martelli called. She tried him at the office with no success. Then, on a hunch, she phoned Mercy Hospital and asked them to look for him in the vicinity of Bert Yankovich. Sure enough, in a moment she heard his scratchy voice.

"You called me?" she said.

"Yep, I did." The end.

"How's Bert? Is he all right?" she asked, too curious to be annoyed.

"Oh, yeah. Seems to be, amazingly enough." Silence.

But before she had to nudge the conversation, Tom continued, "The thing is, Bert admits that he and Levine fought the other night. But he claims that when he drove off Levine was sitting in the middle of the road, very much alive."

Chapter 24

"*What?*"

"Bert says he didn't kill Levine," said Martelli. "What did you expect? That that old buzzard would break down and start to blubber? 'I did it, Martelli, just put the cuffs on me?' Faced with the physical evidence from his truck, he allows as how he *did* talk to Levine real late that night, and Levine *did* tell him he was writing this exposé on farmworkers and pesticides and was going to talk about Bert's abuses. Bert says he told him to a) Go ahead and write it, and b) Fuck himself."

"Publish and be damned," in the words of a more polite era. "Why did Jon even meet with him?"

"Bert claims that Levine tried to shake him down."

"That's bullshit—" she began hotly, but Martelli interrupted her.

"Yeah, yeah, relax. I agree. I figure *Bert* arranged the meeting, to see if he could buy off Levine or otherwise persuade him to shut up. Anyway, there was an altercation—"

"A fistfight," she translated.

"Yup, a real doozy, according to Bert. Which he won—again, according to Bert. But he says that was it. He left Jonathan Levine lying in the middle of the Alta-Woodbury Road and walked to his truck, and when he drove off around midnight Levine was sitting up, looking a little dazed but otherwise okay. It's all crap, of course," he added.

Claire made an ambiguous, muffled noise. The irrational and the rational contended inside her. In her dream, Jon hadn't been left sitting in the road; someone had come up behind him and forced him into the water, and this vision carried the weight of absolute conviction. On the other hand, logic suggested that if Jon *had* been alive when Bert had left him, this might solve the puzzle of the notebook: a Bert acting out of ordinary hot rage rather than cold, murderous calculation might very well have forgotten about the notebook.

But, he had remembered the wallet.

But, it would be a relief to know once and for all that she *had* only been dreaming, not reliving Levine's dying moments.

"What?" Tom was saying in response to her inarticulate grunts.

She groped her way through confusion. "I keep wondering about the notebook," she said. "Because if Bert was ruthless enough to . . . to hold Jon's head underwater for a long time, as you so graphically described it, wouldn't he have grabbed Jon's keys and searched his car? And probably not bothered to tuck the keys neatly back into Jon's pocket, where I found them. But he had to send Moreno after the notebook later."

"So? He might have forgotten about it."

"Yes. But he seems to have remembered to take Jon's wallet—"

"He didn't say nothing about no wallet," Martelli interjected.

"Did you ask him?"

"No."

"Okay," she said, "forget about the notebook. If Bert *did* kill Jon at midnight, what about the coroner's estimate of time of death? You put it at six A.M. at the latest."

"What is this?" he said after a moment. "You're defending Bert? *You* were the one who bonked him over the head because you were so sure he murdered Levine!"

Was she just atoning for that embarrassing lapse from rationality? "Am I right about the time of death?"

"Yes," he admitted. "But those estimates are notoriously unreliable. Especially with the cold water and all. We got a tight case against Bert, and that's that, far as I'm concerned. We ain't gonna get a confession."

"No, but . . . what about a witness? What if I could find a witness to what happened between Bert and Levine?"

"A witness!" he snorted. "Where're you gonna find a witness to a fight in the middle of fucking nowhere in the middle of the fucking night?"

Claire was silent. "Tell me again where Jon's car and Bert's pickup were parked," she said after a moment.

He told her.

"That's what I thought. Maybe I can help you."

He listened for a moment. "Kind of a coincidence," he commented.

"Stranger things have happened," she said wisely.

A plume of gray streamed behind her as she drove up the dirt road toward the battered pickup. The sky was overcast again, but it would take more than a few days of rain to settle the Valley's dust, she thought. An entire Rain Age, maybe, or a new inland sea. . . .

She pulled up and slammed the door. The man leaning against the truck gave her a smile, which faded as the other door slammed behind her. "Howdy, Wayne," said Tom Martelli's voice.

"Wayne," said Claire, gesturing, "you know Tom Martelli?"

Harris nodded. "You an expert on walnut blight, too?" he joked weakly.

"Nope," Tom said, "it's the one thing in the world I don't know nothin' about. But I understand from Claire here that you've been standing night watch in your grove from time to time."

Wayne hesitated, then nodded again.

"Like last Friday?"

"I can't recall," said Harris with the automatic truculence of an adolescent stonewalling the principal. A not-too-bright adolescent; Claire had the sudden intuition that if Wayne Harris had ever fought the law, the law had won.

She intervened. "You told me at the open house that you'd been up the night before, making sure nobody sprayed your trees with defoliant."

"Oh, was it that night?" he said with an unconvincing air of innocence. "Well, yes, then I guess I was. Why?"

Martelli wandered over to the first row of trees. When he

spoke, it was in such a soft voice that the other two had to move closer to hear him. "We think there was a fight that night. Around midnight. In the middle of the road, right there." He pointed down the drive, past Claire's car, out to the Alta-Woodbury Road. "Thought you might have seen something."

Harris was shaking his head before Martelli even finished. "Nope. Sorry."

"That's too bad," Tom said neutrally. "Because right now Bert Yankovich is suspected of murder."

"Murder!" Harris exclaimed. "No way——" He stopped and set his jaw, and Claire had to keep herself from looking exultantly at Martelli. He *had* seen something, she was sure of it! Now the only problem was his powerful desire to keep himself, and his family, uninvolved in any trouble.

"Wayne," she coaxed, "I know Bert Yankovich is your landlord. But if you did see something that could clear him, you'd really be helping him." On the other hand, of course, if he had seen Bert kill Jonathan, Bert would be far from grateful for his testimony. . . .

Her feminine powers of persuasion were definitely anemic; Harris didn't change expression.

"Well," said Martelli, "more to the point, *I* might be grateful. And who knows, Wayne, you might need my gratitude sometime. Maybe even real soon."

Wayne looked at him for a long minute. Then, in a quick, decisive move, he dropped down on one knee as if proposing marriage. After a startled moment Claire and Tom joined him there.

"This is the road," he said, drawing a line in the dust, "an' I was here"—drilling a little dimple with his index finger—"behind the road berm—it's real high along there—watching for anybody who might be fuckin' with my trees. Like I tol' you, Claire. Anyway, after a while this pickup come up the road, headin' north. . . ."

The truck pulled up on the far side of the road, about five hundred yards to the south. He dropped down on his belly and hugged his shotgun—and then recognized Bert's truck. It just sat there, with its headlights on. And then, maybe ten

*minutes later—this would have been about midnight, he
guessed, certainly no later than twelve-thirty—another car
come along, going south. When the driver saw the parked
truck he veered to the other side of the road, as if he was
going to smash head on into it, but in fact he pulled up about
ten yards in front of it. The driver squeezed out his door,
walked to Bert's truck, and climbed into the cab; Wayne
could hear two voices rise and dip in argument. After about
twenty minutes the fellow slammed the door and walked back
toward his car, back toward Wayne. It was maybe a half-
moon that night, and it fell full on this guy's face, and Wayne
was sure he'd never seen him before. Well, to make a long
story short, Bert followed him, and before this feller could
get to his door, he decked him. Just slammed him up against
the car, hard, then whirled him around and whacked him
across the face. They rolled around in the middle of the road
and hollered for a while, but this other guy was pretty
shaken up, and anyway he was a little guy, Bert made two of
him. So Bert ended up sitting on top of him, pushing his face
down into the dirt, and then all of a sudden the heart seemed
to go out of the fight. ("That'll happen," Wayne said know-
ingly.) Anyway, Bert dismounted, walked to his truck, and
drove off.*

*And eventually the feller sat up, held his head, and looked
around him, kinda dazed.*

Claire threw Tom a triumphant look, but he was watching
Harris.

"So I split," Wayne said. "Seemed like it was all over.
And I had a thermos of coffee and a joint back in my truck—"
He stopped abruptly as he remembered who he was talking
to.

"Sounds like a pleasant way to spend the night," was
Martelli's only comment.

"And was that it?" asked Claire, infringing on Tom's territory. "Was that all you saw?"

"Well, no. I checked back in about a half hour, just out of
curiosity. And this guy was gone."

"Gone?" Claire repeated stupidly.

"Gone. No sign of him. I even walked over to look in his

car—you know, just to see if he was all right. 'Cause Bert hit him pretty hard. But he wasn't nowhere around."

"How much of that joint you smoke?" Martelli asked after a moment, and Wayne laughed.

"None of it. Fergit about it, Martelli. I just drank some coffee, was all. And like I said, this Levine dude was gone. So I don't see how Bert could've wasted him. . . ." He trailed off when he saw Martelli and Claire staring at him.

"Thought you didn't know the fellow," Tom said. "How'd you know his name?"

"I . . . maybe I heard it on the news," he said, eyes flickering. "Or . . . or maybe Bert said it! Yeah, come to think of it, Bert yelled his name while they were fighting."

This was plausible. But Tom just kept watching him with those guileless blue eyes, and Wayne's face tightened with anxiety. Claire didn't intervene in the psychodrama. She felt a little sorry for him, but not that sorry; she wanted to know what the hell had happened to Jonathan Levine.

The silence stretched on. Wayne fished in his breast pocket for a cigarette, lit it, and took a drag and then another. Eventually he said, "Look, Martelli, you don't think *I* had something to do with this guy's death? I mean, I woulda just kept my mouth shut!"

"Naw, Wayne, I don't believe you hurt Levine."

Damn braces, bless relaxes, Blake says; Harris, braced for an attack, now slumped with relief.

Too soon.

"I do think you took his wallet, though," Tom continued thoughtfully.

It caught him off guard. "Shit!" he exploded, launching his cigarette far down the road. "Jesus fucking Christ!" He stood there breathing heavily until he was calmer, then clamped his mouth shut, regretting his outburst.

Martelli said, "Look, I told you you'd want my gratitude sometime, Harris. And all I really care about is the guy. So tell me about the wallet if you want to."

Wayne hesitated. "Guess it come out of his pocket when he was fightin'," he said presently. "'Cause it was just a-layin' in the middle of the road. I spot it when I'm walkin' over to the car, and I pick it up—and there's two hundred bucks in the damn thing. Two hundred fuckin' dollars! In a wallet! I ain't got that much in the bank! And this guy was *gone,* man, so what was the harm?"

"Not much," conceded Tom. "Especially as it turned out."

"And as for what happened to the guy—I can't help you," Wayne continued. "I told you all I know. I swear it. You hook me up to a lie detector if you don't believe me."

"I just might do that. So stick around," Tom said. "Don't go back to Oklahoma."

"Texas. And I ain't goin' nowhere," Wayne muttered, looking at his trees.

All this time Claire had, uncharacteristically, kept silent. But as she and Martelli climbed into her car she burst out, "I don't understand why you're leaving him there! Didn't he kill Jonathan over the wallet?"

"I don't believe so."

"You still think *Bert* killed him?"

"Yup. Like you said, Bert's Wayne's landlord. Harris could be protecting him."

"Well," she said after a moment, "I guess I can't see Harris killing Jon over the money, either. Taking it, sure, he's pretty desperate, but not murder, not holding Jon's head underwater. . . . anyway, Wayne's a little guy, too. Not much bigger than Levine."

"No. But he's strong, and he's a fighter," Martelli said, automatically taking the other side of the argument. "And according to the postmortem, Bert hurt this Levine pretty bad. Prob'ly hit him so hard he was completely winky-wonky. Let me tell you something about heads," he continued belligerently, though she hadn't said a word. "Lotta people watch TV, see Magnum, P.I. get knocked unconscious five times in a one-hour episode and never have nothin' worse than a headache. But actually heads is delicate. Boxers die from blows to the head—"

"I know," she interjected. "I knew somebody in graduate school who stumbled in a bathroom, knocked his head against the sink, and was hospitalized for a month—and he never was the same."

He nodded vigorously. "That's what I'm sayin', these things

are *serious*. Bert knocked the shit out of this boy; he might've died from the injury even if *somebody* hadn't pushed him into the water. Which somebody I personally believe to be Bert Yankovich, despite what Harris and you say."

She was beginning to lose faith herself. Bert was the likely man, and just because she had leaped to that conclusion prematurely didn't make it untrue. Because if it hadn't been Bert, and it hadn't been Wayne, who *had* drowned Jonathan? she asked herself as they pulled onto the main road. Did somebody else come by? That was a lot of homicidal traffic in the middle of the fucking night in the middle of fucking nowhere, as Tom had described it. She squinted at the far side of the road as they went past. "Where exactly was his car?"

"We just passed the spot. It's back about ten yards—Whoa!" he exclaimed as she threw the car into reverse and rocketed backward. "Right about here, I think."

She parked along the northbound side, pushed the car door open until it lodged in the soft dirt piled high by the shoulder, and squeezed out. Martelli looked at her curiously. "I just want to see," she explained, climbing to the top of the mound, sinking ankle deep into the silt as she had on that first visit to Wayne's. She teetered there a moment, looking down at the irrigation ditch that had received Jonathan Levine into its waters.

"Tom," she said suddenly, "what if nobody killed Jonathan Levine?"

Chapter 25

"What if nobody killed him," he repeated.

"What I mean is, what if nobody *drowned* him?"

"Wait a minute," he said. "You misunderstood me. There was trauma to the head, but that boy *drowned.* The coroner's report—"

"I know, I know, I'm not saying he didn't drown, I'm saying maybe nobody drowned him."

Silence. Then, "You think he stumbled into the ditch by accident?" he said with a polite curiosity more devastating than scorn.

Instead of answering she said, "You and what's-his-name, Morrie, examined this area, I suppose."

"Of course. And by now the rain will have washed everything out."

Or uncovered something. . . . "Look, humor me," she said. "Let's just search along here for . . . for twenty minutes. If we don't find anything, I'll shut up about Bert. Twenty minutes, okay?"

He grumbled but set off north along the ridge while she walked south, surveying the inner slope. In a minute she heard a sharp curse and turned to see Tom pouring dirt out of his right shoe. "What the fuck are we looking for?" he called impatiently, but since she didn't know the answer, she ignored him.

The rain had revealed a few hidden treasures: A root. A beer bottle. An empty can of 10W-50. A flat smooth object, still half-buried, which, had it been a leaf, she would have described as spatulate and entire. . . .

Gently, like an archaeologist uncovering a shard, she brushed enough silt away to reveal—a rubber sandal with dirty red straps.

"Tom!" she called excitedly, and he came galumphing down the road.

"Looks like the mate to Levine's flip-flop," he said in a bored voice.

"Yes, but look where it is! Doesn't that location suggest anything to you?"

"Suggests I got the position of the car about right."

"But why was it buried on the inner slope?"

"Prob'ly came off when Bert dragged him into the water—Oh." He stopped suddenly. "You mean, why was it *buried*—"

"Instead of just lying there. Exactly! Now, I happen to know from personal experience—actually, I think you just learned this, too—that if you try to walk along the top of this stuff, say, to get around your car door so you can open it, it'll suck your shoes right off. Like quicksand."

Tom stared at her. "You saying that's what happened to Levine?"

There was a pause. "I think," she said finally, "that Jonathan wandered toward his car, climbed up on the bank so he could get around the door to open it. His feet sank, he lost his shoe and his balance, slid backward, maybe hit his head again, and blacked out. Lay there for a while, maybe even till morning—that would explain the lack of rigor mortis and the late estimated time of death."

"Mmm," said Tom. "I s'pose he could've even crawled a ways. That's how you come to find him where you did. But eventually he stumbled, or rolled, into the ditch—"

"And drowned," Claire finished. "Harris wouldn't have seen him—"

"Because he was on the other side of the berm," said Tom. "And anyway, Wayne was a little distracted by the wallet in the road."

"But what about the bruises on the back of his neck—Oh. The fight." Bert had mashed Jon's face in the dirt, exactly like the playground bully she had once imagined.

"Yeah. That explains the scratches on his nose, too."

Tom's voice had risen with enthusiasm in spite of himself, and they stood there grinning at each other.

Then Claire's smile faded. "Oh."

"What now?"

"Tom, do you really think this is what happened?" As usual, she had run with an appealing theory without considering the consequences, but now the thought that Jonathan was lying ten feet from somebody who was looking for him—who could have *saved* him—was somehow more intolerable than the idea of someone deliberately drowning him.

"Hell, I don't know. Do you? I mean"—without waiting for an answer—"Wayne could be lying to cover his own ass, or Bert's; Bert could be lying; some other bastard coulda come along and dunked him in the canal. . . . But I gotta hand it to you, it's what seems most likely. I mean, like you said, Bert runs hot, not cold. And drowning somebody, that's a cold thing to do—Hey, this was your idea!" he interrupted himself, seeing her discomfort. "What's eatin' you?"

"It's so arbitrary!" she cried. "If Wayne had turned his head thirty degrees, he might have seen him. . . ."

"Listen, there's no tellin' what Wayne might or might not have seen, with two hundred dollars whispering sweet nothings in his ear. But as for the other—well, most of the death I see is just somebody in the wrong place at the wrong time. You know, if they hadn't been at that intersection at the moment the drunk maniac went tearing through it; if they hadn't been settin' on their porch when the gangbangers cruised by; if they hadn't been jogging in the park when some dude's psychosexual biorhythms happened to peak . . . By my standards, Levine's death wasn't—what'd you call it?"

"Arbitrary."

"Right, arbitrary, at all. It was kinda, um, inevitable. I mean, he was threatening—by choice, mind you—a man known to have an explosive temper. See, even if we say nobody killed Levine, Bert's responsible, no two ways about it. I always reckoned he'd beat somebody to death someday, and that's more or less what he done. So. Feel better?"

"Yes," she said. She wouldn't tell him that what she was actually feeling was—anticlimax. Lack of catharsis. She had been wrestling with the problem of Jonathan Levine's death for weeks now, and this solution was simply not dramatic—

"One good thing," he was saying. "Levine died a hell of a lot easier than what I was thinking."

Yes. There was that, she thought, suddenly hot with shame. "Oh!" she exclaimed abruptly. "His mother! Did you talk to his mother?"

"Yep."

"Did you remember to ask her where he grew up?"

"I did, as a matter of fact. She said they lived in some place called Rensa—Rensal—Damn, these New York towns have weird names!" This from a man who lived up the road from Weed Patch, Pumpkin Center, and Buttonwillow. "Someplace near Sichen . . . near Albany, anyway."

"Rensselaer?"

"Yeah, that was it! Lived there till he was in junior high, then moved to Sich—"

"Schenectady," she supplied absently.

"Schen-ec-ta-dy," he repeated carefully. "Got it!"

She was late, but she knew Sam would be, too. You had to increase any parent's estimate of time by some complicated formula involving number of kids squared plus some negative coefficient for their ages. In Sam's present situation this meant adding about an hour to his ETA. So she stopped off at the station to call Jeff.

"Claire!" His voice seemed warm and welcoming as always, and her heart bumped in spite of herself. "Thanks for your message! That's great news!"

"I figured you'd want to know right away."

"I'll say. Jesus, what a relief. The end of a particularly bizarre episode in my life."

Did that include her? she wondered, and decided to find out. "I'll probably have to come down to L.A. again in a couple of weeks."

"Oh. Great." He seemed to have moved the receiver several feet from his mouth. "Um, this is a really busy time for me, beginning of the quarter and all that. But maybe we could have lunch."

Lunch, she thought disgustedly. Even if she had missed

the sudden wariness in his voice, *lunch* was a clincher, the safest meal of the day. With a small internal sigh she gave up the last tatters of that fantasy. Either Jeff had a new Earring and just couldn't pencil her in or he had after all been interested in her only for what she could tell him about the Levine murder.

And that wouldn't surprise her. Every other man she had interacted with in the last two weeks had lied to her—Sam, Tom, Emil, Wayne; even Jon Levine had sent her a misleading dream from the beyond, if she wanted to believe that. So why not Jeff?

In fact, it was easier to name the males who *hadn't* lied: Terry, Shannon, Bernie Perlmutter—children and bit players.

And Bert Yankovich, that old reprobate, had played it pretty straight.

"I'll give you a call," she told Jeff, hanging up before he could reply, and walked briskly out to the parking lot.

The books in her car had spilled across the floor and slid under the seat. She was trying to shove them into a pile when her hand encountered the sticky, alligator-textured vinyl of the photo album. She picked it up and laid it on the seat. All on its own it fell open to her fifth-grade class picture, and once again Jonathan Levine's pinched little face looked back at her.

Had he known he was gay even then—no, no, that was the *other* Jonathan Levine. She stopped, hopelessly confused between fiction and fact, knowing she would probably always think of this as the child who grew into the man she had found in the muddy water of an irrigation ditch. Unless she discovered what had actually become of Jonnie Levine of Lenox, Massachusetts. . . . Maybe she should set her mother on his trail. That would at least give them something to talk about, other than the absence of grandchildren.

So. Jonathan was *not* her Jonathan, and Bert had *not* killed him—not really—and she and Sam were *not* happily reconciled, and Jeff was *not* going to rescue her from Kaweah County. Nothing resolved, nothing tied up neatly. On the other hand, in a few weeks Sam would know, within some reasonable confidence interval, whether organically grown peach trees had yields comparable to conventional trees.

Someone else would know whether soil solarization was an effective means of weed suppression. Allen and she would eventually know if *Entyloma seritonum* was practical biological control for *Amsinckia intermedia* in alfalfa.

This was why science was superior to life.

It was four when she pulled into Sam's drive, but he was still there, shepherding Shannon and Terry toward the car.

"You just made it. We were about to leave," he said. "I should be back by eleven or so, if you're interested." He hesitated. "Will you be here?"

"Yes. I checked out of the motel this morning."

"Oh," was all he said, but he kissed her hard on the mouth.

The boys snickered in unison; acting quickly, Claire snagged Terry by the collar and planted a kiss on his forehead—or at least aimed for his forehead and got the brim of his baseball cap as he squirmed away. "Eeuw!" he exclaimed, while Shannon darted to the far side of the car, crying, "Not me! Not me!"

So much for tender good-byes.

But as they were piling into the car, Shannon stopped and said, "When we visit at Christmas can I come to your lab again, and see some more spores?"

Claire and Sam exchanged a quick glance. God only knew what would be happening by Christmas.

"Sure," she said. "I'll try to have lots of gross stuff for you to look at."

"Cool!"

She waved to the car as it backed out of the driveway, then headed inside. As she climbed the porch she thought she heard Terry's high voice singing, "Three away! Three away!"

Claire and Sam were going to be married—just a small, casual affair. Only it turned out that Sam was going to marry Linda, too, later, in a grand wedding. Claire hadn't known this, but everybody else seemed to know, and she felt deeply humiliated. She asked Sam about it, but he wouldn't answer her. He was busy searching the mall for items he would need for his real marriage: a scratchy wool overcoat. A bad-

minton racket. "*But what about me? What about our wedding?*" *she kept saying, following him from store to store. Finally he spoke.* "*I'll marry you if that's what you want, but it won't matter. My great love is Linda.*" *Linda appeared, pale and exquisite; Claire held her fist right up to the perfect nose and said through clenched teeth,* "*I'll smash your face in.*" "*No, you won't,*" *said Linda, and Claire lowered her fist.* "*No,*" *she said. She looked down at the blue-and-orange LustreWare plate she had been clutching to her chest. It had been meant for her own wedding.* "*Here,*" *she said, relinquishing it to Linda.*

When she woke Sam was in fact sleeping peacefully next to her, and the shame and frustration of the dream receded a little. But a residue of sick anticipation remained: now that the drama of Jonathan Levine no longer occupied her unconscious, it could devote itself full time to the melodrama of Sam and Linda and Claire.

It was going to be a long summer.